LAST RUN

LAST RUN

Hilary Norman

This first world edition published in Great Britain 2007 by
SEVERN HOUSE PUBLISHERS LTD of
9–15 High Street, Sutton, Surrey SM1 1DF.
This first world edition published in the USA 2008 by
SEVERN HOUSE PUBLISHERS INC of
595 Madison Avenue, New York, N.Y. 10022.
This first trade paperback edition published 2008 by
SEVERN HOUSE PUBLISHERS, London and New York.

British Library Cataloguing in Publication Data

Norman, Hilary
   Last run
   1. Runners (Sports) - Crimes against - Florida - Fiction
   2. Murder - Investigation - Florida - Fiction 3. Florida -
   Fiction 4. Detective and mystery stories
   I. Title
   823.9'14[F]

   ISBN-13: 978-0-7278-6566-3   (cased)
   ISBN-13: 978-1-84751-036-5   (trade paper)

For my mother, Herta Norman

Acknowledgements
Grateful thanks to: Howard Barmad; Jennifer Bloch; Batya
Brykman; Sheena Craig; special thanks to Sara Fisher;
a great debt of gratitude to Sergeant Paul Marcus of the Miami
Beach Police Department; Helen Rose; Dr Jonathan Tarlow.
Most of all, as always, for putting up with me while I work,
my husband Jonathan.

Except where actual historical events and characters are being
described for the storyline of this novel, all situations in this
publication are fictitious and any resemblance to living persons
is purely coincidental.

All Severn House titles are printed on acid-free paper.

Typeset by Palimpsest Book Production Ltd.,
Grangemouth, Stirlingshire, Scotland.
Printed and bound in Great Britain by
MPG Books Ltd., Bodmin, Cornwall.

Prologue

The beach at night's a cool place for killing.

Biggest bath in the world for washing away blood. Sand ruffling with every breath of breeze, shifting with each passing footfall, sweeping away prints, eradicating evidence.

A crime-scene technician's nightmare.

And a detective's.

One minute the guy was running; nice, easy, loping strides, warm air sucking in, and blowing out of his well-trained lungs, free as a bird and loving it, the way he always felt this time of night, the tedium of his day blown away, his body and mind in peaceful tandem, getting ready for rest, for sleep.

No sense of danger.

Not till it was on him. Something swinging at his face.

Last things he heard were the sounds of his own bones smashing.

And the *screaming*.

Last things he felt were the terror and the agony.

Nothing after that.

One

At least six people heard it (every one of them failing to report it at the time) just over four hours before the body was found – at five a.m. on Wednesday – not far from a jet-ski rental booth on the beach close to North Shore Open Space Park, just south of Surfside.

The crime had been brutal and ugly; the sound, they said, a *kind* of screaming. 'But not the kind a victim would make,' one person volunteered. Which made it either the scream of a witness or, some were speculating, the sound the killer had made.

'Sounded like an animal to me,' said a middle-aged man, who'd heard it through the open bedroom window of his fifth-story, ocean-facing apartment.

'Crazy was what it sounded,' said his less fanciful wife.

Sam had come in to the handsome white building that was 1100 Washington Avenue, and which housed the Miami Beach Police Department before six a.m., planning to dig in for a day at the office, when Lieutenant Kovac had appointed him lead investigator for the North Shore homicide, and agreed to free Martinez from the aggravated assault case he'd been working on, so they could work on the new case together.

Not because Kovac liked either of them any better than he ever had, but that was the way it went; the detectives in the Violent Crimes Section worked a kind of rotation, each man and woman having their turn to take responsibility for fresh cases. Besides which, even Kovac had been forced to admit over the years that Sam Becket and Al Martinez, while not officially a partnership, worked better together than apart.

So, for both detectives, a day at the office had turned into a day at the beach.

No picnic, though.

Especially for the late Rudolph Muller.

*   *   *

No problems with unconfirmed identification (no official ID possible yet with the dead man's face pounded beyond recognition) since Muller had worn a runner's belt, complete with water bottle and a pouch for his keys and wallet. Rudolph F. Muller, a janitor at Trent University in North Miami, living on Abbott Avenue, just a handful of blocks from where he had died.

Had been murdered.

The twenty-dollar bill and three quarters in the wallet, the small size of the wallet itself, and the presence of the man's keys, appeared, at least at first glance, to rule out the likelihood of robbery or a drug deal gone bad.

There were two stages to the assault, according to Elliot Sanders, the medical examiner. The first stage had been a vicious blow to the face – possibly with a baseball bat or some other blunt, club-like object – which had almost certainly rendered Muller unconscious, *after* which his throat had been cut.

'Straight across,' Sanders told Sam, just after six thirty, moments after he'd made his preliminary on-scene examination. 'Nice and clean, probably because the victim was out cold.'

'Surgical?' Sam forced his eyes back down to scan again the horrors that were, to his enduring regret, an integral part of his working life.

'I'd say not.' Sanders stooped again for another look. 'Kitchen knife, maybe. We'll know more later.' He surveyed the facial destruction again, and raised a brow. 'Anaesthesia technique could use some work.'

'Anything else, doc?' Sam was six-three, a rangy African-American, tough-looking, but still grateful he'd missed breakfast that morning.

'Later.' The overweight ME hauled himself back upright, took out his handkerchief to mop his brow, already glistening this humid August morning, and began to move away from the body.

Both men stepped cautiously, the measure ingrained, though they and Al Martinez – currently in conversation with a crime-scene technician over on the sandy path that led to 88th Street and Collins – had all realized on arrival that the crime scene had already been contaminated by an unknown number of passers-by. Certainly by the two joggers whose misfortune it had been to find the body; then, just as inevitably in the circumstances, by the fire and rescue team who'd pronounced the victim dead. By which time, the Miami Beach police officers securing the crime scene had to have known that despite their best efforts all kinds of evidence, most notably any foot impressions that the killer *might* have left (doubtful, in any case, since the instant a foot lifted up on the beach, the soft sand was already shifting) were lost for ever.

Reaching the path outside the taped-off area, Sanders lit a cigarette and grinned, without malice, at Becket's still discernible discomfort.

'Get any paler, Sam, they'll be calling you Jackson.'

'Get any fatter, doc – ' Martinez, slightly built with a rounded face, sharp dark eyes and a lightly accented voice, joined them – 'we can rent you out for shade.'

'Never heard that one before, Al,' the ME said, wryly.

'What's up with you?' Martinez asked Sam as they pulled up outside the ochre-and-cream two-storey apartment building on Abbott Avenue that had checked out as Rudolph Muller's home.

They were friends as well as colleagues, had worked side by side for years with liking and mutual respect. Both of them good, solid, occasionally outstanding detectives, yet neither having won the promotions they might have anticipated in that length of service; Alejandro Martinez, even-tempered till seriously roused, a courteous man with a strong streak of street fighter, never really seeking advancement because, as a bachelor – albeit with an eye for pretty women – he felt responsibility to no one other than himself; Samuel Becket because he had developed a tendency – disapproved of by his superiors – of sailing dangerously close to the wind if department regulations came up against his own strong personal instincts.

'Muller worked at Trent,' Sam replied to his colleague's question.

'Cathy.' Martinez knew that Sam's adopted daughter was studying for a bachelor's degree at Trent's School of Social Work, and was equally aware of how his partner felt when any semblance of danger impinged on her life. 'The guy was a janitor, man. Cathy probably never even saw him, let alone met him.'

'I know,' Sam said.

'And he was killed on home turf, not at Trent.'

'I know,' Sam said again.

Martinez glanced at him. 'She doin' OK?'

'Uh-huh,' Sam said, which was thankfully, so far as he could tell, true.

'Grace?'

Sam smiled. 'Grace is doing wonderfully, thank God, and Saul and my dad, too.'

'Me too,' said Martinez. 'All one of me.'

Sam opened his door. 'Two lucky bastards.' He looked up at Muller's building. 'And now we get to wreck someone else's life.'

'Real lucky,' Martinez said.

Six years had passed since a grisly serial homicide case in the Miami Beach and surrounding areas had finally been laid to rest, bringing to an end a long and hideous nightmare that had personally affected both Sam Becket and Dr Grace Lucca, and had all but destroyed the life of their daughter-to-be Cathy Robbins.

Sam and Grace – a child and adolescent psychologist – had been married for four of those years, living with Cathy in the Bay Harbor Island house that had first been Grace's: a small white stone house with a red-tiled roof, arched windows, a pair of palm trees and a bottlebrush tree at the front, and a deck at the back – Grace's favourite spot – overlooking Biscayne Bay.

It might have felt crowded to her sometimes, this space that had previously been hers alone, but it never had. It just felt right. Marriage – first for her, second for Sam – and their parental guardianship of Cathy had seemed to flow naturally and, for the most part, contentedly; the only real sorrow in their relationship their seeming inability to bring a new baby into the world.

After two soul-wrenching miscarriages, however, Grace's latest pregnancy had made it through to six months, and for both of them joy just didn't *begin* to describe it. Sam had hit forty a while back, and Grace, at thirty-seven, was being termed a *geriatric* in medical jargon. Still, Barbara Walden, her obstetrician, seemed quietly confident they were past Grace's primary danger zone. And if Sam had thought he could get away with wrapping his wife up at home for the duration, he might have tried, but he knew better. Anyone who'd spent much time with Grace knew better than that.

Happy family.

Not so happy as they might have been, because they had lost Judy Becket – Sam and Saul's greatly loved chicken-soup-and-steel mom – to bone cancer last year, and so Judy had never known that Grace was pregnant again, had come to fear that Sam (who had, almost fifteen years ago, endured the agony of losing his baby son) would never be blessed with another child.

'I was trying – ' Saul, Sam's nineteen-year-old brother, had said at one of their family dinners a month or so back – 'to work out the many parts of my nephew-to-be.'

'Racially, you mean?' David Becket, their paediatrician father – Sam's by adoption – had raised a grey eyebrow. 'Too magnificent a mix to waste on calculation.'

They had tried it though, wading through their respective inheritances; Cathy attempting the math and failing. Hardly surprising, they all discussed, laughing, with Sam, an African -Bahamian-Episcopalian barmitzvahed Jew, descendant of a runaway slave, married to Grace, daughter of a third generation Swedish-American-Protestant mother and a second-generation Italian-American-Catholic. Both David and his late wife, Judy, were children of Jewish refugees from Nazism, David's roots in Russia, Judy's in Poland, and Cathy had Scottish and French blood back along her own family line.

'Though that doesn't count for the baby.' She smiled. 'Just as well.'

'More important ingredients than genes – ' Grace's hand lay over her swollen abdomen – 'are going into this particular pot.'

'Whole lot of love,' Sam said, covering her hand with his own.

Mocha on cream.

Happy family.

Two

August 11

By Thursday morning, most of the summer students on Trent's small but lovely, sun-baked campus near Elaine Gordon Park in North Miami were talking about the murder; the majority, so far as Cathy could tell, with more than a degree of morbid curiosity.

None, Cathy could almost guarantee, had a clue what they were talking about. The true horror, the ugly brutality of violent killing. She knew. So much that she sometimes felt as if her mind had become infused with the blood and agony of her memories, as if they had become a part of her.

Grace – back when she had not been her adopted mom; when she had still, to Cathy, been Dr Grace Lucca, kiddie shrink – had tried to help Cathy believe that though the memories were irrevocably hers she would, in time, be able to move forward; be able to push the ugliness farther away and draw strength from her own survival.

Nothing had come easily, for all their kindness and patience. Cathy had found a real sense of belonging with Grace and Sam, had long ago ceased feeling the need to unload daily secrets into the computer journal she'd confided in during the bad times. Yet she still harboured private fears that loss might strike again, and her ongoing insecurities had made it an uphill battle to achieve adequate grades to get accepted at Trent. She had managed it though, and she was now hoping to put her own experiences to good use in social work.

Running still did it for Cathy – better than drink or dope or Tony Roma's baby back ribs, better even than dancing to *Born to be Wild*, better than sex – not that sex had ever come *close* to Steppenwolf. Running had always been Cathy's greatest release, the loss of it during her time in prison had been her greatest deprivation, and any time things got her down or terrified her, she put on her Pumas and got flying.

The news of the Trent janitor's murder had not exactly freaked her out since she'd never met the poor guy. But the fact remained that a man had been slain, a human being with family and friends whose worlds were presumably now being ripped apart. Which was something else Cathy knew too much about; and the *last* thing she wanted to do was think about it. So this morning she'd driven into school, parked her Mazda (Grace's car until Sam had bought his wife a new Toyota), struggled through an hour's study in the library, and then got out on the track.

She was unaware until she had finished running, had done her cool-down stretching exercises and was stepping into her track-suit pants, that she was being watched.

Photographed.

The glint of the lens was what alerted Cathy. And then the camera was lowered, and she saw who had been taking her picture. Kez Flanagan, of all people. If Cathy had a heroine at Trent, it was Kerry – Kez – Flanagan, the twenty-one-year-old powerhouse of the Tornadoes.

Flanagan was standing under a jacaranda tree.

'Hi,' she said.

'Hi,' Cathy said back, pulling on her jacket despite the heat.

'Hope you don't mind?' Kez Flanagan indicated the camera strung around her neck – the kind Cathy thought of as 'real', not one of the dinky digital numbers the whole world carried around these days. 'I was finishing a roll, and—'

'And I got in the way,' Cathy said quickly, embarrassed.

'I like your style.' Flanagan's voice was husky and a little brusque.

'Really?' Cathy heard the surprise in her own voice, and felt even more flustered.

'Nice smooth action,' Flanagan said.

'Thank you.' Thankful, too, that exercise had already flushed her cheeks.

'I'm Kez Flanagan.' The woman held out her hand.

'I know.' Cathy felt the powerful squeeze of the tanned hand, glanced down as it withdrew from hers, noticing its long fingers and intricately painted nails – almost like the late great Flo-Jo's, but very short, the way guitarists cut their nails. 'I'm Cathy Becket.'

Close up, Flanagan's short, semi-spiky hair was almost the colour of the fiery bottlebrush tree in their yard at home on the island, her eyes green-flecked hazel, her chin pointed, mouth straight and even, her nose small but aggressive, like an arrow-head.

'I know,' Kez Flanagan said. 'I've seen you run a few times.'

'You have?' Cathy was finding it hard not to stare at her.

A pair of runners rounding the bend to their right raised their right hands in a salute to Flanagan, who waved back, watched them for a moment or two, then turned back to Cathy.

'You're really not bad.'

'I'm nothing.' Cathy felt a thrill. 'I mean, I don't really compete.'

'Maybe you should,' Flanagan said. 'With some work, a little harnessing, you could be pretty good.'

The huskiness was almost like a smoker's, though Cathy could scarcely imagine a dedicated athlete like Flanagan, her body every bit as hard and lean close up as from a distance, putting crap of any kind into her lungs.

'You run,' Flanagan went on, 'like you're trying to escape.' She saw wariness spring into the younger woman's eyes. 'Which is cool, so long as you're in charge.'

'I guess,' Cathy said.

'Not my business,' Flanagan said.

'No.' Cathy felt flustered again. 'I mean, I don't mind. Not coming from you.'

'I'm no expert, mind.'

'You're the best.' Cathy heard the awe in her own voice, couldn't help it.

Kez Flanagan shrugged. 'Big fish, small pond.'

'You got us gold at Sarasota.'

'Because Jackson busted her ankle and Valdez screwed up.'

'What about the silver at Tampa?'

Flanagan smiled. 'Tampa was special.'

'You're special,' Cathy said.

'I guess I have my moments.' Flanagan paused. 'What I meant, before, about the way you run—'

Cathy waited.

'Sure you don't mind me talking about it?' Flanagan checked.

'No way,' Cathy said. 'I need all the help I can get.'

They left the track, walked together away from the athletic building along one of the palm-shaded pathways, heading for the parking lot. Two tracksuited athletes – red-haired Flanagan an inch-and-a-half taller; Cathy, blonde hair tied back and a slighter build – both walking easily and unconsciously in matching rhythmic strides.

'I'm no coach,' Flanagan said in her matter-of-fact manner. 'But I do know that being in charge of yourself matters. Running away may feel great, but when you're racing it's where you're headed that counts.'

'The finish.'

'And how you get there,' Kez Flanagan said. 'Taking care of your body on the way. Not hurting yourself.'

'OK,' Cathy said.

'You could use someone,' Flanagan said.

'We have Delaney,' Cathy said.

Mike Delaney was the Trent track coach, an all-round nice guy, but not reckoned by some of the students as the man to take the Tornadoes any place higher than two-thirds up the team rankings.

'Delaney's OK,' Flanagan said. 'And he's been good to me.'

'He calls you his star,' Cathy said.

'I've heard him call me other things.' Flanagan shrugged again. 'And he's been right.' They were close to the lot now, less than half filled by vehicles belonging to summer students and teaching staff. 'If you're interested,' she said casually, 'we could run together sometime.'

More than interested.

'I'd like that,' Cathy said.

Three

'We got a two-year unsolved homicide on Pompano Beach,' Martinez said, midway through Thursday afternoon. 'Could be something, maybe.'

'Actually *on* the beach?' Sam checked.

'Uh-huh.' Martinez sat on the outside edge of Sam's paper-jammed desk in his corner of the big open-plan Violent Crimes office and looked at his notes. 'Victim Carmelita Sanchez, bludgeoned with a blunt instrument, probably a baseball bat, then facially disfigured.' His face puckered with disgust. 'Bastard sliced off her lips.'

Sam took a second or two to force himself to mentally confront that image, then tried to file it in one of the mental cabinets in the back of his brain; he turned his gaze briefly to one of the Florida Grand Opera posters on his section of wall, then went back to business.

'Muller's throat was cut,' Sam said. 'Ugly, but not weird like this.'

'Still in two stages, the bat first,' Martinez said. 'Something else too. Same kind of screaming reported by residents.' He looked down at a sheet of paper in his hand. ' "Crazed", one guy said.' He looked back down at Sam. ' "Like an animal".'

'Close enough to go talk to Broward.' Sam was already on his feet.

Four

In his dream, Gregory Hoffman saw it all again. Blurred around the edges by his semi-sleeping brain's unwillingness to process too accurately, too realistically.

The terror, though, was undiminished.

The thing looming out of the night, or maybe not really *looming*, too fast for that, more like a whirlwind, but solid; a figure, a person, he guessed, except it was too dark and too fast to get a real look at, but the *thing* was flying at the other guy and one minute he was running, the next he was down on the sand.

But in the middle of that, in the middle of the guy getting knocked down, there were the sounds, terrible, sickening sounds, and Greg knew, even in the depths of his dream, that they were the sounds of small bones being crunched in the man's face, and of his cry, cut off real fast too, because he *couldn't* make any more noise, and anyway, the ocean got louder after that, the roar of the surf drowning it out, and that was good, that was better.

Except then the damned moon came out from behind the clouds and that was when he saw the knife blade glinting wet-red-black, and that wasn't *so* bad, he could take that more than the sounds of pulverized bones. Except that wasn't all he saw, was it? He wished it was, wished it with every fibre, every goddamned molecule of his body and soul.

He saw the face.

The killer's face. Except it wasn't really a face, at least not one you could recognize or describe, because, like the knife blade, it was wet-red-black, shining in the moonlight, and Greg thought it looked like it was *made* of blood, so much blood that he had to squeeze his eyes shut to try and block it out.

That was when he heard the other, final sound, louder than the ocean.

The screaming. Awful, hideous, crazy, *nutso* screaming that made his own blood, still safely shut in his veins under his skin, thank Christ, run cold enough to freeze.

And he woke.

At two o'clock on Friday morning, in his nice safe bedroom in his nice safe house in North Bay Road in Sunny Isles Beach, Gregory Hoffman woke from his dream, sweating and crying out and shaking and more afraid, more *terrified*, than he had ever been in his whole fourteen-year-old life.

But this wasn't like most nightmares, where things looked better after you were awake, after you got over it. This one was worse, much, much worse, because he knew why he'd dreamed it, knew exactly why he was so frightened.

Because he had seen the killer with the blood-soaked head.

Because if he had seen the killer, then the killer had seen him.

And because he couldn't tell anyone, not his mom or dad or the cops, because of what he'd been doing before it had happened. Because if he told them that then they'd send him back to rehab again, and Greg knew he couldn't stand that; he remembered it too clearly and it had been too bad, much too bad, and he couldn't bear it, and so he didn't know what to do.

Except go on dreaming it again, over and over. Go on waiting for the killer to come for him.

Three in the morning.

Quiet time in Surfside. Nice, peaceful community, predominantly young professional families and retirees. Sleeping now, most of them. Visitors, too, nearing the close of their summer vacations, getting set to take their kids home.

Not a whole lot of traffic on Collins.

One car, already slow, braked to a crawl near 88th Street. Driver taking a look down the side street, towards the beach. Scene of the Muller killing. Thinking about making a right. Seeing another car, in the side road, lights switched off, a woman in the driver's seat, a street lamp illuminating her face. Young, pretty, possibly Hispanic.

Waiting for someone, maybe. Or watching.

Cop, perhaps, the first driver thought.

And drove on more quickly, heading north.

At a little past noon, Kez Flanagan was in the main cafeteria at Trent with a couple of fellow Tornadoes – like her, using the facilities during the summer.

Her eyes were on Cathy Robbins Becket, in line at the counter, buying a salad. Cathy turned slightly, saw her and smiled. Kez lifted her right hand with its blunt, decorated nails, and smiled back.

'You know her?' Jackie Lomax asked.

Kez nodded.

'Know about her past?' Jackie asked.

'Sure,' Kez said.

'Poor kid,' Jackie said.

'Bit of a weirdo,' Nita North remarked.

'Nothing weird about Cathy,' Kez said sharply.

She looked back at the line and saw that the younger woman had gone, and felt something that surprised her.

Empty.

While Judy had still been with them, even during her illness, they had all, when able, come on Friday evenings to the Becket home on Golden Beach, to the old house, comfortable as old slippers and always welcoming.

They came, these days, to Grace and Sam's place, sat at the hand-carved kitchen table, gleaming copper pots and pans steaming on the stove. They all – women and men – took it in turns to light the Sabbath candles and say the blessings over bread and wine, and sometimes it was no more than two or three at the table, with Sam working a case or perhaps Saul or Cathy otherwise occupied. But this Friday, with the first few rounds of intense activity in the Muller investigation having hit dead ends, and with Sam feeling especially needy of Grace's wonderful, essentially Italian cooking, and of his family in general, they were, as it happened, all present and correct.

An extra place laid for Terri, Saul's girlfriend. Saul's *love*. Teresa Suarez. Petite, *very* pretty, and tough. Terri to her friends. Teté – her Cuban nickname – to Saul. No one else close enough to call her that.

Sam knew her, too, as Officer Teresa Suarez, an intensely ambitious rookie working in Property Crimes at the Miami Beach Police Department. To her chagrin, since Terri's aim was to be a homicide cop like Sam.

Her single-mindedness was a little too much, on occasion, for Sam's liking.

'Why shouldn't she want what you have?' Saul had asked his

brother a few months back, after Sam had passed a mildly concerned – and, to his mind, diplomatic – remark about Terri's impatience.

'She has a terrific job now,' Sam had said. 'And great potential.'

'You mean that?' Saul had been mollified.

'Sure I mean it,' Sam had said. 'But Terri's young. She can afford to take her time, hone her skills as she goes. And there's nothing inferior about Property Crimes, believe me.'

'She wants to help people,' Saul said. 'Make a difference.'

'Then she couldn't be in a better section,' Sam had pointed out. 'You know how violated people feel when their homes are burgled.'

What Sam had felt – but had known better than to say – was that he had, for some time, had the disconcerting sense that Terri was one of those young officers with wholly unrealistic expectations of life in a homicide squad. The reality, of course, was exposure to horror, ugliness, sordidness, deep sorrow, pain and frustration. Not forgetting the mind-numbingly tedious chores that detectives in Violent Crimes had to constantly wade through because it *was* so vital to catch these most dangerous of criminals, and because knocking on a hundred or more doors and filling out forms and writing endless reports was part of the process that meant a killer might ultimately be not only caught, but also brought to justice.

The homicide cop's reason for being. The prize that made it all worthwhile. The prize that Terri wanted. And Saul was right, of course. Sam was in no position to blame her for that.

Except that the work had more than its share of risks, and no one knew that better than Sam. Saul, his gentle young adoptive brother, was one of the most important people in his universe and Sam could not help feeling afraid that, in so adoring his spunky, bitter-chocolate-eyed girlfriend, Saul might be storing up pain for his future.

Not yet, though, thank God. Not tonight. Hopefully not ever.

'You look happy, sweetheart,' David commented to Cathy part way through Grace's chilli roasted, Tuscan-rooted version of her late mother-in-law's traditional Friday night roast chicken.

'She's happy – ' Saul got in before Cathy could answer – 'because this Trent track star thinks she's a hot runner.'

'Kez never said that,' Cathy corrected him. 'She said I wasn't bad.'

'You're better than not bad,' Grace told her.

Cathy smiled. 'Kez said we could run together sometime.'

'Would this be Kez Flanagan, by any chance?' David was interested.

'You've heard of her?' Cathy was surprised, since being a star at Trent meant little in the wider college athletics world.

'I used to know her,' David said.

'Patient?' Sam asked.

'Until her father passed away.' David smiled. 'Joey, her dad, was crazy about her.'

'How old was she when he died?' Cathy asked.

'Young – maybe around seven or eight.' David wrinkled his curved nose, thinking back. 'I remember them both so clearly because it was always her father who brought her for check-ups, never her mom.'

Grace offered more rice and salad around the table.

'I've never caught the running bug,' she said to Terri, hoping to draw her into the conversation. 'Do you take time out for any sports?'

'I go to the gym,' Terri said. 'I like to keep in shape for work.'

'Me, too.' Sam grinned, looked down at his waistline, which seemed to have expanded just a little since he'd hit forty. 'I blame Grace's cooking for this.'

Cathy, seated to his left at the table that was used for everything from breakfast to Christmas dinner, reached over and patted his stomach. 'I keep telling you to come running with me.'

'I get exercise,' Sam protested.

'Walking Woody,' Grace said, 'doesn't constitute exercise.'

Her greatly loved old West Highland Terrier, Harry, had passed on three years ago, after which they'd found Woody – part wire-haired dachshund, part miniature schnauzer – in a Fort Lauderdale rescue shelter.

'Saul's the same,' Terri said on the subject of exercise. 'Except his nose is always in some book, which is even worse.'

'What about all the sawing I do?' Saul flexed his right arm.

'Making bookshelves hardly makes you a lumberjack,' Cathy teased, though she loved and admired the fruits of her adoptive uncle's hobby that had made their way into her bedroom.

'Was your father into sports, Terri?'

Sam's question sounded relaxed, though the fact was he'd never heard her talk about either of her parents – both dead in a car accident, Saul had told him – but even if there was maybe some big reason for her reticence, he hoped this was safe territory.

'My dad's only real sport,' Terri answered steadily, 'was beating up on women.'

'I'm sorry,' Sam said, dismayed, watching his brother reach for her hand.

'It doesn't matter.' Terri shrugged. 'Not any more, anyway.'

'I imagine,' David said quietly, 'that it still matters a good deal.'

'Teté always says she was lucky,' Saul said, 'because her grandma pretty much took over bringing her up when her mom and dad died.' He still held her hand. 'By the sounds of it, she was an amazing lady.'

'She must have been,' Grace said warmly. 'Judging by her granddaughter.'

'Thank you,' Terri said.

Awkward moment, come through as well as it could be. And not all bad, Grace reflected, since it represented the first truly personal piece of information they had learned about the young woman Saul so clearly loved.

Not our business, Grace reminded herself, wrapping the chicken carcass carefully so that Woody couldn't get at the splintery bones. No reason on earth for Teresa Suarez to share her deeply private affairs with any of them except, perhaps, Saul, and certainly not Saul's place to betray her confidences.

'Any leads in the Muller case?' Terri asked Sam.

The next troublesome moment, while he was brewing coffee for them all: Supreme Bean Espresso Luna for himself and Terri (who shared his love of the strong stuff, though her personal preference was for *cafecito*, the sweet Cuban coffee her grandmother had taught her to enjoy); latte for Grace and Saul, and a decaf espresso he'd found earlier in the week for Cathy and David.

'Good,' Grace had said when she'd seen the pack. 'Better for you.'

'It's not for me,' Sam had assured her. 'Half the flavour.'

'Half the impact on your heart,' Grace had told him.

Sam had said there was nothing wrong with his heart, and Grace had said that was the way she wanted to keep it, and then they'd gone into their usual routine where she told him he was addicted and he claimed he could stop if he wanted, and Grace told him to prove it and Sam said he didn't choose to.

Terri's question now about the Muller murder case irritated him.

Don't overreact, he told himself.

'Nothing yet,' he said.

'I heard about Pompano Beach,' she said.

'Uh-huh.' Sam tried to focus on the super automatic espresso maker that he'd bought himself last Christmas, and which Grace had renamed his Harley, as if it were some kind of dangerous mid-life-crisis machine.

'No link then?' Terri persisted. 'Victim was a cleaner, I heard.'

'Did you?' Sam turned away from the coffee machine, hoping he'd made his reply discouraging rather than downright chilly, saw right away from her expression that he'd failed.

She looked annoyed – not angry, exactly, but her eyes held a distinct glint of hostility. And then it was gone.

'Sorry,' she said. 'Inappropriate dinner conversation.'

'It's me, Terri,' Cathy said unexpectedly. 'Sam doesn't like talking about murders around me.'

Grace and Sam looked at her, both startled.

'It's true,' Cathy said. 'He thinks he's shielding me.'

'Do you blame him, sweetheart?' David asked gently.

'Course not.' Cathy got up, went over to Sam, and smiled up at him. 'I love him even more for it.'

'Nice.' Terri watched them hug, felt everyone's eyes flick towards her, checking for cynicism. 'It's OK, guys,' she said. 'I mean it.' She shrugged. 'I'm maybe a little jealous, but I think it's great.'

'If it's love she's after,' Sam said to Grace later that evening in their bedroom, 'she's a lucky girl.' He pulled his T-shirt up over his head. 'Did you see Saul's face when she said that? He's just so nuts about her.'

'Why shouldn't he be?' Grace said.

They had covered all the reasons for Saul's passion several times before, and Grace had grown annoyed with Sam for seeming to disparage Terri by implying that it was mostly down to her sex appeal and, perhaps, the fact that at twenty-two, Terri was more experienced. They both knew that it was her career that disturbed Sam most.

'Your trouble,' Grace had told him months ago, 'is that you've typecast Saul as the gentle doctor.'

'It's what he is,' Sam had argued.

'It's only part of what he may well become,' Grace had pointed out. 'And whatever that is, it doesn't dictate who Saul's going to fall in love with, any more than you ought to.'

'Is that how you see me?' Sam had been upset. 'A dictator?'

'You're a protective older brother. Almost as daunting in its way.'

Sam had done his best since then to warm to Terri, hoped he made her feel welcome in their home, but he still felt generally edgy around her, and her questions this evening about the Muller case hadn't helped.

'She should know better,' he said now, sitting on the bed, 'than to pump me for information.'

'She didn't exactly *pump* you.' Grace sat down behind him, reached up to rub his neck, trying to ease out some of his tension. 'Besides, Cathy was right, wasn't she?'

'Sure she was,' Sam admitted, shutting his eyes, loving how his wife's hands made him feel. 'I make no excuses for trying to protect our daughter.'

'Nor should you.' Grace went on gently kneading. 'But I think it's natural for Terri to jump at the chance to ask you questions.' Tired and feeling the baby shift, she stopped massaging, stood up and went across to her dressing table. 'Not that she got any answers.'

'She shouldn't, by rights, have known about Pompano Beach.'

'The cleaner?' Grace sat down. 'Something you were keeping under wraps?'

Sam shook his head. 'Probably not even connected.'

Grace pulled a tissue from a box, eyed him through her mirror. 'You're not worried that Terri might be with Saul partly to get to you?'

'Not for a minute.' Sam looked shocked.

'Only she's told you she wants a transfer to Violent Crimes, and—'

'And I told her first time she mentioned it there was nothing I could do for her.' Sam's grin was rueful. 'Face it, if it was influential pals she was after, she picked the wrong family.'

'Stupid of me, anyway.' Grace felt ashamed. 'Terri's with Saul because he's a beautiful person and she's lucky to have him.'

'Maybe I was too rough on her.' Sam said, remembering what Terri had told them earlier. 'Did Saul ever tell you about her father?'

Grace shook her head. 'He wouldn't break her confidence that way.'

Sam thought about his younger brother and smiled. 'Makes her luckier than ever to have found Saul, don't you think?'

'Oh, yes,' Grace said.

Five

During the first three months of her potentially fragile pregnancy, Grace had cut right back on work, hardly needing, for once, to be persuaded to do so either by Sam or David or any of her team of loving, frequently nagging supporters.

The 'team' reduced, in fact. Teddy Lopez, her former housekeeper and good friend, had moved to Los Angeles with a new lover eighteen months ago. Dora Rabinovitch, her part-time office manager, had taken early retirement six months prior to that. And Claudia Brownley, her sister, had upped sticks with her family and relocated to Seattle where Daniel, her architect husband, had chosen to set up his new practice.

That last departure had left by far the greatest void. She and Claudia still spoke at least once a week, which was little different to when her sister had lived down in the Keys, except in those days Grace had known she could hop in the car and go visit with Claudia, Daniel and their boys. Five thousand-plus miles and a three-hour time difference, however, had made Grace feel not only cut off, but also, more disturbingly, almost remote.

Especially disturbing because she knew, whatever Claudia said to the contrary, that she had failed to settle happily in her new home. That something about her new life reminded her of their lousy childhood and teens in Chicago; that Claudia missed sunshine and palm trees and the ocean and, most of all, the sister who had instigated their escape to Florida all those years ago.

'Any time you feel like making the trip,' Daniel had said before they'd left, 'you know your room's going to be ready and waiting.'

Grace knew her brother-in-law had meant it, but the reality was that even before this pregnancy she had found being Cathy's mother a full-time responsibility. Not to mention being the wife of a frequently overworked police detective *and* a psychologist with a still busy practice.

'You don't charge them enough,' Dora had chastised her before she had been diagnosed with glaucoma and decided to quit. 'Their parents take advantage.'

'This isn't a business,' Grace had reminded her, and Dora had picked up a folder of bills due for payment and given her boss a glare to remind her that she might be the doctor, but it was Dora who kept the ship afloat.

Things were different with Lucia Busseto running the office. Another mature, nurturing woman – Italian mama instead of Jewish mother – but less outspoken than Dora and decidedly more respectful of Grace's patients' privacy, even around the practice.

Every bit as vocal, though, when it came to nagging her employer about taking proper care of herself, which meant that now, in her seventh month, 'Team Grace' was still pretty solid, though the mother-to-be was allowing herself to feel more optimistic and generally available to her patients.

'At least,' Lucia had reasoned with her last month, 'keep your weekend rule.'

Office hours, Mondays to Fridays only.

'Barring emergencies,' Grace had said.

'If they've survived weekends without you till now, Dr Lucca,' Lucia had insisted, 'they can carry on till you and the baby are over the birth.'

Grace had to admit that she liked the sound of that.

Sam, too.

He helped his wife every way he could, rubbed her back, carried for her, cooked for her when she let him, reassured her. He kissed and stroked her belly, spoke to the boy-child within her every day, sang lullabies to him at night in his softest baritone, which Grace loved because Sam's other off-duty passion was amateur opera, something he'd managed in the past to squeeze into his spare time, regularly singing with S-BOP, a South Beach group.

They'd offered him Figaro in their next production, and ordinarily he'd have grabbed it, but he'd turned the role down this time because home was where he wanted to be right now as much as possible, taking care of his wife, fretting silently about the baby's safety, always quietly fearful too of letting them down some way.

One child, his sweet baby boy, long dead and gone and *not* his fault, whatever his ex-wife Althea had believed, yet that searingly painful boomerang of blame still regularly looped its way back to Sam, forcing him to relive and examine the tragedy over and over.

Not the same.

He reminded himself of that frequently, too, because this was his new life and Grace was the antithesis of Althea; he told himself that this son, once healthily – God willing – delivered into their arms, their *care*, would be kept as perfectly safe as humanly possible.

Not like Sampson. Not the same. Please God.

Grace had always agreed with the maxim that rules were made to be broken.

Lucia Busseto's idea that weekends be kept for family and rest was a fine one that she had no argument with. But there were always exceptions.

It was three months since Grace had seen young Gregory Hoffman, and in the two or so years that he had been her patient, his mother Annie had never struck Grace as overdramatic or hysterical. On the telephone at a minute after nine that Saturday morning, however, Annie Hoffman had sounded near the end of her rope because not only had Gregory – now fourteen – woken screaming from nightmares for the past two nights, but he was also, according to Annie, jittery and wrecked.

'And I don't think he's been using,' Annie had answered Grace's unspoken question. 'Though there's no way to be sure, is there?'

'You've both tried talking to him?'

'Jay sat down with him after dinner last night,' Annie said. 'Greg hardly said a word. He's been that way for days, Grace, almost as if he *can't* speak, except he can, at least to tell us to leave him alone.'

'Normal teenager,' Grace said, gently.

'Not this,' Annie said. 'He looks sick, Grace.'

'You sure he isn't?'

'Not in the sense that your father-in-law could deal with,' Annie said.

It was David who had first recommended Grace to the Hoffmans.

'Has Greg said he'd like to speak to me?' Grace asked.

'Not exactly,' Annie admitted. 'But he's always confided in you in the past.'

'Not always,' Grace reminded her. 'And even if he does tell me what's wrong, no quick solutions, remember, Annie?'

'We know the score,' Annie said. 'Grace, will you see him, please?'

'Of course I will,' Grace said.

'Today?' the other woman said quickly. 'I know it's the weekend, and I hate imposing, but something is terribly wrong with him, I just know it.'

Grace took a second. Sam was already out working the homicide, and Cathy was planning a run followed by a trip to the Aventura Mall.

'Noon,' she said.

'Are you sure?' Annie's voice was loaded with gratitude.

'I just hope I can help,' Grace said.

She was dismayed when she saw the teenager get out of his mother's Mercedes, nod a farewell to her and walk up the short white stone path between the palms to her front door.

His walk was the first thing that troubled her. Nervy body language with hunched shoulders, yet not in a belligerent teen manner; something different, odder, about it.

'Hi, doc,' he said as she opened the door.

Closer up, he looked sick. He was tanned enough, but the pallor beneath was noticeable and he was gaunter than she could remember ever having seen him.

Annie had made a point of saying, though, that her son was not sick.

'Hello, Greg.' Grace had a sudden impulse to embrace him, but gave him her hand instead. His grip was firm enough, but his skin felt cold, and he did not, as usual, meet her eyes, and she realized as Woody trotted up to greet him that the boy was using the dog as an excuse to look away from her.

Afraid, perhaps, she felt, of what she might see in his face.

Grace waved at Annie, just driving away, and closed the front door.

'Deck?' She knew Gregory had always felt more peaceful by the water.

'Sure,' he said.

His voice had broken since the last time she'd seen him professionally.

A young man now.

'Something to drink?' she offered.

He shook his head.

They left Woody inside, in the air-conditioning, and made themselves comfortable out on the deck on brightly cushioned cane chairs.

'Still no Sunfish,' Gregory said, after a moment.

'No.' Grace smiled. 'Not sure I'd squeeze into one right now.'

'When's your baby due, doc?' he asked.

'A few months to go,' she said.

She had mentioned to him once, in their early days of therapy, that she'd often had a fancy for one of those tiny sailboats, offering it to Gregory as evidence of at least one pleasure in common. She hadn't told him about a man named Hayman, who had once taken her on a terrifying sailboat ride, more than taking the edge off her appetite for the open seas, but Grace was aware that the troubled boy loved spending time out on the *Pegasus*, the Catalina yacht his parents kept moored outside their home on Dumfoundling Bay.

Common ground between therapist and patient by no means a requirement, but with some more reticent youngsters, Grace had found over the years that it could sometimes assist the opening up of communication.

'Have you guys taken the *Pegasus* out much this summer?' she asked now.

'Some,' Gregory answered.

He was a good-looking boy, brown-haired with long-lashed eyes and a wide, sensitive mouth. Grace had witnessed the gradual return of those looks – lost for a time to the ravages of drugs – and had shared the Hoffmans' tentative relief as the joint forces of rehab, counselling and love had won that battle and returned the nice, sweet-faced kid to his bewildered parents and baby sister, Janie.

The battle but not the war, apparently.

She saw what Annie had meant. There was a haunted look in Gregory's eyes that Grace found quite alarming, that made her wonder if Gregory might not have graduated to something far more mind-altering than marijuana or cocaine.

'Your mom is worried about you,' she said.

Up front, the way she preferred it. Beginning again.

'I know,' Gregory said.

Grace waited, watched his face turn away, the eyes appearing to gaze out over the water, but not really seeing, she thought.

'I don't want to talk about it,' he said.

'Take your time,' Grace said. 'You know the score.'

'I did,' Gregory said. 'This isn't the same.'

'Why not?'

'I don't want to be rude, doc.' He was still facing the water.

'I don't take offence, Greg. You know that.'

'Sure,' he said. 'But like I said, this is different.'

Grace waited again. 'Why is it different, Greg?'

He shook his head. 'I'm tired.'

'I can see that,' Grace said. 'Not sleeping?'

Gregory looked at her for a second. 'She told you about the dreams.'

'Your mother told me you've been waking up very upset.'

He exhaled briefly, a sound that might have been cynical or impatient or despairing, hard to be sure which.

'It might help if you tell me,' Grace said.

'I can't,' Gregory said.

She said nothing, sat still, felt the baby move, controlled the impulse to lay a hand over her abdomen, wanting nothing to disturb the pause.

'Aren't you going to ask me if I'm back on dope?' he asked.

'Are you?'

He shrugged.

In the silence, the baby moved again, pressing on her bladder.

Not now, Grace told herself and her son.

'I don't want to be here,' Gregory said.

'OK,' Grace said.

The baby wriggled again, the pressure relieved.

'So can I go?' Gregory asked.

'Of course,' Grace answered. 'We can call your mom.'

'No,' he said. 'I can take the bus.'

'I'll have to call,' Grace said.

'It's OK,' he said, resigned. 'I'll stay. So long as you know I'm not going to tell you anything.'

'It's up to you,' Grace said evenly.

'It isn't just the dreams,' Gregory said. 'I can cope with them. It's the waking stuff I can't take.'

Hope surged in Grace of a real beginning, but then, abruptly, he stood up.

'I'm sorry, doc,' he said. 'I wish I could tell you, but I can't.'

'I hope you know you can trust me, Greg,' she said.

'Yeah,' he said.

Hope melted away.

Six

A little wariness, even prickliness at first, had emanated from Detective Dave Rowan from the Broward County Sheriff's homicide unit when Sam had first made contact about the Pompano Beach killing, though things had eased up when he and Martinez had gone up there to talk.

Sam understood cops who preferred to protect their more challenging cases, guessed he'd been guilty of that too a couple of times in the past when the FDLE – the Florida Department of Law Enforcement, the agency with state-wide jurisdiction – had first stepped in to help and then taken over a Miami Beach investigation. He had known at the time that it was probably the right thing, but still, when a team had run with a case for a while, had done all the donkey work and was anticipating actually getting someplace, it could be a little hard to take.

No suspects in the Pompano Beach killing, nothing to convincingly tie the murder of Carmelita Sanchez to that of Rudolph Muller. Nothing, that was, other than the beach setting, which meant little, and the bludgeoning before cutting.

'With a baseball bat,' Martinez said later.

No sports fan, neither as a player nor spectator, he had long regarded bats as potential weapons, had set his sights on the missing bat as the piece of proof they most needed to locate in order to link these two cases.

'*Possible* baseball bat.' Sam had reiterated Sanders's report.

A few minute fragments of wood had been embedded in Carmelita Sanchez's forehead. Of ash, the Broward County ME had reported, but since most wooden baseball bats in the US were made from ash, that had rendered the evidence of minimal use to the sheriff's office. The same applied to the finding of alcohol and linseed oil residue, both of which simply meant that the owner of the bat had – at least until it had been used as a club – liked to take care of it.

No wood fragments had been found in the mess of Rudolph

Muller's smashed face, and Dr Sanders had made no mention of either oil or alcohol.

'Doesn't mean it was or wasn't the same bat,' the doctor had said when Sam had called him to double check. 'Could mean the killer noticed a chip and rubbed it down and cleaned it before the next assault. Could also mean, as I said, that it wasn't a baseball bat at all.'

'Or just another bat that *wasn't* taken care of,' Sam said.

'Like my oldest boy's,' Sanders said. 'Never seen so much as a drop of linseed oil since we bought it for him.'

The cutting blade of whatever instrument had been used to slice off Mrs Sanchez's lips had, the Broward County ME felt, been fine and sharp, but was, she had thought, more likely to have been a sharp kitchen knife than, say, a cutthroat razor. Sanders had hazarded at a kitchen knife in the Muller case too, but with no telltale markings or striations in the throat wound, he had been unable to be any more specific than that.

'No sense looking in people's kitchens then,' Martinez said. 'Find a suspect with a bloodstained bat and we got our killer.'

'Piece of cake,' said Sam dryly.

By Saturday afternoon, the Miami Beach investigation team had completed their first round of routine tasks, including the painstaking, frustrating area and door-to-door canvassing of the big apartment blocks overlooking the beach where Muller's body had been found. There still, as usual, remained a considerable number of residences for detectives to return to, perhaps repeatedly, until they found the occupants at home; and being Miami Beach, more than a few apartments might have been occupied by summer visitors, who had now departed.

Add to that the fact that those few people likely to have been wandering along the beach at that time of night might be reluctant to come forward, either because they had been up to no good, or out of it on drink or drugs, or maybe there might have been kids who'd sneaked out of hotels or apartments without their parents' permission. Not to mention that most people in their bedrooms in August would have been unlikely to have heard any unusual noise, most having their air conditioners switched on, windows and balcony doors closed, televisions turned on or just plain, old-fashioned asleep.

Muller's brother and mother had arrived from Pennsylvania on Thursday, both shattered, neither having been in close enough contact lately with the murdered man to be able to offer much insight; and neither his friends – mostly members of the Harding Avenue Gym, where he was a regular – nor his co-workers at Trent had been able to supply any information about enemies or serious problems in Muller's life.

'No bad stuff going on in Mrs Sanchez's life, either,' Sam said as he mulled over things again with Martinez in the office.

'That supposed to be a big coincidence?' Martinez was in a negative mood.

'And we still got the weird screams.' Sam ignored the grouchiness. 'In both killings.'

Martinez shrugged, his personal belief that the sounds had come from the victims.

' "Like an animal," ' Sam quoted again.

'You still think it was the perp screaming?'

'Why not?' Sam said.

'Because it would have been like a fucking commercial for what he was doing.'

'Plenty of crazy people,' Sam said.

'We're getting no place, man,' Martinez said.

'No place at all,' Sam agreed.

'I can't get past this thing with Sam,' Terri said to Saul on Saturday evening as they waited for their Middle Eastern platter at the News Café.

Saul, just raising his glass of white wine, put it down.

'Don't get all ticked off,' Terri said. 'You know it's true.'

'It is completely *un*true,' Saul said, 'and if I am ticked off, it's just because I thought we'd already dealt with all that.'

They'd argued about it last night. Terri had concluded, after Sam's response to her probing about the two homicides, that he hated her. Saul had told her she was exaggerating, that she might have had cause to be a little put out, but it had only been a moment, had been *nothing*. Teté had told him it had most definitely not been nothing, that she had felt humiliated and that only someone who really disliked another person would do that to them.

'Sam does not dislike you,' he'd told her. 'He thinks you're beautiful and smart.'

'He hates that you're dating a cop,' she had said.

Saul had found that harder to deny, and then Terri had told him that Sam made it impossible for her to feel comfortable around his family, and after that it had got out of hand and Saul *hated* fighting with Teté or, even worse, finding himself caught between the woman and brother he adored.

Sex had saved the night, and to say that Teresa Suarez was still the best lover Saul had known would have been the under- statement of the decade. The fact was, he would have done just about anything for her, found it endlessly amazing that a girl like Terri should want him, but she most unarguably did, and Saul was deeply grateful for it.

'Why shouldn't she want you?' his friend Hal Liebmann once asked him. 'You're a decent looking guy, and you're going to be a doctor.'

'I'm a student, still sharing a place with my dad.'

'From what you've told me,' Hal had said, 'Terri probably envies you that.'

Now, in the busy South Beach café, their platter arrived and for a few minutes they busied themselves with their pita and dips, though Saul's appetite had already pretty much waned.

'Please,' he said after a while. 'Don't let's have another fight.'

'I don't want to fight with you,' she said.

'Good,' he said, relieved.

'But I think you should talk with Sam.'

He shook his head, exasperated. 'I am not going to blow this tiny thing out of all proportion.'

'Tiny thing,' Terri repeated, coldly.

'Oh, for God's sake,' Saul said.

He left her at the door of her apartment, on the second floor of a drab mushroom coloured building on Washington Avenue between 14th and 15th Street, waited till she was inside, then headed up Collins towards home, having decided that if the first floor lights were still on at Sam and Grace's house, he would go in and tackle his brother.

The lights were on. Grace was upstairs having a bath. Cathy was out. Sam and Woody had just returned from an evening stroll.

'I'm here to lay this thing about you and Terri to rest,' Saul said.

Sam had been anxious for an instant, seeing him on the doorstep, then pleased to have a bonus visit from his little bro.

Pleasure over.

'I'd like to think,' he said in the kitchen, having given Saul a decaf, himself the real thing, 'that I'm not going to have to watch every word I say to Terri, any more than I do with any of my family.'

'So you don't have to watch every word, but she does,' Saul said accusatorily.

Sam frowned. 'This is because of the work questions, right?'

'She was interested, so she asked a question.' Saul had left his coffee on the table, was pacing back and forth. 'Not such a big deal for you to have answered it, surely?'

Sam stirred brown sugar into his espresso.

'Pretty big deal, as a matter of fact,' he said. 'Not her case.'

'Not her business, you mean,' Saul said.

'Not her place to ask.'

Saul sat down, picked up his cup, took a sip and put it down again. 'I don't like seeing her this upset.'

'I can understand that.'

'I especially don't like the fact that it's my own brother who's upset her.'

Sam took a moment. 'There has to be more to this than a single question I wouldn't answer last night.'

'She thinks you dislike her.'

'I do not dislike her,' Sam said. 'You know better than that.'

'I'm not so sure.' Saul stood up again.

'Don't fight with me,' Sam said. 'Especially not about something like this.'

'This is important to me.'

'Exactly,' Sam said. 'To me as well.'

Saul looked down at him, saw the concern in his brother's face, knew it was sincere and sat down again with a sigh.

'She's sensitive,' he said, 'about a lot of things.'

'She comes from a troubled background,' Sam said. 'I didn't know that until last night, and it's her private business, no reason for us to know.'

'Should it make a difference to the way you talk to her?'

'Perhaps not,' Sam answered, 'but the more you get to know a person, particularly when she's the woman your brother's in love with, the more you can try to understand.'

'You make her sound like a case.' Saul was riled again. 'Like one of Grace's patients. Terri's a great person, Sam, she doesn't need your understanding.'

'Stop being so damned prickly.' Now Sam was growing exasperated. 'We all went out of our way last night to make Terri feel welcome.'

'Grace and Cathy certainly did,' Saul said. 'And Dad.'

'But not me.' Sam's voice was quieter. 'I disagree, Saul, but I'm sorry if you feel that way.'

'I guess I don't,' Saul admitted. 'Not really.'

Sam stirred his coffee some more, then tasted it and found it less pleasing than usual, knew it had nothing to do with the beans or machine, and everything to do with the risk of falling out with Saul.

'Did Terri ask you to come?'

'She said she'd like me to talk to you,' Saul said. 'And I got mad at her.'

Sam smiled. 'And then you figured you'd come kick my ass.'

'I guess.' Saul's mouth twitched in a semblance of a smile.

'What can I tell you, bro?' Sam said. 'Love's the best thing in the world, but sometimes it hurts like hell.'

'You need – we all need – to get past this right away,' Grace told Sam in bed early on Sunday morning. 'Invite them to brunch, maybe.'

'Might turn into a replay of Friday,' Sam said. 'Better to take them out.'

Grace went to see if Cathy wanted to come along – found her on the way out for a run, with a load of study to catch up on later – made the call to Saul, found him just leaving to pick up Terri to take her to Metrozoo.

'The zoo again?' Sam raised his eyebrows.

'Terri loves wild animals,' Grace said. 'Nothing wrong with that.'

'Caged animals.' Sam appreciated animal conservation, but tended to remember the bad old zoos, majestic big cats pacing up and down in tiny spaces behind bars and glorious birds banned from the skies.

'Don't start,' Grace told him. 'Saul said we were welcome to join them.' She saw his face. 'It's OK. We settled on a late lunch instead.'

'Sure you're up to it?' Sam asked. 'You worked yesterday.'

'One session,' Grace said. 'You know it was important.'

'You're important, too,' Sam told her. 'And the baby.'

'One appointment, Sam, sitting down the whole time.'

'Stressing about the patient,' Sam said.

'I'm not going to make a habit of it,' Grace assured him.

'I hope not,' he said.

*   *   *

'I guess it's partly the incorruptibility of animals as well as their magnificence that keeps drawing me back,' Terri said to Grace later at Ocean's Ten in South Beach. 'Makes a nice change from some of the humans we have to deal with.'

'I'll go with that,' Sam agreed. 'Though the dogs I've known may not have been corrupt, but they're—'

'I should think not.' Grace wound pasta around her fork, raising her voice over the insistent thump of the background music.

'But they're certainly mercenary creatures,' Sam went on. 'Woody would do just about anything for a slice of ham or a tummy rub, and Harry was no different.'

'Domestic animals,' Terri said, tucking into her paella, 'dancing to man's tune.'

'Luckily for us,' Sam said, enjoying his swordfish.

'You love dogs, Teté,' Saul said, 'and Woody certainly likes you.'

'Woody's a sweetheart,' she agreed, 'and pets are fine, but I'd rather watch an animal in the wild.'

'Plenty of the two-legged variety in Miami,' Sam said.

'Cliché, bro.' Saul poked at his Alaskan king crab.

'I know.' Sam grinned.

'Did you ever consider a career in wildlife conservation, Terri?' Grace asked.

'Working in the wild was a bit of a fantasy for a while,' Terri replied. 'The two things that make me feel most alive are police work and being around animals, especially primates.'

'So what made you choose law enforcement?' Sam asked.

'Mostly, I think,' Terri answered, 'my grandma's tales about my grandfather.'

'He was a Manhattan cop,' Saul said. 'Died in the line of duty.'

'I didn't know that,' Sam said. 'I'm sorry.'

'My grandmother was so proud of him.' Terri's expression softened. 'She's been gone a while now, but I guess that's one of the things that drives me to be the best cop I can – wanting to make her proud of me too.'

'Sounds like a good reason to me,' Sam said.

'Me too,' Grace agreed.

'Still, going to the zoos – even if it's nothing compared to seeing them running free – but just getting as close as I can to those beautiful animals is the best relaxation I know.' She looked at Saul and smiled. 'Or did know.'

*   *   *

Cathy wasn't certain why she had not told Grace, that morning, that she was going running with Kez Flanagan. A kind of foolish embarrassment, she supposed, perhaps because she'd been feeling so nervous about it.

She had gone on feeling that way when she'd got to the track at Trent and had seen Kez warming up, waiting for her. She was wearing vivid orange shorts, ripped up the seam on the outside of her right thigh, a black cut-down T-shirt exposing a small mauve dragonfly tattoo on her right shoulder, battered Nikes and dark, impenetrable Wileys covering her eyes. The colour of the shorts, clashing with the bottlebrush-red hair, made her look, Cathy thought, funky and amazing, and made her wish she hadn't put on her nearly new Adidas shimmel and shorts.

'Hi.' Kez went on warming up.

'Sorry I'm late,' Cathy said.

'You're not.' Kez glanced at her. 'Looking good.'

'Overdressed.' Cathy felt herself blush. 'Are you sure about running with me?'

'Why wouldn't I be?'

'I'll hold you back.'

'We're not racing,' Kez said lightly.

Cathy set down her bag, took out her blue cotton, red-stitched Trent cap, stuck it on her head, pulling her ponytail through, and started some stretches.

'I told you,' Kez went on, 'I think you have promise.'

Cathy could feel her cheeks reddening again, reached back down into her bag for her own sunglasses, perhaps as much for camouflage as protection.

'And to be honest,' Kez told her, 'I'd like the company.'

'You must have a ton of people who'd run with you.' Cathy went on with her warm-up, knowing that the other woman was ready to go.

'I have people I could run with, sure,' Kez said.

Cathy heard a note of something beneath the briskness, looked up to try to gauge her expression, found it impossible with her eyes masked by the Wileys.

'Not many I want to, though.' Kez pulled a black baseball cap out of a pocket and put it on.

Cathy thought for a moment that she had identified that note, then realized almost as quickly that she couldn't be right.

Neediness. That's what she'd *thought* she'd heard.

Crazy.

Cathy looked at Kez Flanagan, at her lean, narrow frame, watched her beginning to move away on to the track, swinging her arms, flexing, bouncing gently, saw the long, supple, strong yet quite thin legs common to many runners, muscles and tendons clearly definable, even in semi-repose. She remembered seeing her run at Tampa – *'Tampa was special'*, Kez had said the other day, hadn't she? – and she remembered her supreme confidence, the respect and acclaim of her fellow Tornadoes, the applause of the spectators.

Nothing needy about Kez.

Running, for Cathy, had always been, at its very best, a lone experience. It was good in many ways to run with a group or be a part of a team, but her fundamental lack of self-confidence had prevented her from becoming a valuable team member, had blocked her full potential. When Cathy ran alone and unobserved, her legs felt stronger, her body indefatigable, her heart pumped blood more effectively, spread vitality around her body right down to her toes. As a lone runner, she *felt* like a real competitor, capable of winning, but whenever Coach Delaney had attempted to stretch her ability, the winner in Cathy had disappeared until finally the coach had all but given up.

Running with Kez felt different.

Watching her from a distance had been great, but running shoulder to shoulder with a fine and powerful athlete, close enough to hear the sharp, steady rasps of her breathing and feel the heat fanning out from her made everything seem more intense. Cathy could hear the pounding of Kez's spikes in a kind of counter-rhythm to her own thump, felt as if she were almost flying, as if running was *effortless*.

'Doing OK?' Kez slowed them down to a jogging rest after the first quarter mile.

'Great,' Cathy panted back.

'I'm going for it,' Kez said suddenly, and broke away.

Cathy considered for about a half second trying to go with her. *No way.* She watched her go, start to fly, cut loose from her running companion's dead weight, saw the red-black-orange blurring with speed and distance, began to slow her own pace, a peculiar kind of sorrow expanding to fill her chest until, finally, she realized it was her own overexertion forcing her to stop. She doubled over, fighting to control her breathing and pulse till she could look up and pinpoint Kez again, watch the end of her solo flight while she, a lesser mortal, reduced again to third-rate, commenced her own warm-down exercises.

'Feel like doing it again?' Kez asked after they'd downed water and rested for a while beneath the jacaranda where they'd first spoken the previous week.

'God, yes,' Cathy said. 'If you're sure.'

'Why not?' Kez said. 'I had fun. Makes a change from training solo.'

She was running, she said, in the 800 and 1500 meter events at the Trio Club meet up in West Palm Beach next weekend.

'Must be a bunch of guys you could train with,' Cathy said, casually.

'I already told you I don't want to train with them,' Kez said.

Cathy liked the compliment. 'Beach OK?' she suggested. 'Next time?'

'Good for me,' Kez said.

Seven

August 15

'I see Gregory Hoffman's been back,' Lucia Busseto said on Monday morning, bringing Grace a cup of one of the home-grown herbal teas that were her particular speciality.

Lucia called this one 'pregnancy tea', and Grace had long since forgotten much of what was in it; recalled, vaguely, camomile and nettle and alfalfa, had checked with Barbara Walden before trying it and had grown accustomed to its taste.

'Is he doing OK?' Lucia knew that although she had access to some patient files, whatever Gregory Hoffman and Grace had talked about on Saturday was not up for discussion.

Forty-one years old, widowed for a decade, a petite, slim, physically fit and attractive brunette with just a few strands of silver in her curly short hair, Lucia lived alone in the Key Biscayne home she had formerly shared with her husband, Phil. Her greatest regret, Lucia had once told Grace, was not having had children of her own – though she spoke animatedly about Phil's niece, Tina, a trainee nurse over in Naples and the apple of her eye, and told Grace regularly that working for a person whose *raison d'être* was helping troubled youngsters had made all the difference to her life.

'It's been a while,' Grace answered now, 'since I last saw Gregory.'

'Sip your tea, doctor,' Lucia told her, and sat down at her own desk, with the pretty miniature herb pots she'd brought from home over time. 'I'm not asking questions as such – I know better – but I'd so hoped he was doing better, and I just want to say that if you think it appropriate at any time, please would you send him my love.'

'Of course I will,' Grace said.

'Damned drugs,' Lucia said, darkly. 'Lovely boy like that, nice family.'

'Yes,' Grace said.

Lucia changed the subject. 'I thought you'd promised to stop working weekends.'

Grace smiled. 'You're very like Dora at times.'

'Because we both care about you.'

'And I'm grateful,' Grace assured her, 'but I've already had Sam and Cathy on my case about Saturday, and the only person who doesn't drive me just a little nuts on a daily basis is my father-in-law, and he's the doctor.'

'Maybe he doesn't see you overdoing things on a daily basis,' Lucia pointed out, then changed topics again. 'So how are things going for Detective Becket with the new murder?'

'You know I couldn't talk about that either,' Grace said, 'even if I knew anything.'

'I know it,' Lucia said easily. 'But I can't help being interested. We're all going to rest a whole lot more comfortably in our beds when the killer's behind bars.'

'Mr Muller wasn't killed in his bed,' Grace said, knowing that wasn't the point.

'On the beach. Just as bad.' Lucia put on her spectacles to commence some work, then took them off again. 'Cathy runs on the beach a lot, doesn't she?'

'In daylight,' Grace said, though she'd worried about that too since the murder.

'She often runs at sunset,' Lucia said.

'Plenty of people around at sunset,' Grace said. 'I thought you were trying to lower my stress levels.'

'Yes,' Lucia agreed. 'I'm sorry, doctor.'

'No problem,' Grace said. 'And are you ever going to start calling me Grace?'

'Professional women should be respected,' Lucia said.

Grace smiled, knew it was true that Lucia – who did not, so far as she knew, need to work for a living – had a fondness for the idea of working for a *doctor*, even if she was just a psychologist.

The spectacles were raised halfway to Lucia's curved nose. 'Does Detective Becket still think there's no connection with Trent?'

'Lucia,' Grace reproached.

'All right,' Lucia said. 'Sorry.'

Grace relented. 'I'm sure the police are checking things out at Trent,' she said, 'but that poor man's just as likely to have been killed by a stranger as by anyone who knew him, at work or anyplace else.'

'God rest his soul,' Lucia said.

No murderous strangers coming out of the woodwork.

No witnesses making themselves known, despite the televised re-enactments on TV. No calls, anonymous or otherwise, to the police tips hotline or to the *Herald* or any of the local radio stations.

Not an inch more common ground between the Pompano Beach and Muller killings. Carmelita Sanchez had been a homely mother of four, dressmaking when she hadn't been cleaning or taking care of her family. No new information about the janitor's past or private life to nudge Miami Beach's investigation in any specific direction. No convictions or arrest record. No evidence of drug-taking – though with the usual backlog, it was going to take a long while till the full toxicology report was in. No recent or even distant relationships, straight or gay, that anyone appeared to know of; and although it was generally agreed at his gym and at Trent that Muller had liked taking care of his body, no one seemed of the opinion that he had been obsessive.

The ransacking of a murder victim's life was an aspect of his work that Sam had never become comfortable with. The sifting through of everything from bank statements to dirty underwear was distasteful to him, however vital it was to an investigation.

'Victim's past caring,' Martinez regularly reminded him, but Sam felt that made it worse, particularly when, as in this case, the deceased seemed to have been beyond reproach.

Not that *anyone* deserved to have most of the bones in his face smashed and his throat cut, no matter what they'd done. Unless maybe they were child killers, Sam had to allow – privately, as a man, not a cop.

Rudolph Muller appeared to have been something of a loner, appeared to have hurt no one, angered no one, stolen from no one, had never committed a crime. Yet *someone* had done that to him, and maybe it had been a random killing, a psycho's fuse lit and ready to blow the next person they encountered, but Sam doubted that. It was too personal and angry a crime, he thought, though probably not a *crime passionel* because most lovers who killed in the heat of the moment balked at facial destruction precisely *because* of the feelings left in them.

This killing had been intensely violent.

'Rage-fuelled,' Sam said to Martinez.

'Lotta fruitcakes about,' the other man maintained.

Whole lotta fruitcakes, if Carmelita Sanchez had been slain by a separate killer. The thought made Sam feel no better.

Gregory Hoffman came for another session on Wednesday afternoon, half an hour after Lucia had left for the day.

When he had first been brought to Grace, he had come burdened by undiagnosed dyslexia and an accompanying lack of self-confidence, all his problems magnified – though it had taken him months to admit to that – by his marijuana habit.

'But he's just a *child*,' Annie Hoffman had protested when Grace had, with Gregory's agreement, broken the news to her.

Gregory and thousands of others, Grace had told the distraught mother, tens of thousands, probably more. Maybe in big cities, Annie had argued – meaning not in Sunny Isles Beach, not in an affluent, loving, Jewish home from which a twelve-year-old boy got driven to school by his dad and collected by his mom and taken to temple Sunday mornings so he could study for his bar mitzvah.

Grace had never found out when Greg's habit had begun or who had sold him his marijuana; she was his psychologist, not a police officer, and all she had cared about was getting through to him, *helping* him, and she had helped, they all had.

But here he was again, back down in the dark. Yet it was not, she felt, the same.

This was different, seriously so. Annie thought so, and Greg had said as much himself at the weekend.

He looked a little less freaked out, less haunted, this afternoon, but he was still patently disturbed and also physically worn, indefinably *damaged*. It would be easy, Grace realized, to pin this sudden downturn on some new chemical being pumped into his system, and she knew that a bad acid trip, for instance, might still be affecting him long after the stuff was out of his bloodstream – but still, all her instincts warned her that something else was at work here.

She had wondered, ever since Gregory had left on Saturday, what he had meant when he had said that he could cope with his nightmares, but that it was the 'waking stuff' he couldn't take.

'What did you mean by that, Greg?' she asked him now, out on the deck again.

He closed his eyes, and shuddered.

'Take your time,' Grace said.

The eyes remained shut, and his mouth worked for a moment.

'Saw me,' he said, so softly she had to strain to hear.

'Who saw you, Gregory?' Grace leaned forward as far as the baby would allow.

He said it again, the same two words.

'Saw me.'

He opened his eyes, and seemed, for a second, startled, disoriented.

'Greg?' Grace was gentle. 'Are you all right?'

'I can't do this.' He shook his head. 'I'm sorry, doc.'

'You said someone saw you,' Grace persevered. 'Did someone see you doing something, Greg? Is that what you've been dreaming about?'

'I can't tell you,' he said.

'I just want to help,' Grace said. 'You know it would be in confidence.'

He shook his head again. 'Uh-uh,' he said. 'Sorry, doc.'

There was an air of regretful finality about those last words, a sense of giving up.

The thought made Grace shiver.

She had just watched him climb into his mother's car, having agreed to speak with Annie and Jay later that evening, when Cathy's Mazda pulled up.

Grace guessed, the instant she saw the stranger climbing out of the passenger seat, that this was Kez Flanagan. Not just because of the short, vibrantly red hair that Cathy had described to her, but because of the way she moved.

An athlete, definitely, a runner like Cathy, but tougher, leaner, less feminine.

'Hi, there,' she said to them both from the doorway.

'Hi, Grace.' Cathy's cheeks were flushed. 'This is Kez Flanagan.' She smiled at the young woman. 'Kez, this is my mom, Grace.'

'Hello, Dr Becket.' Kez put out her hand.

'It's Dr Lucca,' Cathy said a little awkwardly.

'Grace is fine,' her mother said easily, and looked down at Kez's hands. 'Love the nails,' she said.

They all came inside and Cathy shut the door. 'She paints them herself.'

'That's amazing,' Grace said. 'I can barely manage to get basic colour on without smudging.'

'Woody shut in?' Cathy asked.

Right on cue, the little dog came flying out from the back, leaping up at Cathy in greeting, then turning to check out the visitor.

'Don't.' Kez backed up against the wall, knocking against the small Spanish tile-framed mirror. 'Please,' she said sharply, her voice hoarser. 'I'm not good with dogs.'

'It's OK.' Cathy lifted the mongrel off the stone floor, held him close, let him lick her face. 'Woody's cool,' she told Kez, 'and really gentle.'

'I'm sure.' Kez stayed close to the wall. 'Maybe we should go.'

'We're going for a run on the beach,' Cathy explained to Grace. 'Thought we'd come by for a quick juice first.'

'Put Woody in the den,' Grace told Cathy.

'No need,' Kez said. 'We can just go—'

'It's no problem at all.' Grace felt for her.

They went through to the kitchen, collecting juice and water, taking the drinks out on to the deck.

'I got bitten as a kid.' Kez was clearly embarrassed. 'Badly enough to need stitches and shots. I've never been able to get past it.'

'I don't blame you,' Cathy said.

'It's very natural,' Grace said.

'Doesn't stop people laughing at me, especially when the dogs are cute.'

'I wouldn't laugh,' Cathy said.

Kez smiled at her. 'No,' she said.

The connection between them struck Grace quite forcibly.

The beginnings of something *more* than friendship, she felt, at least from Kez's standpoint; she thought she'd glimpsed a distinct strength of feeling in the young woman's interesting eyes.

They had all noticed Cathy's high excitement last Friday evening when she'd talked about her meeting with the college athlete, and Grace had been aware of a degree of hero-worship in that excitement, but nothing more. More than that now, she realized as the two young women finished their drinks, then sat with her a while longer, exchanging questions and answers about running and their respective majors, Kez seeming genuinely interested in Grace's and Sam's disparate professions.

'Isn't she great?' Cathy whispered to Grace as they were leaving, Kez ahead of them and out of earshot. 'Don't you think?'

Grace looked into Cathy's blue eyes – so like her own that, together with their similarly straight blonde hair, strangers often took them for biological mother and daughter – and realized she'd never seen them sparkle that way before. And then, hard on the heels of that thought sprang another: that Cathy, still quite naïve despite all her experiences, seemed to be in Kez Flanagan's thrall.

The idea disturbed Grace, and not just, she thought, because she felt it probable that Kez was gay – would she mind, she asked herself sharply, almost accusingly, if Cathy was lesbian or even bisexual?

So many thoughts in the blink of an eye.

'She's very nice,' she answered.

She waved them off, then closed the door, still feeling troubled.

There had been, it was true, surprisingly few boyfriends in Cathy's life so far. One spell during which Cathy had come to Grace to share with her the fact that she was dating a guy called Nick Cohen and had decided to take the pill; but that relationship had ended soon after, and since then men seemed – so far as Grace and Sam knew – to have been a little thin on the ground.

It had not appeared to have bothered Cathy.

Certainly no indications at any time – Grace reflected on her way back to her office to commence writing up her notes on Gregory Hoffman's appointment – that Cathy might be harbouring doubts about her sexual orientation. Though then again, Grace knew better than some the myriad conundrums buried in the human psyche. And in some ways, of course, ceasing to be Cathy's therapist and becoming her mother had almost automatically restricted her access to her daughter's inner-most secrets.

There was a possibility, Grace considered, that if Cathy had ever been physically attracted to another woman she might – perhaps keeping faith with her late, devoutly Catholic mother – have felt uneasy with that. And if Cathy had feared that either coming out or even confiding any confusion might have caused her new family the slightest discomfort – surely not, Grace hoped – then she might have chosen to suppress the truth altogether, to keep it buried, perhaps even from herself.

Something about Kez Flanagan had touched Grace. The way she had reacted to Woody, the sudden exposing of a fear some might translate as weakness. In a tough-shelled young athlete, that kind of sensitivity might create insecurities.

Good match for Cathy, then, perhaps.

So long as Kez didn't hurt her.

Getting way ahead of yourself, Grace.

It was her day for unexpected visitors.

Less than five minutes later, Terri Suarez arrived – so swiftly after the other two had left that Grace wondered for an instant if she might have been waiting for them to go.

'What a lovely surprise,' Grace told her. 'Though you just missed Cathy and her friend. You probably saw them, heading off for a run.'

Terri shook her head. 'I should have called first, but I was nearby and I wanted to talk to you, if that's OK.'

'Of course it is.' Grace led the way to the kitchen, releasing Woody from the den as they passed, watching Terri enjoying his exuberant greeting. 'So long as I'm not with a patient, it's open house here.'

She asked if Terri wanted to go out back, but the younger woman said she'd be glad to stay inside in the cool, so Grace poured them both some iced tea and they went into the den, made themselves comfortable in the tranquil room – its walls covered with children's paintings – that sometimes doubled as her consulting room.

Terri wasted no time.

'I want to talk about the way Sam feels about me.'

'In what way?' Grace hid her dismay, had hoped their South Beach lunch might have eased the situation.

'Sunday was fine,' Terri said. 'Nice food, getting to know each other.'

'We enjoyed it,' Grace said.

'And you were great and kind, and everyone was cool. Sam, too, on the face of it.'

'Sam tends not to hide his feelings.' Grace tried not to sound prickly. 'Especially with family and close friends.'

'Thanks for that,' Terri went on frankly. 'I just feel that he still has reservations about me, or maybe just about Saul and me as a couple.'

'Sam's very much a big brother, Terri,' Grace said. 'Perhaps even more of a second dad, in some ways, because of the age difference. You'll have worked all that out for yourself.'

'Sure.'

'He may have had some reservations, but I honestly don't think he has any more.' Grace paused. 'Sam just wants Saul to be happy and safe.'

'That's all I want too,' Terri said.

Grace smiled at her. 'Terri, I truly think you should stop stressing about what Sam or anyone else thinks, and enjoy your time with Saul.'

'You don't get it,' Terri said. 'Not really.'

'Then why don't you tell me what I'm not getting?' Grace was gentle. 'I'd so much like to help if I can.'

Terri got up, walked over to the window, and Grace felt a swift dart of envy looking at the curvy little breasts under the plain white T-shirt, the narrow waist and neat behind, all accentuated by her tight blue jeans. Grace loved being pregnant but couldn't quite imagine ever being slim again; she looked forward, once the baby was born, to feeling less clumsy and to seeing – as pregnant women were always saying – her toes again.

'I've thought about saying to hell with what Saul's family thinks about me.' Terri tossed her dark hair a little. 'I know my own worth, I know Saul loves me and that's what matters most.' She shook her head. 'Except it's not the only thing, is it, when you really care about someone?'

Grace smiled again. 'Not always.'

'I've never met anyone like him before.' Terri sat down again. 'He's so gentle and kind, but he still manages to have this real lust for living, you know?'

'Like his dad,' Grace said.

'I'm not sure his dad doesn't have the same kind of doubts about me,' Terri said. 'Saul says he doesn't, that I'm imagining problems, but—'

'Don't you trust Saul?' Grace asked.

'Of course I do.'

'Then why not believe him?'

'You're telling me I'm worrying unnecessarily, too.'

'Yes,' Grace said. 'I think I am.'

She was not at all certain, when Terri left a few minutes later, that she had managed to convince her of that.

'I think this is where the janitor was killed.'

They had covered less than a mile, running south along the beach, were just approaching North Shore Open Space Park, when Cathy said that to Kez. Then, less than a second later, she let out a cry of pain and jolted to a halt, sending up a cloud of sand.

'Damn,' she said. 'My ankle.'

Kez came quickly to her side. 'Bad?'

'Don't think so,' Cathy said, wincing. 'I just turned it a little.'

'Sit down.' Kez nodded towards an Australian pine. 'Let me help you.'

Cathy shook her head. 'I can walk.' She tested her left ankle. 'Just don't think I should run on it yet. I'm sorry.'

'Don't be silly,' Kez said. 'We should get some ice on it.'

They got a makeshift ice pack and some mineral water at the 81st Street Café on Collins Avenue opposite the park gate.

'I didn't realize your dad was working on the janitor case,' Kez said after she'd organized another chair for Cathy to rest her foot on.

Cathy nodded. 'Working all hours.'

'No suspects yet?'

'I'd be the last to know,' Cathy told her. 'Sam hardly talks about work at home, and never in front of me – ' her smile was self-conscious – 'in case it messes with my head.'

'Your head,' Kez remarked, 'seems pretty well screwed on to me.' She paused. 'Though I guess I can understand why your folks might prefer to keep off that kind of subject.'

Cathy was silent for a moment. 'I presume you know about my history.'

'Some,' Kez replied.

'The edited highlights.' Cathy was wry. 'Freak show, huh?'

'Sad, cruel show,' Kez said.

Cathy saw sympathy in her face and something more besides and, not being quite certain what that was, she averted her eyes and looked down at her ankle.

'Pain?' Kez asked.

Cathy shook her head. 'It's feeling better.'

'Take care of it,' Kez said.

'I will.'

Kez took a minute, then said: 'I've thought about what you must have gone through back then, but it's hard to imagine. Just losing my own dad messed with my head for the longest time, and that was natural causes, or kind of.'

'Kind of?' Cathy felt a touch of guilt. 'Sorry, it's personal.'

'I raised it,' Kez said. 'And yes, it is very personal, but I don't think I'd mind sharing it with you – which is interesting, because I've never shared it with anyone else before.'

Cathy was silent.

'I loved my dad a lot, and I always knew he was pretty crazy about me.' Kez took a breath. 'I thought he felt that way about my mom, too.' Her mouth compressed for an instant. 'But when it came right down to it, Joey Flanagan was no better than a lot of men.'

She was looking directly at Cathy as she spoke, but a veil of something, perhaps of self-protection, had slipped down over her eyes, and Cathy could not tell if it was pain or toughness that lay behind.

'Fact was,' Kez continued, 'he had a massive heart attack in the middle of screwing Mrs Jerszinsky, our next-door neighbour, while my mother was out shopping and I was watching them through the keyhole of my parents' bedroom door.'

'Wow,' Cathy said.

'Not in the same league as your traumas,' Kez said. 'Like comparing a little jolt with an earthquake, I guess, but I was seven years old and like I said, it did a good job of messing with my head.'

'I can imagine. How come—?' Cathy stopped.

'How come I was watching?' Kez said. 'It was a weekend, and my dad thought I was at a friend's house across the street, but we had a disagreement and I came back early, heard some weird sounds and took a look.'

'And your dad—'

'I don't like thinking about that,' Kez said quickly.

'Sure,' Cathy said. 'I can understand that.'

'I guess you can.' Kez shrugged. 'I've often wondered – even if our sexual identity does come pre-packaged with our genes – if that afternoon didn't help put me off men.'

Cathy had heard it rumoured on the Trent grapevine that Kez was gay, but she didn't think it had really occurred to her until this instant that Kez might possibly be attracted to her.

Of course she wasn't, she told herself swiftly, why should she be? There certainly hadn't been too many guys lusting after her over the years – though then again, Nick aside, she hadn't particularly wanted them either.

Slow down.

That wasn't the point anyway, was not what was really startling her. What was throwing Cathy for a loop right now was her own reaction.

Excitement.

'You OK?'

Kez's voice sliced through the mess of Cathy's thoughts, reminded her that the only reason they were here talking was that she had turned her ankle during a run, and Kez was just being kind to her.

'Fine,' she said quickly, taking off the ice pack and lowering her foot to the floor.

It wasn't as if Kez Flanagan was some shrinking violet, shy about coming to the point. She was an independent woman with her own apartment in Coconut Grove; a talented runner with a string of wins under her belt who had just simply and casually confirmed her sexuality while expressing no interest in Cathy's preferences.

'Ready to try walking out of here?' Kez asked.

'Sure.' Cathy stood up and tried out the foot.

'How does it feel?'

Kindness, nothing more.

'Good.' Cathy took a step. 'It's nothing.'

'You should still ice it again when you get home, and elevate it. And no running for the rest of the week, OK?'

Definitely kindness.

Though the hazel eyes were still steady on her face, unwavering. Interested.

Maybe, Cathy thought – and that frisson of excitement hit her again.

She was not entirely sure how she felt about that.

Eight

With Terri working that evening and David at a friend's house playing cards, Saul stayed home in Golden Beach, sanding down the edges of the new desk he'd been making for his room, thinking about how much he loved working with wood and how much he looked forward to having his own place someday – with Terri, if she'd have him – with a spare room or maybe a garage he could turn into a workshop.

'Take any room you like,' David had told him more than once.

No shortage of space here at home, they both knew that, two men rattling around in a house that had comfortably held four; but Saul didn't want to build his workshop in his father's house because it would feel too much like giving up hope of moving out.

Which was no insult to his dad because Saul loved him with all his heart, found him the easiest man in the world to live with. But wanting his own place was natural, and David had made it plain that he understood that, was happy to have his company for as long as it lasted, but would encourage his leaving when the time came.

'You know I could afford to help,' he'd offered not long ago, aware of his son's restlessness, but Saul had said he didn't want that either, and his father respected that.

It was Saul's own self-respect that was a little lacking these days – or maybe it was simple disappointment in himself. He had anticipated his freshman year at the University of Miami with such relish, certain he was ready for the tough but stimulating journey to medical practice. At the end of the first year, the plan was for him to have a high enough grade point average to apply to the Medical Scholars Program, admission into which would assure him of a place, at the end of his third year of study, at UM's School of Medicine.

That was the plan, but truth was as different as hell.

'I don't think I'm going to make it,' he'd confided in Terri that spring.

'Sure you are,' she'd told him. 'You're smart and—'

'Even if I was, it's not just about that,' Saul had said. 'I walk into the Merrick Building every day and I'm surrounded by all these bright, confident people—'

'You just think they're confident,' Terri had said.

'A whole lot of them *are*,' Saul had insisted. 'Certainly far more than I am.'

That was brought home to him at every lecture, as fellow students asked and answered and made worthwhile points or offered salient arguments, while Saul's butt stayed glued to his seat and his mouth stayed shut.

He'd always been the quiet kid at home, content to enjoy the arguments or wit or tales that the rest of his family had brought into the house; his quietness in those days stemming from tranquillity and contentment.

No more. These days there was an ever-growing heap of self-doubt piling up on his head, making it harder and harder for him to think.

Making furniture was a satisfying way to procrastinate, exchanging study for the feel and aroma of smooth wood; the exhilarating, sometimes simply mind-numbing exercise of sawing and hammering and planning. Even the noise and vibration of power tools helped block out unwelcome doubts about his other, real work.

Except *this* was what felt infinitely more real to Saul, and certainly more attainable: making tables, shelves and chairs, starting out real simple, then becoming slowly more confident and creative.

'So quit medicine,' Terri had said. 'Make furniture.'

'It's not that simple,' Saul had told her.

'Sure it is,' she'd said. 'One life. One chance.'

There'd been no real pressure to struggle on from his dad, but Judy Becket had badly wanted Saul to follow David's lead, and then there were Sam's high hopes for his kid brother, and Saul hated falling out with him over anything, which was why this problem between Sam and Terri had really been getting to him.

God, he was so crazy about Teté, but not knowing exactly where they were heading as a couple worried him, too, his anxiety that he wasn't lively enough for her, special enough for her. And that was *another* thing about studying medicine; no prospect of offering her anything tangible for years, though Terri said she didn't care about that. So long as this was what he really wanted, she said, she'd be up for the long haul, and it would all be worth it when he was finally a doctor and helping people.

So why didn't she want him moving into her place?

'We both need our space for now,' she had said.

Saul didn't need space, not when it came to Terri. If she'd allowed it, he'd happily have moved into a *closet* with her.

'Anyway, your dad needs you,' she'd said too.

But that wasn't true, so Saul figured that no matter what she said, the truth was that he probably just wasn't enough for her. Teté was so alive and brave, she had this amazing wild side to her, and he would do just about anything for her. Except he couldn't do *anything*, could he, because he was still a student living at home with his old man, who was a great guy, but still . . .

And how long was Terri going to put up with that?

Nine

August 19

Gregory didn't think he could take this any more, this sense of doom, feeling so *bad*, sleeping and waking. And he knew there was only one way to help himself feel better, he *knew* it, and he'd been so damned scared since *it* happened, had been straight and clean and feeling like shit because he was clean.

Except the truth was he wasn't feeling shit because of not doing coke, was he? It was because of what had happened, because of what he'd seen, because he was scared half out of his mind that he or she or *it* was going to come back for him *because* he'd seen it. And maybe the only thing that was going to help him *was* coke, because the fact was no one else was going to be able to help: no doctor, no parents, no shrink.

What Greg needed now, more than anything – except for it

not to have happened, or at least for him not to have *seen* it happening – was for the memory and the fear to go away.

Cocaine could do that for him.

And it wasn't as if he even had to go looking for it, not as if he had to risk his mom and dad or even the cops finding out he was buying it, because he already had it, didn't he?

Because last night Santa had come down his frigging chimney, metaphorically speaking.

Because when Greg had got up this Friday morning and unlocked the sliding doors to the deck outside his bedroom, he had seen it lying less than eight feet away.

Folded silver paper glinting in the sunlight.

Plastic baggie inside.

And sure, it was kind of weird, *more* than kind of, actually, because how in hell had it got there? And Gregory had wondered if maybe one of the guys who knew how freaked out he was feeling had left it as a gift, because otherwise how *could* it have got there? But bottom line, it *was* there.

It had come just when he needed it. So tonight, if he still didn't feel any better . . .

Tonight.

It was late Friday when Kez called Cathy to ask if she felt like driving up to West Palm Beach for the meet the next day.

'I could use the support if you'd like to come,' Kez said, 'and if your ankle's up to it.'

'My ankle's fine, but I'll bet you'll have a zillion supporters,' Cathy said, though she'd been longing to go up, but suppressing the urge, figuring that since Kez had not asked if she was going, that had to mean she didn't want her there.

Not the case.

'No one but the coach that I know of,' Kez said. 'And I'd like having you in the crowd.'

Excitement shot through Cathy again, warming her. Another kind of longing, she thought, still unsure. About anything.

Except that she wanted to go.

The first hundred metres of the 800 was run in lanes, but after that, as often happened in this race, the runners were bunched so close for the rest of the first lap that had it not been for the fierce red of Kez's hair – no sun, so she was wearing no cap – Cathy might not have been able to pick her out of the pack.

At Sarasota where Cathy had seen Kez win the 800, one of the competitors had gone off fast, driving all the runners into too high a speed in the first lap, and with the favourite laid up with a broken ankle and the other main threat, Maria Valdez, finding herself boxed in on the inside, Kez had been the athlete with the most strength and speed on the last lap. Valdez had come home first in Tampa, but Kez's run had been both tactically near-perfect and almost – even Coach Delaney had felt – inspired, gaining her the silver.

'Tail wind,' Kez had answered self-deprecatingly when Cathy had asked her, at the café on Wednesday, what she thought had made that race so special.

'Why do you do that?' Cathy had asked. 'Make it sound like nothing.'

'Just one race. Greatest buzz in the world at the time, but doesn't mean much on its own.'

Coming right after Sarasota, Cathy had wanted to argue, she'd have thought it meant a hell of a lot. But something – a kind of reluctance to overstep – had held her back, kept her silent.

Later, perhaps, when – if – they knew one another better.

If.

A lot of talent was absent today in West Palm Beach, and even as Cathy saw Kez breaking away from the pack and sprinting into the lead, she guessed that if her new friend broke the finish tape, she'd be the first to point that out.

Which didn't stop Cathy yelling her support, *shrieking* as Kez crossed the line.

'Pal of yours?' the man next to her asked. 'She's not bad.'

'Not bad?' Cathy told him. 'She's *amazing*.'

'Yeah.' The man shrugged and smiled. 'Good for her.'

There was no victory in the 1500, but Cathy was yelling just as wildly, and sure, she was used to cheering on the Tornadoes, but she knew that she'd never shouted this loudly before. Had never *felt* like this before. Watching Kez running in this race, the distance so much tougher than the 800, physically and psychologically; watching her giving her all and *then* some, observing the fiercely working muscles on those tanned legs, the intensity of her focus, the obvious pain on her face from the pounding punishment, the pace and sheer speed of the sprint. Noting her grimace, the moment when fatigue took control, mastered her, then, finally, wiped her out.

'I'm fine,' Kez told her later, shrugging off defeat as she had victory.

She was starved, she said, knew exactly what she wanted – and no, the coach didn't know and would not approve, but she hardly ever broke diet rules and right now, at least sometime in the next hour or two, she wanted *steak*.

They left West Palm Beach and Cathy drove them – Kez had come up in Mike Delaney's car – to Fort Lauderdale and found Ruth's Chris Steak House, because most people agreed their sizzling broiled steaks were the best around.

'You've told me,' Kez said a while later, eating Gulf shrimp, 'why you run, but I haven't told you why I do.'

'Because you're so talented.' Cathy speared a heart of lettuce from her salad. 'Because, I guess, you have no choice?'

'I started out running,' Kez said, 'because I could, went on because I seemed pretty good at it and then, like you, I got hooked.' She finished a shrimp, licked her fingers, met Cathy's eyes. 'But you run partly to get away from things, and I run because I'm afraid that if I stop I'll get ugly again.'

'Ugly?' Cathy could not keep the astonishment out of her voice.

'Oh, yeah,' Kez said. 'I was a real ugly teenager.'

'You can't have been,' Cathy said.

'I'm no oil painting now.' Kez held out her hands, palms down, fingers splayed. 'That's why I do stuff like paint my nails this way.'

'I figured it was a tribute to Flo-Jo,' Cathy said.

'Sure,' Kez allowed. 'I admired the hell out of her – who didn't?' She paused. 'But I also do it because they distract people from the rest of me.'

'That's crazy,' Cathy said. 'You're wonderful to look at.'

'You're very kind,' Kez said.

'No,' Cathy insisted. 'Your face, your body, it's all marvellous.'

Kez shook her head. 'You're too beautiful to understand.'

Cathy laughed.

'What's funny?' Kez asked sharply.

Cathy looked at her in surprise and saw what looked like hurt in her eyes, perhaps a hint of anger too, realized suddenly that Kez might think she was laughing at her.

'I guess I'm embarrassed.' She paused. 'I've never seen myself as beautiful.'

The hurt and anger had already left Kez's eyes.

'Then you're the one who's crazy,' she said.

She was looking at Cathy now with warmth. Making her feel special.

There was no doubting one thing.

Cathy had never met a guy who'd made her feel like that.

'Did you see how she looked?' Grace asked Sam softly.

Cathy had come in a while back and found them settled in the den watching one of the old British sitcoms they enjoyed; Woody on the sofa between them, sharing the popcorn Grace had developed a liking for during the pregnancy. She hadn't said much about her day, just that she'd had a great dinner and was tired and going straight to bed, and then she'd gone upstairs.

'Happy,' Sam said. 'Like she had a good time.'

'Mmm,' Grace said. 'Little more than that, I'd say.'

He watched her for a moment. 'And that's bad, why?'

'Not bad, of course not.' Grace thought for a moment. 'I can't give you a good reason why I feel this way, but I just seem to have this sense that Kez might be having a more powerful influence than Cathy may realize.'

Sam frowned, then leaned forward. 'What kind of influence?'

Grace shook her head. 'I'm probably turning into a neurotic mom, scared of Cathy getting hurt.'

'Nothing neurotic about that,' Sam said, 'especially not in Cathy's case.' He fondled the dog's ears. 'Gracie, just tell me what you're thinking – just say it.'

'I think Kez is gay,' she said.

'And?' Sam waited, looked at her face. 'You're kidding, right?'

'I don't know.'

'Cathy isn't gay,' he said with absolute conviction. 'I know there haven't been that many guys around for a while, but she's only ever dated men—' He broke off. 'Unless you know something I don't?'

'Not at all,' Grace said. 'This is just some kind of instinct.'

'Then I don't get what your instinct is telling you,' Sam said. 'That Cathy might be lesbian?' He paused, his brain working to catch up. 'It's never entered my head for a second, but it would be OK, wouldn't it?' He shook his head. 'It would be absolutely fine with me, so long as it made her happy.' His brow creased. 'Are you saying you think Kez is out to *seduce* her?'

He stood up. 'And if she is, what makes you think Cathy couldn't handle that?'

'Nothing,' Grace said. 'She's a survivor, after all.'

'I think – ' Sam sat down again, moved Woody to the end of the sofa so he could get close to Grace, take her hand – 'you're overreacting, which is unlike you.'

'I know,' Grace agreed. 'They've gone running together a few times – they both go to Trent – Cathy went to see her friend compete at a meet.'

'But your instincts are telling you there's more to it, and for some reason, that's worrying you.'

'Only a little,' Grace said. 'As you said, she looked happy.'

'Which is all we want,' Sam said.

They were both still awake two hours later.

'Feeling OK, Gracie?' Sam turned on his bedside lamp, propped himself up on one elbow and looked at her, lying on her side on the big maternity pillow they'd recently bought in the hope that she might sleep more comfortably.

'Fine,' she said. 'You?'

'I'm not pregnant.'

'No, but you've been lying there wide awake and scared to move in case you disturb your big, fat pregnant wife.'

'True,' Sam said.

Grace rolled on to her back and cuddled closer, Sam resting his hand in its new favourite place, somewhere over what he thought of as the greatest gift anyone had given him since Althea had born him Sampson.

'So,' Grace said, 'your turn to tell me what you're thinking.'

'OK,' he said. 'Do you really think Cathy's still vulnerable enough to allow herself to be coerced into a major lifestyle decision she would not otherwise make?'

'I don't know,' Grace answered. 'I hope not.'

They fell silent. Sam's hand remained on her belly.

'I take it,' Grace went on slowly, 'we're both agreed that if it were to turn out that Cathy wanted to choose that path, we would support her one hundred per cent?'

'No doubt about it,' Sam said. 'A thousand per cent.'

Grace laid her own hand over his. 'But?'

'No buts about supporting her,' he answered. 'Except we both know it's not an easy path to follow, especially when your history's as messed up as Cathy's.'

'Don't forget I may be entirely wrong,' Grace said.

'I don't know,' Sam said. 'I've grown to trust your hunches.'

'Not a hunch,' she pointed out. 'Instinct.'

'Even more powerful.' He sighed. 'It bothers me some, too, that Kez is older—'

'Only by a couple of years,' Grace said.

'Almost certainly more experienced.'

'We can't know that.'

'I guess that's the main point,' Sam said. 'We can't – we don't – know anything about Kez, or the way Cathy may, or may not, feel about her.'

'And Cathy may be vulnerable, but I got the sense the other day that the same could be said for Kez.' Grace smiled. 'Which may just make them a good match.'

'And probably just good friends,' Sam said.

'Perhaps,' Grace said.

'But you don't believe that, do you?'

'I believe that our daughter has a certain wisdom,' Grace replied.

'So we just better trust her,' Sam said.

'And be there for her if she needs us.'

'Otherwise, butt out,' Sam said.

'Definitely,' Grace said.

Sam leaned towards her, kissed her on the mouth.

'Could you sleep now, do you think, fat, pregnant, beautiful wife?'

'So long as you go on holding me,' Grace told him.

Ten

August 21

Annie Hoffman heard her husband's scream, and *knew*.

Just another gorgeous Sunday morning in Sunny Isles.

Jay showering and getting dressed before making coffee, then telling her he was going to see if Greg was up and ask him if he wanted to come buy the papers and pick up bagels and lox.

'Greg?'

She heard that first. The last shred of normality, her husband calling his son's name as he knocked on his bedroom door.

Then the door opening – and for a few more seconds, maybe as many as ten, she was still herself, still Annie Hoffman, wife and mother of two.

And then she heard Jay's scream, primal and terrible, filling the sweet Sunday morning, filling her ears, her brain, *all* of her.

And she knew. Was already picturing Gregory hanging, had never realized until this instant that it was an image she had been harbouring in her mind for a long time; that this was what she had been so terrified of since the time of her beautiful boy's first depression.

Stay here.

A voice in her head was telling her, even as she was already moving, that if she stayed in this room, turned on the TV, volume up high, maybe even locked the door, she need never know, not for sure.

But she was already on her way, had already crossed the hallway, taken a swift, wild look into five-year-old Janie's room, and her daughter was still in bed, just stirring, and swiftly Annie closed the door again and locked it.

The door to Greg's room was open.

She stepped inside.

No one – nothing – bed empty, room empty – not there, not *hanging* – the glass door to the deck open, the sounds of the bay, sweet water sounds, flowing in.

And then another sound.

Her husband, keening.

Annie stopped, stood motionless for one more instant, then walked outside.

Jay was sitting on the deck, turned, saw her.

'No, Annie,' he said, ashen-faced, 'don't look.'

She looked.

At her boy, *their* boy.

The picture in her head had been nothing compared to this.

'Mommy!'

Janie's voice, from inside, frightened by her locked door and the awful sounds her daddy was making.

And her mommy now, too.

Sam was at the department and Cathy – still giving her ankle a rest from running – had gone for a swim, and so Grace was home alone when David called with the news that Gregory had died, most probably of a drug overdose.

'I'd have liked to spare you this,' he said, 'but Jay thinks you might possibly be able to help Annie in some way, maybe just persuade her to take something. I've tried, but she's . . .' His voice was weary. 'You can imagine.'

'No,' Grace said, deeply shaken. 'Thank God, I can't begin to imagine.'

As Gregory's doctor, David had been the first person Jay Hoffman had called, aware there was nothing the paramedics could have done for his son. David had told Jay that of course he would come, but that he needed to call the Sunny Isles police right away, because from what Jay had said this was not a natural death, which meant the cops would have to bring in the medical examiner.

'Do you know what he took?' Grace asked David now.

'I can't say,' he replied. 'I didn't examine him, but—'

'But what?'

'There's no point in speculating, Grace. But if you can stand going—'

'David, please.' Grace persisted. 'You know me well enough to know I won't repeat a syllable of anything you tell me.' She paused. 'It might make a tiny difference to how I try to help Annie.'

'Not a word, OK? This is the ME's territory, not mine.'

'Goes without saying.'

'Definitely drugs of some kind, possibly cocaine – I'm no expert, thank God. But I saw some silver paper and one of those damned little plastic bags near the boy, and . . .' He hesitated again. 'And this probably means nothing, but it looked to me as if maybe whatever he took was bad.'

'Dear God.' Grace's horror was intensifying.

'I'm very likely wrong.' David sounded very upset. 'Gregory's face was very contorted, probably from some kind of convulsion, which could have been caused by any number of things, but—'

This time, Grace waited for him to go on.

'But it wasn't just his face,' David added. 'His whole body looked contorted. I think the drugs might have been cut with something toxic. It happens all the time, doesn't it? Drugs adulterated for a bigger "high". Rat poison added or insecticide, God alone knows what else.' The doctor's sigh was heavy and sad. 'Craziness.'

Grace summoned up the courage to ask the question that seemed, at that moment, to be the most unbearable of all.

'Not suicide then?' She felt the baby kick, laid her free hand over her stomach.

'I can't commit myself to that, Grace.'

'I don't know if Jay told you,' she said, 'that I saw Greg twice last week.'

'He did tell me,' David said gently.

'I couldn't help him,' Grace said. 'Didn't help him.'

'You tried,' David said.

Not hard enough came into her mind, and she dismissed it, angry at herself, because this was most certainly not about her, this was about a fourteen-year-old boy and his parents and little sister.

'I'll go,' she said. 'Right away.'

She drove the familiar route up Collins, passing Haulover Park, dozens of apartment blocks and hotels, steeling herself all the way for the questioning likely to come – if not now, then later – from the distraught, grieving parents.

Some years ago a severely depressed patient of hers had committed suicide, and Grace had never forgotten the agony of that girl's mother and father, nor her own anguish and self-recrimination.

And Cathy, don't forget Cathy.

Who'd cried for help once a long time ago, had tried . . .

Not now.

Fiercely, Grace pushed that terrible memory away, concentrated on Gregory.

Accidental, please. Her desperate need for this boy's death not to be suicide was, of course, primarily for his family's sake, but there was undeniable selfishness in it too as she trawled back and forth through her mental log of those last two sessions with the teenager.

Disturbed, damaged, haunted; above all, scared. Not suicidal. At least not when Grace had seen him, but that didn't preclude a deterioration.

If, say, the unknown cause of his terrors had in some way tightened its grip, Gregory might have found it intolerable. Unbearable enough, at least, to use whatever substance had been in the bag David had seen near the body.

The closing stages of her final appointment with Greg came back to her. Those two words she'd had to strain to hear.

'Saw me.'

He had looked so frightened when he'd said that. More than frightened. Terrified.

Had that perhaps been nothing more real than the product of a drug-disordered mind, something reaching out of his night-mares to grab him by the throat, the awful dreams that had driven his mother to bring him back to Grace for help?

No help given.

Horrors on horrors beyond the palms and begonias in the pretty front garden of the Hoffman family home on North Bay Road.

The body had been taken away, but Miami Dade police and crime-scene technicians were all over the house, coming in and out of the teenager's bedroom, moving to and fro from the deck; evidence bags being sealed, cameras flashing, marine patrol officers visible on the *Pegasus*, all the peace of the bay sickeningly destroyed.

More like a homicide, Grace thought, than accident or suicide, then remembered what David had said about the drugs maybe being adulterated.

Toxic. Enough to kill.

'Oh dear God, Annie,' she said when she saw the other woman.

Ravaged already, the pretty face changed for ever.

'Grace,' she said. 'Thank you for coming.'

Grace stood there uncertainly, wanting to embrace her, but half expecting Annie to strike out at her, rage at her, the person she had come to for help.

It was Annie who put out her arms to her.

'I know, Grace,' she said, weeping softly. 'I know.'

'They can never get over this,' Grace told Sam later, at home. 'I'll never forget what Annie told me, so how will she ever be able to bear it?'

It seemed ineradicably etched in her mind, the description of Gregory's poor body, arched back, the dark colour of his face, the blood from his nose. His terrible grimace. Unbearable.

'There were photos of him everywhere,' Grace went on. 'All his belongings strewn around, as if he was still right in the middle of things, alive and *there*, and Annie and Jay were both extraordinary to me.'

It was early evening and they had come out on to their own deck, letting the sorrows of the day wash over them.

'So kind, I could hardly believe it,' she said.

'They're good people,' Sam said.

'I was expecting them to lash out at me,' Grace went on, 'because maybe they might feel I'd failed Greg, which is true, of course.'

'No,' Sam said firmly. 'It is not true.'

'I saw him twice last week.' Grace didn't bother to wipe away the angry tears in her eyes. 'Two hours, and I achieved nothing.'

'They're not always ready,' Sam said. 'You've told me that.'

'I could have pushed harder.'

'And risked driving him away altogether.'

'I managed that anyway, didn't I?' She tried to get up swiftly, but the baby's weight seemed to pin her down, so instead she slumped back in her chair and covered her eyes with both hands. 'Sorry.'

'Gracie.' Sam was out of his own chair and on his knees, taking her in his arms. 'Don't do this to yourself. You did your best, like you always do, with all your patients.' He prised her hands from her face, and looked at her. 'This must be the hardest thing in the world for you.'

'Forget me.' She pulled one hand free and rubbed fiercely at her eyes. 'That poor, poor boy.'

'And his poor, poor parents.'

She shook her head, brought herself back under control. 'Jay asked me some questions about those last two sessions, and I had so few answers for him, but I could see, anyway, that he was afraid of hearing them.'

'Afraid maybe,' Sam said, 'of being shown what he thinks he should have seen for himself.' He looked up at the darkening sky. 'Ultimate failure, for a father.'

Sampson's small coffin back again in his mind, making him shudder.

'Don't.' Grace leaned forward and put her arms around him.

He tried to smile. 'I won't, if you won't.'

'Not quite that easy, is it?' Grace said.

'I don't suppose,' Sam said softly, 'it's meant to be.'

'Dr Becket called,' Lucia told Grace on Tuesday morning after a bereavement session with an eleven-year-old girl who'd recently lost her mother to cancer. 'About Gregory.'

Lucia had been so deeply upset yesterday morning when Grace had broken the news of Greg's death that Grace had wanted to send her home, but Lucia had said it was out of the question, that if there was ever a day on which Grace needed all the help and support she could get, this was it.

'Besides,' she had said, 'we owe it to Gregory, don't we, to help the others.'

And then she had wiped her eyes, seen the self-doubt in Grace's face and added: 'You do help them, Dr Lucca, you truly do.'

Grace telephoned David as soon as she was alone.

'I have nothing new,' he told her. 'I know the ME's thinking along the lines we were discussing, but we're a long way from knowing more.'

'But?' Grace paused. 'David, I can hear there's something.'

'Only that I didn't tell you Sunday that I'd once seen a similar thing. Came upon a patient recently passed and looking a little like – too much like – this poor boy.'

'It's all right.' Grace felt he was trying to spare her. 'Annie told me how he looked.'

David sighed. 'Poor lady.'

'So what was it, with your other patient?'

'It might not be the same,' he cautioned.

'David, please just tell me.'

'In that case, it was strychnine poisoning.'

'Strychnine.' Grace was horrified. 'Oh my God.'

'Heroin cut with rat poison. His last fix.'

'You think Gregory was using heroin?'

'I don't know what he was using yet,' David said. 'And we don't want to jump to any conclusions, but I gather that even the notion that this kind of deadly stuff might be out there has jolted the ME.'

'Enough to speed up the job?' Grace asked.

'Of course,' David said. 'We'd be looking at a homicide, after all, not to mention other lives at risk. They'll be working flat out on blood and examining liver and kidney samples, and I'm told there was some residue on the glassine bag I saw, which might help some. But you'll know from Sam these things take time, and there's no reason for anyone to keep me posted, by the way.'

'Oh my God.' It all began to weigh in on Grace again. 'That poor, lovely boy, and his poor family.'

'Tell me about it,' David said.

'Are you all right, doctor?' Lucia asked an hour later.

Grace told her she was, went on trying to read case notes on her patient due at eleven. All a fuzz. Words on printed sheets about an eight-year-old boy suffering flashbacks a year after his family home had been destroyed by fire.

Concentrate.

An unbreakable rule among all responsible therapists: one patient at a time, each of equal importance. But Gregory, that lovely, frightened boy, was *dead*. Which meant, of course, that Grace could do no more for him, that what she needed to do, as Lucia had said earlier, was force herself to focus on this living child, to do everything in her power to help him.

But still, the words in those notes kept blurring.

Strychnine.

And if not that, then something taken by Gregory noxious enough, *lethal* enough to end his life in the most terrible way. Clearly the ME feared there might be more on the streets, and taking that line of thought further was horrifying – vulnerable men, women and kids at mortal risk, perhaps a rash of deaths or close calls that might be coming to the attention of the police, maybe even Sam's department.

The other possibility. Even more unthinkable, from Grace's standpoint, certainly more *unbearable* from the Hoffman family's.

Grace gave up, and set the notes aside.

If this was strychnine . . . If this was a *one-off*.

That would make it personal.

Saul woke up in Terri's double bed a little before midnight on Wednesday night and found he was alone again.

It kept happening.

He pulled on some shorts, found her on the floor in her tiny living room, wearing the T-shirt she'd tugged over his head a couple of hours back, looking sexy as hell as usual, but engrossed in files of papers.

He knew, without looking, what she was doing, because she'd been doing little else for the past couple of weeks: poring over every crumb of information she had managed to glean about the Muller and Sanchez killings, building her own case files; even sitting waiting for him outside his house in her Miami Beach PD car, listening to the police dispatchers on the radio, reluctant to miss a trick.

'For God's sake, Teté,' he said. 'Not again.'

Terri looked up. 'Hi, baby.' She saw his face. 'Please don't get mad.'

'I'm not mad.' Saul sat on the rug beside her. 'More worried.'

'No need to worry about me.'

'Every need.' Saul looked over her shoulder. 'You're getting obsessed.'

'Don't say that,' Terri said sharply.

'I wouldn't have to if you'd stop reading that stuff.'

She slammed the files shut, got to her feet, stuck the paperwork in the canvas case on her table and glared down at him. 'Satisfied?'

'Get rid of them,' Saul said. 'Then I'll be satisfied.'

'What is so wrong – ' Terri got back down on the floor beside him – 'with me wanting to learn more about my work?'

'It's not your work, Teté,' Saul said, flatly. 'It's my brother's.'

She eyed him with disgust, and got up again. 'Those files do not belong to your precious brother. They belong to the police department I work in too, in case you've forgotten.'

'You work in Property.' He was not in the mood for giving way tonight. 'Not Violent Crimes.'

'Fuck's sake, Saul, I am getting so *sick* of going down this same damned road.'

'Not the only one,' Saul said, though his stomach was starting to churn, and he wished he hadn't started down it again, wished he'd stayed in bed asleep and let her do what made her happy.

'You knew I was ambitious when you met me,' she flared. 'You said you liked ambitious, strong women.'

'I love that you're ambitious,' Saul said. 'I love you, Teté.'

'Maybe you do.' Some of the anger began to melt. 'I know you do, baby.'

Saul heard the unspoken *but* hover in the air between them.

'But I'm not sure you can cope with it,' Terri said.

'Because I think it's crazy to sit up half the night working on stuff that's nothing to do with you?' He just couldn't let it go. 'I don't want you to make yourself sick.'

'What's gonna make me sick,' she said, 'is you mocking my way of working, *my* way of getting where I want to be.'

'I've never mocked anything you do,' Saul protested.

'Maybe not,' Terri said. 'But you sure don't understand it, and if you can't get over this, then we're really going to have big problems.'

'Maybe we are,' Saul said.

And the churning in his stomach became an actual pain.

Eleven

August 25

With Gregory's body not yet released, there had been no funeral and, therefore, no conventional *shiva* for the Hoffman family's relatives and friends to attend, but having caring people around at least some of the time had seemed the only thing, at present, keeping Annie and Jay from drowning. So Michael and Lynne Hoffman, Jay's brother and sister-in-law from New York, had been keeping a table load of drinks and snacks going for the informal steady stream of shocked, caring visitors, most arriving with offerings of food.

Annie and Jay had all but ceased to eat.

People cajoled them with kind, well-intentioned, idiotic words: 'Gregory wouldn't want you to starve yourselves.'; 'You'll feel better if you eat.'; 'You have to stay strong, for Janie's sake.'

Annie and Jay could see a measure of sense in the last argument, though Annie had already concluded that if she had been a mother worth having, her son would never have needed drugs and would now be happy and alive.

Still, Janie was *everything* now, and their total self-destruction would be outright cruelty to her, and people kept on thrusting food at them, so to keep themselves alive and fob off their well-meaning friends they nibbled at the corners of crackers, drank endless cups of coffee and tea, forced down occasional mouthfuls of soup; and Jay poured himself too many J&Bs, and Annie hid in a corner of the kitchen and drank watered down white wine, and Michael and Lynne followed them anxiously around when either of them picked up their little girl and clutched her close, in case they dropped her.

Grace and Sam went to call on Thursday afternoon.

Jay and Annie both looked like shadows, and little Janie's confusion was painfully evident; one minute being removed from her parents by relatives so that she could play quietly out of sight, the next being carried around by her mother or father, gripped so tightly by Annie, at one point, that Janie cried out.

'Bad scene,' Sam said quietly.

'The worst,' Grace agreed.

The young people helped a little, a handful, she assumed, of Gregory's friends, speaking uncomfortably to his parents and in low voices to one another, but now and again forgetting propriety, raising their voices to more natural, youthful levels. When they laughed, from time to time, they looked around guiltily and Grace felt for them, understanding the impact of this early collision with grief.

She had just used the powder room and was walking back through the hallway towards the living room when she overheard two of the teenagers talking in hushed voices, heads together.

'He was on the beach, man, night of the murder, he was *there*.'

Grace stopped, stood still.

'Ryan, for God's sake, you have to stop freaking out.'

'I can't stop.'

Grace tried not to stare, to keep her stance casual. The boy who'd spoken first, the one named Ryan, the one so clearly scared, was tall and broad-shouldered but with a round, fresh face that marked him as being somewhere near Gregory's age.

'He OD'd, man.' The other boy, a head shorter, skinny and red-haired with acne, took Ryan's arm, tried to draw him away. 'Bad luck, nothing more to it.'

For a moment or two, Grace wasn't certain what had chilled her more, the reference to the murder on the beach or hearing a teenager dismiss a drugs overdose as if it were a common place accident.

'*He was on the beach.*'

Dear God.

She waited a little while, saw that Sam was occupied in conversation with Jay and his brother, Annie nowhere to be seen, perhaps in hiding, seeking brief respite, probably finding none.

The tall, fresh-faced teenager went out on to the deck alone. Grace seized the moment and followed.

'Ryan?'

He turned. 'Yes?'

'I'm Dr Grace Lucca, and I'm sorry to intrude.'

'No problem,' Ryan said.

'Could we talk for a moment?' Grace took a couple of steps

closer to the water, away from the house, and the young man followed, frowning now, mystified.

'I owe you an apology.' She kept her voice low. 'But I really couldn't help overhearing your conversation with your friend a few minutes ago.'

Ryan's eyes, darting past her, sought escape.

'It's all right,' Grace told him. 'You're not in any trouble, but it's clear you're very concerned about Greg's death.'

'Who isn't?' Ryan said defensively.

'Not everyone,' she said, still quietly, 'knows that Greg might have witnessed a murder.' She saw his alarm. 'Truly, Ryan, it's OK. I just want to help, if I can.'

'There's nothing to help with,' he said.

'I think there is,' Grace said. 'Though I have to tell you, if you choose not to explain to me what you were talking about back inside, I'll have to consider suggesting that the cops ask you some serious questions.'

'It's not that big a deal.' Ryan's cheeks were hot now, and again his eyes scanned the doorway and room behind her. 'But if my mom and dad find out – ' his voice was barely more than a whisper – 'that I had anything to do with the kind of stuff Greg was into, they'll kill me.'

'Your parents may not need to find that out,' Grace said, 'though I'm not in a position to guarantee that.' She shook her head. 'But you have to realize that if you have any information that might make a difference to the investigation into Gregory's death, you have to share it.'

'Oh God,' the teenager said, 'this is just not fair.'

'I know.' Sympathetic, but matter-of-fact. 'But I gather Greg was a friend?'

'Sure.' Ryan looked at her properly for the first time. 'Did you say you're a doctor?'

'I'm also a friend of Greg's parents.' Grace's smile was gentle. 'Ryan, please.'

'OK.' He sighed. 'It's just that Greg used to smoke dope, you know?'

'I do know,' Grace said.

A middle-aged couple came out of the house and Ryan waited as they stood for a few moments looking out over the bay, then shook their heads sadly, turned back and went inside again.

'Go on,' Grace told Ryan. 'You were talking about Greg smoking dope.'

'Uh-huh.' He motioned to her to move with him even farther from the glass doors, closer to the edge. 'But a while back,' he said softly, 'he got into coke. I warned him about it – not just me, a couple of the other guys, we all told him to keep off – I mean, we all knew how much shit – excuse me – how much trouble he'd already had.'

'Just tell me, Ryan.'

'But Greg wouldn't listen, he just got so *into* stuff, you know, he couldn't stop. And what he'd do, he'd go out late at night, real late, after his parents were asleep, and he'd take his bike and go a good long way from home and do – you know – and then he'd maybe sleep it off on the beach or go swimming, and then he'd go home again.'

'So what was it that happened on the night of the murder?' Grace thought she detected relief in the young man, finally able to unburden himself. 'I take it you meant the killing on the beach near Surfside?'

'The Muller guy.' Ryan nodded. 'The thing was, I saw Greg next day and he was just so weird, you know – I mean *really* freaked out – and he wouldn't tell me why, wouldn't tell any of us. But that was the day after the guy had gotten killed, and I know Greg used to cycle down that way, near the park, because he liked that the trees were there to cover him while he . . .'

'Right,' Grace said.

'So I've just been wondering, you know.'

'I can imagine.'

'He was just so upset, and now he's . . .'

Ryan turned away, and Grace thought he was trying not to weep.

'It's all right,' she said.

'Except it's not, is it?' he said.

'No,' she agreed. 'It's not.'

He turned back, his eyes red, their expression urgent. 'But you see I wasn't there, doc, so there's no point you giving my name to the cops, is there? Because I can't really tell them anything for sure, can I?'

'OK.' Grace waited a beat. 'Ryan, there's just one person I am going to mention this to and that's my husband, because he's a Miami Beach detective—'

'Oh God.'

'It's OK,' she tried reassuring him again. 'But he's actually investigating the Muller killing, which means he really does need to hear this.'

'But there's nothing *to* hear,' Ryan pleaded.

'Probably not.' Grace laid a gentle hand on his forearm. 'But even if Detective Becket does want to ask you a few questions, Ryan, you have nothing to worry about.' She paused. 'Unless you know where Greg was getting his drugs from.'

'No,' Ryan said quickly. '*No.*'

'OK,' Grace said gently. 'That's all right then.'

Twelve

Sales personnel in clothing stores were accustomed to all kinds of sights. Fat men and women trying to squeeze their big behinds into tight jeans. Flat-chested girls hiking up their tiny titties inside Wonderbras. Old women trying on shell suits, old men climbing into Speedos. The more experienced of them knew better than to laugh or even smile, were conscious that the smallest flicker of mockery would not only upset the customer, but also, much more important, lose them the sale.

Maria Rivera prided herself on being an excellent saleswoman, something she measured not only in transactions, but by the fact that her customers felt she cared about selling them the right clothes and tended, therefore, to come back to her. Maria knew that there were times you needed to lie, or at least to conceal the absolute truth, but there were also occasions when allowing a customer to leave the store with a garment that was going to make them look ridiculous was, so far as Maria was concerned, a real disservice. She liked seeing a perfect or at least a good fit, derived pleasure from seeing clientele becoming more attractive because of the clothes they were trying on.

Thursday afternoon had been particularly busy in the Fratelli store on the upper level of the Aventura Mall, but despite the high volume of customers, every single one of Maria's sales and fails remained clear in her memory; none more so than the one she'd instantly, privately, named The Freezer.

A strange one, for sure. Trying on jeans, a better than good fit, fine on the waist, snug but not too tight on the behind, excellent length.

Maria had looked at the customer and smiled. 'You wear them well,' she had said.

She would have said more, but for the customer's eyes.

A look that could have frozen blood.

One sale Maria had not minded losing out on, that was for sure.

Usually – always – if Cathy wasn't going to come home for the night, she telephoned to let Grace and Sam know they could lock up and go to bed without worrying about her.

Thursday night had been the exception. No show, no call. No sleep for Grace.

She'd told herself over and over that she was being absurd and neurotic, that Cathy was an adult, at liberty to stay out whenever she wanted, but it hadn't helped because it was simply so unlike her considerate daughter.

Not that it was only Cathy keeping her awake. Nor was it the baby, who'd kicked around for a while at around one a.m., but had then gone off to sleep.

'What's up?' Sam's voice came out of the darkness at around three. 'You OK?'

'I'm fine,' Grace told him, stroking his arm. 'Go back to sleep.'

No point in them both lying awake.

She had told him before they'd left the Hoffman house that afternoon about her conversation with Ryan, and Sam had spoken briefly to the boy, learned that his surname was Harrison, had given him his card and told him to get in touch next day if he wanted to avoid Sam speaking to his parents first.

'I'm sure as I can be that he was telling the truth about not being there with Gregory,' Sam had said on the way home, 'so I couldn't see any sense hauling him in right away – I'd rather have him on side when we speak.'

Grace was silent.

'What are you thinking?' Sam had asked.

'I keep remembering what Greg said to me.'

'About being seen?'

' "Saw me." ' Grace had shivered. 'Suddenly it makes more sense, doesn't it?'

'If Gregory saw Muller's killer, you mean? If the killer saw him.'

'Don't you think that's what he might have meant?'

'It's possible,' Sam had said. 'But it's just as likely that "saw me" meant that someone saw Gregory doing coke on the beach.'

'Would that have frightened him so much?' Grace had asked.

'Being arrested would probably have terrified him,' Sam said, 'and the prospect of going back into rehab. And don't forget the kid was probably high as a kite.' He had reached for her hand and squeezed it. 'Don't let this make you crazy, sweetheart.'

She'd tried her best not to, and they'd managed a peaceful enough evening, but now she was lying here with sleep still eluding her, and all her various stresses seemed to be contracting into a single tightly packed hard ball of anxiety focused on Cathy.

She gave it up finally, heaved herself as silently as possible from the bed, heard Sam stir but not wake, and padded out of the bedroom and down the stairs.

Woody came out of the kitchen, still half-asleep, tail wagging.

'Sorry,' Grace told him softly, bent with difficulty to stroke his head, and went to put the kettle on.

One of Lucia's camomile-based teas might just help, though she doubted anything was going to soothe her. Speaking to Claudia might have eased things a little, but even on Seattle time it was out of the question, and anyway they'd only spoken a couple of days ago.

'Where is she, Woody?' she asked the dog as he settled by her feet.

The probability was, she realized, that Cathy was with Kez, and she wondered if that was part of what was so troubling her, then decided she'd have been equally concerned if Cathy had gone missing with a new boyfriend.

Not missing, she reminded herself. Just out.

She went across to the phone, put out her hand to pick it up.

'No,' she said. 'Leave them be.'

Maybe this was the reason Cathy hadn't called. Maybe she had been giving off some air of disquiet since she'd begun seeing Kez, and maybe Cathy was angry about that, or maybe she was uncertain herself. Or maybe there was, simply, nothing to talk about.

In her womb, the baby stirred.

'It's OK, sweetheart,' she said. 'Just your mom being a neurotic mess.'

Plenty more where that came from, she supposed, wondering for at least the hundredth time if she was up to this, if maybe she and Sam were too old, because there was just so *much* responsibility, so much potential for pain alongside the joy.

No going back now, she told herself.

'Nor wanting to,' she told the baby.

And made her tea.

Cathy telephoned at five after seven.

'I feel bad,' she said, 'about not calling you last night.'

'It was so unlike you.' Grace managed to conceal her relief as well as her irritation. 'We were worried.'

Cathy told her how sorry she was, then asked about the Hoffmans.

'It must have been terrible.'

'They're being very strong,' Grace said. 'Plenty of people around them, helping.'

'For now,' Cathy said, perceptively.

Grace waited a moment. 'Are you OK?'

She waited for Cathy to tell her where she had spent the night or, at least, where she was this morning. Managed not to pry. Fastest way to lose her.

'I'm fine,' Cathy answered.

No more than that.

Cathy and Kez had been book buying at B. Dalton in CocoWalk late the previous afternoon when Cathy had spotted Saul and Terri emerging from an exhibit of African wildlife sculptures in a gallery on Grand Avenue. They'd all chatted for a few moments and Saul had suggested they have a drink, and Cathy had been about to say yes when she'd caught Kez's expression and quickly made an excuse. Saul had grinned understandingly and they'd all gone on their way.

'Sorry about that,' Kez had said a moment later. 'I'd like to go home, and I just didn't feel like company.'

Cathy had glanced swiftly at her. 'Would you like me to go?'

'I'd rather go home with you,' Kez had said.

Banyan trees and palms were all around the property on Matilda Street, plenty of grass and stone paths – in need of weeding – leading from the sidewalk to an old white clapboard house with ramshackle looking wooden steps leading up to Kez's home on the second floor.

Just a stone's throw from some of the priciest gated houses in Coconut Grove and in walking distance from the commercial buzz of CocoWalk, yet thanks to a deal Kez had struck with its owner, an artist presently living in Europe, the two-roomed apartment was both affordable and hers for the foreseeable future.

'I shot some photos of her work that she liked, and she said she'd be happy for me to live here and take care of the place while she's away,' Kez had told Cathy as they drank cold white wine out on the porch. 'After Europe, she's planning on some time in the Bahamas, so it could be months till I see her again.'

'Don't you miss her?'

Kez had caught the hesitation before the question, and smiled. 'Cathy, I hardly know her.'

'I didn't mean . . .' Cathy stopped.

'I know what you meant,' Kez had said.

That was when the awkwardness had really begun to drift away.

Cathy loved the apartment, the minimalist, almost spartan, feel of the decoration and furnishing sitting comfortably with the posters of Florence Griffith Joyner and other athletics heroines on the walls, with just one blown-up black-and-white photo of Kez triumphantly breaking tape in a race.

'Any of your own work?' Cathy enquired.

'Not worth hanging.'

'I'll bet you're a great photographer,' Cathy said. 'You said you wouldn't have got this place if the owner hadn't loved your pictures.'

Kez shrugged. 'I like this stuff better.'

'Is that your dad?' Cathy looked at the only other photo of Kez, aged four or five, standing beside a smiling fair-haired man with his arm around her.

'That was Joey, yes.'

'He was handsome.' Cathy peered closer, saw Kez's sharp arrow nose in the man's face, saw that Kez's natural hair colour was the same as her father's. 'Any pictures of your mom?'

'No,' Kez said.

Cathy remembered the grisly tale of Joey's *in flagrante* heart attack, remembered Kez saying her mother had been out at the time – and she hadn't mentioned her since, so heaven knew what had happened after that. Her mom must have been distraught, maybe she'd even resented her daughter witnessing the scene – people were complicated, after all, as she'd learned.

Better, Cathy decided, not to ask.

She had never known a night like it.

They'd eaten pizza – or rather, *she* had eaten several slices, Kez scarcely one sliver – but they'd both drunk plenty of white wine and smoked some weed, and Kez had painted Cathy's nails for her – black and yellow, like tiny bees – and finally they'd fallen into bed together and slept.

And even when they'd woken for a while in the night, it had all been about companionship, warmth and comfort. Nothing more.

'It's OK, you know,' Kez had told her. 'I know you're not sure.'

Cathy had been glad of the darkness, hadn't known what to say.

'I'd never push you into anything you didn't want,' Kez said.

Hearing her say that had been wonderful, had made Cathy even more relaxed and happy because it had seemed to her to confirm not only that Kez did *want* her, but also that she was considerate and patient and exactly the kind of person Cathy had believed her to be.

Except that now – just now – this Friday morning, when Cathy had phoned home and talked to Grace, Kez had been in the room. And perhaps she picked up on the touch of strain in the conversation, because the instant Cathy ended the call she saw that something was wrong, something had changed.

'I think,' Kez said, 'maybe you should leave.'

'Leave?' Cathy was dismayed.

'I think,' Kez went on, 'you need to take some time, think this over.'

'I don't need to think anything over,' Cathy said.

'I think you do.' Kez was adamant. 'You have issues to resolve.'

Cathy didn't answer, was too afraid of saying the wrong thing.

'When it comes to self-doubt, I wrote the book,' Kez said. 'But I do know who I am, Cathy, and I know that I'm gay, and I have no problems with that at all.' Her smile was quirky. 'And I know what and *who* I want.'

'I think . . .'

'What do you think, Cathy?'

'I think I want you,' Cathy said.

'That's fine,' Kez said, 'but it's not enough. Not for me, not for you.'

'So what do you want me to do?'

'Take the time you need. Do your thinking – no pressure – decide how you feel, about me, about having a gay relationship.' There was a new, flatter note in Kez's voice. 'I'm not interested in being an experiment.'

'I would never—' Again Cathy was dismayed.

'I don't suppose you would,' Kez said. 'Not deliberately.'

'I'm sorry.' Cathy wasn't certain why she was apologizing, but Kez was upset, and that was bad enough.

'Don't be sorry,' Kez told her. 'Just be honest with me.'

'I will,' Cathy said.

'And with yourself,' Kez said.

Cathy looked at her, saw how calm she was, how steady, and felt a surge of admiration, wished for just a little of the same, wished for her own heart and mind not to be in such turmoil. Realized that Kez was right to want to wait.

Except that Kez had told her to *leave*, which was the last thing in the world she wanted to do. To walk away.

'Couldn't we just go on?' Cathy asked.

'Maybe we could,' Kez said, 'but then we might both get hurt.'

'Isn't that a risk worth taking?' Cathy persisted.

'Not for me.' Kez's smile was wry. 'I don't like that kind of pain.'

The word was in on what had killed Gregory Hoffman.

Rat poison. Strychnine, to be exact, as David Becket had suspected. Not so uncommon as a mix in itself, rodenticide being used on occasions to lace cocaine in the hope of a longer, more intense high; and the potential for serious health risks was always present, especially the risk of uncontrolled bleeding, often intracranial haemorrhage. That was when the mix was moderate.

In Gregory's case, the ratio of strychnine to cocaine had been much higher. The almost indisputable intention, therefore, to kill.

No other similar deaths so far in the county, which indicated at least the possibility that the teenager had been targeted.

About the only thing Sam Becket was not entirely sorry about – when he went with Al Martinez to interview Ryan Harrison with regard to the Muller murder – was that despite the potential cross-over between cases, the Hoffman investigation was not in the hands of Miami Beach.

The Miami-Dade police had – in the immediate aftermath of Gregory's death – gone through Gregory's belongings, read his private journal and talked to all his friends in and out of school. Ryan Harrison had given no hint at that time of what he had later told Grace, but having since established a potential connection with the beach killing, the teenager had already been re-interviewed by Miami-Dade detectives before Sam and Martinez had arrived on his parents' doorstep. And had left again, less than an hour later, no wiser.

Ryan and his parents had been keen to help; no prickliness, no wariness, just up-front, decent people, posing no problems.

Offering no real help either.

'Kid doesn't know zip,' Martinez concluded after the interview.

'He could be right, though,' Sam said, 'about Greg having seen something.'

'But Ryan didn't, so that gets us no place.'

'It gets us talking to all of Gregory's friends,' Sam said, grim-faced. 'Never know, he might have told one of them what he saw.'

'Don't hold your breath,' Martinez said.

There were few things Sam disliked more than questioning young people in the line of his work. Bad enough when they were just witnesses to a violent crime; ugly and depressing when they were suspects. Right now, there was only one thing he hated the idea of more, and that was having to return to the Hoffman home and confront those grieving parents with another search of their dead son's room and possessions – let alone having to ask them questions relating to Gregory as a possible *suspect* in a homicide inquiry.

Yet unthinkable – and improbable – as that was, with the teenager now conceivably placed at the Muller crime scene, and with nothing new discovered to link the Miami and Pompano Beach killings, it had become something he and Martinez had been forced to consider, even if just to eliminate the possibility from the inquiry.

'*Saw me.*' Still not a lot to go on, especially if all Greg had meant was that someone had seen him doing drugs.

'Unless Muller was the one who saw him,' Martinez hazarded over a cup of coffee in the office, 'and the kid was so off his face, he killed him to keep him quiet.'

'But then, if Greg *was* targeted with the strychnine mix, who wanted him dead?' Sam countered. 'And why?'

'One of the other kids, maybe,' Martinez theorized. 'In over his head and figuring Greg was a loose cannon.'

'I don't buy it,' Sam said.

'Me neither,' Martinez said. 'We're not the ones who have to, thank God.'

'Sure we do,' Sam said, 'if the killings are linked.'

Thirteen

August 27

A body was found in Hallandale Beach early on Saturday morning.

Right on the beach, like Rudolph Muller and Carmelita Sanchez. Bludgeoned first, possibly, probably, with a bat – just like the other two.

Another female – *not* like the Miami Beach killing. No weird screaming sounds reported this time either, no screaming at all, even though that part of the beach was close to several high-rise residential buildings. And no cutting.

But the victim's teeth had been smashed. And not, according to the ME's initial findings, as a part of the primary bludgeoning. This demolition job had been done as a secondary assault, after death, *just* after death.

Hallandale Beach PD had responded to the first report, taken care of the preliminaries while waiting for the Broward County Sheriff's office to take over the homicide investigation. With Broward already in charge of the Sanchez case, Detective Rowan was paying full heed, but Sam and Martinez had only gotten to hear about it through Elliot Sanders, who'd had a call from the Hallandale ME, a friend who knew about the other beach cases and figured Doc Sanders would be interested.

Not quite as interested as Sam Becket and his team.

*   *   *

Sam and Martinez drove up on Sunday afternoon to meet with Rowan again and learn a little more: victim's name Maria Rivera, identified by the contents of the small purse still strung diagonally across her body, the way many women wore their bags for security and hands-free walking. Nothing apparently stolen again.

She had been a sales clerk working in Fratelli, one of the one hundred plus clothing stores in the Aventura Mall. An excellent saleswoman according to her supervisor, well-liked by her colleagues. Unmarried, thirty-two, no children, but parents, brothers and sisters who all seemed crazy about her, and several neighbours in her high-rise building close to Magnolia Terrace and Ocean Drive who all seemed to like her too.

No motive anyone could dredge up.

It had been Miss Rivera's habit to get home from her long day's work at the store, take off her uniform suit, change into T-shirt and shorts or the like, and go walking on the beach – pretty much like Muller, pretty much like thousands of Florida residents – then sometimes pick up a TV dinner and go home to chill.

Random, or someone watching her, knowing her pattern, *again*.

No link between them though, Mike Rowan said.

'No *known* link,' Sam said.

'No known link between any of the cases,' Rowan added. 'And even less to connect the others with this one.'

'No cutting,' Martinez said.

'Exactly,' Rowan said, seeming pleased by that.

Still eager to keep his cases to himself, Sam figured, though the Broward homicide unit certainly had no shortage of murders per capita by comparison with Miami Beach.

'Mouth again, though,' Sam pointed out.

'And all bludgeoned first,' added Martinez.

'I don't know.' Rowan still dubious. 'Certainly not where your Muller's concerned.' He shrugged. 'All you got there's a guy clubbed on a beach and his throat cut. Nothing too weird about that.' He tugged at his moustache. 'Now *we* got two women, same county, both on the beach after work, both bludgeoned, one with her lips cut off, the other with her teeth smashed to pulp.' He gave a wry smile. 'I guess we should keep each other posted, but I don't think we got more than that.'

They came away half glad to still have their own ball to run with, knowing that Rowan might be right about the lack of connection.

'Except you don't agree with him,' Martinez said as he drove them back towards the station, staying on A1A, always preferring to stay close to the ocean.

'No.' Sam's mind was working. 'I think we need to focus on the mouth and throat link.' He stared out of his side window, not really seeing the palms or blue sky and ocean or glitzy towers along the way. 'Speech. Speech-making. Public-speaking classes.'

'Acting,' Martinez offered. 'Singing.'

'If Muller belonged to an amateur group,' Sam said, 'we'd probably have found something – a poster or script or libretto maybe – in his apartment.'

'Not everyone gets all the parts, like you,' Martinez said. 'Muller could have gone to auditions and gotten rejected.'

'Let's do some cross-checking,' Sam said. 'Night schools again, that kind of thing.'

'Mouth, throat.' Martinez continued the process. 'Could be eating or drinking. One of those gourmet groups?'

'Could be just about any damned thing,' Sam agreed. 'Could also be some kind of symbolic silencing. Victims maybe *said* too much about something or someone – or maybe just knew too much?'

Martinez was sceptical. 'I can maybe accept that about our guy – I guess Muller could have been a snitch. But a dress-making cleaner and a sales clerk?'

'All kinds of people see things someone doesn't want them to,' Sam said.

They slowed at traffic lights at Bal Harbour, watched an elegant, elderly couple make their way slowly, with fancy shopping bags, from the glitzy mall to the Sheraton.

'Political groups,' Martinez added to the list.

'Maybe they were all in therapy,' Sam came up with. 'Or all seeing different therapists at the same office.'

'Can't imagine Carmelita Sanchez having time for therapy.' Martinez paused in thought. 'Dentists. Doctors.'

'Chat rooms,' Sam said abruptly.

'OK.' Martinez liked that idea better. 'Nothing on Muller's phone bills or PC so far, though.'

'Internet cafés,' Sam said.

'I'll call Rowan,' Martinez said. 'He'll be thrilled.'

'One good thing,' Sam said after a while, 'if there is a link between Maria Rivera and the other two killings.'

'Rules out young Gregory as a suspect.' Martinez was already there.

'Still our only possible witness to Muller's murder though,' Sam said.

And unable, poor kid, to tell them a damned thing.

Fourteen

August 30

Tuesday night, and Saul, spending the night at Terri's, was restless, though she for once was sleeping like a baby beside him.

He got up carefully, picked up his T-shirt and shorts and padded silently out into the living room, closing the bedroom door behind him. He poured himself a glass of water, snaffled an oatmeal and raisin cookie from Terri's jar, and was just about to settle down on the couch and switch on the TV, sound low, when he noticed the photograph on the floor over in the corner near the old dented filing cabinet in which Teté kept her work.

He hadn't noticed it earlier when they'd come in after a great evening at Casa Juancho over in Little Havana, probably because they'd both been so intent on shedding their clothes and falling on to Teté's bed.

Saul stooped to pick up the photograph – and froze.

It was a picture of a dead body on what looked like sand; an appalling photograph. A woman, though it was only possible to see that from her bare limbs and clothing – her head, her face, too bloodied, too *destroyed*, to make out – if one could stand to look at it for more than a second.

Saul thought – putting things together despite his shock – that it might be a photograph of the woman who had been found murdered on the beach up in Hallandale. He'd read about it a couple of days back in the *Herald*, seen more on the local TV news. The assault had been described as 'brutal' and 'shocking' – the kind of words people were all too accustomed to hearing used about crimes.

Different seeing it like this.

Sickening.

Definitely not a branch of medicine he was ever going to be attracted to. Though being squeamish was hardly the greatest quality for any doctor.

No blood in furniture making, give or take the odd cut finger or hammered thumb.

He sat down at the table, wondering how come Terri had this in her possession, already aware that, given how fired up she'd been about Sam's murder case and the poor woman up in Pompano Beach, she might have found a way to obtain – maybe even *steal* – this picture from Violent Crimes.

Except this didn't look like the kind of professional crime-scene shot that Saul had, from time to time, seen Sam looking at over the years. This looked more like the kind of snap one might get from a regular camera, maybe even a disposable.

But surely Terri could not have snapped the body, would never – even if she'd managed to escape her own work schedule and make it up to Hallandale Beach (if this actually *was* that poor woman) – but even if she had gotten herself there, surely she would never have been allowed to get in close enough to take this kind of picture.

No one more charming than Teté though – or more deter-mined. So maybe she had persuaded some Hallandale detective – or more probably one of the officers securing the scene of crime – to let her have a glimpse.

Maybe he'd even agreed to look the other way long enough for Terri to whip out a camera and take this *snap*.

Saul shuddered.

'Nice.'

Terri's voice behind him made him jump.

'Lovely to know this is what my boyfriend gets up to while I'm sleeping.'

Saul turned around, saw her standing in her short, sheer black robe, hair tousled, raw anger in her eyes. 'I just—'

'You just happened to go through my files—'

'Of course not,' Saul protested, standing up. 'This was on the floor.'

Terri snatched it from his fingers. 'I cannot *believe* you, Saul. I thought I could trust you.'

'You can trust me.' He was more than dismayed by the accu-sation. 'You know I'd never touch your private stuff.'

'So this – ' she held the photo up – 'conveniently flew out of the filing cabinet?'

'For God's sake, Terri, I told you it was on the floor over there.' He pointed at the corner. 'You probably dropped it before dinner, or whenever it was you felt like looking at something this awful.'

'Murder is awful, Saul, ugly.'

'Murder is not your *business*.'

'Not this again, please, not this *again*.' She shook her head, turned away from him, flung herself down hard in one corner of the couch.

'So where did you get it?' Saul asked.

'None of *your* business,' Terri flashed back.

'This is the woman up in Hallandale, isn't it?'

She didn't answer.

'So how come a rookie working Property, even an *obsessed* rookie – ' Saul used the word knowing it would inflame because now he was mad, too – 'managed to finagle her way on to a murder scene in a different county, for God's sake?' He was shaking now, hating his anger, hating this whole thing. 'And why in *hell* are you still putting your own job on the line this crazy way?'

'Because the great Sam Becket and his team – ' Terri was back on her feet – 'and the Broward County Sheriff have managed diddlyshit, and this might just be my chance to prove myself. You still don't get how important that is to me, do you?'

'I think looking at stuff like that, taking pictures like that, is *sick*.'

'You think I'm sick – ' she got right up close, practically in his face – 'maybe you better get out of my home.'

'Terri, for God's sake—'

'In fact – ' her eyes were blazing – 'maybe you better get out of my *life*.'

'Teté, stop this!' He wasn't pleading, he was too angry to plead, but he couldn't stand the way this was going, knew it was out of control. 'We need to talk.'

'I don't want to talk with a guy who says he loves me but doesn't want to even try to understand me, who doesn't even *trust* me.'

'You're the one who just accused me of going through your things.'

'I want you to leave,' Terri said. 'Go home to your daddy and your books, and don't forget to tell big bro all about me.'

'Teté, this is nuts.'

'Get the fuck *out*!' she screamed.

He went.

It was Saul's turn to go to Grace for advice.

Everyone ended up there sometime, David had once joked.

'Shrink wisdom,' he called it.

'Wisdom shrunk,' Grace had said recently, self-deprecatingly. The more her pregnancy advanced, the more she felt that was true.

If Saul needed advice, the last thing she wanted was to sell him short.

'I may not be the best person to speak to about this,' she told him when he showed up at lunchtime on Wednesday with a pastrami on rye for himself, and turkey for her, from the Rascal House. 'But I can*not* say no to that sandwich, especially since Lucia the healthy eating queen's off sick today.' She looked down at her sandwich. 'Except you're going to have to split your pastrami.'

'Isn't it bad for you?' Saul asked.

'Half a pastrami, nearly seven months gone? Nah,' Grace said. 'But don't tell anyone.'

Grace ate heartily, but Saul found he was too upset to do more than pick.

'This is between us, right?' he said. 'You won't tell Sam.'

'I'm not too thrilled by that,' Grace said frankly. 'We tend to share.'

'Pretend I'm a patient,' Saul said.

'You're not.'

'It's nothing he needs to know,' Saul told her.

'And more than probably I'll agree with that,' Grace said. 'But I'm not going to make promises I can't keep.'

Saul looked even more disconsolate, tugged at the crust of the half a turkey sandwich Grace had foisted on him.

'You really need to unload, don't you?' Grace said.

'Yes,' Saul said. 'But I really need you to keep quiet with Sam, too.'

She sighed. 'OK. Tell me.'

'You're sure?'

Grace shrugged. 'You haven't left me much choice.'

He told her about the photograph and the fight.

'She's obsessed by these killings,' he said. 'But if I say anything like that, it's a real red rag to a bull, you know? She says I've always known how seriously she takes her work – which is true, of course I know, and I've always respected that about her.'

'That's the impression I've had,' Grace said.

'But she's also always known how to have the best time.' Saul shook his head. 'I've never met anyone like Teté, so full of life. She's always left me way behind, flying ahead of me, which just bowls me over.'

'And that's changed?'

'Not completely, of course not. Just last night, before our fight, we had a great evening, great dinner, great music, amazing—' He broke off, a little embarrassed.

'I get the picture.' Grace smiled.

'And then I found this photo – and it was just lying on the floor, so I picked it up, and I'd never go through Teté's things – but she came in and saw me looking at it, and she lost it, accused me of invading her privacy, and that made me mad, and we just went from there.' He paused. 'All the way to her screaming at me to get out.'

'Have you talked to her since?'

'I called this morning, got voicemail. She hasn't called back.' Saul looked suddenly miserable enough to cry. 'I'm not sure she will, Grace.'

'Maybe not after one message,' Grace said gently. 'Maybe Terri might need a little more than that.'

'But I didn't do anything wrong,' Saul protested.

'I'm sure you didn't,' Grace said. 'But Terri clearly felt you did, which is something you're both going to have to address.'

'Her not trusting me, you mean.'

'Goes both ways, Saul,' Grace said. 'You ought to know, better than most, what it's like for police officers sometimes. It's a given that there are going to be times when Terri – just like Sam – gets completely wrapped in a job.'

'But that's the whole point.' Saul was frustrated. 'This isn't *her* job. It's Sam's work I think she's trying to do. It's these murders that she's completely obsessed by, and I don't know what to do about it.'

'And you don't want me to talk to Sam?' Grace asked.

'Absolutely not,' Saul said. 'Please, Grace.'

'OK,' she said. 'Then, if you really feel you're right about this, you have to go on talking to Terri.'

'I'm not sure there's anything left to say,' Saul said.

'Then unless you find something,' Grace said, 'you're in a lot of trouble.'

Fifteen

Cathy was missing Kez.

Missing her so much she was finding it hard to focus on anything else. Since being asked to leave; to go make up her mind about how she felt about a *real* relationship with Kez. About having a lesbian relationship.

About being gay.

'I'm not interested in being an experiment,' Kez had said.

The words were all still rolling around in her head, driving her mad. She hadn't been able to face summer school, had done little but run since then, racing herself to exhaustion before heading home and being a pain in the ass to everyone there, even being unforgivably curt to Lucia when she'd asked if she was OK. Sam and Grace weren't too impressed with her and she couldn't blame them, though she felt that they were upset *for* her, too, sensing that her lousy mood had something to do with Kez, and for some idiotic reason, that pissed her off even more.

Acting like a child.

Which meant, of course, that Kez had been right to tell her to leave, which conclusion made Cathy feel *even* worse. And it wasn't helping one bit that she didn't feel able to speak to Grace or Sam about her feelings and emotions, but the fact was she *knew* they were relieved that this relationship appeared to be over.

Or maybe they didn't feel that way at all, maybe she was just reading things that weren't there. Neither of them, in any case, seemed to be thinking too much about *her* at all. Sam's mind was jammed full of work and Grace and the baby, and Grace wasn't really herself, which Cathy knew was mostly the pregnancy and hormones, and she was still busy with patients, and the horrible thing that had happened to Greg Hoffman had really freaked her out. And Cathy couldn't have been happier they were finally going to have a baby together, knew how miserable they'd both been after the miscarriages, and the last thing in the world she wanted was to upset them. But this whole thing, this *mess* with Kez, was confusing the hell out of her, and she wished she knew what to do for the best. What was right . . .

Long after Saul had left on Wednesday afternoon, Grace had found her mind straying back again to those last appointments with Gregory, trying to read between the lines. So *few* lines, so little said.

And then something else had come back to her. The afternoon of that last session with Greg, Cathy had brought Kez home to meet her, and then moments after they'd gone Terri had arrived, making Grace wonder if she might have been waiting for them to leave so they could be alone.

A new possibility had just sprung to mind, unbidden and unwelcome. Maybe Terri had been waiting outside the house because she'd known that Gregory was with her. Greg, who it now seemed might possibly have seen Rudolph Muller's killer.

Nonsense.

Terri had come to see her because she was upset about Sam. And even if she had been trying to pump him and Saul for details about the homicide investigation, at no time had she attempted to do so with Grace. Anyway, back then no one had known there was any chance that Greg might have seen anything or anyone connected with the Muller murder.

Coincidence, therefore, Terri arriving when she had; nothing more.

Poor Teté, Grace decided. Everyone down on her for that most heinous of female crimes: ambition.

Nothing new there then.

Still no break in the Muller homicide – nor any success linking the three recent victims. Nothing more in common than the nature of the crimes themselves, their beach locations and South Florida.

And, of course, the continuing lack of evidence.

That one fragment of wood in Broward's first case – no such luck in the Rivera killing – though as Doc Sanders had said at the time of that discovery, the fact that no sliver had been found after the other assaults did not rule out the possibility of the weapon being the same.

Not if the killer was taking good care of his weapon between attacks.

Organized, then, if that was true. Even if the ferocity of the beatings indicated frenzy, the secondary attacks, on lips, throat and teeth, seemed, Sam thought, to point to possible premeditation. And the more he thought about it, sweated it, the more he believed they *were* linked. Even if Detective Rowan did not agree.

Proving it was the problem. Not to mention finding the son-of-a-bitch behind it.

The chief didn't like it when this amount of time had passed without so much as a sniff of a result. Captain Hernandez didn't like it when the chief was unhappy, and Lieutenant Kovac was grouchier than ever. None of the detectives liked having the captain or Kovac busting their chops, nor did they like failure.

Failing themselves, but most of all, the victim.

No one had come to learn much of great interest about Rudolph Muller, either good or bad, yet to their credit it bugged them a whole lot that an apparently honest, hard-working man with a possible weakness about his appearance, but with no rumoured major narcissism or perversion – it bugged them that a guy like that, a regular guy, should go for a run on the beach, *their* beach, get his face smashed in, his throat cut, and not have anyone brought to book for it. Not the kind of victim, Muller, who got cops fired up as a rule, made them line up for overtime night after night. But the Miami Beach police valued their city and were fond of their safe beaches, and they'd be damned if they were going to let some low-life scum or maniac get away with splattering the sand with blood and brains, never mind scaring off innocent people.

So, for Muller's sake, and, of course, his family's: 'Work harder, *think* harder, don't give up.' The whole unit's motto at times like these, Sam's in particular right now. His case, after all.

Work harder.

Saul had decided he needed to take some special action.

Find a way, the *right* way, to make Terri understand how much she meant to him.

He hated the idea that she could even *think* he might snitch on her to Sam about the photograph, about anything; hated even more that Teté seemed to feel she was much less important to him than his family.

Lonely girl, deep down, beneath the sharpness, behind the defensiveness. Saul knew how much she still missed her grandmother, and he sensed in her sometimes the kind of envy she'd admitted to, though more often a touch of resentment of his close, loving family. If he thought about her violent father he could understand that.

He thought, for the most part, that he understood *her*. Knew, without question, that he loved her, would do anything to keep her.

Romance, for now, was his best bet. It was their greatest strength, after all, their love, their passion. Terri had three passions, of course: work, animals, and him – he hoped, still him. Fact was he only really had her.

Which was why he'd taken a chance and made reservations for the weekend.

He knew how much she had always wanted to drive over to the Gulf coast to visit the fifty-two acre Caribbean Gardens zoo in Naples. A big primate exhibit – one of her passions. Most people said that Naples was a romantic place, which made it two out of three, provided she agreed to come.

Going away together might be just what they needed to get back on track.

Saul knocked on wood.

Cathy had finally concluded that the only sensible, adult thing to do was to talk to Kez.

Even if Kez had seemed to think the mature thing was for Cathy to go away and make up her mind on her own.

The more she thought about it, the more Cathy realized that, right or wrong, that was never going to happen. And maybe that did emphasize her immaturity or at least her inexperience, but to hell with it, she *was* young, and this was entirely new to her, and surely the right way for her to make this kind of pivotal decision was *with* Kez.

Problem was, Kez wasn't answering her home phone, and Cathy had left two messages already, to which Kez had failed to respond. Which meant either that she wasn't there (and though she owned a cell phone, she'd told Cathy she seldom took it with her, could hardly remember its number), or that she had decided she didn't want anything more to do with Cathy.

One more attempt, one more message, and after that, more waiting.

Down to Kez now.

Try as she might, Grace had not been able to get her concerns about Terri out of her thoughts. Not so much because of the day she'd come to the house, but because of the photograph that had so disturbed Saul.

Grace knew why she was so troubled by the picture.

Saul's worst case suspicion had been that Terri might have gone up to Hallandale Beach and snapped that photograph herself, had talked her way on to the crime scene, maybe charmed some young officer alone on duty.

Almost impossible, in Grace's opinion.

Grace knew a little about how impeccably crime scenes were preserved, and frankly she doubted that even the most inexperienced cop turned on by the gorgeous Officer Suarez would have been willing to risk his career by letting her screw up potentially crucial evidence.

Besides which, while the body was still there the place had to have been crawling with *experienced* cops and technicians. No way Terri could have got close enough to take a picture. Which presumably meant she had merely taken it, perhaps *stolen* it, from Violent Crimes. Still a much less disturbing notion than the alternative.

So why had Saul, who loved Terri, made more of it rather than less? Instinct, perhaps, that something was very wrong. More than he could cope with – more than he could bear to admit to.

That was what was going around and around in Grace's mind. The photograph and the whole deal about Terri's obsession with the killings was beginning to give her a seriously uncomfortable feeling – more than that, actually, more of a great *unease* – about Teresa Suarez.

Hormones.

Grace hoped so, with all her might.

She didn't want to think about what it might mean, otherwise.

Sixteen

S aul had wanted to book them into the Hotel Escalante on Fifth Avenue in Naples, had wanted to give Terri a weekend of pure pampering and luxury, but she had not wanted that, had told him she'd rather go to the Cove Inn at the city dock.

'Let's just be us,' she'd said. 'We don't need all the frills.'

Saul had said he guessed not, though frankly frills were what he'd been hoping might help soften a few of those sharp, spiky edges of hers that he seemed to have been raising recently. But the fact, for which he was most thankful, was that Terri had agreed to come with him, and so wherever she wanted to stay was great with him.

The inn at Crayton Cove was, as it turned out, exactly what they needed. Wonderful location right at the marina, comfortable room overlooking Naples Bay, two great restaurants and bars a stroll away, a pool and an easy-going atmosphere.

'You were so right,' Saul told Terri, after lunch on Saturday of scallops and stuffed crêpes at the Boat House.

'Usually am,' she told him.

'*So* right,' he said again when they were back in their room, lying naked on the bed, closer and happier than they'd been in a long while.

'Thank you,' Terri murmured against his ear.

'For what?'

'This,' she said. 'Everything.' She smiled. 'You.'

'I'm not such a bargain,' Saul said.

'Me neither,' Terri said.

'True,' he agreed.

She took a gentle swipe at the top of his head, then kissed him on the mouth.

They began making love, and stopped talking.

*   *   *

He didn't know until he woke alone in the bed and saw her, wearing her short scarlet satin robe, sitting hunched over on the couch near the balcony, that she'd even brought her laptop with her.

'No way,' he said, real anger swamping him.

She looked up, startled. 'Just checking over a few—'

'Not here.' Saul was out of bed, still naked, still mad. 'This is nuts, Teté.'

'Don't start, Saul.' Her eyes were already flashing.

'Not starting,' he told her. 'Finishing.'

'You're overreacting again.' She shook her head, looked back down at the computer. 'You don't even know what I'm—'

'I don't care,' he snapped. 'It's work, and this is meant to be our time.'

'You were asleep.' She closed the laptop. 'Jesus, Saul.'

'What's so important?' Saul came across, glowered down. 'Show me.'

'Why should I?' Terri picked up the silver machine, tucked it under her arm. 'So you can tell me I'm obsessed again? Crazy?' She found her weekend case, stuck the laptop into it and pulled out a pair of white jeans and a strawberry coloured blouse. 'Maybe I am, you know? For thinking you might have started accepting what's important to me.'

'I'm the crazy one round here.' Saul felt suddenly exposed, and located his own jeans on the chair where he'd tossed them an hour or so back. 'For imagining you were capable of choosing me – *us* – over three murders that have nothing to *do* with you!' He stepped into the jeans, almost tripped, was grateful in the midst of his anger to have spared himself that small humiliation. 'Not for one single weekend.'

'For fuck's sake.' Terri already had her jeans on, and was fastening the buttons of the blouse, her fingers shaking. 'You were *asleep* – you're always going to *sleep*.'

'Pardon me for being human.' Saul sat back down on the edge of the bed. 'Pardon me for wanting – for thinking it's *normal* – to fall asleep with the woman I love.'

'Pardon *me* for the great sin of waking up.' Terri stuck her feet into her moccasins. 'Pardon me for not being overjoyed to just lie in your arms and gaze at your not *so* handsome sleeping face.'

Saul stared at her, used to passion from her, positive and negative, but not a bit used to real, hard bitchiness.

'Hurt your feelings?' Terri found her bag and slung it over her shoulder. 'Well, I may be a cop, and I may be more ambitious than you think I ought to be, but I have feelings too, and right now all I really feel is sick to death of begging your goddamned pardon.'

It seemed to Saul that one or other of them was always walking out the door.

The weekend had arrived, and still no response from Kez.

She'd blown it. No doubt about that now, Cathy realized.

She found it curious, in a way, that until now she'd never understood quite how lonely she had been despite the warmth of her adoptive family surrounding her. Always there for her when she needed them, because they loved her.

She knew how lucky she was to have that kind of love. To have lost her first family so comprehensively, to have lost the trust of everyone who had ever known her in that other life, and then to have been drawn in, welcomed in with such unstinting faith and generosity by Grace and Sam and David and Judy and Saul.

No one could have asked for more. Which was probably why she had never thought of *needing* any more. Why the absence of intimate relationships had not appeared to matter much to her.

Until she had met Kez and discovered that there was, after all, something more – some*one* more – that she did want.

Blown it.

Saul had waited a long while, his thoughts a precarious balance between anger and guilt, before he'd gone looking for Terri.

Obvious places first, close at hand; the bar at the restaurant where they'd eaten lunch, the bar at The Dock nearby, the hotel's own marina-side Chickee Bar.

Nothing that easy, not where Teté was concerned.

He called her cell phone, got voicemail, left no message – not feeling ready to grovel – then began to move further inland, on foot to begin with, heading for the Third Street shopping district, with no real belief that he would find her there. Nor was she *anywhere* that he looked, and he had picked up his car and was starting to check out approaches to the beach when it struck him that the most probable place – the place most likely to have drawn Terri – was the one they had planned to visit together.

He went back to the Cove Inn, asked if Ms Suarez had called

for a cab to take her anyplace, but no one at reception had taken a request from her, though she might, they suggested, have taken the CAT bus or rented her own car.

She might have done that – Saul had been trying *not* to consider that – and left Naples altogether; might be back on Alligator Alley right now on her way home.

She hadn't taken her things, though.

Saul got directions and headed for the zoo.

It was lush, sub-tropical, and, if you got past the Subway Café, a pretty damned good-looking zoo, Saul supposed, except he wasn't here to look at tall, aged trees, amazing plants and gorgeous flowers, or even what every other visitor in the place was here to look at, namely the animals and birds.

Terri was all he was here for.

He checked out the café first, went back to wait outside the restroom for several minutes just in case, then walked back out past the Subway Pavilion and the children's play area, a small map of the zoo in one hand, taking the main trail that would have taken Teté to her number one goal, the Primate Expedition Cruise on Lake Victoria.

'Lemurs and spider and colobus monkeys,' she had read to him when they'd been setting up the trip back home, excited as a child. 'And siamangs – they're lemurs too, but the biggest there are – and all endangered.'

Saul had enjoyed her thrill at the time, but now, beginning the walk she'd mapped out for him, he wasn't sure he'd have noticed or cared if the rarest species on earth had swung off a palm right into his face.

Macaws, alligators in the bay to his left, dorcas gazelles to his right, a grey parrot, zebras, a porcupine dozing in the hollow of a tree trunk. Humans, too, parents and children wandering through, some pushing buggies, many on their last days of vacation: pointing, enjoying, relaxing.

No dark-haired beauty in a strawberry-coloured blouse.

The catamaran had just sailed as he reached the lake, with half an hour to wait before the next departure. Saul screwed up his eyes, trying to make out the passengers, saw a flash of red – but the *wrong* red – knew it was hopeless, and guessed he had no option but to go on walking around till the cat returned.

He turned to his right, moving into Lagoon Loop, could see the catamaran through the trees, the passengers on the nearside of the vessel quite clearly visible to him now, but still no sign of Terri. She might, he realized abruptly, just have disembarked from the previous cruise, so what he needed to do while the cat made its round of small islands was to go on looking for her on land, and maybe this was just a wild goose chase, but it was, for now, the only game in town.

Left over a small wooden footbridge to Look Out Point, and Saul paused, took a look, could see over to one of the dozen small islands in the lake that the catamaran was now approaching. A gardener was mowing grass over there, and he thought he saw a few monkeys, though he could have cared less which they were.

No Teté. That was all he cared about.

He sighed, turned around, walked back over the bridge, scanning left to right, passed a sable, way back from the fence in its nice spacious enclosure and then, a little further along, another enclosure, of spotted hyenas.

He stopped dead. Totally thrown.

She was over to the left in a corner, crouching, almost huddling, her face right up against the lower, outer perimeter fence of that enclosure. She was watching a spotted hyena padding out of the distance towards her, completely absorbed by it.

More than just absorbed, he felt.

She turned, suddenly, saw him staring at her.

The look in her eyes threw him even more, but he managed a smile.

'Hi,' he said.

Her expression turned to ice.

'You OK?' he asked tentatively, and took a step forward.

She bolted. Just straightened up and ran towards the clearing over to his right, dodging a group of visitors and melting into the old palm trees and banyans behind them.

Saul followed, walking fast, then sprinting, passed the group, saw the Subway Pavilion, the building that housed the zoo's shop and restrooms, but saw no sign of her.

She had gone.

'What's up with you, Gracie?' asked Sam late on Saturday afternoon.

They were in the den, both taking time out, Grace with her feet up on the couch, Sam on the floor close by, Woody draped over his long legs, snoozing.

'Nothing's up.'

She was unaccustomed to lying to him, did not like it one bit.

'Something's wrong,' he persisted.

'The baby's auditioning for the City Ballet.'

'Really?' Sam reached up a hand, put it back on the side of her ever-expanding bump, where it had been resting up until a few moments earlier. 'I thought he was feeling pretty laid back this afternoon.'

'With respect – ' Grace removed his hand, sat up with her now usual effort – 'how would you know?'

'If you want something,' Sam said, 'ask me.'

'I'm pregnant, Sam, not sick.' The irritation in her tone was unmistakable.

'That's what you say,' Sam retaliated, 'unless I *don't* offer to help.'

'I don't ask you to do much,' Grace said. 'If I did, it wouldn't help, since you're hardly ever here.'

'I'm here now,' Sam said.

'You want a medal?'

Sam got up off the rug. 'Come on, Gracie.'

'I'm not in a "Gracie" mood,' she said.

'Tell me about it,' Sam said wryly.

'What's that supposed to mean?'

He held up his hands in surrender. 'Forget it.'

'How can I when you bring up my hormones every chance?'

'I haven't *mentioned* them. I wouldn't dare.'

Grace sank back on to the cushions again. 'Sorry.'

'It's OK,' Sam said. 'It's part of it.'

'Hormones again,' Grace said, this time smiling.

'Hush.' Sam raised a finger to his lips. 'The kid might hear.'

'The kid's a boy,' Grace reminded him. 'He'll probably be on your side.'

'Lord, I hope so,' Sam said.

This thing with Terri – this probably non-existent thing – was beginning to get to Grace despite her best intentions. She had grown so used to sharing even the smallest problems with Sam, had always thought that one of the most precious aspects of their partnership. But in this case her thoughts were so unclear, and even *she* had told herself it was hormones.

The main issue for her right now was that the instant she raised her concerns with Sam there was a real risk that everything would spin right out of control, because as wise as he was, that wisdom tended to go clean out the window if he feared any of his family was under threat. And if Sam asked Terri a single question about that photograph and how she had come to be in possession of it, then Saul might end up hating him for ever.

A dilemma or several in the making. Which was why Grace was planning to go on doing what she seldom did.

Nothing.

There was no sign of Terri back at the Cove Inn, but her clothes were still there, and Saul didn't know if he was more angry now or worried.

Worried enough to call her cell phone again and leave a brief message: 'I need to know you're OK. Please call.'

No response as yet, and all Saul was increasingly certain of was that this situation needed to be resolved, and he hoped to God that would not mean ending their relationship; yet being in love with Teté was becoming ever more painful as time went on, and the last thing he wanted was for it to become destructive.

He went out to the bar at the Boat House, sat on a stool drinking a Miller Lite and gazing up at some ball game, hardly taking it in, his eyes turning to the door each time it opened. And then it struck him that Terri might that very minute be back at the Cove Inn wanting to make up with him, and if he wasn't there that might be the clincher, she might pick up her things and leave for keeps. So he paid for his drink and sprinted back to the inn, half convinced he was going to find her there in their room.

Breathless when he got through the door.

Empty room.

He called her number again, left a second message, half wished he had not, realized abruptly that the gnawing sensation in his stomach was hunger, but knew that the only way he was going to be able to relax long enough to eat a sandwich would be to leave her a note.

> *Terri, I'm over at The Dock having a snack – come find me, please.*

He stuck it right in the centre of the bed, a bottle of her shampoo weighing down one corner of the sheet of paper in case it blew away when she opened the door, went over to the bustling restaurant, ordered himself a grilled yellow fin tuna sandwich, downed it too fast with a Bud, and went back yet again to the inn.

The note had not been touched.

Crayton Cove, he decided, through no fault of its own, was swiftly losing its charms.

It was the first Saturday evening Cathy had spent at home with Sam and Grace for a while, and she had enjoyed it, acknowledging privately that she had been ducking out on them too much lately.

It was good to be with family, and just the three of them for once. Sure she loved Saul – found it hard sometimes to believe just how much. And David too, of course, she adored him for all his kindness and wisdom and incredibly generous heart. But it was a little different with these two.

Her adoptive parents on paper, yet *more* than that, in her heart – her greatest friends in the world, willing to do anything for her, wanting to protect her, urging her on. She still thought about her real mom and Arnie, her *first* adoptive father, still loved and missed them, would have given anything to have them back, safe and happy – though then she'd never have known Grace and Sam and the others, and . . .

The complexities of her life were still often too much to contemplate, bore down on her sometimes like great blanketing clouds. Easier, better for her, she had decided long ago, not to dwell on them, to take each day as it came, and she was a survivor these days rather than a victim, and lucky, so lucky, to be that.

Kez was a new complexity. Out of her life now, as swiftly as she'd entered it, and maybe that was as well, maybe there would be less pain this way.

'I don't like that kind of pain,' Kez had said.

The last thing she'd said to her, right after she'd told Cathy to go away and think. Except that what Kez had really meant – Cathy could see that now – was that she should just *go* altogether because she was too young, too inexperienced, too uncertain. Maybe Kez was right.

If only, Cathy thought, she really believed that.

By eleven o'clock Saul had become seriously worried about Terri.

Storming out had been just like her, as had going off on her own, staying out, making him sweat, he guessed. But it had been too many hours now, and even if she didn't care about the few clothes and personal possessions she'd brought from home, Terri had also left her laptop behind – presumably with her precious *work* loaded. Even if she'd been trying to score points, perhaps leaving it there to see if he could resist taking a look – which he had no intention of doing – surely enough time, almost nine hours, had passed.

Something could have happened to her – he was becoming increasingly afraid that something *had* happened, and was increasingly agitated too, because there wasn't a single thing he could do about finding her. The Naples police weren't going to be concerned about a grown woman – not to mention a fellow officer – who'd walked out after a fight with her boyfriend. And if Terri ever got to hear about his making that kind of a report, she would most certainly never forgive him.

Calm down.

He went out again, no real purpose in mind now other than to try ridding himself of some of the tension that had built up in him, not even looking for Terri now because there was no point. In all likelihood nothing had happened to her, and she was probably not even *in* Naples any more, had just decided to make him suffer, had known he would take care of her belongings and take them back to Miami. And for all he knew, she might have gone to call on some cop colleagues – people who might understand what made her tick more than he did – maybe she'd even gotten a ride back to Miami with one of them.

His walk was taking him along quiet affluent streets lined with large and lovely residences, exemplary homes with nothing to hide, no high walls to shield them from scrutiny, only perfectly tidy front gardens. Saul had seen similar houses driving into town with Terri, and they had been happy then, looking forward to checking in and sharing a little vacation time and making love and . . .

Cut that out.

Saul shook his head, irritated by his own self-pity, and turned a corner, heading towards the beach, and that was the best idea he'd had all day, getting some sand under his toes and a stiff ocean breeze in his face. And after that he thought he'd buy himself a nightcap back at the inn and get some rest and then, first thing, if Terri still wasn't making contact, he'd check out and head back home.

It was wonderful.

Stars littering the black sky, a half moon silvering the already white sand, and Saul had taken off his sneakers and was gripping them by their laces, swinging them a little as he walked, the feel of the sand as good as he'd known it would be.

A few people around, not many, but still too many for his mood.

Couples, almost all of them, hand in hand or arms around each other, one pair laughing with pure joy as he passed them.

He went on walking, wanting to escape the lovers, all those happy, normal people, and Saul knew, of course, that in reality at least half of those people were probably nowhere near completely happy, and that there was no such thing as *normal*. In any case, what he and Terri were going through was nothing so special, just a case of two people who'd been crazy about each other coming to the slow, painful realization that things might not be going to work out for them, after all, and it was no big deal. Except it felt, right this minute, like the biggest damned deal on earth.

Suddenly, the people were all gone. He was, as he had wished, all alone.

Saul sat down facing the ocean, knees drawn up, arms hugging them, hands still holding on to the sneakers which knocked gently against his shins, blown by the wind. There was a little sand in the air, mixed in with the salt from the ocean, and it stung his eyes, but it didn't matter because there were tears in them already.

He dug his toes into the sand, thought back to how it had been after lunch, in bed with Teté, allowed himself to think about her beautiful breasts and wonderful skin, about the way she always wrapped herself so close to him.

He said her name, not shouting it or whispering it, just *said* it, into the wind.

'Teté.'

And then he heard the sound from behind, footsteps hurrying over the sand towards him.

Saul turned, too late, saw it coming a split second before the first blow struck his right shoulder, sending spears of agony through him and knocking him on to his back.

He started to cry out . . .
'*Why?*'
Cut off by the foot coming down, stamping hard and viciously on his Adam's apple, destroying his voice and wiping out his breath.
The last thing he heard as he sank into oblivion was the scream.

Seventeen

September 4

They travelled together in the darkness, one silent carload skimming Interstate 75 – aka Alligator Alley: Sam driving, Grace beside him, David and Cathy in the rear.
David had got the call, Saul's wallet, intact, having given the Naples police and People's Hospital the information they needed.
Not many details given on the phone; just the bare essentials.
Saul was badly injured, had been attacked on the beach.
Get here fast.
No one was speaking. Sam sat rigidly, hands clenched around the wheel. Cathy wept softly, wiping her eyes occasionally with a saturated tissue. David was praying, silently for the most part, his lips moving now and again.
Grace, her hands clasped over the child in her womb, her eyes focused straight ahead, kept stealing glances at Sam, felt as if her private thoughts and fears were drilling holes in her head; and she *knew* she had no choice now but to tell Sam without further delay about her suspicions of Terri.
Not while he's driving, you can wait till you get there.
Yet having waited this long, surely she would have to wait a little longer than that, until she saw Terri's face, her expression, her *eyes*, before she said anything so damaging, so potentially shattering. She owed it to Saul to wait till then, now that she'd held on to it for so long, had to try and get it right.
As to the greatest, the most terrifying of her fears . . .
That if her suspicions were *not* unfounded, then this terrible

thing might not have happened to Saul if she had spoken up before now. Grace could not bear even to contemplate that.

On the beach.

Like the others. The ones Terri had been so obsessed by.

No!

A silent cry in Grace's head.

Please, God, no.

Terri was pacing outside the ICU, visible from the far end of the long fifth floor corridor, vivid in her strawberry blouse and white jeans.

'The surgery went OK,' she told them hoarsely as they approached.

'And now?' Sam's voice was a lash in the quiet air as his eyes went to the glass window, strained to see his brother, saw two beds occupied by strangers, Saul – if he was in there – out of view. 'Where is he?'

'Far end.' She looked wrecked, mascara streaked, hair messed up. 'I don't know how he is. He's unconscious and hooked up to machines, and he looks so *bad . . .*'

Sam turned on his heel, disappeared into the ICU, and David, with a swift, despairing look at Grace, went after him.

Grace waited another moment, composing herself, then faced Terri.

'Tell us,' she said.

'How much do you know?'

'Very little.' Grace kept her eyes on the younger woman's. 'We know Saul was attacked, and that it's bad.'

'They – someone – battered him.' Terri's mouth worked for an instant or two, but she brought herself back under control. 'They broke his shoulder and beat him around the head.' She took a juddering breath. 'A doctor told me he thought they might have stamped on his throat, Grace.'

Cathy gave a gasp of pure horror.

Terri looked at her with sympathy, then back at Grace.

'His larynx is smashed.' A whisper now. 'That's how hard they stamped on him.'

Cathy made a brief, shrill, terrible sound, and Grace, her own heart pounding so hard she feared she might pass out, looked away from Terri for a moment to check that her daughter was not about to collapse. Then, struggling for self-control, she returned her gaze to the other young woman, searched the red-rimmed, distraught eyes. The anguish looked true, it looked *real* – and suddenly pure instinct took over, propelled Grace's arms up and out, and Terri all but fell into them, allowed herself to be held for a moment before she pulled away again, trembling violently.

'You need to sit.' Grace nodded at a bench to their right.

'I can't.'

'You should,' Cathy said. 'You look like hell.'

'I have to keep *moving*.'

Grace asked the dread question. 'What about his head?'

Terri shook her head. 'I don't know.' She looked from Cathy to Grace again. 'You two should sit, especially you, Grace.'

What Grace desperately wanted was to be with Sam and David in the ICU, to be with poor, poor Saul, but she also needed, she knew, to stay here with Terri and go on observing her for just a little longer, to be *certain* that she was what she appeared: Saul's traumatized, horrified girlfriend.

'What about you, Terri?' she asked quietly. 'They didn't hurt you?'

Terri shook her head. 'I wasn't there.'

'How come?' Cathy was bewildered. 'Where did it happen?'

Finally Terri moved over to the bench, sank down. 'Saul was walking on the beach.' Her voice was almost a whisper again. 'I wasn't with him.'

'Why weren't you?' Something inside Grace began to chill.

'We had another fight,' Terri said.

'A man found him on the beach near the pier,' David reported to Sam after he'd talked with one of the ICU team. 'The paramedics came fast, thank God, got his airway open, saved his life. The CT scan showed a blood clot, but they got him into surgery, dealt with that.'

'But all this.' Sam was staring down at Saul, at the bandages and the plastered shoulder and upper right arm and the awful bruising, at all the tubes and wires, the catheters and electrode pads on his chest, the ventilator and monitors, the bags of blood and fluid, administering and taking away; the blessed horrors of modern medicine. 'He looks as if he's on life support.'

'All there to help him through,' David reassured. 'The monitors are his friends right now, son. If the machines report a problem, the team can jump on it right away.' He didn't know how he was managing to speak so calmly, didn't know how he was still upright. 'They've done some preliminary fixing up, too, in his throat. Fragments of cartilage had to be removed, tiny plates and wires put in to stabilize the area.'

'And now?' Sam's own throat felt constricted, his chest tight.

The emotional agony spreading through him as he looked down at his brother was all too sickeningly familiar. He had experienced it three other times, the first when Sampson had died, the next when his dad had been in the ICU at Miami General after someone had stabbed him six years back; the third when he'd heard the death knell of Judy's terminal cancer prognosis.

Not the same, he told himself, and tried in vain to shove it away. Tried, but failed, to put away the greatest of his fears.

'How long was it, before they got his airway open?'

One part of the fear. Sam did not, could not, look at his father.

David knew what he was really asking: how long Saul's brain might have been deprived of oxygen. Two bites of the poisoned cherry, he thought, with a new, silent rush of agony: head trauma and suffocation.

'No way of knowing how long.' He paused. 'The EEG looks OK.'

Finally Sam dared to look at him, feeling like a boy again, craving reassurance from the man he trusted most in the world.

'But it's early days, son.' David needed to be honest, for all their sakes. 'He took a hell of a beating. More than a single impact.'

'Is he in a coma?'

His father shook his head. 'But they're going to keep him under heavy sedation for quite a while, to give everything a chance to settle.' He struggled for a few more crumbs to throw to his older son. 'I know it doesn't seem that way, but we've actually been very lucky.'

'Lucky.' Sam's face twisted.

'He's alive,' David said simply. 'Another few minutes, maybe less, he'd have been gone if the paramedics hadn't done such a great job. The procedure they used can be risky, a hollow needle in the perfect spot, but they had no choice, and they got it right, thank God.'

'So all in all, he could be OK?' Still like a kid, begging for good news.

'It's early, Sam,' his father told him again. 'There's no cervical spine injury—'

'Jesus.' That horror hadn't even occurred to Sam.

'But however it goes, they're going to have to do a lot more work on him.' David's face was a mass of lines, each seeming more deeply etched than it had been a few hours ago. 'More surgery to repair and rebuild, then physio for his shoulder, and speech therapy.' He looked at his older son's face. 'This minute, though, he's out of danger.'

'But things could still go wrong.' The pleading child had disappeared again, melted back into the core of Sam, the man, filled with fear and a growing, seething rage.

'They could,' David said. 'And he could have died right there on the beach.' He reached for Sam's big hand, squeezed it, felt his skin hot against his own cold fingers. 'But our boy's strong, right?'

Sam looked at his father, recalled again his time in ICU, tethered by tubes and wires, remembered him surviving.

'Like you.' He squeezed his hand back.

And then, abruptly, his mind started working again, and he let the hand go. 'Them,' he said. 'You said a man found "him" on the beach, but surely you meant *them*. Saul and Terri.'

'No,' David said. 'Just Saul. They said he was alone.'

For the first time, Sam looked around the unit, his gaze passing over the other patients and the vigilant nursing team, searching for another kind of uniform, guessed that the police had been and gone, figuring there was no point coming back till there was a chance of Saul waking.

The Naples PD officer walked in as if Sam had conjured him up, began to walk across the room, but Sam beckoned him quickly into a corner near the door where no one would overhear, showed his badge and saw the other man's expression change from irritated to compassionate.

His own cop's mind had begun to tick horribly.

'Do you know,' he asked, 'if there's a chance it was a bat?'

'You mean, like a baseball bat?' The guy saw Sam nod. 'I wasn't at the scene, but word is it could have been something like that, or a club, maybe.'

Something in Sam recoiled.

It made no sense, none at all. Different coast, no possible connection.

Except through *him*, through his involvement in the investigation.

'Son?'

David was at his side, looking at him with new anxiety.

'It's OK, Dad.'

He put an arm around his father's shoulders, went with him back to the bed.

This had to be random, surely, his mind went on ticking; a brutal, random assault.

Except there was no getting away from the fact that it had all the ingredients of another attack by the same individual who might have already killed three people on the Atlantic coast.

All the ingredients but one, thank the Lord. The most fundamental difference of all: Saul was still clinging to life.

Grace was coming down the corridor, heading for the unit as he came out.

'How's he doing?' Her eyes searched his face. 'Terri told us what happened.'

Sam looked at the awful strain in her face, and put his arms around her.

'He's strong,' he said. 'He'll make it.'

'I know he will,' Grace said. 'I know.'

'I want to see him.' Cathy was just a foot away, still white-faced.

'Sure, sweetheart,' Sam told her. 'Dad's still in there.' He pulled gently away from Grace, laid a hand on Cathy's arm. 'You have to be prepared for all the tubes and wires and machines, OK?'

Cathy nodded.

'He's unconscious because they're keeping him that way, because it's the best thing for him.' He looked at Grace. 'You holding up?' Sam asked Grace.

'Don't worry about me,' she said, tension building in her by the second.

Sam turned away, walked across to where Terri still sat on the bench by the wall.

'Where were you,' he asked, 'when it happened?'

Behind him, Grace remained motionless, let Cathy go into the ICU alone.

Bad mom.

Bad wife, worse sister-in-law.

Terri had stood up slowly, was facing Sam.

'We had a fight,' she told him.

'Another one,' Sam said, and shook his head.

He began to turn away from her; then swivelled slowly back around.

'You must have noticed the similarities, too,' he said.

'Of course,' she said.

Grace was watching Terri again. The young woman was wrecked, there seemed no doubt about that, and it was *impossible* to conceive that this horrific crime could have anything whatever to do with her.

Yet all the outward distress in the world might mean nothing. *Might.*

Grace knew she had no choices left.

She took a deep breath. 'Sam,' she said. 'I need to speak to you.'

He was pulling his cell phone out of his pocket, starting to walk away from the ICU, where he might get away with making calls without going outside.

'Just give me a minute,' he said.

'Now,' Grace told him, and her voice shook just a little. 'Please.'

Eighteen

G race had never seen Sam look at her like that before. As if he hated her.

It passed swiftly, disbelief taking its place.

'I don't believe you could have kept this to yourself.' He shook his head. 'Though I have to say I don't believe in what you've been thinking.'

'Thank God,' Grace said.

They were in a small room, someone's nondescript office. They had slipped in there because she had said, softly, that no one else must hear what she had to say.

'It's craziness,' Sam went on now. 'Based on virtually nothing. The fact that Terri came to see you just after Gregory left that last time.'

'And the photograph of Maria Rivera,' Grace reminded him painfully, desperately wanting him to swat that away too. 'And her obsession, most of all, with the killings.'

'The obsession of an ambitious rookie taking all the wrong paths,' Sam came back. 'We've talked about all this before, Grace.'

'And you said – ' she wanted to give way, to drop this, but she had to get it all said so that they could, God willing, leave the awful suspicion behind – 'that Terri oughtn't to have known anything about Pompano Beach.'

'More obsession, Grace.' Sam was impatient to get out of the room. 'She's had a pretty screwed up life, she's maybe a little needy because of—'

'What about the photograph?' Grace asked doggedly.

Sam was silent.

'Oh God,' Grace said. 'That's getting to you too, isn't it?'

'What's getting to me is why Saul didn't tell me about it.'

That look returned; a dagger straight into Grace's heart.

'You know why,' she said weakly.

'Yes,' he said, 'and I can understand that.' His mouth was set hard. 'What I can't, will never, understand is why my own wife kept it from me.'

He stopped then, did not say out loud what Grace knew he had to be thinking.

The same as she was. That if – *if*, heaven forbid –Terri was to blame, then this terrible thing need never have happened.

That if Grace was right, it was her fault that Sam's brother was lying there now in the ICU with head injuries and a crushed larynx.

Her fault.

'Sure, we spoke with Officer Suarez,' the detective told Sam, 'right after she showed up at the Cove Inn.'

He had only just exited the elevator at the fifth floor, had paused at the nurses' station for an update, when Sam had jumped right on him.

Detective Joseph Patterson of the Naples PD, a young man with keen blue eyes, a cleft chin and brown hair in early retreat from his forehead, investigating the aggravated battery of Saul Becket; all available fellow officers – he had swiftly assured Sam – out on the streets doing everything in their power to get the assailant locked up as quickly as possible.

No evidence, meantime, was the word from the crime scene, and nothing on Saul's body, no fragments under his fingers, though his clothing had been taken away for analysis.

They'd moved out of the corridor into a waiting area, currently empty.

'We knew about the inn,' the detective told Sam, 'because your brother had a note of the reservation in his wallet. Mr and Mrs Saul Becket.'

So old-fashioned and just plain Saul it made Sam want to cry.

The people at the Cove Inn had reported that Saul had been in and out all afternoon and evening looking for Terri, plainly upset, and everyone Patterson had talked to there had been deeply shocked to hear what had happened, particularly as they had found him such a very nice young man.

'Anything we should know?' Patterson asked him.

Sam shook his head. 'Nothing I can tell you.'

'Regarding the relationship with Officer Suarez maybe?'

'She's told me they'd had an argument – ' Sam picked his words carefully – 'and that she'd walked out, that she didn't come back till . . .' He paused. 'You know when.'

'That's what they figured at the inn,' Patterson said. 'Lovers' tiff.'

'The relationship has been a little up and down.' Sam kept his tone even.

When Saul woke up – *when* – if he learned that Sam had laid so much as the smallest finger of suspicion on Terri, he'd prob-ably never forgive him. Without real, *realistic* justification there was simply no way on earth Sam was going to risk that. Not with nothing more than his pregnant wife's almost certainly irra-tional doubts and a photograph.

Not just any photograph, though.

'Where was Terri Suarez, out of interest?' he asked, almost casually. 'When my brother was looking for her?'

'Hasn't she told you?' Patterson asked.

'I didn't ask her,' Sam said. 'She's too shaken up.'

'As you all are,' Patterson said.

His judgment, Sam felt, was being torn to bits. His first impulse was to shove the Naples detective out of the hospital and on to the street to get the job done; but bitterly angry as he was at Grace, he still knew better than to completely dismiss her instincts. The photograph of Maria Rivera *was* disturbing him, as it had clearly disturbed Saul, and Joseph Patterson had already quizzed Terri so Sam *needed* to keep him here at least until he had his answers.

Not that Patterson was under any obligation to tell him a damned thing about his case – even if Sam was a fellow cop, and even if there were, as Sam had already briefly told him, some similarities with the Miami Beach and other east coast killings.

Most of all right here and now, Sam was a *relative*, which meant that Patterson and his colleagues were going to be particularly reluctant to tell him too much, let alone permit him any involvement in their investigation.

The sympathy was there though, and professional courtesy.

'She said she was walking around the city.' Patterson finally answered Sam's question about Terri's whereabouts. 'Had a drink in a bar, no proof of that, but then she says she took a bus ride and got off at a pizza place just a little way from here – she showed us the receipt for that.'

'You're making her sound like a suspect,' Sam remarked.

'Not at all,' the other man said quickly. 'She's one of us. But fact is they came into town as boyfriend and girlfriend, had a bust-up big enough to keep them apart all afternoon and evening, and next thing your brother's in the hospital. So we had to ask a few routine questions, you know?'

'Sure,' Sam said, grateful someone else had.

His thoughts turned back to Saul, to the ugliness of his injuries, the ferocity of the assault, the strength needed for such an attack. Terri had told them that she went to a gym, liked staying in shape, and she was certainly that; a curvy, beautiful young woman, tough enough for her job, but nothing more than that.

'She was on the beach, too, you know,' Patterson told him.

Sam didn't say anything.

'I noticed the sand on her moccasins when she came into the inn. She said she took the bus back after her pizza, went walking on the beach for a while, then sat down to do some thinking.' The detective shrugged. 'The kind of thing people – young lovers – do after a fight, I guess. Mooch on the beach, looking at the moon.'

'So where was she,' Sam asked, 'when it happened?'

'About a mile north of where your brother was attacked.'

'Anyone to corroborate that?'

'Any reason we'd need to, Detective Becket?'

'Of course not,' Sam said. 'Force of habit. Routine, like you said.'

'She said there were other people walking. We'll be asking around.'

Sam was silent again, the question he'd wanted to ask for the last several moments still hanging heavily in his mind – but then Patterson answered it anyway.

'Just sand and grit on her moccasins,' he said. 'No blood.'

Sam felt a sick kind of relief wash over him.

'Not that it would prove much,' Patterson added, 'if Terri Suarez was a suspect. Not with the doc saying it was probably a bare foot that did the stomping.'

The relief, paltry as it had been, went away.

He had to ask, *had* to.

'I don't suppose you asked Terri – Officer Suarez – to show you her feet?'

'No.' Now Patterson was looking curiously at Sam. 'Sure there's nothing you want to tell me?'

'Nothing,' Sam said.

'Something about Ms Suarez I should know?'

'Not a thing.' Sam shook his head. 'I can't believe we're having this conversation.' His jaw felt stiff, his eyes were burning. 'But then I'm still having trouble believing what's happened to my brother.'

'What kind of a guy is he?' The question was kind. 'Is he a fighter?'

'He's a med student,' Sam said. 'Our dad's a doctor.' He took a breath, needing to control himself. 'My brother's a sweetheart of a guy. I'm praying he's a fighter, too.'

'By the looks of your family, at least he'll have a whole bunch of supporters in his corner.' He saw Sam's battle for composure starting up again, put out a hand and gripped his arm briefly but supportively. 'Meantime, we're going to find this bastard.'

'I'd like to help.' Sam already knew how the other man would respond.

'Best way you can do that,' Patterson said, 'is be here for Saul.'

Sam nodded. 'Right,' he said.

Lying through his teeth.

Sam checked on Saul, confirmed there was no change, then left the others to take it in turns to sit with him, and went downstairs and out into the warm air.

Dawn was well on its way, delicate and fragrant, heightened by the scent of the flowerbeds bordering the driveway at the front of the hospital. The urban section of Route 41, the Tamiami Trail, lay straight ahead, vehicles skimming to and fro, traffic still light at this time.

Sam took out his cell phone and called Martinez, the only

person outside the family he'd already told about Saul. Kovac and the captain could wait till later.

'How is he?' Martinez sounded as if he'd been waiting for the phone to ring.

'Holding his own. Still in ICU, still critical.'

'What can I do for you, man? Anything, name it.'

'It's a strange one, Al,' Sam said, 'and off the record, OK?'

'Shoot,' Martinez told him.

'Anything out of place you can find out about Teresa Suarez.'

'Saul's lady?' Martinez was confused. 'The cop?'

'That's right,' Saul said. 'This is a little off, I know, but . . . '

'We're not IAD, Sam.' Martinez sounded upset. 'And I wouldn't find anything if I looked. She's had all the checks, same as we all do when we're starting out.'

'I know,' Sam said. 'I thought maybe you could have a discreet word with one of your girlfriends in Property or Personnel.'

'You want me to try to look at her file?' Martinez was patently reluctant.

'I don't know if that would help, Al.' Sam began pacing the broad driveway, fighting the sudden wall of fatigue that felt about ready to collapse on him. 'I already know some family stuff – abusive father, both parents killed – life with her grandma – grandfather was NYPD, line of duty death.'

'Jesus, man.'

'I know,' Sam agreed. 'I don't like it either, and the hell of it is I don't even know what I'm looking for.'

'It's not so much *what* that bothers me as *why*?' Martinez said. 'You need to help me out here, tell me what's goin' on in your head.' He paused. 'You're thinking Suarez had something to do with what happened to Saul?' He sounded incredulous.

'Not really,' Sam said. 'I hope not. With all my heart.'

'But if that is what you're thinking, that means you're tying this up with the beach murders.' Martinez paused again. 'Are you kidding me?'

'I'm not in a kidding mood,' Sam said. 'And I can't say any more right now. What I want is to *know* she's OK. Most of all, that she loves my brother as much as she says she does.'

'And that she isn't a secret whacko,' Martinez added.

Coming out of the elevator back on the fifth floor, he saw them right away. Standing outside the ICU. Body language unmistakable.

Terror clamped around Sam's heart. David had his arms around

Cathy, her face buried in his chest. Grace had already seen him, started to move towards him but then stopped, uncertain if he wanted her close, and stricken by the doubt.

Terri was leaning against a wall a few feet away, her face a mask of fear.

Apparent fear.

Sam felt leaden as he walked towards them, by-passed them all, asking nothing, needing to see for himself, to *know* . . .

He went through the door.

Saw a whole team around Saul's bed, working on him.

Please, God, no, please, God no.

He heard Grace's step behind him, felt her hand on his arm, looked around at her, saw the awful fear in her eyes.

Stepped away from her.

Nineteen

It had been a seizure, a bad one, but they had him back, stable again.

David told them it was possible it could happen again, but that he was in the best place and Saul was young and fit and tough.

No more surgery, he said, until he was stronger.

'What can we do for him?' Cathy asked David.

'Be here,' he told her. 'Let him know we're here, that we all love him.'

'Need him,' Terri said.

'Can he hear us, do you think?' Cathy asked.

'Maybe,' David answered. 'We can't be sure.'

'What about you when you were unconscious that time?' she asked him. 'Could you hear people talking to you?'

'I don't know,' he said. 'But that's because I can't remember because of the drugs. It doesn't mean I didn't hear.'

Cathy hardly stopped talking to Saul after that, told him every little thing that came into her head – talked to him, when no one

Hilary Norman

else was around, about her feelings for Kez, about how much she was missing her.

'I keep thinking about the afternoon we met you and Teté in CocoWalk and you said we should all go have a drink, but we didn't because Kez wanted us to be alone. But afterward she was worried you might have been upset, and I told her you wouldn't be offended about something like that, but still, you would have gotten to spend some time with Kez, and then you'd understand how I feel about her. So when you're better I hope we can do that anyway, though I'm not too sure that Kez is ever going to want to spend time with me again.'

She paused, hoping for some tiny response, the smallest movement of a finger, *anything*, but there was nothing, would be nothing for a long while yet.

And if there had ever been the smallest doubt in her mind as to the depth of her feelings for Saul, it was entirely extinguished now.

They took rooms at a motel near the hospital, taking it in turns to go there to shower and sleep for short periods before going back again.

David was practically immovable, for which Sam – anxious as he was that their father not make himself sick – was profoundly grateful, since so long as that grey-haired, hawk-nosed old guard dog was on duty, it freed him at least to liaise with Patterson, check in periodically with Martinez (nothing so far of any interest on Terri) and take a couple of late night walks on the beach – about all he felt he could get away with without arousing the irritation, or worse, of the local force.

Sam did not want a grain of bad feeling between himself and Joseph Patterson or his colleagues. He wanted them on this case with as much motivation and goodwill as humanly possible. For now, at least, they were still in what many cops called 'the first seventy-two' – the period during which new cases were most likely, statistically, to be solved, after which, with manpower as stretched in Naples as in Miami Beach – though there were exceptions, especially in particularly high profile cases – the only detective likely to be left with the case was the lead investigator, most people returning to work on other old cases and, of course, new crimes.

Saul might be one of the most important people in Sam's life, but there was nothing remotely high profile about him – and he wasn't even dead.

Sam still felt torn between the urge to get out on the streets – as a private citizen, not a cop – and his need to keep Terri under a degree of surveillance.

Not that he actually believed she was the one.

He'd had occasion to see the soles of Terri's feet early the first morning, an hour or so after he'd talked with Detective Patterson.

They had been taking a few minutes in the relatives' room – David and Grace sitting in the ICU – and Cathy had fallen asleep on the couch.

Terri had taken off her moccasins, lifted one foot at a time and rubbed it.

Neat, tidy feet with red toenails. Smooth soles and heels.

Not a blemish.

That ought, Sam thought, to have been a turning point, the instant he should have felt able to drop the notion for keeps and let her off the hook, yet it had not been, for there was no real reason why the foot which had stamped on his brother's throat should have been injured or marked in any way.

So he was still watching, just in case.

He blamed her anyway.

For not having been with Saul when he'd been attacked. For having had another quarrel with him. For walking out on him, leaving him distressed enough to spend the rest of the afternoon and evening out searching for her.

Though even if they hadn't fought, Sam tried to rationalize, if Terri had not walked out, they might still have taken a night-time stroll along the beach, and maybe the attack might still have taken place.

Not if they were prowling, looking for a lone victim. All three of the others had been alone on the beach, all after dark. Which meant that the chances were that it would *not* have happened to Saul if Terri had been with him, and Sam didn't know if he could ever forgive her for that.

Which made him no better than Althea with her unforgiving heart, because he had not been there when their little boy had pulled away from *her* grasp and been run down by the drunk driver.

If – when – Saul got better, Sam would have to find a way to forgive Terri. She was looking about as ripped apart as he felt, had told Sam how much she wanted to stay close to Saul, yet wanted at the same time – just like him – to be out there helping find the scum who'd done this.

She had told Sam, too, how much she hated herself for running out on Saul. Had told Grace the same thing.

'I hate myself for that,' Terri had said to her, 'more than I could ever have believed possible.'

And Grace, still in pieces, had gone straight to Sam and repeated every word to him, verbatim. All she could do right now. Too little, too late.

He had not actively rejected her again, not in the same painful way, since that moment outside the ICU early that first morning, but neither was he sharing his innermost feelings with her as he usually did, and sometimes when he looked at her she noticed that he swiftly looked away again, and she was terribly afraid that it was because he no longer loved what he saw.

As frightened for Saul as she was, Cathy was feeling guilt, too.

She felt so caged, the long hours of vigil in the hospital, the bad atmosphere between the others – only David seeming at all himself, and he, of course, was consumed with fear for his son – taking their toll on her.

She wanted – needed – to do what she always did under stress. Run, keep on running.

She wanted Kez, too, was utterly certain of that now. To talk with, be with. To be close to her, have her strong arms around her, and not only for comfort.

She made the call on Tuesday afternoon, went outside to the hospital driveway, checked her voicemail for the umpteenth time, found nothing and, steeling herself against further rejection, keyed in Kez's number again.

'I can't take your call right now . . .'

Kez's voice, but no warmth in it, a message spoken swiftly, perhaps recorded in a rush, and if Kez didn't like cell phones, maybe she disliked telephones altogether.

But Cathy *needed* her.

'Kez, it's me, Cathy,' she said. 'I really, really need you to call me.'

The whole thing, she had to tell her what had happened to Saul, throw it all in, let Kez understand how much she meant to her.

'Saul was attacked, in Naples, and he's in really bad shape, and we're all over here together, all the family, but there's only one person I really want to be with, to talk to, and that's you, Kez, and I miss you so much, and you told me to make up my mind about how I feel about you, and I have, I really have.'

Pitiful.

Cathy hated herself already.

Kez would despise her even more.

'Please call,' she said.

Needs must.

'I've said it before,' Grace told Lucia on the phone, late on Tuesday evening, 'but it's never been quite as true. I do not know what I'd do without you.'

'You'd cope,' Lucia said.

She had left a message for Grace, wanting primarily to check on Saul, but also to let her know that she had cleared her entire list for the next week so Grace didn't need to worry about her patients, and yes, Lucia had remembered that the more fragile would need to be seen by Dr Shrike (Magda Shrike, Grace's old mentor, and one of the best psychologists she knew).

'So all you have to think about is Saul and your family and yourself,' Lucia went on. 'And please, Dr Lucca, promise me you will take care of yourself and the baby. And Tina's not at People's Hospital, of course, but if there's anything you think she could help with, just tell me and I'll get in touch with her.'

Grace had forgotten, in the horror, all about Lucia's favourite niece.

'That's so kind,' she said, 'but I can't think of anything right now.' She wanted to get back upstairs to Saul, but Lucia deserved consideration too. 'If Tina has something that she'd like us to bring back to you, or if you think of . . .'

'You can stop that this instant, doctor,' Lucia chided her. 'Didn't I just tell you to take care of yourself?'

Grace mustered a smile, felt the baby move, thought of him as an anchor in all the dark distress; thought, too, of the incomparable value of good friends.

'I almost forgot,' Lucia said, 'to tell you that Claudia called yesterday.'

A new wave of guilt jogged Grace.

'You haven't told her about Saul,' Lucia said.

'No,' Grace said. 'Did you . . . ?'

'Of course not,' Lucia said. 'Not my place to interfere and I know you feel your sister has a lot on her plate, but I do still think it's time you let her know. Problems or not, she's family. She should at least be given the option of getting on a plane.'

'You're right,' Grace said.

'I know I am,' Lucia said.

Grace made the call right away, but the instant she heard her sister's voice, heard the dullness she'd been noticing far too often lately, she knew she still wasn't going to tell her the whole truth.

'What's going on?' Claudia asked. 'Where are you?'

'We're in Naples,' Grace told her. 'Saul's in the hospital.'

'What happened?' Distress replaced the dullness. 'Is he OK?'

'He will be,' Grace said. 'He was attacked, sis, and we had some scary moments, but he's going to be fine.'

Claudia began firing questions: what exactly and when had it happened, why hadn't Grace told her right away, because she would have flown across, could have been with her through such a dreadful time. There was nothing she could have done, Grace told her, and quite frankly the last few days had been a blur.

She did not tell her how bad Saul was, told Claudia that the reason she couldn't speak to him was because he was sleeping much of the time.

'I'm going to book a flight,' Claudia said.

'There's no need,' Grace said. 'They'll probably be moving Saul soon.'

'Discharging him?' Claudia jumped on the words.

'Moving him first, I expect,' Grace said, 'back to Miami.'

'Why can't they discharge him, if he's OK?'

'Because he's been concussed, and he's going to need some surgery.' Grace was fighting to blend truth with white lies. 'He has a fractured shoulder.'

'Oh, poor Saul,' Claudia said. 'He must be in such pain.'

'Anyway – ' Grace took the subject back to Claudia – 'it's not as if you can just jump on a plane.'

'I can find a sitter for the boys,' Claudia said, 'or Daniel will just have to work from home for once – he used to be happy enough doing that.'

'Before he had the new practice,' Grace said. 'Not just himself to look after now, sis, a whole bunch of responsibilities.'

'Me and the boys, most of all, I'd have thought,' Claudia said.

Grace's heart sank a little deeper, as it tended to whenever she spoke to her sister these days. *Not* her imagination that things had been difficult between Claudia and Daniel since the move, and maybe after the baby was born she was going to have to be the one to stir herself and fly up there to see if there was anything she could do.

For now though, her hands were more than full, and frankly, the way Claudia was sounding, having her here was unlikely to be any help at all.

She told Claudia that she loved her and missed her, told her that she and the baby were fine, but that she didn't want to have to stress about creating upheavals for her and Daniel and the boys, and that she had Sam and Cathy and David to take care of her, so there was no need to worry. And Claudia sounded a little aggrieved, but a little relieved, too, no question about it.

'Promise you'll call if anything changes, or if you need me,' she said.

'The instant,' Grace said.

'Nothing new,' Martinez told Sam early Wednesday morning.

'Nothing?'

'Nothing you don't already know. Dirtbag dad and drunken mom, grandma saved the day, like you said. And maybe that could all have been the start of some screw-up psychosis, but I don't buy it because the kid hauled herself up and became a cop like her grandpa, didn't she?'

'Yes, she did,' Sam said.

'So, can I stop this now?'

'I guess,' Sam said.

'Fuck's sake, man, do you *want* her to be a serial killer?' Martinez sounded exasperated. 'Would you rather she'd been the one to beat the shit out of your brother?'

'No,' Sam said. 'Of course not.'

'So now you can focus on Saul and Grace and Cathy and your dad, and you can leave the investigation to the Naples guys, right?'

'Sure,' Sam said.

'Why don't I believe you mean that?' Martinez asked.

'Have I done something to upset you?'

Cathy asked Grace the question as they took a walk outside in the hospital gardens early that afternoon. All kinds of gorgeous trees and flowers, a typically, beautifully cared for

Naples setting, the kind of grass that looked as if every blade had been hand-trimmed, carved memorial benches at intervals along the pathways.

Neither of them noticed the loveliness, both had too much on their minds.

'Why would you think that?' Grace asked.

'I don't know,' Cathy said. 'I mean, we're all feeling so bad about Saul, but you seem—'

'What do I seem?' Grace stopped walking, looked at Cathy. 'Sweetheart, tell me, please, what have I done to make you think you could have upset me?'

'Nothing terrible.' Cathy took her hand and squeezed it. 'Except ever since we got here you seem as if you're a thousand miles away from us.' She shook her head. 'Not just from me, either. I can see David feeling it too, and I can't tell about Sam, because he's half crazy about Saul anyway.'

'I'm so sorry.' Shame heated Grace's cheeks. 'I swear to you, Cathy, this has absolutely nothing to do with you. I'm just not dealing with things as well as I ought to be, that's all.'

'I don't buy that.' Cathy's clear blue eyes were challenging. 'Grace, if this were the other way around, you'd want me to share my problems with you, wouldn't you?'

'Of course I would, but—'

'So why won't you do the same?'

For just a moment Grace was tempted, because Cathy was right, of course, and she wasn't a kid any more, she was an adult with more life experience under her belt than most of them.

Still, she could not tell her, could not share this with her. Neither her doubts about Terri, nor Sam's anger with her for keeping them from him. She had finally handed her anxieties over to Sam and they had, necessarily, to be kept private for everyone's sake, especially Saul's. As to the trouble between her and Sam, that was just as private, and it was up to her to find the right way to bridge the gap between them.

'Because there is nothing to share,' she said. 'Except what you already know about, which I think is more than enough, don't you?'

Cathy gave it up, and they walked on in silence, Grace not the only one with guilt loading her down; Cathy aware of more than a touch of hypocrisy in herself, given that she had not exactly been sharing her own emotional problems with Grace.

'OK now?' Grace asked her, gently.

'Fine,' Cathy answered.

They walked back inside the hospital.

Two hours later, taking another break, by herself this time in the cafeteria, Cathy checked her phone and saw Kez's home number on her missed calls.

Voicemail, too. From *her*.

'I only just got your message about Saul – I've been at a meet up in Jacksonville, thought I'd told you about it, but anyhow that's not important. I hope your brother's OK, and if I'd known, I'd have called right away.'

Warmth and the greatest relief coursed through Cathy.

'So anyway,' the husky voice went on, 'what can I do to help? Would you like me to drive across to be with you or is this strictly family?' A pause. 'Whatever you want, just call me.'

Cathy left the cafeteria without finishing her juice, went out of the hospital, walked around to the parking lot, made the call from there, and Kez picked up right away, her voice filled with concern, listening as Cathy brought her rapidly up to date.

'So there's no need for you to drive across, because they've been talking about moving him to Miami if he stays stable for another twenty-four hours.'

'Oh,' Kez said. 'OK, that's good.'

'But just knowing you're going to be there for me – ' Cathy forged right on – 'is already helping, because I do know now just how badly I need you.'

'That's all I've been waiting to hear.'

Cathy heard pleasure colouring Kez's voice.

Felt the same.

David noticed the change in her instantly, said that she was looking better, then noted her flush, and took her aside.

'Would this have something to do with Kez, by chance?' he asked softly.

'How d'you know?' Cathy felt awkward, but impressed.

'I'm happy for you, honey.' David gave her a gentle hug. 'I found Kez quite a special young person when I knew her.'

Cathy drew away, and smiled at him. 'Thank you.'

'My pleasure,' he said.

Sam arrived then, Grace right behind him, and just watching Sam stroking Saul's cheek, so much tenderness in his big strong hand, got Cathy all choked up. But then Terri walked in, less than a minute later, and Cathy saw Grace's eyes shift to her, her expression suddenly wary. Not like Grace at all.

Something was going on there, Cathy thought. Something bad.

Twenty

September 11

It was early Sunday morning before they transferred Saul, still under heavy sedation, to Miami General, the plan to give him time to settle down before allowing his levels of consciousness to rise; after which the first of the remaining operations would begin.

The Naples police had been hoping to have some form of communication with Saul before his departure, hoping that he might at least have been able to give some small clue, even ID his assailant.

No one wanted that more than Sam.

'Only when the doctors say he's ready,' he told Joe Patterson. 'Not a minute earlier.'

They were Joe and Sam now. On good terms, all things considered, not withstanding Sam's frustration and sense of powerlessness into which he had managed, somehow, not to rub the noses of the Naples PD. He'd stuck like glue to Saul's bedside, especially when his dad had gone to get some rest, even when – especially when – Terri had been there, which had been most of the time.

He couldn't fault her devotion – if that was what it was.

Though even if she did love her man, Sam knew all too well that didn't mean she might not be capable of savagery in the *name* of love.

Not his kind of love, God knew, and maybe – he hoped with all his heart – not Teresa Suarez's kind either.

On Sunday afternoon, Cathy came out of Miami General and saw her right away.

Kez Flanagan looking as Cathy had never seen her before. No ripped shorts and T-shirt, no Nikes, no tracksuit. This Kez was wearing black silky pants and a semi-sheer black silk top with a single flash of red the exact colour of her hair.

She was wearing make-up too. Just a touch of aqua eye shadow that brought out the green flecks in her eyes, black mascara and a hint of lip colour.

'You look amazing,' Cathy said.

'Thank you.' Kez looked pleased. 'You too.'

'I look like hell,' Cathy said.

'A little tired,' Kez admitted. 'But you could never look like hell.'

They were standing outside the main entrance of Miami General where a steady stream of vehicles drove in and out from Biscayne Boulevard, dropping off and picking up patients and visitors.

'How's he doing?' Kez asked.

'Still out of it,' Cathy said. 'But they say he'll be fine.'

Kez eyed her. 'You don't buy that?'

'I guess it's a question of perspective. From their point-of-view Saul's doing OK, and any time now they're going to let him wake up properly, but then they're going to knock him out again and start operating.' Cathy shook her head. 'So far as I'm concerned Saul won't be doing really OK until he's ready to come home.'

'Day at a time,' Kez said. 'All you can do, right?'

Cathy made an effort. 'So where are we going? Do I need to change?'

'No way.' Kez surveyed her jeans and cornflower blue T-shirt with FAST embroidered on it in fuchsia. 'I told you, you look great.'

They had prearranged for Cathy to leave her Mazda in the hospital parking lot so Kez could pick her up and they could go have some dinner.

'If I tell you,' Kez said slowly as they got into her old green Golf, 'that I can't remember the last time I felt this happy to see anyone, would you mind?'

'Are you kidding?' Cathy's warm cheeks grew pinker. 'I feel the same.'

'Do you like Indian food?'

'Love it.'

Kez drove out of the parking space, glanced at her. 'Sure?'

'I don't say things I don't mean,' Cathy said.

'No,' Kez said. 'I don't think you do.'

They went to Anokha in Coconut Grove, and sat outside; Cathy relishing the relaxing ambience, finding to her surprise that she was ravenous, though Kez watched her devouring her *aloo chaat* and *patrani machchi*, but ate very little of her own dishes.

'We didn't need to have dinner,' Cathy said, 'if you weren't hungry.'

'You were starved and I had lunch,' Kez said. 'And I need to drop a few pounds.'

'You're kidding,' Cathy said. 'You look great to me, I told you.'

'Trust me,' Kez said. 'My times were shit up in Jacksonville.'

'God,' Cathy said. 'I haven't even asked you.'

'Other things on your mind,' Kez told her. 'And believe me, the eight hundred wasn't worth reporting on, and the fifteen hundred was even worse.' She took a sip of white wine. 'I guess I missed my training mate.'

'I'm sorry,' Cathy said.

'Not your fault,' Kez said.

They decided against dessert, picked up some Oreo cheesecake from the Cheesecake Factory in CocoWalk and headed back to the apartment on Matilda Street, where they talked for a long time out on the porch, drinking coffee, Cathy eating cake, Kez refusing any. And then she went inside for a few minutes and came back with a pretty carved walnut box out of which she took the makings of a joint.

'OK with you?' she asked first.

She had not asked the last time – but then everything today seemed different between them, Cathy felt. Easier. Better.

'Sure.' Cathy smiled. 'I like sharing with you.'

She wasn't sure afterwards if it was the dope that might have made at least part of the difference, if it had heightened her responses, the intensity of the lovemaking. All she knew for sure was that she had never, *never*, known anything like it, and not just, she thought, because it was with another woman.

The marijuana had, she supposed, helped her to relax about that, had eased her inhibitions and helped tip her over the edge of her uncertainty. But the thing was, Cathy thought a little fuzzily, while they were still at the early stages of their lovemaking – foreplay, she guessed, though it didn't *feel* like that, she already felt so folded into a warm, amazing cocoon of sensuous joy . . .

The thing was that wondering about being gay or straight seemed suddenly to have nothing to do with *this*. This was something else, something entirely separate; this was about Cathy and Kez being together, simply being *themselves*.

She had imagined – and she *had* done a lot of imagining, she realized now, even in Naples in the hours when she'd been trying to rest and keep her mind off Saul, when thinking about Kez had helped blot out the awfulness of what had happened to him. But she had *imagined* that she might find Kez's body – a woman's body – too soft, even a woman as athletic and toned and lean as Kez. She had thought she might miss the power of a male body, the different texture of a man's skin, had thought she might find the softness of a female mouth too strange, maybe too *weird*; she had thought she might miss that moment of first awareness of erection – though the truth was that the few men Cathy had been with had started out burning her face with their stubble and ended up hurting her with their dicks.

Nothing to miss.

Kez led the way and Cathy followed, learning swiftly, finding nothing strange or remotely weird, finding exactly the opposite as Kez rubbed her face over her breasts and licked her nipples – and Cathy did the same, discovering another small tattoo in the shadow beneath Kez's left breast, a tiny black and yellow wild cat.

'Cheetah?' Cathy asked, kissing it.

'Jaguar,' Kez told her.

'It's beautiful,' Cathy said. 'Are there any more?'

'Consider this,' Kez said, 'a voyage of discovery.'

And then she kissed her so deeply and passionately that Cathy forgot to think about the fact that she was kissing another woman, began to find it impossible to *think* at all, and they might almost have been young animals cavorting and nuzzling and fondling, any remaining inhibitions being cast off as swiftly as their clothes had been when the marijuana had kicked in.

'A boat!' Cathy delighted in a third tiny tattoo on the inside of Kez's right thigh, a delicate blue boat with a white sail. 'How many more?'

'Just one.'

Kez wrapped herself tightly around Cathy, stroked and tantalized and simply *held* her, and Cathy did the same right back and felt the other woman shiver with pleasure and moan, and Kez was touching her in places, physically and emotionally, that Cathy realized she'd never let anyone touch or uncover before. She was on fire, she was *melting*, and all the old doubts she'd had about her own ability to love sexually were being blown away; those fingers were inside her again and Cathy was open and wet and crying out, and she wanted to do the same for Kez, but right now she was powerless to do anything but respond, all her thought processes blown away to kingdom come.

'How do you feel?' Kez asked, after they had slept for a while.

It was after nine, and dark, but the street lamps on Matilda Street cast a pale glow into the bedroom, picking out the shapes of the lovers curled together beneath the white sheet, the rest of the room inky black.

'I feel – ' Cathy's voice was soft – 'like I've been on a long journey, and now I've come home. To you.' She paused. 'Is that too corny, or too much?'

Kez didn't answer.

'If it's too much,' Cathy said, 'tell me, please.'

'You have no idea,' Kez said, 'how special that was for me.'

'I think I do.' Cathy smiled into the dark.

They were silent for a few minutes, and then Kez said: 'I want to tell you something I've never told anyone else.'

Cathy waited, stroking the inside of Kez's left forearm, its skin as soft as her own, wondering idly if this kind of similarity, familiarity, might be part of what made this so special, so right.

'I needed the dope,' Kez said. 'Really needed it.'

Cathy stopped stroking, became still, waited to be told her lover was an addict.

'I needed it,' Kez went on, 'because I was afraid that when it came down to it, you might be turned off by my body.'

'Are you serious?'

'Oh, yes.'

Cathy recalled the evening after the meet in West Palm, when they'd had dinner together in Fort Lauderdale and Kez had said she painted her nails intricately to distract people from the rest of her, and she'd called Cathy beautiful and Cathy had laughed, and for a moment Kez had looked so hurt.

Cathy sat up, the sheet falling from her, exposing her breasts.

'Didn't you feel – while we were making love – couldn't you tell what was *happening* to me?' She sought the right words. 'How blown away I was?'

'It's OK,' Kez said.

'No,' Cathy said. 'It's not. Not unless you believe . . .'

'I do. That's the point. That's how I was able to tell you that about me. Because I think you feel – you give me the idea that you feel – I'm more special than I am.'

'You are,' Cathy said. 'Very special.'

'Thank you,' Kez said. 'Feeling's mutual.'

They lay down again, Kez resting her spiky red head against Cathy's breast.

'I can hear your heart,' she said.

'Is it fast?' Cathy asked.

'Nice and steady,' Kez said.

'OK,' Cathy said. 'That's about how I feel now.'

In their bedroom back home, Grace was lying beside Sam; wide awake.

It wasn't the baby keeping her from sleep. Nor the knowledge that Cathy had met up again with Kez earlier and had not come home, because right now Grace was grateful if Cathy was managing to grab a piece of happiness. It wasn't even Saul keeping her awake, because David was staying overnight at Miami General, wanting to stay close on his son's first night there.

Her thoughts were just too torn up.

No possibility of talking to Sam either, even if he had been awake.

There had never, throughout their marriage or before, been this kind of emotional distance between them, and it was hurting so badly. Grace had tried repeatedly to explain the motivations behind her secrecy about Terri, had told him she understood his anger. Sam had said he knew *exactly* why she'd acted as she had, but that did not lessen the impact on him of discovering that they did not – as he had previously believed – feel the same way about sharing.

'Everything,' he'd said. 'Rough and smooth.'

'I know,' Grace had said. 'And I'm sorry.'

'I know you are.'

So she'd waited to be forgiven, for him to get past it, over it, but he had not.

Which was, if she was honest, starting to piss her off just a little.

'I've apologized,' she had said yesterday soon after they'd got home. 'You know I mean it.'

'I know,' Sam had said.

'So can we please put it behind us,' she'd asked. 'Learn from it.'

'Sure,' he'd said.

'Why don't I feel you mean that?' Grace had asked.

'Because I can't just forget it, not just like that,' Sam had told her.

'What do you want from me, Sam?' she'd asked.

'I want,' he'd begun, then stopped.

'What?'

'I want it not to have happened,' he'd said frankly. 'Which is absurd and childish and not the way I'd like to be with you, of all people. Not any time, and certainly not now.'

'So can't you try?' Grace had asked him.

'I have.'

'Try harder.'

'I am. I will.' He'd paused. 'It'll be OK.'

'I hope so,' Grace had said.

He had taken her hand then and pulled her close, and for a moment or two she had believed they were mending. But then he had stepped away again and the gap had felt even wider, and a little deeper, which had scared her.

Which was why she was awake.

Claudia had called again this evening – had been phoning regularly since Grace had told her the half-truth about Saul – and Grace had told yet more lies, saying that they were all coping, but now she was lying in bed questioning her motives for that deceit, too. She'd thought it was for Claudia's sake, but maybe it had been for her own, because she couldn't face listening to her sister right now telling her that leaving the sunshine and Grace and moving to Seattle had made her remember the bad old days in Chicago.

Not just a liar, then.

Selfish, too.

The baby moved inside her womb.

'Some mom,' Grace murmured.

'Mmm?' Sam said.

'Nothing,' Grace said. 'Go back to sleep.'

* * *

At three o'clock on Monday morning Cathy was roaming around Kez's living room with a cup of camomile tea in one hand, knowing already that it wasn't going to be enough, which was a damned shame, since all she really wanted to do was go back and cuddle up to Kez; but she had fallen asleep a couple of hours back and Cathy had lain still for as long as she could stand it, and then she'd slipped out of bed and crept out of the bedroom, managing not to wake her.

No sense in both of them losing sleep.

She'd taken a bathrobe from a hook on the bathroom door – Kez had told her earlier to make herself at home – and had gone out on to the porch, opening the creaky door with care, and it had been lovely to sit for a few minutes out there in the warm darkness with the gentle night breeze stirring the banyans and ruffling her long hair. Suddenly though, she'd experienced a sense of feeling landlocked and oddly claustrophobic, which was why she'd come back inside, gone into the small kitchen and made her tea.

Too much excitement.

Cathy remembered her mom admonishing her about that when she was a child, back in the still happy days after Arnie had entered their lives and they'd lived in their house on Pine Tree Drive.

The house in which they'd been murdered.

In the past now, where it belonged. Another world now, another family.

And now, Kez Flanagan.

Another drag or two of dope, she thought, might help retrieve that wonderful, suddenly elusive, relaxation.

She looked around for the small carved box, then remembered Kez bringing it out earlier from what she had called her junk room.

'It's supposed to be my dark room,' she'd said, 'but mostly I use the facilities at Trent, and everything seems to end up getting stashed in there.'

Cathy hesitated briefly, then opened the door.

Junk room was about right, clutter and dust the most noticeable features – and the broken mirror in the corner by the window, an old cheval glass with a large, jagged crack right through it. Cathy had already noticed the absence of a real mirror in the bathroom, only a powder compact standing open on the shelf; something to do perhaps, she had supposed with a rush of protectiveness, with Kez's inexplicable dislike of her own appearance.

The photographic developing equipment stood on a table over to the right, bottles of fluid dusty, everything dusty, trays empty, no signs of any work having been done in a long while, and that surprised Cathy a little, because even if Kez did use the facilities at college, she'd have expected an enthusiastic photographer to work when impulse took her. Though maybe the photography major was more of a cover, a needs-must, because what Kez wanted most from Trent was the athletics side – which went, if Cathy was honest, for her too.

More in common all the time . . .

She went in search of the dope, not easy among the cardboard boxes and bin bags and old running shoes – a whole pile of them, and that certainly made perfect sense to Cathy who had her own heap at the back of her closet at home.

There was no sign of the box, but in the corner opposite the mirror stood a large walnut chest carved in a similar style – a few fingerprints in the film of dust around the lid, making it the most likely place to look. Cathy was only intending to search for the marijuana and rolling paper, but once she had the chest open and saw two silver trophies and two certificates, it was impossible to resist. She knelt and began rummaging gently through, swiftly striking gold: old snaps of Kez as a child running in what looked like elementary school races, more at high school age – and oh, the *intensity* of the concentration on her face, even then, and Kez had said she'd been an ugly teenager, but that was so *untrue*, and if she'd felt like that, there must have . . .

Something else caught her eye.

A kind of a package, a curious looking long thing, wrapped in material rather than paper, and as Cathy leaned in for a closer look she realized that the wrapper was an old, stained, pinstripe sports jersey.

Intrigued, she lifted it out of the box, felt its weight, unrolled the jersey at one end, wrinkled her nose as its strange, pungent smell reached her nostrils, then peeked inside and, more fascinated than ever, drew out a bat.

An old baseball bat. Scuffed, scraped and badly stained in places.

The darkest stains of all at the thick, batting end.

'What the hell are you doing?'

Kez's voice came out of nowhere.

Cathy dropped the bat and jersey.

Twenty-One

September 12

Dozing fully clothed on a bed in a doctor's room at Miami General, David woke with a start – his first fear for Saul – then realized that it was something entirely different that had dragged him out of his sleep.

Something to do with Sam's beach homicides. And to do with Saul.

He got up slowly, trying to ignore the ever-growing army of aches that seemed to assail him these days whenever he rested for more than half an hour or so, put on his shoes, went down the corridor to check on his boy, found his condition unchanged, gave him a kiss and took the elevator down to the hospital library.

Closed.

Of course it was closed at three-twenty in the morning.

He thought about leaving it till next day, but found he could not.

He went slowly out to the parking lot, got in his old Mercury, drove out on to Biscayne Boulevard, south a little way to 192nd and over the William Lehman Causeway, then left again towards Golden Beach and home.

He needed his own bookshelves.

Needed to look something up.

'It's OK,' Kez said to Cathy for the third time.

'But it isn't.' Cathy was still deeply ashamed. 'And I did start out just looking for the box with the dope . . .'

'Which was a good idea,' Kez said.

She had already picked up the bat and jersey, and now she reached down behind the walnut chest and retrieved the smaller carved box.

'One I could go for right now,' she added.

She led the way back into the living room, set the box on the coffee table, sat on the couch and looked up at Cathy.

'My robe suits you,' she said.

'Oh God,' Cathy said. 'I shouldn't have borrowed it.'

'Sure you should,' Kez said. 'I told you to make yourself at home.'

Cathy looked down at her. 'You look nice too.'

Kez had pulled on a man-sized grey vest with My Camel's In Bed printed on it in maroon. Her legs, maybe not classically beautiful, made Cathy want to kiss them. But she wasn't done apologizing yet, felt that despite Kez's reassurances, damage had been done, trust lost, and she couldn't stand to think she'd done that.

'I'm not normally a snoop – I *hate* it when people invade my privacy, and I am really so sorry, and if you do feel like kicking me out I'll be miserable as hell, but I'll understand.'

'I don't feel like it,' Kez said.

She was calm and kind, but Cathy still felt something else beneath the kindness, something that told her Kez *did* mind her snooping – and why wouldn't she, why wouldn't anyone? Yet Kez was already rolling a joint, patting the couch for Cathy to sit beside her, and Cathy was starting to hope that maybe things were all right after all, maybe she hadn't screwed up irrevocably.

'I want to know,' Kez said suddenly, 'if I can trust you with something else.'

'You can.' Not OK. 'Kez, I promise I won't ever—'

'Forget that,' Kez interrupted her. She lifted the joint to her lips, licked the edge of the paper, finished rolling it, shaped the tip and put it down. 'I'm asking if I can trust you with something very important to me. Very private.' She paused. 'What do you say?'

'I say,' Cathy said, 'it would mean a lot to know you still trust me that much.'

She waited while Kez lit the joint and inhaled deeply.

'The bat you found belonged to my dad, Joey,' Kez began. 'He was in the garment trade, but he was crazy about baseball, always talking to me about it, taking me to games, watching them with me on TV.'

'He sounds nice,' Cathy said.

Kez passed the joint to Cathy, who took a drag and gave it back.

'When I was six,' Kez went on, 'a year before he died, I had a fancy dress party to go to and I told my dad I wanted to go as Reggie Jackson – you know?' She saw Cathy nod. 'My father laughed, said Jackson was a guy and I was his little girl, and I got upset, told him not to laugh at me, because even back then I guess I had a problem with what I looked like, felt like people were laughing at me.'

'But he wasn't,' Cathy said quietly.

'Joey told me he'd make me a Reggie Jackson jersey.'

Kez had been holding the bat and jersey close, but now she laid the bat down on the couch beside her, took a long drag from the joint, handed it to Cathy and smoothed the jersey out on her knees, and Cathy saw now that it was a kid-sized Yankees pinstripe with a big black **44** on the back.

'He told me too – he was very serious, I remember – that he would never, ever laugh at me, that I could depend on that. That if anyone ever did, I could just come and tell him and he'd deal with them for me.' Kez's smile was ironic. 'Only when it came to it, he wasn't there to do that, was he?'

'Can I hold it?' Cathy looked at the jersey.

Kez gave it to her in exchange for the joint, saw Cathy's nose screw up as she caught the odd chemical smell again. 'That's just some dry-cleaning stuff I used on it once. However often I wash it, it still lingers.'

'I understand,' Cathy said, handing back the jersey, 'about keeping precious stuff safe. There weren't many things I took from our old house after my parents were killed, but I did keep my old Raggedy Ann chair, wouldn't throw it out for anything.'

'I knew you'd understand,' Kez said. 'I knew first time we spoke you were going to be someone I could really share with.'

'Thank you,' Cathy said.

Kez put down the jersey, twisted around and stretched out on the couch, her feet in Cathy's lap.

'Oh,' Cathy said. 'The last tattoo.'

Two small, intricate designs on the sole of Kez's right foot.

'Chinese characters?' Cathy asked. 'What do they mean?'

'*Lieh gou*,' Kez said.

'You speak Chinese?'

'Not a word.'

'So what do they mean?' Cathy asked again.

Kez smiled.

'Come to bed.'

* * *

'Don't worry,' David told Sam when he called him on his cell phone – hoping to avoid waking Grace – at six a.m. 'Nothing's happened.'

'Something must have happened,' Sam said, 'or you wouldn't be calling.'

He was in the kitchen drinking his first espresso of the day, had already taken Woody for his morning stroll, trying his best to relax before his first day back at work. He'd figured on leaving in a few minutes and running into the hospital to check on Saul before heading on down to the office; hoping – probably in vain – to be allowed to ease back into the job, knowing that Lieutenant Kovac would probably consider that the time already taken in Naples amounted to more than enough compassionate leave.

'I think I may have come up with something,' David said, 'that might just possibly be a link between your beach killings and the attack on Saul.'

'Jesus,' Sam said.

'Can you spare me fifteen minutes?'

Sam glanced at the clock on the wall, thought how badly he wanted to look in on his brother, do all he could to make sure Saul was never left unobserved for long. 'Can't you just tell me now?'

'I need to show you one of my books,' David told him. 'I guess I could bring it down to your office, or—'

'Dad, it's fine.' Sam was up on his feet. 'I'm on my way.'

'The physiological production of laughter.'

David had brought the book into the living room and Sam was sitting on the old battered sofa, staring at the page his father had pointed to.

'Like me to précis for you, son?'

'Always,' Sam said.

'OK.' David sat down heavily beside him. 'This is probably off the wall, so just shoot me down any time, right?'

'Go on, Dad.' Sam glanced at the clock on the mantelpiece, hating the idea of being late first morning back but knowing at the same time that his father would never have brought him here if he had not believed it important.

'A lot of that – ' David gestured at the book – 'is too complex to get into and probably irrelevant, but did you know that fifteen facial muscles get involved when you lift your lips just to smile? And that when a person laughs the epiglottis half shuts off the larynx, which results in that kind of *gasp* you get with laughter? And so on . . .'

'OK.' Sam's concentration was sharper already.

'So it came to me in the middle of the night, you'd had *lips* in the case of Mrs Sanchez, and the *throat* in the janitor's case—'

'And teeth in Maria Rivera's case,' Sam came in.

'So there's the smiling connection, too,' David said. 'And all kinds of facial bones smashed in all three murders.'

They both fell silent, thinking on the same lines.

Saul's larynx.

No facial injuries though.

It was, in Sam's experience, relatively uncommon for an intimate assailant to damage the face that they loved – even if hate had come to outweigh that love.

Another possible strike against Terri?

'It could be nothing at all,' David said, 'but just in case, I . . .'

'You did right, Dad,' Sam said.

The phone began to ring, and David got up to answer. 'Dr Becket.' He listened for a moment or two, then said: 'On our way.'

Sam was already on his feet. 'Saul?'

'They're letting him wake up,' David said. 'They want us there.'

Twenty-Two

'You're dressed already.'

Cathy, having woken again at six thirty to find the bed empty, had dragged Kez's grey vest over her head and emerged to find her out on the porch dressed in a sleeveless black T-shirt and chinos, a plate of toast, jug of juice, freshly cut melon slices and a pot of coffee laid out on the small table before her.

'Wow, that looks so good.' Cathy bent and kissed Kez on the mouth. 'Why didn't you wake me?'

'It was early and you looked peaceful.' Kez picked up a slice of melon. 'I figured you needed some rest after what you've been through.'

Cathy tweaked at the vest. 'Is this OK?'

'It's great. Looks better on you.'

'No, it does not.' Cathy sat down beside her, poured herself some of the purplish juice and drank a little. 'Mmm . . . Pomegranate.'

'Healthy start before we go somewhere,' Kez said.

'Where?' Cathy picked up a melon slice.

'A place that's special to me.'

'I'd like that.' Cathy bit into the slice.

'It's something else I've never shared with anyone else.' Kez drank some coffee and stood up. 'But we need to go now.'

'Right now?' Cathy looked at the breakfast. 'What's the rush?'

'It has to be now,' Kez said.

'OK.' Cathy drained her juice. 'Do I have time to shower?'

'Sure.' Kez sat down again.

'And I'd really like to swing by the hospital first,' Cathy said.

'Can that wait till later?' Kez looked up at her. 'Please?'

'I just want to see Saul for a moment or two.'

'And you will,' Kez said. 'But it's very early. Hospitals don't like early visitors.'

'We visit all hours.'

'All the more reason,' Kez persisted. 'If we leave soon you'll have plenty of time to see him later.' She paused. 'This is important to me, Cathy.'

There was no mistaking the urgency in her eyes.

'All right,' Cathy said.

'Dad's gone ahead in his own car,' Sam told Grace on the phone, heading south again on Collins, 'and I've told Terri I'm going to pick her up and bring her to the hospital.'

'Because you want to see Saul's reaction to her,' Grace said.

'I do,' Sam said. 'Though we don't know if Saul saw his attacker – or if he'll remember even if he did.' He paused. 'We don't even know if he'll know us.'

Grace wished she was with him, wanted badly to hold him.

'Would you like me to call Cathy?' she asked.

Sam had already made up his mind on that. 'Not till we know what shape he's in. I think we should let her have a little more time out, don't you?'

'I do,' Grace said. 'I'll join you soon as I can.'

'Are you OK to drive?'

'Fine,' Grace said. 'If he's awake before I get there, give him a kiss from me.'

'You got it,' Sam said.

Looking good so far, David was told when he got to the hospital.

Rancho Levels – an assessment tool that did not require cooperation from a patient unable to communicate, but monitored their reaction to external stimuli – were promising. Saul was able to follow simple commands, his agitation and confusion in keeping with the traumatic situation to which he was waking to.

Still sedated, for which David was thankful.

Thankful not the word for how he felt altogether. No words could be enough for that.

He had decided to wait until Sam arrived with Terri before he went in. Sam still hadn't told him what was going on where she was concerned, and something inside David had recoiled at the thought of what it might be, which was why he hadn't pushed it either with Sam or with Grace who was, he sensed, up to speed on that. Now at least he could focus on such things – had not been entirely aware of how much he had been blotting out until Saul's awakening.

Thank God.

The trouble between Sam and Grace was something else that had been worrying the hell out of him, and once the worst was over with Saul – God willing – he was going to get to the bottom of that too, knock their damned-fool heads together if he had to. There was a *baby* on the way, for pity's sake, and even if there hadn't been, two people more crazy about each other than Sam and Grace would be hard to find, and David would be damned if he was going to let them put that at risk.

'Thank God,' Sam said when David told him about the Rancho Levels.

Grace here now, too, her golden hair tousled, the shadows beneath her eyes more pronounced than they would have been if she'd had time to put on make-up. Still as lovely as ever in most ways, especially, David thought, all swollen up with child.

Fear etched on her face, though – and not just for Saul now.

Time to fix that, David thought again, Saul permitting.

'Can we go in yet?' Terri asked, her beautiful dark eyes loaded, too, with anxiety.

'Two at a time,' David said. 'And we're not to tire him.'

He and Sam went in first.

They were both overwhelmed immediately with the mightiest relief.

Saul knew them. That was plain as day, not just from the cardiac monitor beeping and showing its wavy, spiky excitement, but from the look of relief in his eyes, despite their still-sedated fuzziness.

He *knew* them.

'Thank God,' David said, softly.

'Amen,' Sam said, and walked around the bed to the other side.

'You're OK, son.' David stooped over his son, stroked his cheek, and kissed his forehead. 'I know the doctors have already told you this, but I'm telling you, too. Don't be afraid. All of this is temporary. It's going to take some time, but you're going to be just fine.'

'Damn straight you are,' Sam told his brother, and took his good left hand.

And there it was, love for them both alive and clear in Saul's eyes.

David went on talking to him, telling him a little more about what was being done to help him, just enough information, not *too* much, reassuring at every step, knowing his son was more likely to believe him than any other doctor, because David had made it a rule not to lie to his wife or kids, had stuck to it all through Judy's illness. So if David told Saul it was going to be lousy for a while, but *only* for a while, after which he would be better, then it was his hope that Saul might rest just a little more comfortably than he might have otherwise.

'OK, Dad,' Sam said quietly, when he was done talking. 'If you're ready, do you think you could ask Terri to come in?'

Saul nodded urgently, his eyes avid.

'And Grace?' David said.

'Just Terri for now, OK?'

More of the strangeness, David thought, but did not question him, just kissed his younger son again, told him he'd be back soon and left the room.

Sam stepped away from the bed and moved over to the back

wall, the best vantage point in the room from where he would be able to see Saul's expression clearly, because the monitors weren't going to tell him much, would be unlikely to distinguish waves or spikes of great joy from fear.

The door opened and she came in.

The cardiac monitor beeped faster.

Hard *not* to look at it or at her, but Sam kept his eyes on his brother's face.

'Hello, baby.' Terri bent to stroke his cheek, then to kiss it, then straightened up. 'I'm so sorry, Saul – ' her soft voice trembled a little – 'for everything. For getting so mad and walking out. For not being with you.'

Sam watched Saul till his own eyes ached.

He saw not so much as a hint of wariness in his brother's eyes.

Certainly no fear or anger.

Just love.

Sam felt himself begin to uncoil, then tensed up again, ready now for the next big moment, the sixty-four thousand dollar question.

He stepped closer to the bed again, opposite Terri, looked down at Saul.

'I need to ask you something, bro.' He kept his voice calm. 'It's real important.'

Saul tore his eyes from Terri, looked up at his big brother.

'Do you know who did this to you?' Sam asked.

The monitor beeped erratically, and the pupils in Saul's brown eyes dilated.

'Saul,' Terri said, softly. 'Baby. Do you remember?'

Urging him, encouraging him; not a trace of a threat.

Sam's eyes flitted to Terri's face, saw nothing but intensity.

'Saul – ' he took his brother's left hand again – 'can you squeeze my hand?'

He felt a small movement, then a weak but definite squeeze.

'That's fine.' Sam waited another moment. 'Saul, if you know who did this to you, if you remember anything at all, squeeze my hand again.'

Pressure from Saul's fingers, and Sam's own heart leapt, except that Saul's eyes were filled with distress now, and so, for all Sam knew, the squeeze was just that, distress brought on by thinking about what had happened.

'Saul, was that a squeeze? Do you remember something?'

Saul made a sound, an awful, choking sound, and the monitors reacted accordingly, and the door opened and a doctor – name-tagged Lucy Khan – strode in, glaring at Sam and the monitor.

'That's it, folks,' she said. 'My patient needs rest.'

'That's OK,' Sam said, looked at Terri, saw she was weeping, looked back at Saul. 'It's going to be fine, man.'

'This is too much, too soon,' Dr Khan said. 'I need you to leave.'

'Going,' Sam told her, heading for the door. 'We're going to find whoever did this, don't you worry about it.'

'Better believe it.' Terri wiped her eyes, and managed a smile.

'Out,' Lucy Khan told them.

In the corridor, Sam went directly to David and Grace.

'He remembers what happened.'

'Are you sure?' David asked.

'I'd swear to it,' Sam told him.

'Can I go in now?' Grace asked.

Sam shook his head. 'Dr Khan kicked us out. Says he has to rest.'

'Nice woman,' David said. 'Smart, too.'

'Seems to want to take good care of Saul,' Sam said.

'Which is all that matters,' Grace said.

Sam saw the way she was looking at him, saw a neediness in her eyes that he'd seldom seen there before, and shame jabbed at his conscience.

'It's OK,' he said softly.

He turned around, saw that Terri had vanished.

'She went to the restroom,' David told him.

Sam looked at his father, saw from the wry lift of his eyebrows that he'd figured out that something was up between him and Terri.

'I didn't have to be a genius.' David looked at Grace, then back at Sam. 'And right now, you two need a moment alone.'

'Hey, Dad,' Sam said, quickly. 'I haven't forgotten your theory.'

'My theory, Einstein's, Wolfie Cohen's, I don't care – ' David walked towards the nurses' station – 'so long as it helps.'

'Theory?' Grace enquired.

'I'll tell you later.' Sam checked over his shoulder. 'Right now I need to tell you something else.'

'Terri?'

Sam saw the awful tension around Grace's mouth and eyes, and knew that he, almost as much as Saul's assailant, had put it there. He felt a sudden great urge to kiss it all away, but knew he had to wait.

'It wasn't her,' he said. 'I can't prove it, but I'd bet the farm.'

The relief, the release, almost floored her, and Sam saw her start to sway, reached out to catch her, but she was already recovering, pulling away – and suddenly there was something else in those blue eyes, a spark of anger, of resentment.

'So now I'm off the hook?' she said. 'Now you can touch me again.'

'Grace, I'm sorry.'

'I understand.' She shook her head. 'I understood all through.' Her attempt at a smile didn't work. 'Didn't stop it hurting, though.'

'Gracie.' The name was loaded with regret. 'I have to go.'

'Oh,' she said. 'OK.'

'Something I have to check into.'

'Your dad's theory?' Again she tried to smile. 'Go ahead.'

'You'll be all right?' He was anxious as hell now about her.

'I'll be fine,' Grace told him. 'I'll call Cathy about Saul.'

'You should,' Sam said. 'Great to tell her something good.'

'And then if we can't get to see Saul, I'll go home.'

'Get some rest. You look tired.'

'I am,' she said, 'a little.'

Sam was vacillating.

'So go,' Grace said.

'I want to make sure you're OK,' he said. 'And the baby.'

'We're both fine,' she said.

'I'm sorry,' he said again.

'Me, too,' she said.

'Where exactly are we going?' Cathy asked at around seven thirty, a mess of signposts coming up ahead.

'Wait and see,' Kez told her.

'Only I really don't want to leave town today.'

The Golf turned on to the Florida Turnpike.

'Kez, please, just tell me . . .'

'Like I said,' Kez broke in, 'you'll be back in plenty of time.'

Cathy felt irritated. 'I'm not a little kid or a package.'

'I know.'

'Then please tell mc where we're headed.'

'Naples,' Kez said.

'No way,' Cathy protested. 'Of all places.'

'I know,' Kez said again, laid her right hand briefly on Cathy's knee, then brought it back to the gear shift. 'It's probably the last place you—'

'It has nothing to do with that,' Cathy cut in. 'I don't blame Naples for what happened to Saul, but I told you I didn't want to leave town and I don't appreciate—'

'Hey.' Kez glanced at her. 'It's OK.'

'It's not.'

'I mean it's fine. If you want me to I'll get us turned around and straight back to Miami General.' Kez's eyes flicked between Cathy's face and the road ahead. 'I'm sorry.'

'OK. I guess.'

'I shouldn't have assumed you'd be cool with being whisked away without a moment's notice.'

'I guess I would be cool, ordinarily.' Cathy was regretting her overreaction.

'It's just this place I wanted to show you means so much to me, and we wouldn't have to stay long. But you're right, we can go some other time.'

Except, Cathy was painfully aware, times like this, nights like the last one, *magic* like that, only came along once in a very long while – had not, face it, ever come along for her before.

'Maybe if I just call home,' she said.

'Sure,' Kez said easily. 'If that helps. Or we could still turn around.'

'No.' Cathy pulled her cell phone out of her bag on the floor. 'This'll be fine.'

'Good,' Kez said.

Heading for Alligator Alley.

Grace sat in her car in the hospital parking lot. The air-con already blowing cool and more than welcome. Cell phone in one hand ready to use.

Her tears had startled her, like an old pal hitting on her unexpectedly, the instant she'd finished hauling herself in behind the wheel and shutting the door. She had not really allowed herself to weep since they'd first heard the news of Saul's attack. But now the good news about Saul, and Sam's sharing with her his belief in Terri; his forgiveness, the relief of it *all*, and then in the midst of that, her own flaring of resentment.

All a little too much for one almost 'geriatric' mom-to-be in her eighth month.

The brief tear storm had shaken her up a little, but had helped, too. Steadied her enough, now that she'd wiped her eyes and taken a drink from her small on-board Evian bottle, to make the call to Cathy.

She pressed the speed-dial key for her daughter's mobile.

'I'm sorry I can't take your call,' Cathy's voice said.

Voicemail.

'Sweetheart, it's me,' Grace said. 'Calling with wonderful news.' Part of her mind flashed to how great Cathy would feel hearing her words. 'Saul's awake and according to the doctors, he's doing really well all things considered.' About to sign off, she added: 'No point rushing over to Miami General though, because they want him to rest, which is very frustrating for us all, but they know what they're doing.' The baby kicked her hard and she smiled, went quickly on. 'Have a wonderful time, whatever you're doing, and say hi to Kez from us all. We love you, Cathy.'

'It's the machine,' Cathy said to Kez.

'Leave a message,' Kez told her.

'What if something's wrong?' Cathy ended the call.

'It's not the middle of the night.' Kez sounded irritated.

'Sam'll have gone to work,' Cathy said, 'but Grace ought to be home.'

'Gone shopping,' Kez suggested.

'Too early,' Cathy said. 'Not Grace's thing.'

'Taking a shower,' Kez said. 'Walking the dog.'

'Could be, though that's usually Sam first thing.'

'First day back,' Kez said. 'He probably left earlier than usual.'

'I guess Grace could be walking Woody or taking a shower.' Cathy paused. 'She sometimes makes house calls too, pre-school.'

'There you are, then,' Kez said. 'No need to worry.'

'I'll leave a message.'

Cathy called again, waited a moment.

'Hi, everyone, it's me. Hope Saul's doing well – hope you're all OK.' She considered apologizing for staying out, then decided against it. 'I just wanted to let you know Kez and I are going to Naples for a couple of hours – yeah, I know I just got back, but we have to go see something important. If there's any news, any change with Saul, can you please, please call me right away.' She paused again. 'Love you.'

She ended the call, tucked the phone back in her bag.

'Better?' Kez asked.

'I guess,' Cathy said.

She had stayed in hiding in the restroom, going in and out of cubicles, washing her hands when other women came in and then, when she was alone again, opening the outer door a crack now and again until she was sure they had all gone.

Sam first, then Grace, then David.

She waited while Dr Khan went back into Saul's room, came out again, wrote up some notes at the nurses' station, handed over a folder, then disappeared into one of the elevators.

And then, while all was quiet, she slipped into the room.

Saul was sleeping.

Terri sat down quietly on the visitor's chair nearest his bed.

Watching him. The tubes and electrode pads, the padding and bandages around his neck, the whole dreadful, life-saving picture.

Her mind was almost numb. Not numb enough.

The machines droned and beeped, Saul's chest rose and fell, and Terri began to realize how tired she was, and if he didn't wake again soon she was going to have to rouse him, and she hated to disturb his rest, but this might be the only time she had to be alone with him and she needed that so badly.

Saul opened his eyes.

They smiled as soon as he saw her, warming her through.

'Thank you,' she said.

His left hand moved to the tube in his neck.

'Leave that, baby,' she told him gently, took his hand in hers and held it.

He made a sound, from some place between his throat and chest.

'It's OK,' Terri told him. 'You're going to be OK.'

He closed his eyes briefly, and when he opened them, they were filled with tears.

'I'm so sorry,' she said. 'I need you to understand how much I mean that. I love you so much, but it's all my fault, I know that.'

Saul shook his head as well as he could, and another sound, more like a moan, escaped him.

'It's true.' Terri bent her head over his hand, kissed it, held it to her cheek. 'If I hadn't walked out on you, if we'd been together, this wouldn't have happened to you.'

Saul pulled his hand away.

'You hate me,' Terri said, 'and I can't blame you. And if you hate me for ever, I'll understand, but I need you to understand how much I love you, baby.'

She realized suddenly that something was happening.

Saul had not just withdrawn his hand out of anger.

He was pointing. Past her.

'What is it?' Terri asked. 'Something you need?'

He made another sound – of effort, she thought – pointed again, and Terri half rose from her chair.

'Want me to find someone?'

He shook his head again, and now she saw that he was pointing at her bag, at the shoulder bag she'd dumped on the floor when she came in.

'My bag?' she asked. 'Something in my bag?'

She got up, went to fetch it, held it out in front of him.

Saul pointed again.

'This?' Terri took out the *Miami Herald*, rolled and sticking out of one corner of the canvas bag. 'Is this what you want?'

He flattened out his hand.

'OK.' She laid the newspaper out on the bed. 'Like this?'

Another grunt of effort and he was pointing again, his eyes straining.

'Closer?' Terri moved the paper further up the bed, wary of the tubes, conscious too of the risk of infection, certain that if a nurse or Dr Khan were to come in right now, they would kick her straight out.

She could see that Saul was having some problems focusing on the front page, was at a loss to know how to help him – but suddenly his index finger was straight out, shaky but pointing at one of the headlines.

'This?' She motioned to it with her own hand.

He shook his head again, and the cardiac monitor sent out beeps, and Terri knew that any minute now a nurse would come in, but there was nothing she could do . . .

And then she realized he was pointing at a single word in the headline.

KIDNAPPER

'Kidnapper?' She said the word out loud.

Saul shook his head yet again, pointed again.

At the first letter.

'K?' Terri asked.

A nod at last, another wince and his finger was travelling to the right, so shakily that it took another moment for Terri to establish which letter was next.

'E?'

Saul let his hand drop, exhausted.

'K.E.?' Terri was perplexed. 'Is that it?'

His eyes were moving, roaming over the whole front page.

'OK,' she encouraged him. 'You're looking for more, right?'

Back and forth, up and down, and Saul was paler, sweating, and Terri cast a glance back at the door, willing medics and nurses to stay out just a little longer.

His hand lifted off the covers again, finger back at work targeting one more letter, finding it, it seemed, in a piece about a drowning.

Down to one word again.

CAPSIZED

One letter.

Z.

His hand dropped down again and he lay back, drained.

'Z?' Terri said.

Spelt it out.

'K.E.Z.'

Realized what she had said, forehead creasing, bewildered.

'Kez?' She stared at Saul, scarcely able to believe it. 'Is that it? Is that what you're telling me?'

His eyes told the rest.

'Oh dear God,' Terri said.

Twenty-Three

Grace was back home in her office, had just finished playing back her messages when a new call came in from the hospital.

She listened briefly, heard the caller tell her that Saul was in an increasing state of agitation and that Dr Khan now felt that it might be helpful if one of the family could return to Miami General.

'Of course,' Grace said. 'I'll contact my husband and Dr Becket right away, and we'll be there as soon as we can.'

'Can I help?' Lucia came through the door, Woody still at the end of his leash, tail wagging after their walk – often Lucia's first chore of the day – as Grace got back to her feet. 'Is it Saul?'

'Nothing terrible, don't fret,' Grace told her. 'But I need to call—'

'I heard.' Lucia bent to unclip the leash. 'Shall I make the calls for you?'

Grace shook her head. 'I can do it on the way.'

They went out into the hallway together.

'I didn't see Cathy's car outside.' Lucia said. 'Would you like me to get hold of her? I'd like to be of some use.'

'There's no point.' Grace picked up her keys from the hall table. 'I just had a message from her saying she's en route to Naples with a friend, so I think I'd rather wait a little while before I yank them back, see how Saul's doing first.' She opened the front door. 'God knows Cathy could use a day away.'

She caught Lucia's expression just before she turned away.

Barely veiled disapproval, reminding her strongly of how Dora had been in Cathy's early days with them. And though Grace realized that Lucia's only sin was in feeling that Cathy's place right now was with family, not friends, the look annoyed her nonetheless. It seemed to her, as she got back in the Toyota and slammed the door, that where Cathy was concerned, even some of the nicest people – people who ought, therefore, to know a damned sight better – still tended to judge her.

Which frankly made Grace even more glad that Cathy had found someone she cared about and who, she hoped with all her heart, cared about her in return and would not let her down.

Terri sat in her car, thoughts whirling.

What to do first?

Find Cathy, tell her.

Can't tell her if she's with Kez.

So just *find* her.

She scrolled through her phone book, called the Becket house. The machine picked up – Grace's voice, giving her cell phone number in the message for emergencies. Terri tried that number, got voicemail, cut off again.

What she needed was Cathy's cell phone number. What she

had to do was find out where she was and if she *was* with Kez. One-two-three. Find her, get her away from Kez, then take it from there.

Not the right approach for Officer Teresa Suarez, of course. The right approach, the *only* one, for her as a cop was to pass this on – to Sam, first, she guessed, or maybe to go over his head to his sergeant or lieutenant, maybe even higher.

No way she was going to do any of that, not yet at least.

For one thing, this was *it* at last, her big chance – the biggest she was ever likely to get – to prove herself. Besides which, slowing things down by calling it in, reporting it to anyone at the department was not going to help Cathy if she was with Kez. Only finding her quickly was going to do that.

Anyway, after what had gone on in the hospital this morning, with Big Bro keeping his eyes glued to Saul's face, checking out the way he reacted to her in *case* – that had not been her imagination any more than the suspicious looks she'd been getting from Doc Grace lately – and Terri did not appreciate being treated that way, no ma'am.

No, sir.

Not Cathy's fault, though.

She waited a moment, called Saul's father's house, not sure what she was going to say if he answered, not wanting to give him more heartache – of all of them, she had most time for David, who always treated her with respect.

His machine was switched on, too, which made Terri wonder if maybe they'd all been called back to Miami General, which had to mean that Saul, having found a way to communicate with her, wanted to do the same with them.

Which meant that the big detective was going to know about Kez soon enough, with or without Officer Suarez's help.

Which was not going to stop Terri from heading over to Golden Beach right now.

Fast as the wheels of her Ford Focus could take her.

Sam, Grace and David were all back at the hospital waiting to go in to Saul's room, because they'd chosen that time for their routine changing of IV and other bags and dressings, and Sam was pacing.

'Go on like that,' David told him, 'and you'll be needing your own room.'

'I'm fine, Dad,' Sam said, and went on pacing.

'Well, I'm not,' David said. 'I'm old and I'm tired and I need my son to be calm around me instead of aggravating my ulcer.'

'You don't have an ulcer, do you?' asked Grace.

'Not till this morning,' said David.

No trouble getting into Saul's house because the place was virtually hidden from Ocean Boulevard by its white stone wall, and because Saul had complained that his dad never turned on the intruder alarm that Sam had put in for him, which meant it was easy for Terri to stroll around to the back and get in through the old sliding patio door.

Property Crimes had its uses, after all.

Inside, she didn't hesitate, knew where to go, directly into the kitchen where she knew that David Becket kept his list of family numbers on the refrigerator door – and bingo, there was Cathy's cell phone number.

Which she called right away.

Heard it ringing.

A little way past the signs for the Miccusokee Indian Reservation, Cathy heard the phone ringing in her bag, dug it out and answered.

Heard Terri's voice, and panicked. 'Is Saul OK?'

'He's more than OK,' Terri told her. 'He's awake.'

'Oh my God,' Cathy said. 'That's wonderful.'

'Cathy, there's something I . . .'

'Call her back later,' Kez said.

'Terri, hold on.' Cathy covered the phone's mouthpiece and frowned at Kez. 'I want to hear what she's saying.'

'And clearly what she's just told you is *wonderful*, so now I'm asking you to wait a little while,' Kez said brusquely. 'Not so much to ask, is it? Just a couple of hours alone together before we go back.'

Cathy put the phone back to her ear.

'Terri, we're on Alligator Alley on our way to Naples, but I'll be back in Miami Beach later, so if you . . .'

Kez reached across, snatched the phone from her, looked at it quickly, hit the cut-off key, then opened her window and threw it out into the grass on the central reservation.

'For heaven's *sake*.' Cathy couldn't believe it. 'Kez, why did you *do* that?'

'I'm sorry.' Kez closed the window, her eyes back on the highway.

'Stop the car.' Cathy couldn't remember the last time she had felt so furious.

'I can't,' Kez said.

'Pull over and stop the *car*.'

'Calm down,' Kez told her. 'I'll replace your fucking phone.'

'I don't care about the phone,' Cathy said. 'I care about my brother and I care about what you just *did*.'

'I know, and I told you I'm sorry. But Saul's obviously doing better, which is great, which is why I'm asking you to put me first for a few short hours.'

Cathy shook her head, still seething.

'But I guess,' Kez went on, 'if you're not happy to do that for me, better I know that now, and I'll turn around soon as I can and we can call this whole thing a day.'

Cathy was still silent, trying to absorb what had just happened, to comprehend what could possibly lie behind Kez's extraordinary intensity.

'Is that what you want?' Kez asked.

Cathy wanted to turn around, not to end things.

'Is it?' Kez's voice was a little softer.

Cathy looked sideways at her, saw the vulnerability again.

Shook her head again, let out a sigh.

'Let's just get to Naples,' she said.

Terri knew now that she had no alternative – *damn* it – but to get help with this. She'd wanted so badly to make this case her own, to show them all what she was made of. But if she compounded the danger Cathy was already facing, the Beckets would blame her – and screw Sam and Grace for even *thinking* she could have done that to the man she loved, but if anything happened to Cathy because she failed to call this in, then Saul would never forgive her, and that she could not bear.

Back in the Focus, her break-in behind her, Terri made her first call to Sam's office, in case he was there rather than at Miami General. Sam wasn't there, and she considered briefly telling his pal Martinez what she'd learned. Except then he would almost certainly put out a Locate and Notify on Kez Flanagan, and that in itself might endanger or compromise Cathy.

She called Sam's cell phone. Got his voicemail.

'Shit,' Terri said.

Then took a breath and left a message:

'Sam, it's Terri. Call me back the instant you get this, please. Life or death, Sam, so please call me *now*.'

David had gone in first, deemed by far the most likely family member to calm Saul's agitation, especially if the whole physical hell of his situation had finally kicked in and freaked him out.

'Your dad will help him,' Grace said.

Sam felt his cell phone vibrate, snuck it out of his pocket, looked at it.

'Message from Terri,' he said.

And read it.

'What?' Grace saw new tension tautening his facial muscles.

'I have to go call her,' he said.

'Why? What's happened?'

'I don't know.' He was already walking away. 'Don't worry.'

He passed a vacant office, stepped inside and shut the door.

Made the call, heard what she had to say.

'Terri, thank you for this,' he said.

'Don't thank me,' she said. 'Thank Saul.'

'Don't do anything, OK?' Sam got no response. 'Terri, I'm telling you not to go off half-cocked. Just sit tight till I call you back. Have you got that?'

'Yes, sir,' Terri said.

Grace was still in the hallway waiting for him, too anxious now to go in to see Saul, and Sam felt for her badly but he wasn't going to tell her this, at least not until he'd found a way to validate the information.

'I have to talk to Saul,' he said.

Grace's expression was fearful. 'You think it was Terri, after all?'

'No.' That much he could do for her.

Sam's thanks had been something, Terri supposed.

But then he'd blown that by telling her to wait, do nothing. Giving her orders.

Not her boss.

And she had no intention of waiting – was already past Toll Plaza and on I-75.

With no idea where to go once she hit Naples, but at least she'd be there ahead of Sam, and she wasn't losing sight of the fact that she needed help, that Cathy's safety was the thing that counted most for now.

But she'd *be* there first.

David looked up at Sam as he came into Saul's room.

'Maybe you can settle him, son. They upped his sedation some, but he still seems a little too upset for my liking.'

'Maybe I can.' Sam saw fear and frustration on his brother's face. 'I need a moment alone with Saul, Dad.'

David saw his grimness. 'What's happened?'

'It won't take long,' Sam said.

Their father stood up, realized he was getting no more, at least for now, and nodded. 'He doesn't need any more upset,' he said quietly, and left the room.

Sam waited a moment and then sat down.

'Terri called me,' he said. 'Told me something.'

The expression in Saul's eyes changed. He nodded with difficulty.

'I have to ask you this, and I need you to nod or shake your head, OK?'

Another nod, a wince of pain.

'Is blinking going to be easier?' Sam asked.

Saul shook his head, irritated.

'OK.' Sam paused. 'Is it true that Kez Flanagan did this to you?'

The pain in Saul's eyes seemed to spread, to grow more intense.

'Saul, is it true? Was it really Kez?'

Saul nodded, lifted his left hand, fingers trembling a little.

'All right.' Sam took the hand, squeezed it gently. 'You can rest now.'

His brother's eyes expressed urgency.

'You're fretting about Cathy?' Sam saw another nod. 'She's fine, Saul, you don't have to worry any more. I'm going to take care of things now.' He stood up. 'I love you. We all love you.' He stooped and kissed his brow. 'All you need to think about now is getting well and coming home.'

'Ever going to speak to me again?' Kez asked Cathy.

Mile upon mile of grey topped highway, flat grassy land to either side.

Over halfway there, but Cathy had hated every yard because

it reminded her of the journey after they'd got the news about Saul.

'I might,' she said.

It wasn't Kez's fault that she hated the road.

'Ever going to forgive me?' Kez asked.

'Not if you're going to be sarcastic about it.'

'I won't,' Kez said. 'I'm not.' She waited. 'Say you forgive me.'

'I don't want to,' Cathy said, 'until I mean it.'

'Couldn't you just say it now, so I can start enjoying *us* again.'

Cathy smiled, despite herself.

'OK,' she said.

'Thank Christ for that,' Kez said.

Sam took the stairs so he could call Terri again on his way down.

'I guess you couldn't know whose car they were in.'

Terri told him she couldn't.

'Did you maybe get an impression of who was driving?'

'Hard to say,' Terri said. 'If I had to guess, I'd say Flanagan.'

'OK, thanks.'

'What do—?' Terri began to ask.

He was already gone.

Sam was getting into his Saab when he saw it.

Grace's old Mazda. Cathy's now.

He smacked his forehead with the palm of his hand. He'd wasted questions to Terri just now, wasted precious time. Grace had told him yesterday that Cathy was going to leave her car in the lot here because Kez was picking her up.

All he needed now was to find out the make, model and license of Flanagan's car, though she might not own a car, might have rented.

He shook his head as if that might clear it and called Martinez on his cell phone.

'Where are you, man?' his partner wanted to know.

'Not coming in.'

'Saul?'

'Saul and a whole lot more,' Sam said. 'He's doing better, but something's broken here, and I need your help.'

'Let me guess.' Martinez was dry. 'Off the record.'

'You got it.' Sam paused. 'Woman by the name of Flanagan.'

'Cathy's new friend?'

'That's the one. First name Kerry, aka Kez.'

'Kez, that's the girl,' Martinez said. 'The runner.'

'Al, I need you to run a Triple I and FCIC.'

'You gonna tell me why?'

'Are you alone?'

'Uh-huh.'

'Saul says she attacked him.'

'Cathy's friend?' Martinez sounded shocked. 'Holy smoke.' He paused. 'So why is this off the record? Don't you want a BOLO, or at least Locate and Notify?'

'Not yet,' Sam told him. 'She's with Cathy right now, possibly on the road to Naples, so the last thing I want is cops on the look-out tipping Flanagan off.'

'So Suarez is off the hook?'

'She's the one who got this from Saul, and I just confirmed it.'

'Jesus.' Martinez was absorbing the ramifications. 'You still think there could be a connection with Muller and the others?'

'Let's just focus on Saul for now,' Sam said. 'On finding Flanagan.'

'Want me to try Auto Track?'

The privately run organization was frequently used by the police, a fast and useful tool, collecting information from a variety of sources and linking it all up.

'Definitely,' Sam said. 'And ask around at Trent, but be discreet.'

'You said they're going to Naples?' Martinez checked.

'Do *not* tell the Naples PD,' Sam told him. 'The danger to Cathy aside, if she's voluntarily travelling with Kez, they might figure she's some kind of accomplice.'

'Her record's been expunged,' Martinez reminded him.

'It's still a risk.' Sam's mind was reeling with alarming possibilities. 'And if we turn this into a possible abduction and something bad happens to Flanagan, Cathy may never forgive me.'

'We could ask the Highway Patrol to pull them over on a minor . . .'

'We can't tell anyone, Al,' Sam cut in.

'Jeez,' Martinez said. 'Let me guess. You're going to Naples.'

'I have no choice,' Sam said.

'You know this is a bad idea, don't you?'

'Sure it is,' Sam said. 'But it's all I have right now.'

He went home before leaving town, had briefly considered returning to the hospital to tell Grace and David what was happening, aware that they might learn of it from Saul, which would be gratuitously upsetting, even cruel.

Still better to wait though, he decided, until he was on his way; no chance for them then to try to talk him out of going.

At the house he set the machine to fix himself an extra strong espresso, then went upstairs to change out of his working suit into jeans, sneakers and a laid-back looking, loose fitting, chocolate brown linen shirt so he could keep his Sig Sauer holstered but unseen (since he was going to be out of juris-diction) without roasting alive in the heat. After which he headed into Cathy's room and began taking it apart, hating himself for doing it but desperately needing something to take away with him; tried checking her computer journal but quickly gave it up, unsure if she still kept one, knowing in any case that in the past it had been password-protected and he had no time for code-breaking.

Two bonuses. A credit card bill – another intrusion, but one that might help him track the young women down. And a note of what just might possibly – written beside a carelessly scrawled letter that might be a K or an H or an R – be Flanagan's cell phone number.

He withheld his own number and called it – found it switched off with no voicemail – and went on looking.

No photographs on or in Cathy's bedside or dressing table. A bunch of printed sheets though, on her desk, about the Trent Tornadoes. Sam whipped through them and found her – no doubt, her name captioned. The funky, spiky, violently tinted red hair framed a sharp-nosed, tough little face with interesting eyes. She looked strong-willed, possibly aggressive, yet still he thought he could see her appeal. Would have said, he imagined, if Cathy had shown him the photo, if he hadn't known the truth, that he rather liked the look of her.

A wave of sorrow rocked him for Cathy. For their sweet, kind-hearted, bafflingly unlucky adopted daughter.

'Jesus,' he said, tidying up the mess he'd made, though at least he now had a photograph to show around when he reached Naples.

He went downstairs to slug down his espresso, wondered, not for the first time, about his judgment over not calling this in to Detective Patterson. A good guy, no doubt about that, who'd probably jump right on the vital new information and have as many pairs of eyes as Naples PD could afford scanning the city for Flanagan.

None of those people, though, would be a hundred per cent sure of her companion's innocence. None of them was going to care enough about Cathy's heart and soul or even her physical safety, the way Sam did.

No call to Patterson then.

Back in the Saab, and on his way.

'I understand,' Grace said on the phone to Sam right after he'd given her and David the news, 'that it could be dangerous for us to tell Cathy outright, but couldn't we call to say she has to come back, maybe because Saul's worse?' She thought. 'You could ask the hospital to confirm that if Kez calls.'

'What if they've already called, know he's OK?' Sam asked. 'More to the point, what if Kez doesn't want her to come back?'

'His condition could have changed since they called,' Grace said. 'And Cathy wouldn't accept Kez trying to stop her.'

'Which could make Kez mad,' Sam said.

'We have to do *something*,' Grace protested.

'We are,' Sam said. 'I am.'

Grace went back with David to Saul's room, both in agreement that what they had to do was stay calm around him, give him no cause to suspect the kind of danger Cathy might be in.

Not that tough with Saul sleeping again, mercifully.

This was hardest now, Grace realized, for David.

'I told Cathy – ' he had just said to Grace out in the corridor – 'just a few days back, while we were still in Naples, that I thought Kez was special.'

Special.

Grace had seen the pain in his eyes, had empathized.

She wanted to scream.

One of the things Sam badly wanted to do, he thought, driving west again on I-75 – after he'd got Cathy safely home and put Kez where she belonged – was to put things right between himself and Terri. Even if he did still feel she'd brought their suspicions on herself with her inappropriate approach to cases that had nothing to do with her.

Still, he could call her, *had* to call her.

'I want to thank you again,' he said, 'for what you've brought to us.'

'Saul brought it to us, like I said.'

She sounded curt and Sam winced, felt that even if she hadn't realized the extent of their qualms, she'd almost certainly felt a heap of negativity.

'I also want to tell you, off the record,' he said, 'that so far as I'm concerned, right now we're both on the same team.'

'Both out of our jurisdiction,' Terri said.

'Both wanting the same end,' Sam said.

'What do you want, Sam?'

'I want you to promise me that if you find them first you'll sit tight, wait for me.'

'I can't promise you that,' Terri said. 'It's going to have to depend on what the circumstances are. I'm sure you agree.'

'Better for everyone if you wait.'

'Assuming I do find them,' Terri said, 'which is pretty unlikely since I don't have the first idea where they'd be headed – and you're more likely to find out if Flanagan has people in Naples than I am. '

'But just for the heck of it,' Sam persisted, 'let's say you do happen on them . . .'

'If you still can't trust me to do the right thing, Detective Becket,' Terri said, 'then screw you.'

He swallowed it. Even understood it.

'OK,' he said. 'Then at least promise me that if anything happens, you'll share with me before you decide on any course of action.'

'So long as you guarantee – ' she didn't hesitate – 'you'll share everything your contacts give you.'

'No problem,' Sam said.

'You do that,' Terri said, 'then I'll tell you if I find them.'

Back in beautiful, sweet-scented Naples again.

No hospital this time. A residential street lined with houses of charm and character, set well apart.

Spacious. Tranquil.

A little after ten to ten as the Golf slowed to a crawl outside a pale peaches and cream two-storey house with a pretty walled veranda around the whole second floor, clearly divided into sections, the only indication from a distance that the once single dwelling had been converted into apartments.

'Is this it?' Cathy asked.

Kez opened the glove box, withdrew a small remote control, drove slowly around the house to a palm sheltered bank of garages, pushed a button, waited for the door of one to open, nosed the Golf inside and switched off the motor.

'Sanctuary,' she said.

Twenty-Four

'**Y**ou should go home,' David said quietly to Grace, just before ten a.m.

'I'm fine,' she told him.

Lying. She was, in fact, more than a little uncomfortable, had been feeling unwell for some time, quite nauseous and shaky and in need of either some gentle exercise or an hour or so of sleep, probably the latter. Except that sleep was out of the question until they knew Cathy was safe and Kez Flanagan was in police custody.

Something else was worrying hell out of her. Sam's decision not to pass on Saul's accusation to the Naples police. Not that she hadn't understood his reasoning – *anything* that might keep Cathy out of even greater danger was fine with her. But the knowledge that Sam was out there on his own without permission or, more significantly, without back-up, scared her so much she could hardly bear to think about it.

'Grace, sweetheart,' David said gently. 'Worrying isn't going to change anything, we both know that.'

'And you're not worried to death, I suppose?' Her voice was still hushed, since the last thing she wanted to do was wake Saul.

'I'm not nearly eight months pregnant,' David said.

'I'm a whole lot younger than you are,' Grace countered.

He smiled, reached over and patted her hand. 'Old folk need less sleep.'

'Do you have patients today?' Grace asked.

'This afternoon,' he said. 'Plenty of time to rest before.'

'So leave with me now.'

'In a while,' he said easily.

'But if Saul's going to be sleeping for a long . . .' She broke off as a new thought struck her. 'You're not worried that Kez might come here?'

'Hardly, since she's on the way to Naples.'

'What if she isn't?'

'Sam said it was *Cathy* who told Terri that, remember?' David smiled again. 'We have enough real stuff to worry about without inventing more.'

'You're right.' Grace stood up with even more effort than usual.

'Want me to drive you home, tuck you in?'

The thought was incredibly tempting.

'I'll be fine,' she said. 'And if I need anything, Lucia's around.'

He walked with her to the elevator, told her he was going to stay a little while longer, speak to Lucy Khan when she did her rounds.

'Then I'll go home, see if I can dig up any old stuff about Kez and her family.'

'Maybe I could help you,' Grace said.

An elevator opened and David pushed her gently inside. 'Go rest, Mommy.'

'Please don't overdo it,' she said.

The door began to slide shut.

'You stop worrying,' David said.

'I will if you will,' Grace said.

It was so *different*.

Pretty furnishings, pastel colours, gorgeous clematis on the veranda – and it struck Cathy when Kez showed it to her that there was something vaguely familiar about it.

'Almost as if I'd been here before,' she said.

'Like a zillion other balconies all over Florida.' Kez shrugged. 'All over the world.'

Maybe that was the thing that made Cathy feel so surprised by the whole apartment. Kez had referred to it as her sanctuary, and it was certainly lovely to look at; it possessed a certain tranquillity, which was perhaps why it appealed to her. But Matilda Street was peaceful too, and perfect for Kez – at least, Cathy thought so – with its simplicity and posters and photographs of what mattered to Kez.

This was too . . . *pretty*.

'So what do you think?' Kez asked, back inside the living room.

'It's lovely,' Cathy answered, which was only half a lie, but if she'd told her what she was really thinking, Kez would almost certainly have been hurt.

'It's very different,' she added. 'To Matilda Street, I mean.'

'I know,' Kez said.

'It could almost,' Cathy ventured further, 'belong to another person.'

'In a way,' Kez said, 'I guess it does.'

That was when Cathy noticed the photograph in a polished wood frame on the end table by the sofa. The only photograph she could see in the whole place.

It was of her, on the track at Trent, one of the shots Kez must have taken that first day just before they'd met.

'Like it?' Kez asked.

'I do,' Cathy said, touched, and it was a good action photo, the best she'd ever seen of herself, long ponytail streaming, face concentrated, legs pumping.

Kez smiled. 'Guess it must be my place, after all.'

They went to check out the refrigerator because Kez said she was hungry, but there was nothing inside but a pack of ground coffee, two wrinkly apples and, wrapped in tin foil in one of the salad crispers, some marijuana.

'Perfect.' Kez took out the dope.

'You said you were hungry,' Cathy reminded her. 'We could go out.'

'Uh-uh.' Kez went ahead of her back into the living room.

'Or I could go buy something, if you're tired from the drive.'

'I'm really not that hungry.' Kez sat down on the sofa, carefully unfolded the foil, then leaned back and smiled up at Cathy. 'What I want far more than food is to smoke and talk for a little while.'

Cathy sat down beside her.

'I've been alone a long time,' Kez said. 'Had no one to share things with.'

'I'm here now,' Cathy said.

'I'm glad.'

'Me too,' Cathy said.

Which was true enough – yet even as she said it she felt a small unease, realized now that she'd felt that way ever since she'd noticed that Kez had stuck the 44 jersey and bat in the black duffel bag she'd brought along from Matilda Street, which had struck Cathy as a little off – though then she'd figured that maybe Kez took them along wherever she travelled because of her dad.

Not *off* then, at all, just touching.

Except the way Kez had acted on the road was still worrying Cathy a little, and she had believed she was more than OK with this relationship, but if that was true, then why was a part of her wishing she were home right now on the island, with Grace to talk to?

'Where's the phone?' she asked.

'Don't have one,' Kez said.

'What about your cell phone?'

'In Matilda Street.'

'I'll have to go out soon then,' Cathy said. 'Use a payphone.'

'Sure,' Kez said easily. 'No problem.'

At ten fifteen Sam had Terri on the line again, doing his best now to keep her on side by sharing David's laughter theory with her.

'I hate to rain on his parade,' she said, 'but I came up with that a while back, and if you'd been willing to talk to me about the killings, I'd have told you.'

Sam felt an impulse to tell her that acting like a spoiled kid now, trying to score points, was going to make him even less inclined to talk to her, but right this minute there was no question that he *needed* Terri, so he bit down the response.

'So how,' he asked instead, 'do you think it might connect to Flanagan?'

'I only met her one time for about a minute,' she answered, 'so I guess I have to throw the ball straight back to you.'

'Fair enough,' Sam said.

'You come up with anything else about her?'

'Not yet,' Sam told her, 'though a friend's working on it.'

'Detective Martinez,' Terri guessed. 'Off the record, I take it?'

'You take it right,' Sam said.

Since arriving back home, Grace had experienced a few cramps.

Stress, she told herself. She was pretty sure the cramps didn't signify a problem. If she took it easy, maybe did a little breathing, the pains would disappear. She certainly wasn't going to worry either David or Sam with it, both of them with more than enough to deal with – and what she ought to be doing was going back over her one and only encounter with Kez, in case she'd forgotten even the smallest detail that Sam could use now. The trouble was she was finding it unbearable to think about Cathy with Kez and in danger – and up until this morning it had been Terri she'd been stressing over.

'Guess I'm not quite myself today,' Grace said to the dog.

Too much, too *much*.

Maybe after a sleep . . .

'People don't laugh at you much, do they?' Kez asked Cathy.

It was just after ten thirty, and they were in the pretty sitting room, and she was still smoking, while Cathy was staying with coffee, intent that one of them keep a clear head for the return journey.

'Sure they do.'

'So what do you do about it?'

'Mostly,' Cathy said, 'I turn my back on them.'

'Not me. Not even when I was a little kid. Someone laughed at me, I let them know how I felt about it.'

'How?' Cathy asked curiously.

'All kinds of ways.' Kez held out the joint to Cathy, shrugged when she shook her head. 'It's good stuff.'

'You shouldn't smoke so much. It can't be good for your running.'

'The cat was the first.' Kez took another drag and stood up. 'Way back when I was very young there was this cat used to visit, sit on the window ledge and watch me.' She walked over to the glass doors and stared out. 'That day, I was lying on my bed fooling around, touching myself – not masturbating exactly, just playing.'

Cathy sat in silence, wondering where this was going.

'But this damned cat kept *watching* me, and it made me think of Alice's Cheshire cat and the way it grinned.' Kez turned around. 'So I got the idea it was laughing at me.' She shook her head. 'I've never forgotten that cat and getting the better of it, wiping the damned grin off its silly face.'

'How did you do that?' Cathy's unease was back, not just because of the strangeness of the tale but because of the *way* Kez was telling it, as if it were just a regular childhood story.

'I pushed it,' Kez answered simply, 'off the window ledge.'

'Did you?' Cathy said, feeling sick.

'It isn't true what they say about cats always landing on their feet,' Kez said. 'Or about them having nine lives.'

Twenty-Five

B y eleven, Terry was getting closer to Naples, listening to her radio, staying off her phone in case Sam called again, and thinking about how she was feeling. Anxious about Cathy, sure, and a little excited, too, contemplating the fact that she might be closing in on the beach killer.

Mostly, though, she was pumped up with rage because of what Kez had done to Saul. The way his family had been around her hadn't helped her state of mind one bit, but bottom line it was Flanagan's brutality to the man she loved that had lit Terri's flame so sky high that it was scaring her a little, because she was not entirely sure what she might do if she was the one to find her first.

When she'd started out on all this, on her personal parallel homicide investigation, it had really just been ambition fuelling her, her need to show everyone what she was capable of. Now it was *personal*.

And Teresa Suarez, granddaughter of an NYPD street cop, knew enough about police work to realize that was dangerous.

Sam had decided a while back to break his own order, had tried Cathy's phone, unable to bear *not* trying it a moment longer, hoping his acting skills were up to playing the game – God forgive him – about Saul's worsening condition.

Voicemail. Goddamned *voice* mail.

He'd ended the call, thought about it, then called again and left a convincing enough message: her brother wasn't doing so well, they hated to drag her back, but they knew she'd want to be there.

And after that, of course, he'd had to call Miami General as Grace had earlier suggested, make sure they knew what to say if either Cathy or Kez called in; and then he'd had to speak to Grace and his dad again, tell them to be sure to check their caller displays and *resist* the urge to answer any call from Cathy so she'd think they were at the hospital, just switch to voice-mail and pass on any messages directly to him.

He'd heard nothing new from Martinez, just one useless call to say that Kovac had been on his back all morning and surely it would be smarter and safer to call this in. Sam had told him that no, it would *not* be safer, and he trusted Martinez not to say a word to anyone, he trusted Martinez with his life, but what he needed was *facts* now, not more fucking advice.

Which was when it had occurred to him to call his old pal Angie Carlino. She was based in Tampa, not Naples, but they'd always had a soft spot for each other, and Angie had a history of helping Sam when push came to shove. Today was no excep-tion; no questions asked, but Angie said she had a pal in Naples she could ask to keep an eye out for the young women, though without a license registration there wasn't too much hope.

'Soon as I get it, you'll have it,' Sam had told her.

'And I'll pass it straight on, kiddo.'

'Off the record,' Sam had reminded her.

'Gotcha,' Angie had assured him.

'I have a cell number that might be Flanagan's,' Sam had remembered. 'Any chance you could do something with that unofficially?'

'As a matter of fact,' she'd said, 'I do have another friend with access to Triggerfish, so if she's willing and has time, we might just be able to track that. But she's not one of us so it could cost.'

'Anything,' Sam had said.

'Maybe we should go out for a while?' Cathy suggested again.

She had decided not to believe the story of the cat, thought it was probably just a grisly fairy tale spun, or at worst exag-gerated, by Kez because of the dope.

Kez shook her head, rolling a fresh joint. 'I'm fine here.'

'I'd like to go running soon,' Cathy said.

And find a phone, she added silently.

'We can run any time.' Kez's fingers moved nimbly, her whole demeanour excitable now, a woman in a rush. 'I need to go on talking.'

'OK,' Cathy said. 'So long as—'

'Did I tell you about the kids?' Kez went straight on. 'The ones who poked fun at me when I was around thirteen because of the way I looked, all legs and no breasts – no big change there then.' She didn't wait for Cathy to speak. 'I showed them too, and I was stronger than they were, so showing them was a cinch.'

Cathy didn't want to hear another tale.

'I'm really going to have to think about going back soon,' she said.

'I know,' Kez said. 'Am I making you uncomfortable, telling you this stuff?'

'I think you're smoking too much weed,' Cathy said. 'And you know I want to get back to see—'

'Maybe I have this relationship wrong,' Kez cut in again. 'Only I thought you meant it when you said you wanted to share.'

Cathy felt instantly guilty, supposed that another half an hour or so wouldn't make any difference, especially with Saul doing better.

'You don't have it wrong,' she said.

'How are you doing, sweetheart?'

David called Grace at eleven fifteen.

'Fine,' she said.

Only half a lie, because the cramps had gone a while back, and the backache and weariness she was experiencing now were, in her opinion, nothing unexpected in her particular circumstances.

'I managed to dig out some of the Flanagan records,' David told her.

'Anything useful?'

'Afraid not.' He sounded glum. 'Dad's name Joseph, mother Gina, dates of vaccinations, that kind of thing.'

'How's Saul doing?' Grace asked.

'Sleeping,' David answered. 'Anything from Sam?'

'Nothing yet,' Grace said.

'You're looking very tired,' Cathy told Kez. 'Maybe you could use a nap.'

'No time,' Kez said.

She got up, found her duffel bag and foraged in it, took out a foil-wrapped tablet and swallowed it instantly, without water.

'That'll do it,' she said.

'What was that?' Cathy was afraid it might have been speed or maybe E, hated the idea of either, especially on top of all the dope.

'Don't stress.' Kez came to sit beside her on the couch.

'I'm just worried about you,' Cathy said. 'Because I care.'

'Me too. That's why I took it. I don't want to waste our time together sleeping.'

'But what was the tab?' Cathy persisted.

'Don't make a big deal,' Kez said.

'I'm not,' Cathy said. 'But I think it's time I went home.'

'Soon,' Kez said. 'Know what I'd like first. More than anything?'

Cathy did know, could read it in her eyes, but she didn't answer.

'Don't you want to make love again?' Kez asked.

'I don't know,' Cathy said. 'Not if it's just because of the pill you took.'

'I didn't take anything last night, did I?'

Cathy looked at her, saw that she seemed more amused than pissed off, wondered again what the pill had been.

'It's OK,' Kez said. 'I understand.'

'Do you?'

'Cathy, I told you I'd never push you into that.'

'I know,' Cathy said.

'That's something at least,' Kez said.

She took hold of Cathy's hand, folded it in her own and held it against her heart, and all Cathy's agitation melted away.

'That's lovely,' she said.

'I love you, Cathy.'

Cathy heard the words and was startled.

'You don't have to say anything,' Kez said. 'Only would you mind if we just rest here together for a little while, and then we can go out and you can call home again.'

'I'd like that,' Cathy said.

Kez leaned back against the cushions and put her feet up, and Cathy curled against her and thought, with sudden, overwhelming sleepiness, that this was the warmest, most comfortable place she'd ever been.

'Where are you?' Sam asked at eleven twenty-five.

'Still on 75,' Terri answered.

Lying.

Because she was already in Naples, but if she told him that Sam would start issuing orders, and while she accepted that he *appeared* to be keeping his side of their bargain he still hadn't given her a single new scrap of information, and *maybe* that was because he didn't have anything, but she couldn't be sure of that. Besides, whatever he said and meant now, if something did go down in Naples it would be the local cops that Sam Becket would ultimately trust in, not the *rookie*, and even if he did ask for her to be involved, the Naples PD weren't going to take any real notice of what the Miami Beach detective wanted.

So for now she had to go on playing it her own way, take any crumbs he might toss to her, but go on working solo, drive around for a while, get her bearings, check out the place in a way she hadn't had time to do while Saul had been in hospital here, try to figure out the possible districts someone like Flanagan might be drawn to.

She had called Miami General a while back, asked one of the nurses on Saul's floor how he was doing, and she'd acted a little weird, asking if she was family. They'd stopped doing that with her after day one, and this new attitude had not only bugged her, but *scared* her. And what Terri wanted, desperately, was to go back to Saul with the news that *she* had brought in Kez for his sake.

That was what Teresa Suarez wanted now more than anything.

Except for Saul to get up out of that hospital bed and come home to her – to *her*, not to his daddy or his brother or the rest of his doubting family.

'No news at all?' Grace asked Sam.

'I wish I had something for you,' he told her.

'Not just for me,' she said.

'I know,' Sam said. 'How you holding up?'

'I guess I'm doing as well as you,' Grace said, 'except at least you're out there trying to find them, and all I can do is sit here and try not to go out of my mind. And please don't tell me to relax or take it easy, because I can't.'

'I know,' he said. 'Is Lucia taking care of you?'

'She will,' Grace said, 'if I need her to.'

It wasn't exactly a lie, though Lucia had not been here since Grace had returned from the hospital, and Grace was on the whole content to be alone, but it would have been good right now to have her comforting presence about the house. Except she couldn't summon the energy to try calling her, and anyway Lucia must have had a good reason for leaving, so she didn't want to hassle her.

'Will you do something for me, please?' Grace changed the subject. 'Take care.'

'I promise,' Sam said. 'You too.' He paused. 'Give the baby a kiss from me.'

'Doing it right now.' She kissed her own fingertips, pressed them against her abdomen.

Then he was gone again, and though he had been kind, almost loving, she still felt that he had not been quite his normal self. And Grace couldn't remember ever feeling quite this needy of him before. She supposed she liked thinking of herself as being fairly self-sufficient, a sounding board for others, remembered hoping in the early weeks that advanced pregnancy might have an empowering effect upon her.

'I wish,' she said wanly to the dog.

Woody thumped his tail.

Judgment shot to pieces, and energy too, Grace thought with a heavy sigh.

Heavy was the right word.

'I'm in Naples,' Sam told Terri at ten to noon, 'so it stands to reason you've been here a little while.'

'I guess it does,' she said.

'Want to get together?'

'Soon,' Terri said.

'You have a good reason for playing hard to get?' he asked pleasantly.

'You have a good reason for wanting to get together?' she countered.

'I have a photograph of Flanagan,' Sam told her, 'that I plan to get copied at the first print shop I see. At least we could both have something to hand out.'

'The beach where Saul was attacked,' Terri said. 'Near the pier.'

'Give me a half-hour,' Sam told her.

On the pretty couch in the pretty sitting room in the pretty apartment in the peaches and cream house, Cathy and Kez slept on.

The deeper their sleep, the more entwined.

Faces peaceful, cares left behind.

Innocence personified.

The former crime scene on the beach was, Sam and Terri both agreed, probably the last place Kez would come with Cathy.

'But not necessarily without her,' Sam said, basing it on the old chestnut about killers returning to the scene, scanning around, searching for long blonde hair and a short spiky red head, but almost certain that nothing so simple was going to happen in this case. Certainly not Kez Flanagan offering herself up to them on a plate with Cathy safely out of the way.

'I talked to Detective Martinez,' he told Terri. 'He's been tied up all morning, but he's finally stolen some time, has a friend at DHSMV trying to get a license number for Flanagan's car. Nothing else yet.'

It was overcast, sticky and very warm, with a whole lot less people around than there would have been before Labor Day. Still plenty of blonde heads walking, none of them Cathy.

No one even vaguely resembling Kez on the horizon.

'I could kill,' Terri said, 'for a decent cup of coffee.'

'Two things we have in common,' Sam said. 'Espresso's my poison.'

'*Cafecito*,' she said. 'Strong and sweet.'

They settled for a couple of Cokes and sat for a while on the sand, exchanging thoughts and possible theories about why Flanagan should have wanted or needed to attack Saul, of all people.

'I can't see the laughter connection working in this case,' Sam said.

'Me neither,' Terri agreed. 'I've presumed that Flanagan takes her running seriously, and maybe her victims were people who didn't, who maybe laughed at her.'

'Or maybe Kez just perceived them as laughing at her,' Sam suggested.

'Neither would fit with Saul,' Terri said.

Sam shook his head, agreeing. 'Saul doesn't laugh *at* people, just with them.'

'Except,' Terri thought on, 'if Flanagan is nuts, maybe she imagines people laughing at her.'

They got up, began to walk away from the pier, both continuing the constant search, eyes darting back and forth, pausing whenever they passed the walkways and small footbridges that connected the beach to the streets. Sam wondered which of them Saul might have crossed on his way to disaster, wondered if Kez had been following him, how long before the attack she had targeted him as her next victim, if it had been impulse or part of some as yet unknown plan.

'Maybe,' he hypothesized, 'Saul found out something about her.'

'But when?' Terri shook her head, the notion too painful for her. 'If he'd known something before we argued, he'd have told me.' She glanced at Sam, saw the doubt on his face. 'And even if he didn't want to tell me, he'd certainly have called you right away because he'd have been afraid for Cathy.'

'Unquestionably,' Sam agreed. 'And I think you're right, by the way. Saul wouldn't have kept something that huge, that frightening, from you.'

Terri stopped walking. 'Which means if he did find out something, see something maybe, it happened after our fight. While he was out looking for me.'

Sam said nothing, saw the bleak guilt deepening in her dark eyes, felt conflicting sympathy and anger, and was unsure if he was ever going to be able to help her with that guilt, or if he even wanted to.

'There's another possibility,' he said. 'Saul might have unwittingly seen something before that weekend. Flanagan might have followed you both to Naples, struck lucky because of your fight just because it made Saul an easier target.' He paused. 'Not your fault, after all.'

'Nice try,' Terri said. 'No cigar.'

They went on walking.

'First time,' Sam said after a few minutes, 'we've worked together.'

'How was it for you?' Terri asked ironically.

'I liked it,' Sam said gently.

Found it to be true.

When Cathy woke Kez was already up, smoking again, sitting at the small, white, fake marble-topped table in the little kitchen, her father's old bat and the jersey laid out in front of her.

'I can't believe I slept so long.' Cathy glanced at her watch, saw it was after two. 'I must look wrecked – I used the bathroom, but there's no mirror.'

'Never use them if I can help it,' Kez said.

No mirror, no phone.

No big deal, either, Cathy decided.

'Mind if I make some coffee?' She stooped, kissed the red hair. 'I wish you wouldn't smoke so much weed.' She went to the sink, turned on the cold tap. 'You put far too much crap in you for an athlete.'

'Remember when I told you how my dad died?' Kez said.

'How could I forget?' Cathy said, filling the jug for the coffee maker.

'Wasn't quite the whole truth.'

'No?' Cathy opened the refrigerator, took out the packet of coffee.

'The sex happened the way I said it did. And my father's heart attack, too.' Kez fingered the handle of the bat. 'But I didn't just stay outside watching through the keyhole.' She paused. 'What actually happened was I did watch for a while, watched them fucking. And then I opened the door real quietly, and Mrs Jerszinsky saw me first, before Joey.' Kez looked up at Cathy. 'You'd think she'd have been ashamed, right?'

'I'd think,' Cathy agreed quietly.

Kez shook her head. 'Not her. Not a bit of it.'

Cathy had stopped making coffee.

'She saw me standing there, saw the way I was looking – and I guess I must have looked shocked.'

Cathy stood quite still, wanting the story to stop.

'But that cow, with her great big tits and ass – ' Kez's fingers curled around the handle of the bat – 'looked right back at my face, and then she looked down at my skinny kid's body. And she smirked.'

The room was very silent.

'But not for long,' Kez said.

The unease came back again.

'You've never really talked,' Cathy said quickly, 'about your mother.'

'What about her?' Kez asked.

'Is she still alive?' Cathy asked.

'I've never heard otherwise.' Kez shrugged. 'Though she might just as well be dead for all the difference she's ever made to me.'

The shrug did it, changed things again. The sad, wan little gesture.

That and the expression in Kez's eyes of utter loneliness.

Suddenly all Cathy wanted to do was weep for her.

She went back to making coffee.

Terri and Sam had split up again, searching out on the streets, showing Kez Flanagan's photograph around like relatives looking for a missing loved one, neither getting any response so far.

Sam had decided not to bother with the high-priced areas and had come to Crayton Cove, partly because it was where Saul and Terri had chosen for their ill-fated weekend, but also because it seemed to him that if Cathy was being allowed a say in where she and Kez spent their time – if they were out and about at all – she'd probably find this dockside area attractive.

He had taken a look around the bar at The Dock, talking the bartender into promising to call him if anyone fitting Flanagan's or Cathy's description came in, and was just coming out of the Naples Ships Store when Martinez called.

'Give me something, please, Al,' Sam said. 'Anything.'

'I'm sorry, man,' Martinez said.

'Motor vehicles?'

'Not yet.'

Sam swallowed his frustration, thanked his friend, told him to keep trying, to share with Angie if he thought it might help, and then he called home, his greatest need now to talk to Grace, his greatest wish to get back home to her with Cathy.

'No news yet,' he told her right off. 'I'm sorry, sweetheart.'

'Don't be sorry,' Grace said. 'Just find her, please.'

The helplessness in her voice jolted him. 'You feeling all right? Cathy aside?'

'I'm fine.' She gave a small wry laugh. 'Cathy aside.'

'The baby?' Something, he felt, was wrong. 'Any pain?'

'Nothing,' Grace told him firmly. 'Sam, you have more than enough to take care of without worrying unnecessarily about me. Do you believe me?'

He told her he did, told her to be careful and rest, told her he was checking in regularly with the hospital so he knew Saul was still peaceful; told her that what he was hoping for was that come late afternoon or evening, if not before, when people started emerging from their homes, hotels and work places to come out to bars and restaurants, they would happen upon the two young women and get Cathy away from Kez without any significant problems.

'What if they don't come out?' Grace asked. 'What if Angie's friend can't trace Kez's phone and Cathy doesn't use her credit card and you and Terri aren't enough?'

'Then I guess I'll call in the troops,' Sam said.

'You will, won't you?' Grace said. 'We can't just leave Cathy with her.'

'I know that,' Sam said. 'Trust me, please.'

'I do,' Grace said.

Small mercies.

'One of the things,' Kez told Cathy, 'I knew made you special, soon as we met, was I felt you respected me. That you weren't the type of person who would ever try to ridicule me or laugh at me.'

'No,' Cathy said. 'I'm not. I wouldn't.'

She felt, suddenly, as if she needed to tread carefully, and disliked the feeling.

'He did,' Kez said. 'This man.'

The blood flowing through Cathy's veins felt suddenly colder.

'He was watching me run one evening,' Kez went on. 'He had this grin on his face that reminded me of the kids at school who poked fun of me, and the boy who laughed at me when he found out I was a virgin.'

There was more coming, and Cathy knew she didn't want to hear it.

'All trying to make me feel the same way,' Kez said. 'Inferior, stupid, different. What they didn't get was that I *was* different. He learned that the hard way, same as they all did.'

He.

'They laughed at me,' Kez said, 'but I laughed louder.'

Cathy's mouth was dry.

'I screamed louder too,' Kez said, 'because I hated what I was doing, *hated* it. Do you believe that, Cathy? Can you understand that?'

'I don't know,' Cathy said.

'I hated it, but I needed it, too,' Kez said. 'More than anything.'

'Kez.' Cathy tried again. 'I have to go back soon.'

'To your mom, the shrink,' Kez said.

'To Saul,' Cathy said.

'I know,' Kez said.

She began rolling another joint.

Sam and Terri were exchanging periodic calls, the afternoon moving uncomfortably swiftly. Sam had already been in Naples for three hours with nothing to show, and Martinez had been doing as well as he could with Kovac almost glued to him, but everything he'd learned about Flanagan thus far, Sam had already pretty much learned from David.

'Sad stuff, mostly,' Martinez had told him a while back. 'Only

child. Joseph Flanagan, her dad, died of a heart attack when she
was seven; Gina, her mom, seems to have dropped the parenting
ball, there when she had to be, but no frills.'

Kez, it seemed, had been no great shakes academically, but
the running had made up for that, all kinds of prizes, and no
major failures on that front, no serious injuries. Nothing, Martinez
said, to grievously shake young Flanagan or wreck her confidence.

'Relationships?' Sam had asked.

'Getting nowhere on that score,' Martinez had answered.

No big affairs or painful break-ups; no known discrimination
because of her gay lifestyle.

'Fuck's sake,' Sam said, 'there has to be *something*.'

'There always is,' Martinez agreed. 'Doesn't mean we're going
to find it.'

Stealing a glance at the front door it occurred to Cathy that Kez
might, perhaps while she'd been asleep, have locked it.

There was no key in the bottom lock now, and she *thought* –
though she wasn't certain – that Kez had left a key there after
they'd first come in.

If it was locked, that meant the only other way out was over
the veranda.

She told herself to calm down, that there was no need to think
that way, not if this was all story-telling, all dope-induced.

Except she wasn't as certain of that as she had been. And one
of the many curious things about this was that Kez had been
telling these disjointed and incomplete tales as if she believed
them commonplace, as if she believed that Cathy could listen to
them and then say: 'Hey, that was interesting, now let's go get
some food.' As if there was no risk at all in telling Cathy – or
at least *implying* – that she had done things to people who had
ridiculed her.

Unless she didn't consider it a risk because Cathy was in love
with her.

Cathy was finding it harder by the minute to know how she
felt about Kez, about her stories, about anything.

Just one thing she was certain of.

She wanted to get out of this place. The sooner the better.

'Why don't we go out,' she said, 'get something to eat?'

'I thought you wanted to go home,' Kez said, and took a drag
of her joint.

'I meant – ' Cathy amended – 'on the way home.'

'You hate me now, don't you?' Kez said, suddenly flat.

'Of course I don't,' Cathy said, stomach clenching.

'So what, you love me?' Kez asked.

The irony alarmed Cathy.

'Maybe,' Cathy said. 'I think I do.'

'I'm glad you said "maybe",' Kez said. 'I'm glad you can still be honest. It's one of the reasons I chose you to share with.'

Chose you.

'Can I ask you another question?' Kez said.

'Sure.'

'Are you going to tell anyone what I've told you?'

'Of course not.'

'Not quite as honest there,' Kez said.

'I am being honest,' Cathy said. 'And you haven't really told me anything.'

She wondered what would happen if she walked to the front door right now and tried to open it.

'Food sounds good,' Kez said abruptly.

She put down the joint, stood up, went into the kitchen and picked up the bat and jersey. And then she walked out of the room over to the front door, slid the latch sideways and opened it.

No key needed.

The tension drained out of Cathy like air from a decompression chamber.

The door had not been locked, and they *were* leaving this apartment. Which meant that Kez truly trusted her, had no hidden agenda. Had been sharing her deepest secrets with her, the woman she loved.

Relief and warmth filled Cathy as they walked together downstairs and out into the warm, humid air.

They turned towards the garage.

Cathy looked at the jersey and the baseball bat under Kez's left arm.

Thought about the dark stains.

Kez took the remote control from her pocket. 'You do know, don't you,' she said, 'that I'd never hurt you?'

The door opened and Cathy looked into Kez's eyes. The sun turned the irises almost golden, exposing the intensity of the hope behind them, making Cathy feel almost overcome by the enormity of her trust.

They went into the garage and got back in the Golf.

'You OK?' Kez asked.

Gentle and caring.

'I'm OK,' Cathy answered.

More confused than she had been in a very long time.

But with the woman she loved.

Who loved her.

Twenty-Six

At a quarter to four, Grace was making herself a late lunch. Not that she was hungry, but she owed it to the baby to eat, and anyway Lucia had called a little while back, apologetic for taking time out for an electrical problem at home.

'I'll bet you haven't eaten anything,' Lucia had said.

'Not much,' Grace had admitted.

'You have to eat, Dr Lucca, you know that, for the baby's sake.'

Grace had made herself a small pasta salad, but now that she'd sat down to eat it at the kitchen table, Woody by her feet, she found she could hardly see the food for tears.

Too much.

Their son had been meant to come into the world with a young doctor-to-be for its uncle, and God only knew what would become of Saul's plans now, his study on hold for many months, at least. The baby's big sister was out somewhere with the person who had *done* that to Saul, who might even, it seemed possible, be a multiple killer.

And what had happened to her own judgment skills? After this, after her awful, shameful suspicions of Terri, and even worse, *much* worse, her inability to help poor Gregory, maybe it was time she considered taking down her shingle and concentrating on full-time motherhood – and who was to say she was remotely fit for *that*?

Grace pushed away her salad, unable to imagine being able to eat anything until Cathy was safely home, Saul through all his operations and Sam back here with her.

Not just *with* her. Able to look her in the eye when he told her he loved her.

Kez had relented, had let Cathy take over at the wheel.

'You really can't drive,' Cathy had told her as soon as they were out of the garage, 'not with all that junk in you.'

And to her great relief Kez had said that she was right, and just being in the driver's seat had made Cathy feel even better, more in control, and her thoughts were starting to clear a little.

Whatever Kez might or might not have done in the past, Cathy felt they would find a way to cope with it together. Grace would help her, she was certain, or maybe David was the one they should approach first because he had, after all, once been Kez's doctor, had said how much he had liked her. And once they saw how far back her problems had started, Grace and David would both want to help, and if not entirely for Kez's sake, then for hers. And yes, it would be hard for Kez, but she would have Cathy standing by her, proving her love for her.

Now if she could just find the way to get back to I-75 . . .

'I know you want to go home,' Kez said suddenly.

'I have to,' Cathy said. 'You know that.'

'I know,' Kez said, 'and it's cool, but . . . '

Cathy glanced at her. 'But what?'

'I have one more thing to ask of you, just one more, before we go.'

The dashboard clock read 3.54, and Cathy was acutely aware that she still hadn't called home or the hospital, and she figured there was little point stopping to use a payphone now if they were on their way, but . . .

'Let's go to the beach,' Kez said. 'The sand here is amazing and we could run – we don't have to go far, just run together one more time before . . . '

'There'll be plenty more times to—'

'No,' Kez said. 'There won't.'

Cathy sighed, checked the mirror, pulled over to the right.

'I know,' Kez said, 'that what I've told you has to change things. And I know you meant it when you said you'd keep my secrets.'

'I did mean it.' Guilt was already rising again.

'It's OK,' Kez said, 'you won't have to stick to that.'

Cathy said nothing because she felt as if Kez had been reading her mind, and she didn't know *what* to say.

'If I turn myself in,' Kez said, slowly, 'and if they lock me up—'

'They won't,' Cathy said. 'You'll get help and . . .'

'*When* they lock me up,' Kez said, 'maybe in prison, maybe some institution, will you come see me sometimes, do you think?'

Prison.

Not storytelling after all.

Cathy's heart began to break.

'Will you come see me?' Kez asked again.

'Yes,' Cathy said. 'Of course I'll come.'

'I believe you,' Kez said.

They sat in silence.

'Want to hear the rest of it?' she asked.

'I don't know,' Cathy said. 'Do you want to tell me?'

'In a way,' Kez said. 'It might help you understand a little more.'

Cathy was silent again for a moment, and then she said:

'Which way to the beach?'

Terri had called the hospital again, and this time they had told her that Saul was still sleeping, which was the best thing for him right now. More than ever while Cathy was missing.

She had asked them to send her love when he woke.

She did love him, no question about that, and it had hurt so badly whenever they'd fought, but the trouble was, as much as she wanted to make a pact now with God or whoever, promise never to fight with Saul again so long as he made it out of hospital and was able to talk again, walk again, be *him* again . . . As much as she wanted to do that, she had realized that last day before the attack that they were too damned *different*, that as much as they loved one another, they were always going to fight.

Maybe that didn't matter.

She certainly wasn't going to bail out on him now. She was going to stay by his side for as long as he needed her, maybe even for ever.

Maybe. The rub. The nub.

She looked at her watch. Three fifty-seven.

Where *were* they?

'I always knew how wrong it was,' Kez said. 'How wicked.' The old Golf moved slowly south down another lovely, peaceful residential street. 'But they laughed at me.'

She made it sound simple. Matter of fact.

'When people do that to me, Cathy, it feels like they're stripping me naked. All the ugliness gets exposed when they laugh, and I hate them so much for that. I hate them more than you could ever begin to imagine.'

Cathy knew she had to say something.

'I know something about hate,' she said.

'Next right,' Kez told her.

Directions in the midst of *this*.

Cathy turned right.

'That's how it was with the janitor,' Kez said.

Shock juddered through Cathy, turning her blood to ice.

The janitor. Muller.

Sam's case.

'And that's how it was,' Kez said, 'with the woman who came into the changing rooms at the gym I used to go to.'

More to come, Cathy thought, *more*, dear Christ.

'It was late,' Kez went on. 'I thought everyone else had left, so my guard was down, you know, so I came out of the shower and dropped my towel, and this woman was there cleaning, and she snickered when she saw me, and that was it.'

Cathy stopped at a crossroads.

'I got myself dressed and out of there. I can do that now, keep myself under control. I don't fly into rages the way I did when I was a kid. I get away and I think about it, and if I'm sure I'm right – if I know they *were* laughing at me, mocking me – then I keep it all together and wait for the moment.'

Cathy crossed the junction.

Her brain was hurting. One minute the pain was soothed away, bathed in the novocaine of Kez's trust and love, and then another brand new wound shocked her back into fresh pain and uncertainty.

Fear now, above everything.

She tried to stop listening, tried running lines in her head: '*The beach, then home, a run, then home . . .*'

Kez was still talking, something about an aunt who used to help her, though it was hard for her, she said, hard for anyone to understand.

'Which is why I always try to do it near the ocean so I can wash myself after.'

Washing off the blood.

Don't think about that.

Cathy had seen enough blood, more than enough for a life-time.

Don't go there.

There was a dead-end ahead, the road widening before it with spaces on both sides for two or three cars; a small, curved foot-bridge ahead, tall palms on either side.

The beach ahead, the ocean.

'*The beach, then home . . .*'

She nosed the Golf into one of the spaces.

'The woman in the mall didn't laugh out loud – ' Kez was still talking – 'but she knew those jeans made me look ugly, and . . .'

Get out of the car, run, find a cop.

She couldn't do that to Kez, not when she was so sick.

You can walk away though, leave her behind.

But then what would Kez do? Abandoned, betrayed, what would she *do*?

What would Grace do if she were here? Forgetting about love, focusing on friendship and decency and what was *right*.

Grace would probably go on listening.

Angie called Sam at ten after four.

'Martinez got a license number for Flanagan, and we just got a sighting. Eighth Avenue South, heading for the beach. Green VW Golf, two young women.'

His pulse rate soared as he grabbed a pen, wrote down the number.

'Blessings on you both.'

'Blonde driver,' Angie went on, 'so probably Cathy.'

Good and bad news. Cathy safe for now, but no easy way, if things got ugly, to persuade the Naples PD she'd been with Flanagan against her will.

He called Terri thirty seconds later. 'Meet you there?'

'I'd say we start where we met before,' she suggested. 'Move up that way from there. Flanagan might be revisiting the scene.'

'They might just be going for a run,' Sam said. 'It's what they do.'

'What they *did*,' Terri said. 'Could all be different now.'

'You see them first,' Sam warned, 'keep your distance.'

He was conscious of *not* asking if she'd brought her firearm along for the ride, thought he probably knew the answer, was maybe better off *not* knowing for sure, could hardly castigate her for something he was equally guilty of.

'You'll be there before me,' she said. 'Traffic's pretty snarled up.'
'On my way,' Sam told her.

Kez got out of the car, the jersey over her left shoulder, the bat in her left hand, and came around to the driver's side, waited while Cathy locked the door and tucked her right arm through hers.

They strolled over the tiled paving and up on to the foot-bridge.

'Hey,' Kez said softly, stopping halfway across. 'You going to leave me?'

Cathy looked into her face, her lover's eyes, saw the plea.

Nothing matter of fact now. Nothing simple.

She knew that the answer was no, even now. She was not going to run out on her. She was going to stay by Kez's side for as long as she could, as long as they let her. And it wasn't at all like novocaine now, not a numbing of judgment or common-sense; it was something else entirely, something wholly devoid of sense . . .

'I'm not going anywhere,' she said.

They walked on to the other side of the bridge and down past the long grasses on either side on to the beach. The sand was whiter, seemed softer underfoot than in Miami; the ocean looked and sounded and smelled wonderful, and the wind was high, whipping through their hair, a warm, sandy wind; there were people around living real, normal lives, and it felt just a little like being on vacation, except that Cathy had to keep forcing herself not to think about those dark stains on the bat that was still in her lover's left hand.

Trying to forget that Rudolph Muller had been killed on a beach.

And then suddenly she realized where they were.

On the beach not far from Naples Pier.

Where Saul had been attacked.

Stamped on. Bludgeoned. Almost destroyed.

Cathy stopped walking, pulled her arm out of Kez's and stared at her.

Kez looked right back at her.

Knew that Cathy had realized.

She knelt down on the sand, laid the bat down on the ground before her like a samurai laying down his sword.

'Come sit with me, Cathy.' She dropped the 44 jersey by her

side. The sleeveless black T-shirt she'd put on hours before was stuck to her skin with perspiration, her arms and shoulders and the tiny dragonfly tattoo glistening with it. 'Come sit with me one last time.'

Cathy sat, her movements very slow, and now this *was* numbness, and dumbness too. Though something that felt like a great scream of anguish was building deep inside her mind, walled up by disbelief.

'I've never forgotten the cat,' Kez said, 'but I've never felt bad about it either. I've grown to hate it more over the years because it was the first to mock me, to make me feel like that, and even if it all was just up here – ' she tapped her head – 'I'm not a fool, Cathy, I know most of my problems are in *here*, but even so, even so, it was that cat made me see I was ugly and ridiculous.'

Cathy looked away from Kez, gazed out at the ocean, thought about its power, thought that if the Gulf of Mexico were to rise up now and swallow them it might feel welcome to her. And then a man and his small child crossed her line of vision, the boy in a too-big white T-shirt that billowed in the breeze, the man holding his hand as they walked through the surf – and Cathy felt ashamed of the thought she'd just had.

'I guess maybe that's why I've never much liked animals,' Kez said.

'Woody.' Cathy was unsure if the word had escaped her lips, not that it mattered now, nothing mattered except . . .

'Except the *real* thing, you know, the stronger, wilder kind, like jaguars and hyenas.' Kez was speaking softly now. 'Jaguars are shape-shifters, Cathy. They hunt in water and they're so beautiful; and people think hyenas are ugly and cowardly, but they're not, and they don't let anything get in their way, they fight to get the last laugh, and I admire that in them, don't you?'

It was getting harder to hear her over the wind and waves, or maybe Cathy didn't *want* to hear her any more, and anyway Kez was rambling on now about animals, and maybe soon, Cathy thought, she might find the strength to stand up and walk away, but right now all she could seem to do was sit, half listening, and gaze out to sea.

'That's where Saul saw me,' Kez said.

Cathy heard *that*.

'That's where he did it,' Kez went on. 'At the zoo, here in Naples.'

Cathy turned and stared at her again.

'I was just sitting minding my own business, taking a little time out with the hyenas because I like watching them, being near them. And then I looked up and there he was, standing there, doing what they do. Laughing at me.'

'No,' Cathy said. 'Saul wouldn't do that.'

'Maybe not out loud,' Kez said, 'but I saw his eyes, knew what he was thinking.'

'What was he thinking?' Cathy felt very ill.

'That I was a weirdo,' Kez said. 'Sitting there on the ground talking to animals.'

'Saul wouldn't think like that,' Cathy said faintly.

'Don't you get it yet?' Kez's voice and eyes were suddenly sharp and clear. 'This isn't about Saul, Cathy, this is about *me*. My confession. This is what I've known I needed for a long, long time, so I can finally stop. So I can *be* stopped.'

'That's all I know,' Sam told Grace. 'Will you pass it on to Dad?'

'Right away,' she promised, heart racing.

'She'll be OK,' he said, then honked his horn at an old guy meandering serenely ahead of him up Tenth Avenue South.

'Sam, please take care.' Grace had heard the horn, knew how desperate he must be to get to the beach.

'Don't worry.' He winced at the foolishness of that. 'At least try not to make yourself crazy.'

'I'm fine,' she told him. 'Your son and I are both fine, but we want you – we all want you and Cathy home, safe and sound.'

'I want that, too,' Sam said.

'No risks,' Grace said. 'Please.'

'Kid gloves all the way,' he told her. 'I love you, Gracie.'

'Me, too,' she told him back.

'I don't want you thinking I'm not sorry about Saul. I hate what I did to him more than any of the others, because no matter what he did to me first, I know you care for him.'

'He didn't do *anything*!' A tiny, sharp hammer had started pounding painfully in Cathy's head, like the kind that struck the inside of a bell, but the faintness was gone and she scrambled up from the sand. 'And I don't just care for Saul, I *love* him, we all do.'

'I know,' Kez said, still on her knees. 'And maybe I'll never be able to make myself care about him, but I do care about you.'

'*Screw* your care!' Cathy bent down and shoved her as hard as she could, and Kez fell sideways, made no move to defend herself. 'And if you think by *confessing* to me there's going to be any kind of forgiveness for *that*, any absolution, you're—'

'Crazy?' Kez finished it for her.

A family walking by heard their raised voices, saw the small violence and moved away, giving them a wide berth.

'I don't *understand*.' Cathy's hands were up in her hair, pulling at it as if the pain might help her, ground her. 'I don't understand any of it.' She'd pushed away the other parts of the *confession*, the killings, couldn't begin to think about them. 'Why were you at the zoo anyway? You told me you were in Jacksonville – so that was a lie, like everything else has been a goddamned lie!'

'Not everything,' Kez said, her voice flat and calm. 'Not my feelings for you.'

'Shut up,' Cathy said. 'Why were you here? Were you following Saul?' Her mind was fighting to make some kind of sense of it. 'Was it because he was with Terri, because she's a cop? Did you think they knew about you?'

Kez shook her head. 'Nothing like that. It was just the way I told you. I often go to the zoo when I'm staying at my place.'

'Your *sanctuary*.'

'That's right.'

'So what, you were in hiding?'

'In a way.' Kez stood up, finally, picked up the bat, slung the jersey over her shoulder again. 'It was after the woman at the mall.'

'Oh God,' Cathy said. 'Oh, dear *God*.'

A child playing in the surf turned to look at her.

'Doesn't this prove how much I care about you?' Kez took a step closer, winced as Cathy backed off. 'I held back with Saul. If I hadn't, he wouldn't be in the hospital, he'd be in the morgue.'

Cathy let rip a cry and Kez reached out, grasped her right hand, held on to it.

'One more run,' she said. 'You promised me.'

'You're out of your mind,' Cathy said.

'You think I don't know that?'

Sam saw the Golf, checked it out, then parked where he knew he could beat Flanagan out of the dead-end back into the avenue, and called Terri.

'I've found the car, beach end of Eighth Avenue. Where are you?'

'Still snarled up, too far to come on foot.'

'Right.' Sam got out of the Saab, and looked around. 'I'm going on ahead.'

'Why don't I park closer to the pier and walk up towards you?' Terri suggested.

Sam hesitated, knew he was in no position to give her any kind of an order.

'If you see them, stay out of sight,' he said, 'and call me.'

'Here's hoping,' Terri said.

'I know – ' Kez still gripped Cathy's hand – 'that I'm sick.'

The bat in her left hand began to swing a little. Not fast, but Cathy saw the sinews tightening in her arm.

'I know,' Kez went on, 'what has to happen.'

She let go of Cathy's hand.

'One last run first,' she said. 'It's all I'm asking for.'

She saw Cathy's eyes on the bat, stopped swinging it.

'It's the very last thing I'll ask you for.' She held the bat out. 'You want it?'

Cathy shook her head, felt a sick shudder pass through her.

Not just fear of Kez now. Fear of what was coming next, whatever that might be.

Kez laid the bat down on the sand, took the old stained jersey from over her shoulder, draped it around her narrow waist, stretching and knotting the sleeves, then bent and picked up the bat again, and suddenly Cathy wondered if the other woman might be playing a game with her. She knew better than most about those kinds of games, had been toyed with in the past by a master of them.

'Please,' Kez said.

Not a game, Cathy thought, except that the bat was swinging again.

'No,' Kez said clearly. 'I would never hurt you. Never.'

Cathy dragged her eyes away from the bat to her lover's face.

Sick, and wicked, too, she knew that now, knew what she had done to Saul, to those others. Yet the hell of it, the hot, boiling *hell* of it, was that a part of her still loved her. And she believed, as much as she could any longer believe in anything, that Kez meant what she had just said. That she would not hurt her.

And anyway, Cathy did not know what else to do.

So she nodded.
They lined up, shoulder to shoulder.
And began their run.

Twenty-Seven

G race had been lying on the couch, Woody draped over her feet, since Sam's last call.

Had she not felt so unwell, she would have been finding ways of *dealing* with this dreadful wait. Pacing and cooking, making something healthy and consoling and probably Tuscan for their return. Speaking to David, persuading him to come over for the long haul, taking it in turns with him to go back to Miami General and sit with Saul.

But Saul was still out for the count and David was, she hoped, having the rest he needed. She was too tired to cook or pace, and the fear in her soul seemed to be invading her like a sapping force, and she was beginning to wonder if she ought not to speak to a doctor other than David, but Barbara Walden, her ob-gyn, had been in Europe for a week and Grace had no real wish to speak to a stranger.

She ought, she supposed, to have gone upstairs to bed by now, but the fact was she was too superstitiously afraid that if she did that and fell asleep, something terrible might happen, something even worse than had already befallen Saul.

Ridiculous, of course.

Rest, for the sake of the baby.

Tell that to a mom-to-be whose daughter was not out with a probable killer.

Tell it to a wife whose husband was not out there hunting for them.

Sam was on the beach, trying to slow himself down, fighting the urge to run.

Just a man out for a stroll.

He hadn't seen Terri yet, but he wasn't looking for her. He

was looking for a slim young woman with long, straight golden hair and . . .

There.

There.

Hair glinting in the afternoon sunshine, her figure unmistakable.

Flanagan beside her. Side by side, running real close a couple of hundred yards ahead of him, kicking up low sand clouds in their wake.

Flanagan had something in her left hand. A baseball bat. *The* bat.

Sweet Jesus.

Sam slid his right hand beneath his shirt, closed his fingers around his Sig Sauer, unsnapped the holster – instinct, almost reflex, taking over, and he knew that using his firearm would be his last resort, knew he had no right to use it, was out of jurisdiction, and there were people around, innocent bystanders. His eyes flicked back and forth, took in with a fragment of gratitude that this Monday afternoon there were no crowds and, thank the Lord, no *kids* in sight.

They neared the old wooden pier and Sam willed them to pass it by. If he could just follow on the beach, he would have more time and opportunity to make decisions, pick his moment, whereas if they got up there, the chances were they'd end up being cornered, Flanagan *feeling* cornered, worst case scenario . . .

They took the steps two at a time up on to the pier, and stopped.

Sam swore quietly, slowed his own pace, staying right back, trying to keep them in sight, saw them jogging on the spot. Maybe, he hoped, they'd come back down again, hoped, too, that if Terri saw them she'd have the sense to keep back.

Kez was panting – they were both panting – and Cathy looked around, relieved that there were other people up here on the boardwalk. Not many, but enough, some strolling, some fishing over the sides, some watching a surfer catching waves.

'I want to go now,' Kez said, swinging the bat again.

Cathy stared at her, not understanding.

'Now,' Kez said. 'Hard and fast.'

Cathy saw where she was looking, straight ahead to the end of the pier, and realized suddenly, with a wild gripping of her stomach, that Kez wasn't planning on stopping when she reached the end.

Not certain if she meant to go alone, or take her along for the ride.

'No,' Cathy said.

'Only way to go,' Kez said.

'*No*,' Cathy said again.

'For me,' Kez added, and smiled at her.

A tender, sweet, sad smile.

And then she took off.

Cathy waited a half second.

And took off after her.

Sam, pacing down below, saw them go.

'Oh, Christ.'

He broke into a sprint, trying to keep up, to keep them in view – but the goddamned ocean was in the way, and he knew he was going to have to get up on the pier with them. He flew up the steps, his sneakers pounding the old timber, his eyes frantically scanning.

Kez was much too close to Cathy for him to risk a shot, but it was happening too fast. The temptation to shout out Cathy's name was intense, but he knew how dangerous that might be – *cop, not dad* – so he ground his teeth and stayed silent, edging towards them, hand under his shirt, pistol in his grip, ready if he had no choice . . .

Terri had seen them too, from way off, had started running right away, had already drawn her own pistol, gripping it in both hands as she tracked the women, barrel pointed down. Remembering her training, trying to push Saul out of her mind – *cop, not girl-friend* –

Not sure if she could do that.

Cathy knew now, *knew* that Kez wasn't going to stop, that when she hit the end she was going to jump – and in her mind's eye Cathy could already *see* it, could picture Kez injured and struggling in the water, people trying to save her, cops coming, and Kez didn't *want* that, Kez wanted to . . .

'*No!*' she screamed, kicked like crazy and got *ahead* of Kez, swerved into her path and stopped dead. 'I won't let you!'

'Get out of my *way*!' Kez pushed at her, trying to get past.

'It'll be all right.' Cathy tried to grab at her.

'Let me *go*!'

*   *   *

Sam ducked into the small squared-off recess, halfway along the pier, knelt behind one of the tables in the area, drew his Sig Sauer and kept it down by his side, kept his eyes focused on Cathy and Kez, prayed for enough space between them – not knowing what he was going to do if he got it because it was too *dangerous* to shoot, there were too many people around . . .

Terri saw it happen from down below, from way back. Saw Kez break free, saw her raise the baseball bat . . .

Terri crouched, dug her feet in the sand, brought up her gun and took aim.

Sam saw Kez swing the bat right back.

Heard the shot.

Saw the bat fly out of Kez's hand, soar through the air and plummet down into the waters of the Gulf of Mexico.

Saw Kez launch herself at Cathy, grab hold of her.

Saw, rather than heard, Cathy start to scream, saw her wide open mouth, saw her horror and fear, saw her step back.

Giving Sam space.

A clear shot. He raised the Sig Sauer, took aim . . .

Kez came at Cathy again.

And Sam fired.

'*No!*' Cathy screamed.

Kez already falling.

No pain in her face, something else, something fierce.

But fading out.

People were yelling, shrieking, running in panic, ducking, some right down on the boards, terrified of more shooting.

'No,' Cathy cried out, her voice carrying on the wind.

She was on her knees beside Kez, cradling her.

Sam reached her, stooped, tried to draw her up. 'Let me,' he said.

'No,' she said, quieter now, knowing it was too late.

Kez was trying to speak.

Cathy bent over her, put her ear against her mouth.

Felt the blood, still warm, on her own cheek.

Heard only two words.

'Thank you.'

'Oh God, Kez, hang on,' Cathy said.

But she was already gone.

Twenty-Eight

Chaos in the aftermath.

Cops coming from everywhere along with the local media, and all kinds of hell breaking loose, professional and personal.

Naples PD and Collier County Sheriff's office. The medical examiner, crime-scene techs, uniforms, detectives. Word out to Miami Beach, to Sam's unit, and Terri's and to Internal Affairs.

Sam and Terri were being questioned there at the scene, Sam losing it big-time and not caring because the professional hell could wait, he'd deal with that when the time came. The *personal* hell was something else. He had seen them leading Cathy away and she'd been so damned quiet, no weeping or protestation, just blankness, just *nothing*, and Sam wanted to be with her, to hold her, try to comfort her.

The thing he was most afraid of, now that she was safe, was that Cathy might never forgive him for what he'd done to Kez. He was more afraid of that now than of losing his job or facing charges, or even of going to jail; except then he thought about Grace and their baby and not being with her, with *them*, when the time came, and that was every bit as frightening.

He ran it all over and over in his mind while he and Terri – kept well apart, of course – answered their questions, first out on the pier with Kez's body still lying there, cameras zapping every angle, the ME doing her first exam, members of the public having been hustled away behind crime-scene tape, names and witness reports being taken. Because this was a crime scene, a shooting, and Sam was one of the people behind the shooting, the man who'd shot Flanagan to death, and the only good thing, the only real *blessing* was that no one else had been hurt, no innocent blood spilled, and even in the midst of all this blur, this awful unthinkable reality, Sam was managing to be grateful for that.

They were taken, a while later – he didn't know how long, time had ceased to register – to the Collier County Sheriff's office, and Sam went on cooperating, answering questions, making a voluntary statement, being cautioned that what he told them now could be used against him criminally, civilly and administratively, telling them it was OK, he knew, he *knew*.

But his mind wasn't working properly, he knew that, too, because all he kept on doing was replaying the scene, going back over the build-up, back to the shooting and Flanagan's dying and Cathy's cradling her and Cathy's *face* with the other woman's blood on her cheek, over and over and over . . .

Long evening.

It was almost seven p.m. before Sam was able to call Grace. 'She's safe.' The two words he knew she needed to hear. 'It's over, and Cathy's not hurt.'

The unspoken *but* seemed to pound the air.

'And Kez?' Grace asked.

All downhill from that point on.

'Kez is dead,' Sam said. 'I shot her.' He got it out fast, the only way. 'I thought she was going to hurt Cathy, and I shot her.'

'Oh my God, Sam.'

Her voice was low, horrified, stunned, and Sam – whose own mind had finally begun working properly again – knew that in that one thunderclap moment Grace had understood all the potential ramifications of what he had done.

'Sam, are you OK?' she asked. 'You're not hurt?'

'No, I'm not hurt,' he said, 'but we're all at the Collier County Sheriff's office – Terri, too, because she was there.'

'Was she involved in the shooting?'

'It's a little blurred.' Sam paused. 'Grace, Saul mustn't hear any of this.'

'Of course not.'

'How's he doing?'

'No change. Sam—'

'Grace, I only have a few minutes.'

They had allowed him to phone from an unoccupied office, but he knew they wouldn't give him long. He felt as if he'd been answering questions for ever, knew it was only the beginning, that though he'd been advised against giving a statement at this stage because of the policeman's bill of rights, once the team of investigators out of Miami Beach arrived, things would get heavier before they got better.

If they did get better. He could hardly count the strikes against him. He had been out of jurisdiction. He had not notified the Naples police of his reasons for being there. He had fired his weapon in a public place, endangering innocent bystanders. Had used deadly force against a young woman who had, when the Naples and Collier County officers had arrived, possessed no weapon, the baseball bat being somewhere in the Gulf of Mexico.

And that young woman was dead.

'What about Cathy?' Grace was scrambling, needing to ask questions fast. 'She must be shattered. Does she know what Kez did?'

'I don't know.' Suddenly Sam felt unspeakably weary, like he could lie down on the linoleum floor and sleep forever. 'I'm so sorry, Grace.'

'You did what you had to do.'

'I know,' he said. 'Doesn't necessarily make it right.'

'If you saved Cathy's life that makes it *more* than right in my book.' A new thought, a new horror, hit her. 'Sam, was anyone else hurt?'

'Thank God, no.' He waited for her to speak. 'Grace, are you OK?'

'Are they holding you there?' she asked.

'For a while, I guess,' Sam answered.

'Can I come to you?'

'No way,' Sam told her point-blank. 'I don't want you making the drive, and anyway, by the time they let you see me I'll probably be on my way back.'

'And Cathy? Surely they'd let me see her?'

'She's making a statement right now,' Sam said. 'But I'm hoping they'll get her home ahead of me, and that's why you need to stay there.'

'Of course.' Grace's mind was in turmoil. 'Should I call David?'

'I think so,' he said. 'It might be a while before either of you hear from me again, but you're not to worry about me.'

'How about a lawyer?'

'I've already seen one,' Sam told her, 'and there's a whole posse coming over from our department.' He paused. 'Internal Affairs included.'

'Oh my God, Sam, what a mess.'

The door opened and a young, fresh-faced officer came in.

'I have to go now,' Sam said.

'I want to speak to Cathy,' Grace said urgently.

The officer cleared his throat.

'I'll ask someone,' Sam said.

'Don't forget.'

'I love you, Grace,' he said. 'I'm sorry.'

'I love you, too,' she said.

They let Sam see Cathy.

Not alone. An officer present too.

'We're not allowed to talk about what happened,' she said to him.

She looked pale, hair dishevelled, her eyes filled with deep pain, but she seemed under control. Sam put out his arms and she came into them, and he offered up a swift prayer of gratitude because she was letting him hold her.

'I'm so sorry, sweetheart,' he told her softly.

'You're shaking,' Cathy said.

'I've been so afraid,' Sam said, 'that you'd hate me.'

She pulled back. 'You don't understand,' she said.

There was something else now in her eyes besides the pain, something less easily readable, something that reminded Sam sickeningly of the blankness he had seen in her face the very first time they had met years ago, just after her parents had been killed.

'You don't understand,' she said again, 'that it was what she wanted.'

'OK,' the officer said. 'Change the subject or that's it.'

Cathy nodded. 'I'm sorry.' She thought. 'Am I allowed to tell him stuff that happened before?'

'Is it connected with the shooting?' the young man asked.

'In a way, sure,' she said.

'Then no, I don't think so.' He smiled at her. 'I'm sorry, it's not my rule.'

'Sure,' Cathy said.

'How're you holding up, baby?' Sam asked. 'Have you seen a doctor?'

'I don't need a doctor.'

'If it gets too much, if they're asking too many questions, you can tell them you want to take a break. Tell them if you change your mind about seeing a doctor.'

'Have you told Grace?' Cathy asked.

'I have and she's hanging in, but what she'd love most is to hear your voice.'

'She probably thinks I need her as a shrink again,' Cathy said.

'She thinks you need her as a mom.' Sam put her straight.

'I'm not sure,' Cathy said, 'that I don't need both.'

They all wanted to talk to her.

Collier County wanted to talk to her about the shooting, mostly in her capacity as chief witness to a police-involved shooting, even if the fact that the shooter was her dad was almost certainly going to muddy the waters. And they didn't especially want to talk about the crimes to which the victim had allegedly confessed, but Cathy's account of those multiple confessions had formed a major part of her statement, so they had no choice but to listen.

Detective Joe Patterson and his colleague from the Naples police department did most definitely want to talk to her about Kez's admission of guilt in the assault on Saul, particularly since it seemed their best chance of closing the case.

Mike Rowan from Broward County was going to be interested as hell in talking to her in relation to the murders of Carmelita Sanchez and Maria Rivera – and with Sam otherwise occupied for the foreseeable future, Al Martinez would want to listen to every word Cathy had to tell him about Kez and her dad's old baseball bat and what she'd said about Rudolph Muller.

All hearsay, of course, and almost certainly inadmissible.

The bat was lost somewhere in the Mexican Gulf. The only possible, known, forensic proof of Flanagan's link to the victims were the residual stains on the repeatedly washed Reggie Jackson jersey tied around her waist at the time of her death.

They all wanted to talk to her and Cathy *wanted* to talk, wanted to release it, get it all out of her head, because even Kez had accepted that she would do that, and because it was too much for her to bear on her own. Because of Saul and all he was going through. Because of Kez's other victims. Because if she tried to conceal the truth, not only would those deaths weigh on her conscience, but the cops might come after *her*, decide she had been an accomplice in some way, even if she hadn't even known Kez when poor Carmelita Sanchez and the Trent janitor had died.

And because Cathy had done time, known prison and knew, too, that she could not endure it again, and so she had to co-operate, had to talk.

And then there was Sam.

Sam-the-cop, armed and dangerous. Sam-the-killer, who had blown away Kez in the blink of an eye. And there had been witnesses to that – Cathy had heard their voices, even in the cacophony of ocean and wind and sirens and screaming; one woman telling everyone who would listen that Kez had been unarmed and doing nothing to provoke anyone when 'that man' had shot her; one young, hippy-looking guy in tears because of the 'maniac who shot into the crowd' and could have killed *anyone*.

Except in reality he was Sam-her-dad, the gentlest man in the world, who loved his wife and his father and his brother, and *her*. And if Cathy did not tell the investigators everything she knew, there was a far greater chance that Sam's troubles might multiply all the way to *murder*. And she couldn't do that to him or to Grace, or to Saul or David, or to her unborn baby brother.

She doubted if talking would get the things out of her head. Things Cathy thought she would not forget even if she lived to be a hundred.

Feeling Sam tremble when she'd let him hold her had been small fry by comparison to the rest, but she had felt his fear and known it was because he loved her so much, and that had moved her enough to tell him that it had been what Kez had wanted, to be dead, *out* of it.

But if she had told him that she would not remember, to her own dying day, that he had taken aim at Kez's heart and pulled the trigger, Cathy would have been lying. Because she could never forget, and never forgive.

Except it wasn't Sam she would not be able to forgive. It was *herself*. Cathy Robbins Becket, always the *survivor*, always managing to walk away, trailing bloody footprints behind her.

She had brought Kez Flanagan to her family, which made it her fault, because she was naïve and needy and desperate to be loved. Which made it her fault that Saul was lying wrecked in that hospital bed. Her fault that Sam might be fired or have charges brought against him. Her fault that Grace might not have her husband with her when their child was born.

Her fault that Kez was dead.

And *not* talking would not set Kez back on the track in her orange shorts and battered Nikes, her funky hair fanning as she ran on those fabulous lightning feet. *Not* talking would not warm her poor dead arms, give them life again so she could wrap them around Cathy, help set the fire burning in her again.

Not talking would not change the fact that Kez had spent her whole life feeling ugly and mocked and letting it make her crazy.

Crazy and wicked, and knowing it, and hating it enough to want, in the end, to die.

So Cathy did what they all wanted, and talked.

Twenty-Nine

Nine o'clock had passed when Grace finally heard her voice. 'Thank God,' she said.

Standing in the kitchen, her legs were suddenly so weak that she had to sink down on to a chair. David had come over a while back and ordered her to bed. She'd promised him she'd do that and then he'd left to visit with Saul, but still Grace had not gone upstairs, because even though Sam had told her Cathy was safe, until she actually *spoke* to her, it wouldn't count.

'How are you?' Cathy asked.

'It's not me who's been through hell,' Grace said. 'And I'm not going to ask you if you're OK, because I know you can't possibly be.'

'I don't think I really know how I am right now,' Cathy said. 'I'm so tired from all the talking, from everything, but I'm glad to be tired because it's keeping me from feeling too much. Does that make sense?'

'Absolute sense,' Grace said. 'I'm so sorry, sweetheart, about Kez.'

'Me, too,' Cathy said.

Grace wanted to ask about Sam, but suddenly the fact that Sam had shot Cathy's probable lover seemed to open up a gulf between them, which frightened her all over again.

'Sam's with an attorney,' Cathy said, helping her out.

If Grace had been with her she would have flung her arms around her.

'And then I think we're supposed to be going someplace to sleep, or at least they're taking me somewhere. I'm not sure about Sam, but he's doing OK, Grace, don't worry too much.'

'I think I should come over there,' Grace said. 'Sam said I

should stay home, but that was because he thought they might let you go this evening.'

Woody came padding into the kitchen and lay down at her feet.

'He didn't know how much I have to tell the cops,' Cathy said. 'And they're not making me stay, I want to. I need to tell them.'

'About Kez?' Grace was careful.

'She confessed things to me, Grace. Terrible things that she'd done.'

'Are you allowed to tell me, sweetheart?' Grace asked. 'Do you want to?'

'I think so,' Cathy said. 'Except I'm too tired right now.'

'Then it can all wait,' Grace said. 'Till you're ready.'

Cathy was silent for a moment and then she said: 'You already know about Saul, don't you?'

'Yes,' Grace said. 'Saul told Terri, spelled out her name.'

Cathy didn't speak.

'Cathy, sweetheart,' Grace said. 'If you want to stop talking, it's—'

'She killed those people, Grace.' Cathy's voice was thin and bewildered. 'The janitor at Trent, and two women. She said it was because they'd *laughed* at her – she had this thing about everyone mocking her, she'd had it since she was very small because she thought she was ugly, can you *believe* that? She thought her body was ugly, and it wasn't, Grace, she wasn't ugly.'

'No, she wasn't,' Grace said.

'I think she brought me to Naples,' Cathy said, 'just so she could confess to me. She brought me to an apartment that she said was hers – except it didn't feel like it was hers at all, but she called it her sanctuary, and it was very pretty, all flowers and . . .'

She stopped, went silent.

'Cathy?' Grace was anxious.

'I just remembered something, that's all,' Cathy said. 'A weird little thing that happened when I first saw the apartment.'

'What kind of weird?'

'It was nothing, really, just something about it that felt familiar, but then so much was going on and I forgot about it. But I just realized why it happened – Grace, do you remember a photo Lucia used to keep on her desk, right next to the one of her husband?'

'The one of her with her niece.' Grace did vaguely remember

it, but mostly because Lucia had taken it to be repaired when the frame had broken, and it troubled her a little now that Cathy should be latching on to that in the midst of so much horror.

'Only that was what looked familiar,' Cathy explained. 'They were standing on a balcony in the photo, and it looked exactly like the veranda at Kez's place. And I don't know why I'm even talking about it, because it's nothing, *less* than nothing – thousands of balconies must look like that, with clematis or flowers like that wound around so prettily, and I don't know why I'm babbling about that when poor Kez is *dead*.'

'Sweetheart,' Grace said, gently, 'take it easy.'

'I'm going to have to go in a minute.'

Grace said, 'It's been so wonderful for me to hear you.' She thought about family then, about the emotions that bound people together. 'Is Kez's mother still alive, do you know?'

'I think so,' Cathy answered. 'But Kez hadn't had anything to do with her for years, though she said something about an aunt who used to help her, and I think she meant she helped her after she'd done terrible things. I guess because she understood that Kez was sick, that she couldn't help what she did.'

Grace heard a sound in the background, like a door closing, and then a man's voice – Sam's voice – and the baby kicked hard at that instant, almost as if he'd heard his father, and she laid her left hand over him and smiled.

First time she'd smiled for a long while.

'Sam's here,' Cathy told her. 'He wants to talk to you.'

'Sweetheart, please try and get some rest,' Grace said quickly. 'Call me any time, collect if that's easier, any time.'

Then Sam was on the line.

'Good to hear her, right?'

'Can she hear me now?' Grace asked him.

'No,' Sam said, 'she's just left the room.'

'I want you to answer me honestly,' Grace said.

'Of course.'

'Does anyone there think she might have been involved with what Kez did?'

'No one's implied that to me,' Sam said. 'But the fact that Cathy was driving Kez's car in Naples, running with her on the beach just before . . .'

'She says Kez confessed to the killings,' Grace said.

'But only to her,' Sam said. 'Right now Cathy's being treated simply as a witness to the shooting, and until someone digs up something solid to back up her story about the confessions, that's all it's going to be, her story.'

'Does she need a lawyer?' Grace asked.

'Not yet,' Sam said. 'Grace, you don't need to worry about that. Even if a few people do want to sniff around Cathy for a while it's not going to take too much time to show that Flanagan was killing long before she ever met Cathy.'

'But they were both at Trent for a while before they met,' Grace pointed out.

'It won't come to that,' Sam said. 'They have another Becket to roast first. One who might deserve it.'

'Don't talk like that,' Grace said. 'Please.'

'Can't quite seem to help it,' Sam said.

'You saved our daughter's life,' Grace said.

'Maybe I did,' he said. 'Maybe I needn't have done what I did.'

'Sam, *please*,' Grace said, violently.

'I'm sorry, Gracie,' he said.

And hung up again.

For a long while after that call, Grace sat in the kitchen, thinking.

Claudia had rung about ten minutes later, and Grace had let the machine pick up; the breakdown of communication between them was something she knew she needed to deal with soon, but not now.

Inside her womb, the baby kicked and squirmed.

She spoke to him calmingly, lovingly, and he settled.

Not so Grace.

She stood up, finally, wandered out of the kitchen into the little hallway and into her office. As she looked at Lucia's desk, at the dainty pots of herbs on the shelf above, then back down at the letter and filing trays, and jars of pens and pencils, all neat and tidy beside the computer, Grace found that she was missing her again, felt that it might have brought a degree of comfort to have Lucia here.

She thought about the photograph Cathy had talked about, thought she'd like to see it again, just so she could know what Kez's balcony had looked like, because visualizing the place might help her feel less cut-off from Cathy, might perhaps even make it easier, in the longer term, to help her.

She sat down on Lucia's chair, idly slid open her top desk drawer in case the broken frame might have been tucked in there, found only a notepad, more pens, some sticky tape, general stationery.

She tried the bottom drawer and found it locked.

Which surprised her, because aside from the filing cabinets containing patients' confidential files, nothing in her office had ever been locked to her knowledge.

She had never regarded Lucia as the secretive type. Then again, she hadn't ever thought of herself as nosy. Though some might say psychologists, in general, were just that.

Maybe they were right.

Grace had seen characters on TV open locked drawers like this easily enough.

She got up to get the paperknife from her own desk, came back and sat down again. She knew she had no right to do this, had no real understanding of *why* she was trying to do it, but it wasn't too hard at all. A little jiggling and sliding around, then just a small amount of force and – with a rush of guilt and an instant mental scramble for a suitable excuse – the drawer was open.

The photograph was there, right at the back.

The frame not broken, after all – or maybe it might have been fixed, there was no way of knowing, except then why would it have been put away?

The picture was, as Grace had vaguely recalled, of Lucia, taken about ten years ago with Tina, her niece, who must, she guessed, have been around twelve or so at the time.

Tall for her age, long-legged, fair-haired – unlike her Aunt Lucia – her smile for the camera a little strained, looking the way many youngsters do when forced to pose.

Grace realized suddenly, guiltily, that she had never taken time to look as closely as she might have at the girl who had always, after all, been so special to her aunt.

There was, now that she did look, something familiar about her. Which was what Cathy had said about the balcony. She looked away from Tina Busseto to the background, saw the flowers – clematis, perhaps, though flowers had never been Grace's strong suit – and thought that they might have been standing on any balcony anywhere the sun shone.

She looked back again at the young girl.

And felt her heart miss a beat.

Thirty

September 13

'It really is all over, son,' David told Saul.

He had been there when Saul had woken again just after midnight, had seen agitation resurface almost immediately, had thanked God that he was able to reassure him without resorting to lies.

Almost. No reason he could see to give him the whole ugly picture.

'Cathy's safe and sends her love, and your brother, too. And your Teté is fine, but she's still with them in Naples, and Grace is resting, but she's doing fine, and they'll all be back here to see you soon as they can.'

No reason on earth to tell his suffering boy that Kez was dead because Sam had shot her. And David had not yet been quite able to establish what part exactly Terri had played in the whole tragic fiasco, but it sounded to him as if she might have fired her weapon, too. Both out of their jurisdiction, in a public place, and it didn't take a legal brain to know they were almost certainly in all kinds of a jam. And Sam had been suspended before, six years ago, after he'd gone down to the Keys to rescue Grace from Peter Hayman, and a man had ended up dead then. And it cut David right to his *soul* to think that anyone might regard his tough, brave, but fundamentally gentle and decent son as some kind of rogue cop.

But shit happened, didn't it, and that was the likely outcome.

And David would be damned if Saul was going to hear about it from him.

Grace hardly slept.

She called the hospital just after one a.m., heard that Saul was comfortable, thanked God for that and for Cathy's safety, and Sam's, and sent up a prayer for Cathy's broken heart and

strength. And then a little later she surprised Woody by clip-
ping on his leash and taking him for a walk around the quiet
island roads.

Thinking.

It couldn't be, she must be wrong.

Yet Cathy had recognized the balcony.

And Grace thought, just *thought*, that she might have recognized the girl in Lucia's photograph.

Which had disappeared, if she ransacked her brain, at around
the time Cathy had first met Kez Flanagan. Around the time
when Cathy had brought Kez home to meet her.

No Lucia that day, Grace remembered.

It couldn't be. What she was thinking couldn't possibly be right.

Phil Busseto's niece. Tina, the apple of Lucia's eye, the
daughter she'd never had, as she had once told Grace.

Cathy had said, hadn't she, that Kez had told her something
about an aunt?

An aunt who used to help her.

Kez Flanagan. Given name Kerry Flanagan.

Tina Busseto?

Couldn't be.

She struggled through the rest of the night, slept a little out of
pure exhaustion, a fitful, useless kind of sleep, knowing already
the call she was going to make as early as possible come Tuesday
morning.

'Grace, what's up?' Martinez asked.

'A hell of a lot,' she said, 'as I'm sure you know.'

'Own worst enemy, our Sam,' his friend said. 'But there's no
guy in this world I'd rather have looking out for me, and I'll
testify to that till hurricanes stop blowing.'

'Thank you, Al,' Grace said. 'Let's hope you don't have to.'

'Me, too.' He surmised from her tone that nothing bad – at
least nothing worse – had happened, and waited to hear what
she did want from him.

'I'm looking for a little help with something,' she told him.
'And I apologize, in advance, because I know how burdened you
must be.'

'True enough,' Martinez said, 'but if I can help, I will.'

'I was hoping you might be able to run a check on someone
for me.'

His sigh was audible. 'What kind of a check?'

'Nothing complicated,' Grace said. 'At least, I don't think so. The kind I might want to run on, say, a future nanny.'

'OK.' Martinez was relieved. 'Name?'

'It's Lucia Busseto,' Grace said.

'Your Lucia?' He sounded surprised.

'I know it's a little strange, but we never ran any checks when she first began working here because she came through Dora.' Grace hesitated. 'Al, I don't want to tell you why I need this, but it would just put my mind at rest.'

'And your mind can't be getting too much of that right now,' Martinez said. 'No problem.'

'Her niece, too,' Grace added quickly. 'Her late husband's niece, in fact. Tina Busseto. She's a nurse, living in Naples, that's about all I know. And Lucia lives in Key Biscayne.'

'And you still don't want to tell me why.' Martinez didn't wait for a reply. 'Anything special I should be looking for?'

'Nothing in particular. Just family stuff, I guess, anything unusual.'

'Criminal records?' The surprise came through again.

'As I said, the kind of thing we'd do for a nanny.'

'No problem.'

'One more thing,' Grace said. 'If you talk to Sam—'

'Let me guess.' Martinez cut her short. 'Don't mention it to him.'

'Only because he's got too much to handle as it is, and this really is just something I need to do because I work with Lucia every day. And, of course, the most important thing is that *she* does not find out, because that might be really hurtful.'

'How urgent is this?'

'Very,' she said. 'I'm really sorry, Al.'

'Leave it with me,' Martinez told her. 'I'll do what I can.'

The bat was found by a surfer just after eight a.m.

Something, maybe, to help Sam's case a little. Proof, at least, that there had *been* a baseball bat – though none of the witnesses who had mentioned it, even the two who'd seen Kez swinging it, had felt the action had in any way justified her being shot.

The ingrained stains were still there, though only time and testing would tell if the ocean, and Kez's multiple cleanings, had left behind any conclusive matches with blood or DNA of any of the victims. Certainly something to compare with the fragment left in the mess of Carmelita Sanchez's forehead.

Not that helping prove Flanagan's guilt was necessarily going to save Sam from losing his job or, conceivably, from a civil suit that might be brought against him by some, as yet unknown, member of Flanagan's family, maybe her long lost mother. Or even from going to jail.

But at least now they *had* the bat.

Sam had just called – a snatched couple of moments – when Martinez phoned Grace at nine twenty-five.

'No record and no skeletons,' he said, getting right to it, 'if that's what you were nervous of. Husband Philip Busseto died of heart disease way back, not too long after they lost their daughter.'

'Daughter?' Grace, sitting in her office, was startled.

'You didn't know?'

'Tell me.'

'Could be too hard for her to talk about,' Martinez said. 'Little girl named Christina, drowned in their bathtub. No suspicious circumstances. The coroner was very clear on that, no blame attached to her mom or dad. But Lucia had a breakdown afterwards. Guess you didn't know about that either?'

'Not a thing,' Grace said, her heart already aching for Lucia.

'The niece is going to take a little longer to track down,' Martinez told her. 'Unless you know different, I figure I'll check out Christina Busseto, too, in case this Tina was named for the dead child.'

'Sounds sensible,' Grace said.

Though her mind was wandering. She remembered David saying that Kez's mother had been named Gina.

By no means necessarily an Italian name, but . . .

Kez in the photograph with Lucia.

Perhaps Kez – hard to say, for sure; so young and with fair hair.

But Grace had looked again and again, then shut her eyes, trying to pull Kez back to the forefront of her mind, remembering a sharp nose, greenish-hazel eyes and a pointed chin, and then she'd opened her eyes again and seen those features in the girl in the picture.

Which was utterly bewildering, but *seemed* to say that Kez was Lucia's niece. Daughter of Joey and Gina Flanagan. Gina *perhaps* then being Phil Busseto's sister.

'Grace?' Martinez's voice, sharper than usual, jolted her. 'Anything else?'

'No,' she said. 'Nothing.'

She tried to sound normal as she thanked him – poor man, already beleaguered enough, and now being asked to take on weird-sounding nanny checks for her. But as she ended the call, Grace felt quite dizzy with confusion, struggling to make some kind of sense of it all.

Lucia had always talked so *much* about Phil's niece. Tina, the wonderful, happy young nurse in Naples. But if – *if* – Grace was right about this, then surely that had to mean there was no such person as Tina Busseto. That she was some kind of invention of Lucia's, perhaps because the bereaved mother had needed a replacement for her poor drowned little girl so badly that she had made up a perfect niece.

Or maybe the reality of her *actual* niece, Kez, had been too hard to cope with.

'Guesswork,' Grace said, out loud. 'Nothing but conjecture.'

She knew though, with sudden certainty, that what she had to do now, as Lucia's friend, was to find her and speak to her.

Because if by chance she was right, then poor Lucia must be desperately in need of a friend. Because if she did turn out to be the aunt who Kez said had '*helped*' her in the past, then Lucia must have been through the most unimaginable hell on earth. And now, after all that horror, to be so brutally bereaved.

If she even knew yet that Kez was dead.

Terri had been suspended from duties pending further investigation into her actions, but was now free to leave Naples, and though she knew that some time down the track the possibility that she might have wrecked her precious career might break her heart, for now all she cared about was getting back to Saul.

'Anything you need,' Sam had told her hastily in a corridor between interviews, 'any time.'

'I'll be fine,' she had told him.

'I doubt anyone in Internal Affairs is going to pay any attention to anything I have to say,' Sam had added quietly, 'but I guarantee I'll do my best for you.'

'Somehow,' Terri had said, 'I can't see your best being quite good enough.'

Grace had accepted that she *had* to call Sam to share her thoughts with him, and had tried to do so before hauling herself back into the Toyota and heading west over Broad Causeway. But his phone had been switched to voicemail, which had tempted her momentarily to leave no message, anxious that if she worded it badly Sam might send in the troops – or at least the Village of Key Biscayne police – to deal with Lucia without giving her a chance to speak to Grace first.

Sins of the niece.

The injustice of that rankled, but then so did the risk of making Sam feel yet again that she had not trusted him. And hurting him was a far worse prospect than hurting Lucia, much as she sympathized.

She kept the message simple. 'I've gone to see Lucia,' she told him, 'who may just possibly turn out to be Kez Flanagan's aunt by marriage.' She paused, then added: 'Ask Martinez.'

And now, her conscience less cluttered, she was turning south on to Biscayne Boulevard on her way to Key Biscayne, trying as she drove to gauge how she really felt now about Lucia, and to work out what she planned to say when she found her.

To reassure her, if possible, that she could not be blamed for her niece's crimes.

If she was right about Kez being the niece.

Yet Grace's instincts told her that she was right, and she'd trusted to them more often than not in the past – though they had certainly been appallingly off when it had come to mistrusting Terri.

Play it as it comes.

Best thing to do when she got there, look the other woman in the eye and take it from there.

The real best thing to do might be to turn the car around and go home.

Grace went on driving south.

Cathy didn't know how much more she could take.

The questions were still going on and on, everyone being kind and polite and considerate, and she'd volunteered for it, *wanted* to get it all out and finished with. But each word stabbed at her, at her heart and at her psyche, her character, her pitiful lack of judgment.

All she wanted now was to go home, lick her wounds and be allowed a little time to grieve for Kez. But returning to Miami would mean going to see Saul, witnessing his pain again, knowing that *her* friend, her lover, had done that to him.

So how *could* she contemplate grieving for that person?

She really didn't know how much more she could take.

Thirty-One

Though Dora Rabinovitch had once told Grace that Phil Busseto had left Lucia well provided for, the dainty white waterfront house on a Harbor Drive corner plot – Lucia's scarlet Audi coupé in the driveway as confirmation – still came as a surprise.

It had the *works* – a pretty backyard, deck and mooring complete with a pale blue speedboat, all just visible through palms from the road – and it had to be worth a small fortune in today's market. Though all the money in the world, Grace thought, could never have made up for what this woman must have – *might* have – gone through.

She took her cell phone off its hands-free cradle and hesitated – she'd told Sam where he could find her, after all. She turned it off, dropped it in her bag and got out of the car, walked slowly up the path, took a breath and rang the bell.

Three seconds later, the door opened.

'Grace,' Lucia said.

Grace had the sense, instantly, that she had been expected.

'I hope you don't mind,' she said.

Lucia wore a black linen trouser suit, her curly, silver-threaded hair as kempt as ever, but her face was drawn and tired, her eyes bleak.

Grace's heart went out to her.

Lucia opened the door wider, stepped back to let Grace in and closed it quietly.

'You know,' she said.

'I'm so very sorry, Lucia.'

Grace put out her arms and the other woman, almost a head shorter, allowed herself to be held for a moment or two before she drew away again and moved ahead of her visitor towards the rear of the house.

Everything was white and graceful except for the greenery, which seemed the overwhelming feature throughout. Plants everywhere of all shapes and sizes, a glasshouse visible through the doors at the back of the sitting room – and no surprise to Grace there, given Lucia's gift for indoor and outdoor gardening.

Yet in spite of the flowers and herbs, there was an absence of the cosiness Grace might have expected in this woman's house, which only seemed to compound her new sadness for Lucia, emphasizing her solitary state, her lack of family. Everything neat and in its place, the antithesis of the Lucca–Becket household, making Grace more thankful than ever for the rich overcrowding of home.

'Tea,' Lucia said, leading the way into her kitchen. 'My special.'

'Let me help.'

'No,' Lucia said. 'I'm better keeping busy.'

'I know that feeling,' Grace said.

She looked around at more white surfaces, softened only by herbs, the air lightly fragranced with their myriad scents, and she recognized a few, those she used in her own cooking: rosemary, sweet basil, mint, thyme, and saffron perhaps, though she was less sure of that, and coriander and . . .

She shook her head, cut away from the compelling aromas back to Lucia, who had filled an old-fashioned white enamel kettle from a spring water dispenser; Grace was accustomed to Lucia insisting on using bottled, not tap water to make her herb teas when she was at the office.

'The first time I've been able to make you a true *tisana*,' she said, turning on the gas beneath the kettle. 'Very simple, of course, if you're using leaves or seeds or flowers; just pour boiling water over and steep.' She nodded towards a white cooking pot standing on a low light beside the kettle. 'If you're using harder seeds or berries, or sometimes bark, it takes longer to release the oils.'

'So many scents,' Grace said. 'I've been trying to identify them.'

'Some you never could,' Lucia said, 'unless you were a herbalist yourself.'

'I hadn't quite understood – ' Grace looked around, took in the shelves of small white porcelain apothecary jars, the mortar and pestle on the worktop, the scales – 'how important this was to you.'

'It's just a hobby.' Lucia indicated the white table and chairs.

'Please, Dr Lucca, take the weight off your feet. I'll bring the tea across in a moment.'

'I thought we'd got past this,' Grace said gently. 'Please call me Grace.'

'Old habits,' Lucia said.

It was a relief to sit down, though Grace felt that the tension still building inside her would only begin to be eased once they started talking properly.

She knew, already, that she would not have to push hard.

'*You know.*'

That had said it all, or had at least begun the process.

However much Lucia might or might not know about the things Kez had done, whatever the *help* Kez had spoken of to Cathy might have involved, Lucia was almost ready to talk.

Needed to talk.

All Grace had to do was wait.

Saul was awake and agitated again. His drug levels had been decreased, partly to prevent future dependency, but his stress levels were inevitably rising again, and he was running a slight fever.

'Nothing to be concerned about,' Lucy Khan had told David when he'd come in a while ago, and had peered at him critically. 'You're looking very tired, Dr Becket. Couldn't one of the others take over for a while?'

'Sam and Cathy are both still out of town,' David had said. 'And I've told Grace to take things a little easier for a while.'

He liked Lucy Khan a lot, but he didn't know her well enough to share their new family emergency.

'What about Saul's girlfriend?' Lucy Khan had persisted.

'Terri called me an hour or so ago,' David was glad to tell her something positive. 'She's on her way back to Miami.'

He had given Saul that piece of good news as soon as he'd come into his room, and it had certainly helped, but David could see in his eyes that nothing less than Terri's *and* the rest of his family's physical presence in his room would convince him that they were all truly safe and well.

Given that David felt much the same himself, he couldn't blame Saul.

It had begun, Lucia was telling Grace, with a cat.

'You hear, don't you, that these things start out with animals.'

These things.

The words alone made Grace feel abruptly sick, brought the reality of what she now realized she was going to hear sharply, horribly into focus.

'Kez was staying with me here in this house,' Lucia was saying, 'when it happened. She was very upset – I'd never seen my niece so upset. Yet the fact that she blamed the *creature* rather than herself should have been an early warning – what they call a wake-up call these days.'

They had moved, with their teacups, into the sitting room, where Grace had noticed a group of photographs on a lamp table in the corner, some of Phil Busseto, and some of a baby girl with curly dark hair. Not Kez.

Christina, the daughter, she supposed.

'Why did you never tell me that you had a child?' she asked gently.

'Because I've never been able to bear the pain of talking about Christina.'

'And was your niece named for her?' Grace saw no purpose in prevaricating. 'Was Tina your pet name for Kez?'

Lucia shook her head. 'Kez was born Kerry, as you probably know, to Phil's sister Gina and her husband Joey Flanagan. Kez was what she called herself as a small child, and after that everyone used it.'

'And Tina?' Grace was fascinated now.

'Tina – ' Lucia's small smile was sad – 'was my fantasy.'

The candour of her admission both surprised and impressed Grace.

'Tina Busseto.' The first hint of tears had sprung to Lucia's brown eyes. 'My "good" niece. A fine young person.'

'The kind of person,' Grace ventured, 'Christina might have become.'

'Perhaps,' Lucia said.

'You used to say that Tina lived in Naples.'

Lucia nodded and sipped her tea.

'The photograph,' Grace said, 'that used to stand on your desk in the office.'

'Yes,' Lucia said. 'That was taken in our apartment in Naples.'

'Of you and Kez?' Grace wanted to be certain.

Again, Lucia nodded. 'She grew up over there with Gina and Joey. And then after Joey died and Gina didn't really want to be a mom any more, Phil and I took over the payments on the

Naples apartment, and paid for a housekeeper, and had Kez over to stay with us as often as was practical.'

'Lucky for Gina to have you,' Grace said. 'And wonderful for Kez.'

Or maybe not, went through her mind.

'So that was how you found out,' Lucia said, 'about my being her aunt. From the photograph.' She paused. 'You opened my drawer – you must have, to see it. You'd never have remembered, otherwise.'

'No,' Grace said. 'I'm sorry for invading your privacy.'

Lucia shrugged. 'I should have taken it away. I wonder why I didn't.' She paused again. 'Maybe I wanted you to know.'

'Maybe you did.' Grace looked down at her shoulder bag. 'I brought the photograph with me, in case you wanted it.'

'You keep it,' Lucia said. 'You never know, you might find a use for it.'

They sat for a few moments in silence.

'It went on from there.' Lucia returned to the past. 'You know how it can be; the more you do for some people, the more they expect. Gina was like that. We put Kez through school and encouraged her with her running, and then later, when she went to Trent, I helped her get her own place in the Grove because Gina had gone off with another man by then and Phil was dead.'

'But you still kept the Naples apartment.'

'Because I knew by then,' Lucia said steadily, 'that Kez needed it.' She paused. 'She always went there afterward. Like a creature going to a burrow to lick its wounds.'

Afterward.

The word and its implications and, even more, Lucia's unnatural calmness, the total absence of any pretence or denial, jarred Grace's own composure, fragile as it was.

'I know that Kez did terrible things,' Lucia continued. 'But I always felt that she was wounded, too.' She paused. 'Is your tea all right, Grace?'

'It's fine.' Grace drank some, hardly aware of its taste, just sipping it to be polite, the way she often did. 'Thank you.'

'I said Tina was my fantasy niece and that's true, because of course she never existed. Yet there was a kind of crossover between Tina and Kez, with them "sharing" that Naples apartment, and of course I loved them both.' She sipped her own tea. 'I did love Kez, with all my heart, but I knew she was a bad person.'

'From what little Cathy's told me,' Grace said gently, 'she was unwell.'

'No doubt about it,' Lucia said. 'She had this sickness – I looked it up in your books, read all about a disorder – body dysmorphic disorder – that seemed to describe her problems.' She sighed. 'She thought she was ugly, you know.'

'I wish you'd talked to me about it,' Grace said. 'If Kez did suffer from that, it's a very cruel syndrome. Some people suffer from it in relation to specific parts of their body – often the face, sometimes the whole body.'

'Not too many go around killing people because of it, though, do they?'

Grace said nothing.

'Silence,' Lucia said. 'Standard psychologist's reaction.' Her smile was very wry. 'This must be hard for you. You're being very kind, considering.'

'You're my friend,' Grace said.

'Kez did a terrible thing to Saul,' Lucia said.

'But *she* did it, not you. And as we've already agreed, Kez was very sick.'

'I'll bet your husband doesn't feel like that,' Lucia said.

'Perhaps not yet,' Grace said.

'Perhaps not ever,' Lucia said.

One of the parts of the process Sam knew he was going to have to go through was seeing a shrink – and not his wife.

He had killed a woman. Whether or not it was finally decreed just or wrongful, he had still caused Kez Flanagan's death. Cops in such situations, whether they readily admitted distress or not, were, for the most part, well looked after. They would be seen by the appropriate physicians or psychologists, partly for their own good, partly for the purposes of reports that would either sit on their files or, on occasions, be used in a court of law.

Sam supposed that a shrink was probably a good idea. He could not imagine returning to work without resolving at least some of his self-doubt. Was not certain, any longer, about his fitness for his job.

A man trusted with a firearm had no business acting as he had. No real doubt in his mind about that, even if he had done it because he had believed Cathy in grievous danger. Especially since he thought that, given the identical set of circumstances, he would probably do the same again.

But if that made him unfit to be a policeman, was he any more fit to be a husband and father? Was a man who'd done what he had, but who felt no real shame, entitled to bring new life into the world?

The prospect of going home – when they let him – unnerved him because going home would mean spending *real* time with Cathy. Not just snatched moments; swift supportive exchanges in the presence of, or hiding out from, other police officers and attorneys and counsellors.

All too soon there would be no one left to suppress the hate that had to be living, *had* to be, quiet but primed in Cathy's heart. Because no matter what she had said so far, Sam had wiped out her lover.

Far worse than that, he suspected, her *love*.

And how could she truly forgive him for that?

'The day it really began,' Lucia said, 'was the day her father died.'

Up until then, she said, no one – just the cat – had lost their life. There had been fights, Kez had got into some trouble because of her temper, but no one had been badly hurt. No one had been *killed*.

'Until Kez walked in on Joey while he was making love to Lindy Jerszinsky – his and Gina's next-door-neighbour – and Lindy laughed at her – sneered at her, Kez told me. And Kez always had this problem with being laughed at, you see.'

'Yes,' Grace said. 'Cathy told me that much.'

'Did she tell you what Kez did to Lindy?' Lucia shook her head. 'I didn't think so.' She was silent for a moment, and very still. 'She took a pair of scissors from her mother's dressing table and she stuck them in that woman's mouth, all the way in.'

Grace felt sick.

'I'm sorry,' Lucia said. 'Maybe I shouldn't . . .'

'No,' Grace said. 'You need to talk.'

'Maybe I do,' Lucia said. 'And then Joey had a heart attack and died, and Kez went to the phone and called her Aunt Lucia.'

'Not her uncle?' Grace asked.

'Kez never confided in Phil, always in me. She always seemed to know I was the one who would help her.' Lucia shook her head. 'I knew what a huge decision I was making. I know now that it was the wrong decision, but back then, with this poor little girl crazy and covered in blood it seemed like the only thing to do.'

Grace waited a moment. 'And now, all these years later, what do you think you should have done differently?'

'I don't honestly know,' Lucia said wearily. 'If I'd known someone like you, told them, they'd have had to call the cops – same thing if I had called Dr Becket – and that would have been the end for Kez.'

'Not necessarily,' Grace said.

'You think?' Lucia was ironic.

'What about Gina?'

'She'd have had hysterics, thought of herself, not Kez. Whereas I'd already betrayed my own daughter by letting her die – I knew I could never let down another child depending on me.'

'I can understand that,' Grace said.

'Can you?'

'Of course.' Grace felt intrigued, despite herself. 'So what did you do, Lucia?'

'I called Phil. He'd once done time for fraud, you know. He'd been squeaky clean ever since, but he still *knew* people back then, and he knew how important Kez was to me, so he kept Gina out of the way and paid to have the whole scene taken care of – I don't know how, never wanted to either.'

The intrigue was all gone now. Grace felt chilled to the bone.

'But Phil told me after that if Kez ever did anything bad again, anything at all, it would be down to her and her mother, nothing to do with us.'

'And Gina never found out?'

'Only about Joey's heart attack,' Lucia said. 'Lindy Jerszinsky had "gone away unexpectedly", or whatever Phil's pals had arranged. I don't think Gina ever had an inkling of what was happening inside her daughter's head. And as Kez grew up and went on having her . . . *episodes* . . . she knew better than to tell her mother, and it was always her Aunt Lucia she turned to instead.'

'But Phil had said never again.' Grace paused. 'So what did he say the next time Kez came to you for help?'

'He died,' Lucia said.

Thirty-Two

Terri was back in Miami, exhausted and drained, but needing, more than anything, to see Saul before she could think of going home to rest.

His expression when he saw her walk through the door was enough to heat her right through, enough to lighten her load, ease her fatigue and make her certain – if there had been any real question – that she had done the right thing by helping Cathy and avenging him.

'Hi, baby,' she said, light and bright as if she'd come from a shopping trip, bypassing his dad, going straight to the bed, gladder than she'd ever been in her life to see anyone. No doubts left about how much she loved him, she knew that now, though she was not certain that Saul, when he could speak again, would agree with her actions.

Not an eye-for-an-eye type of guy, her Saul, nor likely to appreciate her having put herself in danger, especially not for his sake. Maybe for Cathy's sake, he might go for that – or maybe he might just understand how it had been for her, simply because he loved her. That much, anyway, was clear in his eyes.

The rest of them, his family and Internal Affairs – anyone else who didn't approve of or understand what she had done – could all go hang.

Lucia had made more tea and invited Grace out on to her deck, and now they were sitting on neat white chairs near the glasshouse, not far from where the sleek speedboat was moored.

Its name, Grace now saw, neatly lettered, was *Christina*.

'It's a relief,' Lucia said, 'to talk.'

'Talk as much,' Grace said, 'or as little as you want to.'

'I've learned over the years that people can't, for the most part, be trusted. Kez knew, instinctively, early on, that she couldn't trust her own mother.' Lucia paused. 'I learned that I couldn't trust my husband.'

'But Phil did so much to help Kez,' Grace said.

'Only the first time. The next time he refused.'

She could have coped with that on its own, Lucia told
Grace. She *did* cope, felt that she had no choice but to help
Kez by herself, though it cost her, physically and emotionally as well as financially – not that the money bothered her;
she'd have found that, somehow, even if she hadn't had enough
to manage.

'But Phil wouldn't leave it at that,' she went on. 'He said we
had to go to the police, turn Kez in. He said it was his decision
to make, after all, because she was his niece, his sister's kid, *his*
family.'

A breeze sprang up, enough to ruffle their hair and stir the
palms and ripple the water, gently rocking the *Christina*.

'I couldn't let that happen,' Lucia said.

Grace sat motionless. She had believed in coming here that
the very worst thing she might discover was that Lucia had aided
and abetted her niece by shielding her in some way.

Worse was on the way, she realized now, *much* worse.

'I couldn't betray Kez,' Lucia went on. 'Partly for her, but
also – ' she gave a wry shrug – 'believe me, I know how irra-
tional this sounds, but partly because I remember feeling as if
Christina wanted me to help her cousin.'

Grace said nothing.

'So that was that,' Lucia said. 'I knew what had to happen. It
was only a question of how.'

'You look so tired,' Terri told David after they'd both been shooed
out while Saul was given a sponge bath. 'Why don't you take
advantage of my being here and go home, rest a while?'

'Excuse me,' David said, 'but it isn't me who's just been
through that whole ordeal and then driven from Naples.' He
smiled. 'This is just sitting for me, sitting with my son, and
frankly I'm thankful I can still do that.'

'Same goes for me,' Terri said.

'I well believe it. But truthfully, the way you look right now,
if you don't mind my saying so, you're going to be much better
company for Saul once you've had some sleep.' David smiled
again. 'He's had the greatest present already, he's seen for himself
that you're safe, and he's the last person who would want you
to make yourself sick, now of all times.'

For once, Terri believed that one of Saul's relatives actually meant what he was saying; so for once she didn't feel the need to dig her heels in.

'OK,' she said. 'You win.'

'My relationship with Kez was never the same again,' Lucia said. 'Part of me hated her after that, for making me do such a terrible thing to Phil.'

More than anything now, Grace wanted to leave, to stop listening, just get out and go home to sanity. Yet at the same time she knew she *had* to ask.

'What was it you did to him?'

'It was all very simple,' Lucia answered. 'Strange, in a way, because I started out trying to work out far more complicated ways, using my herbs and plants – quite a few of them are poisonous, you know.'

Grace wished fervently that she hadn't asked.

'I was just about to settle on beautiful foxglove when I realized how foolish that would be, because Phil was already taking digitalis for his heart condition, which meant all that was needed was an overdose.'

Hearing it, Grace thought, but not believing it.

'His own *mistake*,' Lucia went on, 'made while he was out here – ' she gestured at the charming setting around them – 'without a phone, his wife out shopping. Which meant poor Phil was all alone, no one here to give him the atropine that would have stabilized him.'

Not *wanting* to believe it.

'And by the time I did get home,' Lucia said, 'it was too late.'

Terri had not gone directly home as she'd told David she would.

There was something she wanted to check out before she could rest.

Matilda Street.

There were a couple of Miami Beach PD cars and one from Collier County parked outside the white clapboard house she knew Flanagan had lived in.

That was fine, that was good, meant the job was being done.

Then, abruptly, one more thing – she wanted to see Grace.

Wanted to see her reaction when faced with her own prime suspect. Not really expecting or even needing an apology, just wanting to get it over with so they could move on.

But there was no one home, just Woody barking inside.

Finally, ready to admit total exhaustion, Terri turned around and drove home.

'Kez felt it, too,' Lucia said. 'The awful strain that doing something so dreadful to Phil had placed on me and on our relationship. She became much more remote after that, confided in me less often.'

'Did that make it harder?' Grace asked. 'Or easier in some ways?'

She was shell-shocked by the discovery that the woman she'd worked with for two years was herself a killer. Finding it hard to speak, but with a developing awareness that she needed to get into this dialogue, keep her wits about her.

'Nothing made it easier,' Lucia said.

'No,' Grace said. 'Of course not.'

'I think Kez felt I was deeply ashamed of her, which was true.' Lucia paused. 'I think that from that time on, she both loved and hated me. Loved me for having helped her till then. Hated me for knowing her so well.'

'You said she became remote,' Grace said. 'So did you still know what was happening in her life?'

'I made it my business to know. Not everything, thankfully, and I guess it would have been easier just to shut myself off from her, but I felt responsible.'

'So it went on?' Grace felt sick again, with dread.

'I hoped for a while that she'd stopped,' Lucia said. 'But I found she'd just learned to do a better job on her own, without me. And the more *efficient* she became, the harder it was for me to go on believing that she couldn't help herself.'

'I'm not sure that efficiency necessarily means that she *could* help herself.'

The word 'organized' had come to Grace's mind, a word criminal profilers used about some categories of killer. She thought about Sam, wondered if he had listened to her message yet, how angry he would be with her for coming here.

'It's kind of you to say that,' Lucia said, 'except that, you see, the younger Kez would fly into these great rages, but as she matured she seemed to find the self-control to walk away, take her time, plan her revenge, if that's what it was.'

'Is that what you think it was?' Grace asked.

'Revenge or punishment, or just paying them back.' Lucia paused. 'She once told me she was wiping the smiles off their faces.'

'Like a child, still,' Grace said.
'A monster child,' Lucia said.

Mike Rowan from Broward County had been the last to arrive in Naples. He might just as easily have waited and let Cathy come to him, but the way things were, he figured it made more sense to get her account sooner rather than later, before time and grief or some other intense emotion distorted some or all of it.

Sam had been told he could leave any time.

'Not without you,' he'd told Cathy at noon, over a sandwich.

And right after that he'd checked his voicemail, listened to two messages, then tried and failed to reach first Grace, and then Martinez.

'What's wrong?' Cathy had seen the new tension in his face.

'Nothing, sweetheart,' Sam said. 'Everything's fine.'

'You're lying,' she said. 'Something's up with Grace, and when are you ever going to understand that I'm not a kid and I can *take* bad stuff?'

'OK,' Sam said. 'One question.'

'Sure,' Cathy said.

'Can you shed some light on a couple of weird messages Grace and Al left me about Lucia Busseto maybe being Kez's aunt?'

'What?' Cathy turned ashen. 'What did you say?'

'Come on.' Sam led her to a chair, sat her down. 'What's going on?'

'I don't know.' Cathy shook her head, trying to piece things together. 'Sam, I don't *know*, except—'

'Tell me.' Sam drew up a second chair, sat down close to her. 'Just tell me.'

She told him about the photograph on Lucia's desk. And then – getting it out fast, because no one was with them for once – she told him, too, what Kez had said about an *aunt* who'd helped her.

'Helped her,' Sam echoed, fear mounting.

'After the things she did,' Cathy said.

'After the killings,' he said.

Needing to be very clear now, because Grace had left her message before ten thirty, and it was past noon now, which meant that she could have been in Key Biscayne with Lucia Busseto for over an hour.

'You think Grace is with her, don't you?' Cathy said, reading his face.

'Yes, I do,' Sam said.

'Then you have to go,' she told him.

'I don't want to leave without—'

'You have to go *now*,' Cathy insisted. 'You have to make sure Grace is all right, Sam, you *have* to.' She took hold of his hand, held it tightly. 'They'd let me go if I asked them, but it might take time.' She saw him hesitating. 'I've been through a lot worse than this, you know I have.'

'I know, sweetheart, but—'

'But none of this would be happening if I hadn't met Kez, and if anything happens to Grace or the baby I'll never forgive myself, and you know that too.'

He did know.

Listening to Lucia, Grace was starting to feel unwell again, a little nauseous and disoriented.

Hardly surprising, she told herself. Tried telling herself, too, that this was what she did for a living, letting people talk about their problems, their lives.

Not the same.

'I used to wish sometimes,' Lucia said, 'that if Kez couldn't stop, she would die, even kill herself. I've read that some people with body dysmorphic disorder – if that is what she had – do sometimes commit suicide.'

'It happens,' Grace said. 'It's a tragedy when it does.'

She wondered, not for the first time, why Lucia was entrusting all this to her, and finding the answer more than a little frightening, she decided not to think about it.

She asked herself again if Sam had listened to her message, felt he probably had, was almost certainly therefore either on the way here, or had asked Martinez or even the local police to come check on her.

That thought comforted her, though the knowledge that she had turned her cell phone off before entering Lucia's house was less comforting. Especially as the phone was still in her bag, which she had left in the sitting room.

Lucia had just told her that she had murdered her husband, which meant she might not take kindly to Grace retrieving it.

Forget the phone for now.

She asked another question instead.

'Cathy told me that Kez confessed some of these things to her.' Grace paused. 'Why do you think she did that after so long, and why to Cathy?'

'Hard for me to say,' Lucia replied.

'You knew her better than anyone,' Grace persisted.

'That doesn't mean I ever understood how her mind worked.'

Grace said nothing, just waited.

'I think, maybe,' Lucia reflected, 'she came to her confession, and to her end, because of Saul. Because finally one of her crimes came home to her. Because in harming Saul she also wounded Cathy, someone she cared for.' She shrugged. 'Because maybe until Saul, her victims weren't "real" people to her.'

Good answers, Grace realized. Rationally thought through.

Frighteningly so.

Terri was finally home, and she knew that Saul's dad was right, that she ought to give in and go straight to bed.

But she also knew that this was the right time – perhaps the only time she might have – to complete the work she'd set herself, the task no one had wanted her to undertake in the first place, by writing up her final report on the beach killings. And she was fairly certain that no one was ever going to want to read it, that it would probably never be used to help her career as she'd hoped it might, but the fact was she still wanted to do it for *herself*, and for her grandma, and for her 'New York's Finest' granddad. Terri accepted now that she'd screwed up big-time career-wise, that at the very least she was going to get hauled over the coals, but . . .

Cafecito was what she needed, a good strong hit to clear her head.

Then the report.

Then, finally, some rest and back to Saul.

Sam was back on I-75 driving way too fast. They hadn't taken his badge, *yet*, and if he got pulled over for speeding he'd show it to them and they'd let him go; he had no *choice*.

As scared as he was for Grace, he was also extraordinarily pissed at her for heading into this situation without talking to him first. So she'd left him a message, but she *had* to have known when she left home that if she'd reached him, he'd have told her to stay the hell away from Lucia. And all he wanted was for her to be safe, all he wanted was to get hold of her and hug her so hard they'd be *welded* together – and then he'd tell her what he thought.

If Lucia Busseto did turn out to be Flanagan's aunt, maybe even her goddamned *accomplice*, then that had to mean Grace had put herself in real danger.

Heavily pregnant, stressed to the hilt because of Saul and Cathy, and the hard time he'd given her over Terri Suarez, and right this minute – he'd bet their house and both their cars – probably trying to console and counsel this woman she'd regarded as her friend.

If Sam could have gotten the Saab to *fly*, he would have.

Confessions, Lucia had just said to Grace, came in all shapes and sizes.

Fresh cups of tea for them both, though Grace didn't want more tea, thought that after today, she might never drink another cup of herbal tea for as long as she lived.

'I hope you know,' Lucia went on, 'how deeply sorry I am for everything my niece has done, most of all for what she did to Saul.'

It was all beginning to blur just a little to Grace, the incredible horror of it still jagged as a serrated blade, but some of it becoming murkier, harder to penetrate. Her own mind did not seem to be working with its usual meticulous focus; her concentration was flagging, and she was tired.

'But for my own part,' Lucia said, 'I'm sorriest of all about Gregory.'

That felt like a pitcher of ice water thrown in her face.

Grace stared in silence, reeling with new shock.

Gregory.

That young man had been, today at least, out of her thoughts; the vague link that had been part of her spurious suspicion of Terri virtually forgotten. Now, suddenly, she cast urgently around her memory for what she knew about his death.

Timing.

Greg had died on the night after Cathy and Kez had been at the meet up in West Palm Beach and Cathy had come home looking so happy –

'No.' Lucia shook her head, reading her thoughts. 'Not Kez.'

Grace looked at her, confused. 'I don't understand.'

'My greatest personal regret,' Lucia said. 'After Phil.'

She saw the look in Grace's eyes change, saw the last remnants of friendship and compassion disintegrate and fall away.

'The first I heard about the janitor was on the news,' she went on. 'They called it a "bizarre slaying", something like that – I was hardly listening – but then they said Muller had worked at Trent and I started paying attention.' She paused. 'And then Kez phoned.'

Both Grace's hands moved, almost reflexively, over her unborn child.

'That poor boy,' Lucia said, 'must have been there on the beach doing drugs, and Kez hadn't realized he was there until it was too late.' She paused again 'He was down on the sand over by some rocks, three-quarters asleep. But he woke up as Kez was killing Muller. Woke up, freaked out, took off.' Another pause. 'Kez's words.'

Gregory's gaunt face and haunted eyes came back again to Grace, as they had so often since his death.

'She hadn't asked me for help for a long time,' Lucia said.

'So you killed him?' Grace's voice was hushed with disbelief.

She remembered the woman's apparent distress on the Monday after Greg's death.

'I had no real choice,' Lucia said.

'Of *course* you had a choice.' Grace remembered David's description of the hideousness of Greg's dying, and revulsion and rage rose in her.

'I didn't think I had.'

'My God,' Grace said. 'My God, Lucia.'

'I mixed what I needed, waited till after dark, and took the *Christina* through Biscayne Bay, up through the Intracoastal into Dumfoundling Bay. I had to wait a while longer, till I could be sure which bedroom was Gregory's, and then I left it on the deck outside, as a kind of a present.'

'*Present.*' Disgust exploded with the word.

'There was every chance he might not have used it,' Lucia said. 'The wind might have come up and blown it away, or a bird might have picked it up, or he might just not have noticed it. Might even have had the strength to say no.'

'You knew he wouldn't be able to do that,' Grace said. 'You *knew* that.'

Hold on, she told herself.

She was a shrink hanging on by her fingernails, fighting to

remember that this woman might not be sick in the same way as her niece, but she had surely been damaged, her own brand of wickedness some kind of by-product of the horror and helplessness.

But Lucia Busseto had killed her own husband.

Killed an innocent teenage *boy*.

Had known that Cathy was seeing Kez, falling in *love* with Kez, and had made no move to discourage it.

'You've talked about protecting Kez,' Grace said, 'but what about the others?'

'Kez was all I could manage,' Lucia answered. 'If I had let myself think too much about the others, I would have lost my mind.'

'Don't you think you have,' Grace asked, 'lost your mind?'

'I lost myself,' Lucia said, 'a long time ago.'

Grace wanted to get up, wanted to leave but she was feeling nauseous again and a little dizzy, and anyway she had to stay, had to be here when Sam or the local police arrived, had to make sure they understood what Lucia had been party to, what she had *done*. Just because Lucia had told her the truth, didn't mean she was going to tell anyone else, so she had to stay.

And there were questions she needed to ask.

'Why did you need to kill Gregory?' She stayed where she was, sitting in her pretty white chair, willing the dizziness away. 'He didn't know anything, he wouldn't have been a threat to Kez. I'll bet you read my notes, you must have *known* that.'

'No threat then,' Lucia said, 'not yet. But your notes said that he seemed terrified. And there was the thing he kept saying: "Saw me." Which meant he knew Kez had seen him, which had to mean he'd seen *her*.'

'But he didn't say a *word* about the killing, let alone describe the killer.'

'Not that day,' Lucia said again. 'But there could have been all kinds of reasons for that. He might have been too scared, because of what he'd been doing. Or maybe his recall had been blotted out by the fear of what he'd seen. And I knew there was a chance that in time, maybe under hypnosis, or maybe his next time in rehab – which would have come, we both know that – he might have remembered more about Kez. And I couldn't let that happen. However hard you find that to accept.'

'Hard is not the word,' Grace said.

'What if it had been Cathy?' Lucia asked. 'Don't you think you might have done the same thing for her?'

'No,' Grace said. 'I would not. I've asked myself how far I might go for my child, my children, and I expect there are many unthinkable things I *might* do.' She shook her head. 'But not that. Ever.'

'No,' Lucia said. 'I thought that was what you'd say.'

Thirty-Three

'No chance,' Martinez told Sam, who had just asked him if he could get to Lucia Busseto's house before him. 'It's not just Kovac and Hernandez on my case now, it's the chief, too, and—'

'Don't worry about it,' Sam cut in.

'I'm already worried, man,' Martinez told him.

'I'll stay in touch,' Sam said, and cut off.

His partner's first, predictable reaction had been to tell him to call in the Key Biscayne PD – 'haven't you learned *anything* yet, for fuck's sake?' – but moments later, Martinez had agreed how tough it would be, on short notice, to explain wholly unsubstantiated suspicions against an apparently blameless widow. And in any case, no matter what might be going on inside the house, if they *did* send over a couple of regular patrol officers, who was to say they might not just get fobbed off by Lucia?

Terri would go if he called her, whatever she felt about him. If he told that one-woman taskforce that Lucia might be Kez's aunt, she'd burn rubber getting down to the Busseto house, no question. Which really *would* spell the end of her career ambitions, and might just end up placing her in danger too.

Sam put his foot down again, all the way down.

'This must be a horrible jolt for you,' Lucia said. 'All these years of sitting in your nice, cosy office listening to patients, thinking you're helping them. Yet really you have no idea, have you?'

'Sometimes that's true,' Grace said, evenly.

'Quite a lot of times,' Lucia said. 'You've sat with me in that room for over two years, drunk my tea, thanked me for my work, remembered to ask polite questions about Tina and about what I did at the weekend. But you never had the slightest inkling of my pain, of the awful spiral I'd been sucked down into.'

It was the first time Grace had been fully aware of the other woman's hostility towards her.

'More tea,' Lucia said, got up and went into the house.

Grace looked down at her teacup.

Remembered Lucia calling it her 'special'.

Grace looked around at the plants. Everywhere, inside the house and out, and in the glasshouse. Lucia had said that many of them were poisonous, that she'd considered using foxglove to kill her husband before she'd settled on his own digitalis.

Gregory had been killed by cocaine cut with strychnine. Grace struggled to remember if strychnine came from a plant. Then remembered that rat poison had been used. Not a plant.

So take it easy, she told herself. *Don't get crazy.*

She reminded herself how bad she'd felt six years ago when she'd had cause to suspect that she'd been poisoned; how they were never certain afterwards if she hadn't totally imagined her symptoms.

This nausea was probably her imagination, too. Because this was still Lucia, wasn't it, who had always been kind to her and her patients. And maybe the grotesque tales had affected her mind; maybe she had only *thought* that Lucia was being hostile just now. After all, Lucia had been unburdening herself to Grace because she *trusted* her, the way Cathy said Kez had trusted her, which was, in its way, a compliment.

Except this was *not* the Lucia she had thought she knew.

And Grace did feel bad. Less dizzy now, but still unwell.

You felt bad yesterday, too, without Lucia's tea.

Nearly eight months pregnant and going through this was enough to make any woman feel bad.

But just in case, no more tea.

Lucia was in the kitchen making more.

That didn't mean she had to drink it.

Grace thought of her phone again, decided this was the moment to get it, and started to get up.

Lucia came out, holding two cups.

She set one down in front of Grace, moved the used one to a table near the glasshouse, and there was a dish of red and black jellybeans on that, and a jug of water, and more plants, all in white pots.

'Nicer when it's hot,' she said.

Cathy was all talked out.

Drained of facts, details, recollection. Of strength. Of emotion, especially.

They had all continued to be kind to her, had told her several times that she could stop, take more breaks, go home and continue another time, but Cathy had wanted to get it done with. And the kindness seemed to indicate that Sam's and Grace's anxiety about her past counting against her was unfounded.

These people had, she supposed, found her guilty of being a lousy judge of character. Of being a fool and, maybe, some kind of a freak, an oddball.

Right on all counts, she thought. It all seemed completely unreal to her. All that had happened, including her relationship with Kez. The deaths and the pain Kez had left in her wake. The strangeness of her long day of confession. Sam's and Terri's shooting.

Kez dying in her arms. Kez loving her.

Cathy had talked and talked about so much of it; yet, on an emotional level it was as if it had never happened. She knew from experience that the numbness was just a temporary comfort device offered by her brain, a smudging of pain; knew it would not last. But for the present, she was emotionally spent.

There would be more, she realized, much more to deal with and face up to over time. More interviews, more statements, more poking into her privacy. More prodding of her relationship with Kez.

Going home and seeing Saul – who would probably, knowing him, forgive her. Her family would all forgive her, which might be hard to take. Grace and David, concerned for her, assuring her they'd be there for her whenever she was ready. Sam checking every now and again, with wary eyes, to see if she did not, after all, blame him for killing Kez.

All the kindness might just make it worse, though she couldn't be sure of that.

Couldn't be sure of anything.

Except that beneath the exhaustion and temporary emotional paralysis, she was deeply afraid of certain things.

That Kez had only been drawn to her because of her past.

That love of the intimate kind was not for her, because she was somehow flawed.

That people took a risk by loving her.

That she might never be able to feel, properly, intensely, again.

Worse, that she *would* feel again.

'I was there,' Lucia said. 'In Naples.'

A small white boat, with a woman at the helm, deep-bronzed, a pair of sunglasses pushed up into her glossy golden hair, moved sedately past the *Christina*, stirring her and sending small waves bumping up her sides.

'I saw what happened,' Lucia went on. 'What they did to Kez.'

'Oh my God.' Grace was appalled. 'Oh God, Lucia, I'm so sorry.'

And she *was*, despite everything, and it was extraordinary how compassion could return so speedily, even if her heart was pounding crazily at the same time and fear was already pushing the sympathy away again.

'Saul's young lady and Detective Becket,' Lucia said.

No mistaking the hostility now. Though how, thinking of Sam's briefly sketched account of the events leading up to Kez's death, how could this woman *not* feel hostile?

'I'm sorry, too,' Lucia said. 'Truly sorry. For Cathy and for Saul. I've prayed for his recovery, for him to be able to go on with his training. And I can even understand what his girlfriend and your husband did, *why* they did it – I suppose, in a way, I can understand that better than anyone.'

She drank from her cup, then set it down.

'But I can't ever forgive them,' she said.

'They were protecting Cathy,' Grace said.

'Maybe that's what they believed they were doing,' Lucia said. 'But no one's ever going to know for sure, are they, that Cathy *needed* protection. And if Kez was such a great danger to her, why was Cathy on her knees beside Kez when she fell? Why was Cathy *weeping* over my niece as she lay there dying?'

'Because she cared for her,' Grace said, 'very much.'

'At least she was able to be there for her at the end.'

Grace saw, heard, the bitterness.

'Why didn't you go to her, Lucia?' It was her turn to challenge, quietly. 'If you were there, if you knew it was all over, if there was nothing more you could do to shield Kez, why didn't you show yourself, admit to your relationship there and then?' She knew she was taking another risk, found she didn't care, wanted an *answer*. 'Why did you leave Naples and come back here?'

'Because there were things I still had to do for her,' Lucia answered.

'What things?'

'Private things.'

She looked down at Grace's teacup.

'You haven't drunk your tea, doctor.'

'No.'

'Afraid I might have added something?' Lucia asked.

'It has occurred to me,' Grace replied.

'Plenty to choose from.' Lucia indicated the plants and glasshouse. '*Nux vomica.* I'm sure you've heard of that.'

'Yes, I have,' Grace said.

Her heart was pumping even harder now, too hard, she thought, and although they'd been sitting in the shade, she was starting to perspire. What she needed, *really* needed, right now was to get up and walk away while she still could. Off this deck, back through the white house, back to her car.

She thought of Greg again, and her stomach tightened with rage and sorrow.

Unfinished business.

'I believe,' she said, 'that *nux vomica* contains strychnine.'

'Not what I used to kill poor Gregory.' Lucia read the logical progression of Grace's thoughts. 'But you know that already. Ordinary rat poison was easier and more effective.' She looked around. 'All this at my fingertips and I used common rat poison.' She gestured at the glasshouse again. 'Quite a good collection. A kind of fascination, I suppose, rather than a hobby. Not quite an obsession, though.'

'How long have you been practising?' Grace asked.

'I began some time after Christina died. Nature's own pharmacy and death dispensary, and no child any more to be lured by or harmed by them, and many of the plants so pretty.' Lucia paused. 'I don't suppose you'd like a closer look?'

'Not really,' Grace said.

'I love their names, too.' Lucia's eyes glinted a little. 'Winter aconite and dumbcane and nightshade and henbane and rosary pea and angel's trumpet and hemlock – and I have my very own cocoa plant – and do you know, Grace, that tea made from mistletoe berries has killed people—'

'Lucia, I don't—

'Or that rhododendrons can paralyse, or that peach stones contain cyanide?'

'Yes.' Grace felt steadier, suddenly, in the face of something more clearly recognizable now as a psychiatric illness. 'Apricot kernels, too, if I'm not mistaken?'

Lucia smiled at her, an odd, sad little smile. 'You're not really afraid of me any more, are you, Grace?' She paused. 'You were for a little while, but not now.'

'Not really,' Grace said, and found that it was true.

In her womb her baby kicked, and her right hand moved to cover it.

Lucia smiled again. That same, sad smile.

'You're right not to be afraid,' she said. 'I wouldn't harm your child.' The smile twisted, wry and painful. 'I've harmed enough children already, God forgive me.'

She rose from her chair and moved swiftly to the table beside the glasshouse.

Dipped the fingers of her right hand into the bowl of jellybeans, extracted three or four, put them into her mouth –

Grace saw the oddness of her movements.

Lucia's lips clamped tightly shut, one hand over her mouth, the other gripping the edge of the table, white-knuckled as she bit down hard, and cried out involuntarily.

Not jellybeans.

'No!' Grace cried out.

Lucia's face was a grimacing mask as she chewed violently, then moaned again.

Grace struggled to her feet. 'Lucia, no!'

The older woman was already down on her knees, that hand still pressed over her mouth as she swallowed and gagged, fighting against her reflexes.

'Lucia, what have you done?' Grace was down on the deck beside her, prising the hand away. 'Lucia, for God's sake, *tell* me!'

Now Lucia's smile was ghastly. 'I had to be certain,' she said.

A new, great rage pumped through Grace's mind and body.

'Oh, no,' she said. 'I won't let you.'

And not knowing what else to do, she left her side and went, as quickly as she could manage, inside to the phone.

Thirty-Four

Rosary peas. Also known as jequirity beans. Botanical name *Abrus precatorius*. From the family *leguminosae*. Common to Florida, the seeds a pretty scarlet and black, looking like lady-bird beetles. Or jellybeans.

Lethal jellybean look-alikes, abrin, about as toxic as ricin, a given part, these days, newspaper readers were led to believe, of the average terrorist's handbook.

Lucia was still alive – or *had* been when the paramedics had rushed her off to Mercy Hospital on the mainland.

'She took a *handful* of them,' Grace said later to Sam, sitting beside him in the Saab, still shaking at the memory. 'Right in front of me – they'd been right under my nose the whole time and I couldn't stop her, I couldn't *do* anything.'

They were on their way to Jackson Memorial, because a cop at the scene had told Sam that Grace had refused to let the paramedics check her out, even though she'd looked distinctly unwell when they'd arrived. And Lord knew that Sam had experienced one of the most heart-stopping moments of his life when he'd seen the police cars outside the Busseto house, had brought the Saab to a tire-squealing halt and charged into the house – only to start breathing again when he'd seen Grace sitting on the couch, white-faced but *alive*.

'I'm perfectly fine,' Grace had tried to reassure him. 'I *thought* Lucia might have put something in my tea, so I imagined I was feeling bad, but I hadn't been feeling so great before I left home, so it had nothing to do with poison.'

That was when Sam had insisted on driving her to Jackson Memorial. Mercy might be closer, but he was afraid Grace might want to see Lucia – if she was still alive – and with Dr Walden still away, there was no point going further to Miami General.

'I should have realized what she was building up to,' Grace was still berating herself in the car. 'It was textbook stuff she'd lost the last person who mattered to her, she'd done awful, wicked things, and now she was spilling it all before dying. I *should* have known what was coming, found a way to help her before—'

'Grace, stop,' Sam called a halt. 'Lucia wasn't your patient, you're not her psychologist. What you were today was just *human*, a pregnant woman faced with a *killer.*' He glanced sideways at her still taut, pale face. 'Sweetheart, you called the paramedics, you gave them all the facts, you did what they told you to do. There was nothing else you could have done.'

She didn't answer.

Grace was still in shock, though not the kind – according to the doctor who'd examined her – that required hospitalization or treatment. 'Take her home, spoil her and keep an eye on her,' had been his advice to Sam, since there was, so far as anybody could tell at that stage, no evidence that Lucia had poisoned her.

Except that the local police still needed her statement, and – perhaps because they were unaware of what had gone on in Naples – Sam was able to convince them to let him remain at Grace's side during their questioning. And even as he listened to the horrors – filling in blanks in ways almost impossible to reconcile with the *nice* lady who'd been coming to work in his wife's office, in their *home*, for two years – all he really wanted was to keep watching Grace, touching her, holding on to her.

One of these days he supposed he might get around to telling her how mad at her he'd been for getting herself into danger, how frustrated he was by the infuriatingly protective part of Grace's nature that had made her keep her angst over Terri from him and that had made her drive straight to Key Biscayne to comfort Lucia Busseto instead of waiting to talk to him first.

'I left a message,' she'd told him earlier, a little warily.

'Yeah,' he'd replied. 'Big help.'

But then he'd left it alone, because all that mattered now was taking care of her and their unborn baby son, getting police business out of the way as fast as possible, and getting her home.

'I want to see Cathy,' Grace said, the instant the questions were finished.

'She's being driven back as we speak,' Sam told her. 'So all we have to do is get there ahead of her, OK? So you'll let me take you home, put you to bed, lock the front door, turn off the bedroom phone?'

'All sounds good to me,' Grace said.

'And no one's going to come into our house except Cathy and, maybe later, my dad,' Sam added. 'And if anyone – I don't care *who* they are – thinks they're going to ask you another question until after you've rested for a good long time, they'll have to break down the door and take me on first.'

Which was, more or less, how it had gone.

Cathy had arrived soon after they had got home – having looked in on Saul so that Grace could satisfy herself that he was no worse – and they had told her, as briefly and gently as possible, about the drama that had unfolded in Key Biscayne that afternoon.

'So Lucia really was Kez's aunt.' Cathy had been reeling. 'It's all just so hard to believe.'

'Believe it,' Sam had told her grimly.

And then he had heated them up two bowls of Grace's home-made minestrone (which was always on hand in the freezer), after which he had finally tucked up both his girls in their beds, and it was a measure of their sheer exhaustion that neither of them had argued.

So the house was very quiet when, in the early evening, satisfied that Grace and Cathy were both sound asleep, Sam took some time out to switch on the machine and fix himself a super strong espresso.

Strong *exactly* what he needed.

No sleep intended until much later, until he was as certain as he could be that no one was going to need him. And tomorrow, he guessed, was going to be pretty much of a bitch in terms of himself and Terri catching varying degrees of hell from their respective chiefs and Internal Affairs. But with luck and a fair wind at least Cathy ought – as evidence stacked up against Flanagan and Lucia over the next week or so – to find herself wholly accepted as innocent victim rather than suspect associate. That would be tough enough on her, Sam realized, but knowing she'd made an unlucky decision in love had to be a hell of a lot better than facing even one more *minute* of jail time.

The sounds told him his espresso was ready.

Sam loaded his favourite *Tosca* CD (Callas and di Stefano, still sky high compared to the others), set down his cup and two *biscotti* on a small saucer on the low table, sank down on the sofa, slipped on his headphones, picked up the remote and pressed the play button.

The overture began to feed, gloriously, into his ears, a little of the ugliness of the last couple of days seeping away. He didn't plan to listen for more than a few minutes, wanted to be sure of hearing Grace or Cathy if they called him, but he needed just a little beauty, a little tranquillity.

Woody jumped up beside him, snuggled close the way he loved, and Sam fondled his ears for a moment or two, then took his first sip of espresso.

He frowned.

It tasted a little off.

He shrugged, figured it had to be his imagination, his taste buds screwed up by the bitterness of the past many hours.

Took another, bigger drink.

Wrinkled his nose, then sighed, started to shift, to get up, because he'd really wanted this espresso to be the best, so maybe he'd better start over.

Too tired.

Drink this, wake up, then *start over.*

The headache hit him first, right along with the nausea, so violent that he ripped off the headphones and made a run for the bathroom near the staircase, Woody, startled out of contented sleep, following and lying down outside the door to wait.

Sam finally emerged, shaken but sufficiently recovered to make it back to the sofa, where he sank down on to the cushions, trembling and sweating.

'Man,' he murmured.

He looked down at the cup, wondering.

Remembering that Lucia had a key to the house.

'Jesus.' He stood up again as the pains hit him hard, stomach pains as bad as anything he'd ever known. 'Oh, *Jesus.*'

He made it into the hall, staggering, knowing about halfway there that he needed help fast.

'Grace!'

He thought he cried out her name, but something was happening to his heart, something weird and frightening.

The floor came up to hit him.

Thirty-Five

G race heard the barking about three seconds before the phone started to ring.

Still a little groggy she waited for Sam to get it, but after three rings she realized he must have gone out, and answered herself.

'I woke you.' David's voice. 'I'm sorry, sweetheart.'

'It's fine.' Grace had a clutch of anxiety. 'How's Saul?'

Downstairs, Woody was still barking in his shrillest voice.

'He's fine,' David reassured. 'He loved seeing you, knowing you were OK.' He paused. 'It's Sam I'm after.'

'I'm not sure he's here.' Grace decided she'd have to go down to stop the dog's noise before Cathy got up. 'Do you want to hold on while I check?'

'Can you just tell him I'm a little concerned about Terri?' David said. 'Saul asked me a while back to call her to see how she was doing, but she's not answering her phone. I guess she could have turned it off, but that's not so likely with Saul in hospital.'

'Doesn't sound likely,' Grace agreed.

'I was wondering if maybe Sam could ask someone from her unit to go knock on her door? She lives so close to work, after all, and—'

'I'll tell him.'

The scream tore the air.

'My God.' Grace started to scramble out of bed. 'David, something's happened.'

'I heard it.'

Grace had already dropped the phone and was through the door. 'Cathy, I'm coming!'

'It's Sam!' Cathy screamed. 'Grace, call 911!'

The terror felt like ice-lava filling her as she started down the stairs – freezing for a second as she saw them. Woody first, still barking, skittering around. Cathy on her knees, just outside the bathroom.

Sam was on the floor beside her.

'Oh my God!' Grace started towards them. 'Sam!'

'I've got a pulse.' Cathy's first-aid training had kicked in. 'Make the *call*!'

Grace ran for the phone – and she *could* still run – keeping her eyes on Sam all the time, watching Cathy putting him into the recovery position, which meant that he *had* to be breathing, or Cathy wouldn't . . .

'Cathy, is he *breathing*?'

'Yes, but he sounds really bad – ' Cathy was terrified – 'and there's vomit, and . . .'

Grace began to press keys, heard something tinny – her father-in-law's frantic voice, and she'd forgotten he was holding. 'David, Sam's collapsed, so we need you to call the paramedics, get them here *fast*. Woody, be *quiet*. No, I don't know, I don't know *anything* except he's vomited and he's breathing, but he sounds bad, so – yes, I'm sure – Cathy, have you checked his airway?'

'It's clear,' Cathy told her, 'but his pulse is crazy.'

'David, get them here *now*.'

Grace cut off the call, got herself across the hall, down on to her knees on Sam's other side, pushed the eager dog away. 'Sam, darling, I'm here.'

He stirred, moaned, opened his eyes.

'Sam, sweetheart, you're going to be fine,' Grace said, gratitude soaring. 'Don't move.'

He moaned again, tried to sit up, sank straight back, his eyes unfocused, then closing again.

'Oh my God,' Cathy said. 'Oh my God, Grace, what's wrong with him?'

'He's going to be fine.' Grace shot her a look telling her to feign calm.

'I know,' Cathy said, biting back tears.

Sam was trying to say something.

'Don't try to speak, darling,' Grace told him, 'you just rest.'

'Coffee,' he said.

'Coffee?' Cathy, bewildered, stared at Grace.

'Sam, sweetheart, please.' Grace stroked his hair. 'Just rest. Help's on its way.'

His right arm moved, his hand reaching for her, but seeming not to find her.

Coffee.

Grace suddenly remembered Lucia's words near the end of the nightmare afternoon. What she had said about Sam and Terri, about understanding why they had done what they had. But never being able to *forgive* them.

'Oh dear God.'

'What?' Cathy's eyes were wide.

Grace stared down at Sam, saw that he was stiller again, his skin clammy, his breathing laboured, and she tore through her panicked brain, trying to think about the things you were meant to do in cases of poisoning.

'Was he *drinking* coffee?' she asked. 'Before this happened?'

'I don't know, I was sleeping. I don't *know*.'

'Go see. If you find a cup, keep it for the paramedics.'

'You think—?' Cathy got up.

'I think Lucia may have poisoned him,' Grace told her. '*Go*. And don't touch it, just *find* it.'

Lucia's words were rushing back now, names of poisonous plants – hemlock and nightshade and aconite, and if she was not already dead, Grace swore she would kill her, take a pillow and smash it down over her face and hold it there until every last . . .

Sam groaned, jolted, then vomited again.

'It's OK, sweetheart . . .' Grace soothed him, cradled him, supported his head so he wouldn't choke, started to call for Cathy to bring a towel but stopped, because finding the cup – the *source* of this, she was certain – was far more urgent. 'Let it go, Sam.'

'I found his cup,' Cathy called. 'His usual espresso.'

'Is it empty? Did he finish it? Don't touch it!'

'Half full.' Cathy came back out into the hall, took in the situation, ran into the bathroom, brought a damp towel and crouched down on Sam's other side, wiping his mouth, his face. 'Poor you.'

He grunted, too weak and limp to manage more. Grace stroked his hair, took his pulse, found it thready, wished the paramedics were with them.

'Help is on its way, sweetheart,' she told him again.

Sam's moan was the only warning before the seizure took hold, seemed almost to roar through him, its effects terrifying, jerking him around as violently as if some sadistic puppeteer were yanking on his head and body and limbs.

'What do we do?' Cathy's training fell apart. 'What do we *do*?'

'We keep *calm*.' Grace attempted to grasp at Sam's arms, then remembered that was wrong, she had to let him flail; she *thought* she'd learned that you were supposed to place a folded hand-kerchief between the patient's teeth to stop them biting their tongue, but she didn't have one, and anyway this was too *violent*.

It stopped as suddenly as it had begun.

'Thank God.' Limp with relief, Grace felt for his pulse again and froze with fresh overpowering terror, because there was *nothing*, and Sam was motionless – and then it was there again, erratic but *there*. 'Oh, thank you, God.'

'Where *are* they?' Cathy was weeping now.

'Here soon,' Grace said. 'They have to be here soon.'

She bent lower over Sam, stroked the dark hair she loved, tried not to cry, kissed him instead, three soft kisses on his clammy, cold forehead, placed neatly in a curve, as if the placement of them might make a difference.

'You're going to be fine,' she told him again, heard her voice sounding as if she meant it, though all the terror was still there like a boulder in her heart, the unspeakable dread that if help didn't arrive soon, it might be too late.

And then *it* hit her, like a great, crashing wave. Like a cramp, but more powerful, spreading from her uterus all the way into her back, rocking her on to her heels and almost toppling her.

'Oh God,' she said. 'Not now.'

'Grace, what's wrong?' Cathy asked, newly alarmed.

It went away.

'Nothing.' Grace shook her head.

'Was it the baby?' Cathy looked terrified.

'Maybe. I'm not sure. It's gone, anyway.'

'You should go lie down.'

'I'm going nowhere.' Grace looked down at Sam, thought how bad he looked, how sick, and the desire swept over her again to punish Lucia, an urge so violent it staggered her.

The siren bleated out of the night, still a distance away, then grew steadily and swiftly more strident, more recognizable.

'Thank God,' Cathy said.

It came again, a breaker of pain so huge that Grace cried out in spite of herself, and she tried, but failed, to get off her knees – this couldn't be happening, not now!

'It's too *soon*,' she cried.

It was too soon and Sam needed her, had never needed her more than now. It could not happen like this, she would not *let* it happen.

Could not stop it.

Thirty-Six

It was killing David.

His total inability to help *any* of them. The fact that Sam might die. That Grace was soon to give birth to their son *knowing* that Sam might die. That Saul was still suffering, would continue to suffer for months. That Cathy was in pieces.

That while the chances of his still-unborn nephew's survival were better than good, the greatly longed for infant might have to start out on a ventilator, might not be able to nurse, might experience all kinds of difficulties at the beginning of his life . . .

And his father might die.

Sam was on the first floor at Miami General in the Critical Care Unit, his heart rhythms all over the place and causing great concern. He had arrested en route to the hospital, had been pulled back from the brink, but his continuing cardiac symptoms aside, he was still suffering from gastrointestinal and neurological problems.

The doctors knew enough, at least, from what Grace had told them – and from reports from the Busseto house – to accept the high probability that Sam had ingested either leaves, flowers or ground seeds of a plant containing cardiac glycosides – a diverse group of plants fitting that bill, ranging from foxgloves to lily of the valley. If that were true and if more conventional methods of treatment failed to halt the potentially life-threatening cardiac symptoms, they might decide to administer digoxin antibody Fab fragments, but they would need to consult with a toxicologist and, perhaps, the Florida Poison Information Center.

'Ask Lucia Busseto,' David had repeatedly and agitatedly urged every doctor and manager in earshot.

Which was easier said than done since Lucia had been taken to Mercy Hospital, and no one at Miami General seemed certain if she was even still alive, let alone in any condition to answer questions.

'We'll find out what the bitch did to him.'

Al Martinez, sounding shocked and grim, had called David a while ago on his way from the new crime scene to the Busseto house.

'You have my word, doc, believe me.'

David believed him, but he was nowhere near as certain if it would happen in time, or that even if it happened in a minute how much difference it would make, how much damage might already have been done to Sam's heart and other major organs.

'Your son's young and strong and fit,' one of the doctors had told him.

But Sam had scarcely seemed to know that his father was there, even when he'd been standing right beside him, and David had believed, when he had first seen Saul after Kez's murderous attack, that he could know no greater fear than that.

He knew better now, knew that this brand of fear was a bottomless pit.

Because Sam might die.

He had left the CCU for a while because as diplomatic and kind as they were with him, he knew that no one there needed a wrecked old paediatrician underfoot. And he had wanted to spend some time with Grace in her delivery suite on the seventh floor, but she was going nuts between contractions, refusing pain relief, insisting on trying to describe every plant she'd seen at the Busseto house and recall the name of every poisonous plant Lucia had recited to her.

'I don't *care* about the pain,' she said to David and Cathy and to Barbara Walden, who had arrived – *one* piece of good news, at least – back from Europe the previous night and had driven straight in when she'd heard. 'I need to *think* and I don't want to be here, I want to go be with Sam, and if they won't let me be with him, I want to go to Mercy and *make* Lucia tell me what she put in his coffee.'

Nuts was the word, and Doc Walden was as much in control of the situation as Grace was allowing her to be, and Cathy was doing her damnedest to stand in for Sam – and David had never seen that kid look so lousy, and who could blame her.

So he had left them too, because they didn't need him either, had gone down to Saul's floor to be with his younger son. Except now that he was here he found himself unable to muster the emotional strength to actually *be* with him, because he knew he was no longer up to faking that things were fine.

He was beyond doing anything *useful*. Except, perhaps, praying. For Sam and Grace and the baby's safe arrival. And for Saul – and for Terri, too.

He had almost, God forgive him, forgotten about Terri.

At three minutes to nine, the two Miami Beach police officers assigned to checking on fellow officer Teresa Suarez – having been delayed, first when an old guy had rear-ended them, then by a burglary three blocks away on Washington Avenue – finally arrived at the mushroom-coloured house in which their colleague lived, and headed up to the second floor.

They knocked on the door and got no reply.

Called that in and learned from the dispatcher that the perceived risk to Officer Suarez was now *high*. Got ready to bust in but found there was no need, because the Property Crimes officer, who ought to have known better, had a front door a kid could have cracked in seconds.

They found Terri in her tiny living room, face down on the floor. Her laptop computer open on the table close by. Her coffee cup beside it, dark *cafecito* almost drained.

Saul's fiery, dark-chocolate-eyed Teté.

All her sparkle and fire gone for ever.

Thirty-Seven

Nothing had prepared Grace for this, nothing *could* have. She was exhausted, physically and emotionally wrung out, yet as one contraction came to an end, she knew another was already on the way and her fears for Sam were coming even thicker and faster, only submerging briefly beneath labour pains so all-consuming that it was *impossible* to think of anything else.

Physical agony was her only respite. She felt as if she had walked miles around the room since her arrival – had used the bed mostly for brief spells of exhaustion, hardly able to bear to lie down at other times, finding it just a little easier to stay vertical during contractions, letting gravity give a little help. She and Sam had practised her leaning back in his arms, with him kissing the back of her neck and rubbing her back, and when they'd rehearsed that at home, Woody had kept getting involved, wanting to play.

No play now, and no Sam either.

She was taking another weary wander around the delivery suite and had just shaken off Cathy's attempt to support her, when it came to her.

The photograph. Of Lucia with Kez as a twelve-year-old. In the frame Lucia had claimed had been broken and which had, in fact, been whole.

What Grace was remembering now, what had just come back to her sharp as a razor in the midst of her vast fatigue, was something Lucia had said when Grace had told her that she had brought the photo with her in case she wanted it.

Lucia had told Grace to keep it.

Something about it being useful.

'You might find a use for it.'

Grace had thought it an odd remark at the time – but then there had been so much else to think about, she'd forgotten all about it.

Chances were, of course, that Lucia might just have meant that they – perhaps the police – might have used the photograph for identification purposes, in helping establish her relationship with Kez.

But what Grace really thought right now – so strongly that she felt *galvanized* by the idea – was that Lucia might have meant something very different.

Something desperately important.

'The photograph,' she said to Cathy.

'What photograph?'

'In my bag.' Grace stared around the room. 'Where's my bag?'

'We unpacked it,' Cathy reminded her, 'back in the bedroom, the postpartum room, remember?'

Before moving to the delivery suite they had been shown the room in which Grace would rest after the birth, a pretty room with a second bed, space for a bassinet and a lockable closet for personal possessions.

'I mean my handbag,' Grace told her.

'I think it was locked away,' Cathy said.

Barbara Walden walked back into the suite wearing green scrubs, looking fresh as a daisy, not a hint of jet-lag.

'How're you doing?'

'I need you to get it,' Grace told Cathy, ignoring the doctor.

The next flood of pain was already beginning, starting in her back, spreading swiftly down into her legs and all points in between, and Grace was struggling to hold on to her thought processes, because this was more important than the pain.

'I *need* it.' She cried out with pain. 'For Sam – I need it *now*.'

'I don't want to leave you,' Cathy said.

'It's OK,' Barbara Walden told Cathy, coming to Grace's side. 'You go.'

The contraction was past and Grace resting, when Cathy came back in with the bag.

'Thank you.' Grace's hands were trembling. 'Thank you, sweetheart.'

'Let me.' Cathy fished around inside, found the photograph right away and pulled it out. 'Here.'

'Open the frame.' Grace's voice shook. 'Look behind the picture.'

'All right.' Cathy turned the frame over, saw that the back had a velvety cover, the type that slid in and out of grooves at both sides.

'Hurry.' Impatient in case the next contraction overtook her, Grace snatched it out of Cathy's hands, slid the back out, let it fall to the floor.

Brown corrugated card backed the photograph.

Grace began to cry.

'Here.' Cathy took the frame back, lifted the brown card. There. What they needed.

Written in clear blue ink letters on a lined index card.

> *Yellow oleander for Detective Becket*
> *Wolfsbane for Officer Suarez*

'I'll get it to CCU and call the cops,' Cathy said, adrenalin coursing.

'Thank you.' Grace was weeping harder. '*Thank* you.'

Dr Walden gave her a moment and then came over, put her arms around her, rubbed her back gently.

'That'll do it,' she said quietly.

'Think so?' Grace whispered, still weeping.

'It's bound to help,' the doctor told her. 'Which means that you can start helping yourself and your little one.'

'I can't seem to care too much about myself right now,' Grace said.

'You should,' Barbara Walden said. 'Your baby and your husband are both going to need you soon enough.'

Grace nodded.

'For them then,' she said.

She lay back for a moment, closed her eyes, let herself think about her child, their son, labouring so hard to be born, and felt a wave of shame because he had been struggling on this first, dark journey without even so much as the aid of his mother's properly focused thoughts.

Not any more.

She'd be with him now, for as long as it took. With him for ever. *It's all right,* she told her child. *I'm all yours.*

Her mind moved away again, back down to the CCU, to Sam, but with an effort almost as great as the physical labors of birth itself, she dragged it back again.

It's all right, she told her son again. *You can come now.*

Thirty-Eight

The discovery had helped Sam, though not, of course, poor Teté.

They felt such *guilt* about the loneliness of her death, though even if Sam's own collapse had not temporarily wiped David's concern for Terri from his mind, it would have made no difference, because her heart had given out before she could even call for help. The post-mortem might reveal some cardiac weakness, something congenital, perhaps, not picked up in a standard physical exam, but for whatever reason, Terri had stood no chance.

If Cathy had not been at Sam's side so swiftly that, too, might have ended in tragedy, but as it transpired, though he had not been present at or even aware of the birth – on Wednesday,

September 14 – of his son, he had, forty-eight hours later, been well enough to meet him.

Joshua Jude Becket.

Four pounds five ounces, breathing on his own, even suckling. The most beautiful, perfect child in the world, bringing joy with him, and healing, too, at least for his father.

His Uncle Saul's wounds, as much spiritual, perhaps even more than physical, would take much longer to heal. Months of pain and rehab and uncertainty, without the solace of his love to come home to at the end of it.

Lucia was still alive, they heard, but fading by inches.

Multi-system organ dysfunction, they were told, leading to probable multiple organ failure and, ultimately, death.

The doctors were still doing what they were sworn to do.

The police were hoping to do the same, but they and the state attorney were on a frustrating kind of standby, since there was no guarantee that she would live, let alone be fit enough to face charges, which had resulted – to date – in none being formally filed.

'No prospect of speedy trial,' Sam had explained to Grace and Cathy, 'which a lot of defense attorneys file these days.'

'And Lucia's in no condition to run,' Grace had said.

'No flight risk at all,' Sam had agreed, 'which means Martinez and Rowan and the others – ' he was resigned, for now, to excluding himself, since he was still suspended from duties – 'can take their time working up the investigation.'

Time and effort was needed to link the murders of Gregory Hoffman, Teresa Suarez, the probable killing of Phil Busseto, and the attempted murder of Samuel Becket – adding to the mix those other homicides after which Lucia had aided and abetted Kez; and monitoring her medical progress with regard to when – if ever – the time might come to file charges and make a formal arrest.

One multiple killer beyond justice.

The other too sick even to warrant a guard at her door.

Sam Becket more likely than Lucia, at this time, to face charges.

Thirty-Nine

October 6

Kez was laid to rest eight days after Terri's cremation, the funeral in Naples, in keeping with a letter of wishes left by Lucia.

'*It was the place she considered her sanctuary*' – her aunt had written – '*the nearest she had to a real home.*'

Martinez had told Sam about the letter, and Sam, in turn, had told Cathy.

Cathy did not believe Lucia's decision the right one. Kez might have called the Naples apartment her 'sanctuary', but her *home* had been in the old clapboard house on Matilda Street in Coconut Grove, the spartan space with the Flo-Jo posters and the track photograph of herself, running free. That other place had, Cathy suspected, been largely her aunt's creation, somewhere for her niece to escape to when she'd been *bad*.

She kept those thoughts to herself.

'Any time you need to talk,' Grace had told her, 'I'm here for you.'

She had said that several times.

'Same as always,' she had said.

Not the same, though, Cathy had realized. Never the same again.

She did not go to the funeral, even though Grace and Sam had both said they would understand if she did, had even encouraged her to go.

'I can't,' she had told Grace. 'It wouldn't feel right.'

'You loved Kez,' Grace had said. 'That would make it right.'

'Saul couldn't go to Teté's,' Cathy had said.

'Exactly. Because he couldn't,' Sam had said. 'Different.'

Cathy had stayed away from Terri's funeral, too, had told the others that she thought she might go to Miami General to be with Saul during the service and interment, but when the time came she had felt too guilty, had written him a note and gone running instead, which had made her feel even more ashamed.

No one had criticized her, but she had seen disappointment in their faces.

'I guess I'm a coward,' she had said.

'Some things,' Grace had said, 'can be very hard to face.'

Saul was the one who had almost swayed Cathy about Kez's funeral.

She was a sick person, he had typed left-handed into the computer they'd recently given him, and which he had used to write his own eulogy for Terri. *We all know that. It doesn't change how you felt about her.*

'What Kez did to you changed that,' Cathy said.

'If I could,' Saul typed, 'I would go with you.'

'I wouldn't let you,' Cathy told him.

David said much the same thing, and had offered to accompany her.

'You need to say goodbye,' he said. 'It's important.'

'Maybe I will,' Cathy told him. 'But later, some time when it's more private.'

'See that you do,' David said.

It had been a long time since Cathy had felt so alone.

A time of great closeness in the Becket family. Her family.

A time of bonding between Joshua and his parents and grandfather and uncle – and Cathy felt nothing but love for this new scrap of an infant, strong enough to bawl his lungs out and disturb them all, morning, noon and night. His Aunt Claudia had come from Seattle to help out, and there had been a few raw, painful encounters between her and Grace because her sister had felt so wounded by her exclusion during their worst of times.

But all of it, the hurt and the disruption and the worries over Saul, and the ongoing uncertainties about Sam's career, all of it spelled *family* and was, therefore, warming and ultimately reassuring to Cathy. And yet, included as she undeniably was in all of it, and as loving and supportive as everyone had been to her, Cathy still felt isolated by her guilt for having brought Kez to them.

'I have similar feelings, sometimes,' Grace had told her during one of their talks, 'because I worked with Lucia all that time and never recognized her pain.'

Cathy believed her, yet the knowledge brought her no comfort.

'You mustn't blame yourself,' Sam had told her more than once.

'I don't,' Cathy had said. 'Not really.'

She could see that Sam had not believed her, that he was worried for her. She loved him so much, loved them all without reservation.

Yet she chose not to tell them the truth about how she really felt.

Who she *really* blamed.

If she had told them they might have become more concerned, might have thought about watching her more closely, more carefully, in case she did something foolish.

Like going to see Lucia.

Forty

October 12

They let her visit.

They would not have done so had formal charges been filed and a guard placed at the door of Lucia's hospital room. Cathy was not, after all, family – though the lack of any close relatives (Gina had not appeared at her daughter's funeral) had helped in the acceptance that Lucia was no flight risk.

No family or close friends, therefore, to plan a breakout. And Lucia was dying. So they saw no reason not to let Cathy see her.

The nurse she spoke to before her visit had told her it was possible Lucia might understand her if she wanted to talk to her, though she could expect no response.

Kez's aunt's eyes were closed and she was on a ventilator, tubes all over, monitors quietly following her progress.

Cathy waited until they were alone, and then she placed the gift she had brought with her on her bedside table and drew the visitor's chair close up to the bed.

'I have things to say,' she told Lucia.

She waited for a moment, watched the pinched, greyish face, watched the chest rise and fall, watched the tissue paper eyelids.

'I blame you,' Cathy said.

She waited another moment, as if the eyes might open, then went on.

'I blame you, Lucia, because you knew what Kez was and you said nothing. Did nothing to stop me falling in love with her. You put us all in danger. Saul and Sam and Grace, and all the others, too. The ones she murdered, the ones you killed, or tried to kill, in her name.'

No point to this.

It was like talking to a corpse. But people did that all the time in funeral homes and at gravesides.

And Cathy had a little more that she needed to say.

'Most of all, though, I blame you for Kez.'

The pain was flowing again, heat in her veins, raising the pitch of her voice.

'You should have helped her, Lucia. Not the sick way you chose.'

Too loud.

Cathy took a breath and went on.

'If you had got her treatment after the first time, when she was still a child, she could have been *helped* and it would all have been behind her by now. They'd probably have sent her to a psych unit, and they could have taken care of her. Kez could have had a chance to move on and be a great athlete.'

Her palms were damp and she was trembling, feeling sick.

'And all those people would not be *dead*.'

The door opened and Cathy froze, waited to be thrown out.

A nurse, kind-faced, Filipina, offered her something to drink.

'No, thank you,' Cathy told her. 'I'm fine.'

'It's good,' the woman said, 'that someone's here for her.'

'Yes,' Cathy said. 'Thank you.'

She waited until the door had been closed for a minute.

'Grace feels bad for you,' she went on. 'She hated you at first for what you did to Sam, what you'd done to Greg, but she's a shrink and she's *kind* and she tends to blame herself for things that aren't her fault. She thinks she should have known that you were tortured – her word, not mine. She thinks she should have been able to help you.' Cathy shook her head. 'Not me. Just so you know, Lucia. I don't feel any compassion for you. I blame you for destroying Kez.'

The tissue eyelids flickered then and the tracings on one of the monitors jerked a little, then went on as before. Probably just a reflex, she supposed.

The nurse, though, had said that Lucia might just hear her.

'That's it, really,' Cathy said. 'That's what I came to say. That I blame you for everything. Just so you know.'

She stood up.

'I brought you a little something. There's a card, too. It says: "I thought you might find a *use* for these." '

She watched the dying woman, studied her one last time.

'But I guess you're too far gone for that,' she said.

Somewhere nearby a man was weeping, a thin, bereft sound.

'I'll leave them for you, all the same,' Cathy said. 'Then maybe, if you ever do open your eyes, you'll see how pretty they are. If you do, I guess it'll really hurt you not to be able to touch them.'

She went to the door.

'I hope so, anyway,' she said.

Forty-One

October 13

Martinez called Sam next day. Told him what Cathy had done. About the visit.

'Did you know she was going?'

Sam said he had not known.

'Was there a problem?' he asked, already tense.

He had been sitting in the kitchen with Woody, drinking freshly squeezed orange juice. He had not felt like coffee since getting out of the hospital – had told Martinez to tell the guys not to trouble returning his espresso machine when they were done testing – and the only tea he was tending to drink these days came in little bags out of sealed packets from the supermarket.

Upstairs, Joshua – safe with his mom – had been crying for his feed and had now stopped, and just before the phone rang

Sam had been about to go join them, the thought already in his mind of their infant son at Grace's breast.

Sweetest picture in the world, bar none.

'No problem with the visit, as such,' Martinez answered. 'It was the gift she left.'

'Tell me.' Sam's heart beat faster.

'It's OK.' His good friend was swift with reassurance these days. 'It might not have been, might have spelled big trouble for Cathy, if the guy who got what it *really* was hadn't come to me.'

'Jesus,' Sam said. 'So what was it?'

'Bunch of flowers,' Martinez said. 'Pretty things, he said. Pretty colour, the nurse said, when she showed them to the officer – nice young guy called Domingo – checking in on Lucia.'

'Tell me,' Sam said again, tersely.

'Jimsonweed,' Martinez said.

They both knew about jimsonweed – aka Devil's Trumpet and Mad Apple and a whole bunch of other names – from way back, had arrested a teenager only a few months back who'd run amok on a beach after smoking the weed.

'Common as shit,' Martinez went on, 'so Cathy could have picked them at the roadside just about any place.'

Sam's mind went straight there, to an image of their grieving, messed-up daughter gathering toxic weeds by the side of some highway – and they were highly toxic, he knew that. He supposed that if she'd meant serious business, Cathy could have gone to greater trouble, gone in search of something even more obviously deadly, but she had known, of course, that Lucia was beyond the effort.

'She just left them, right?' he asked. 'She didn't *do* anything with them, didn't try to . . . ?'

'She didn't try to ram them down Lucia's throat,' Martinez said, 'or squeeze their sap into her IV, nothing like that. But she left a card with them, wrote on it that Lucia might find a *use* for them.'

Both men had heard from Grace what Lucia had said to her during that afternoon, the words that had jolted her into checking the back of that photograph. '*You might find a use for it.*'

'So I figured it was more of a gesture,' Martinez went on, 'than anything real harmful. Cathy throwing the bitch's gift right back at her, maybe.'

'Sounds about right,' Sam said. 'I guess.'

'To Domingo, too,' Martinez said. 'Which was why he brought the flowers and the card to mc instead of reporting it.'

Silently, Sam blessed Officer Domingo.

'What did you do with them, Al?' he asked.

'What would I want with lousy weeds?' Martinez said. 'I wrapped them up and threw them out with my garbage. The card too.'

'Thanks, Al,' Sam said. 'I owe you. Again.'

'You'd do it for me,' Martinez said.

'Think I should speak to Domingo?'

'I wouldn't,' Martinez said. 'I just figured you should know.'

'Thanks, man,' Sam told him. 'I'm . . . we're very grateful.'

'Nada,' Martinez said. 'No big deal.'

'How much of a problem,' he asked Grace a little while later, 'do you think we have?'

'I think we have all kinds of problems.' She sighed. 'If you're asking me if I think Cathy's gift to Lucia signals a career in poisoning, then no, I don't think so.'

'Think we should talk to her about it?'

'Only in the lightest way,' Grace said. 'So she knows we know.'

' "Heard you left Lucia a little something" – that kind of thing?'

Grace nodded, smiled, looked down at Joshua asleep in his crib beside their bed.

'Sounds about right to me,' she said.

Sam got closer to her. 'What do you think, Gracie? We going to be any good at all at being *real* parents? All the way from diapers up, I mean?'

'I know what you mean.' She kissed him. 'And I have no idea if we're going to be any good.' She paused. 'I certainly hope so.'

'Am I just doing the doting dad thing – ' he leaned across her to look down into the crib – 'or is our son really the most handsome baby I've ever laid eyes on?'

'Yes to both,' Grace answered.

Sam lay back again. 'Do you think Cathy's going to get over this?'

'I don't know.' Grace's eyes were sombre. 'A lot of scars, Sam, for a twenty-year-old.'

'Lot of scars for anyone,' Sam said.

Forty-Two

C athy was in bed in her room. Lying awake in the dark. Thinking about Kez. About the Chinese characters tattooed on the sole of her right foot, which she had since learned were the symbol for hyena, which Kez had told her, in the last hour of her life, that she admired.

That was what she had been doing, admiring hyenas, when Saul had committed the *crime* of happening upon her at the zoo and Kez, in all her madness, had believed he was mocking her. Had that been the foot, Cathy wondered, as she had many agonizing times before, with which Kez had stamped on Saul's throat?

Just one of the questions, one of the thoughts about Kez, some sweet, most acutely painful, that roamed endlessly around Cathy's mind most of the time these days and sleepless nights. And she had tried going back to Trent, ten days after Joshua's birth, and it had been good seeing Coach Delaney – he was shocked, the way everyone was, but his sorrow over Kez's death had seemed genuine – but so far as work was concerned, Cathy had been unable to settle at all.

Today had been a better day, almost a good one. Sam and Grace had spoken to her about her visit to Lucia, had been cool about it, had let her know they knew; that if she wanted to talk some more about it they would be there for her, and if she didn't want to, that was all right with them, too.

She had not wanted to talk about it, had done – was doing – more than enough thinking. About whether she was sorry that the tubes and monitors had made it impossible to do what she thought she *might* otherwise have been tempted to do. About whether or not she might, perhaps, have found some kind of monstrous relief in shoving those flowers down Lucia's throat.

Sick thoughts, burdensome thoughts. Not to be shared.

'I think I pretty much closed that book,' she had told them, and they had seemed to take her word for it.

Joshua was one lucky kid.

She had gone this morning to see Saul, and had felt a little better about him, too.

Done some thinking, he had typed on his computer, *about the doctor thing.*

'What about it?' she'd asked.

'Never was all that sure,' he'd typed, 'I'd be any good.'

Cathy hadn't said anything, was afraid of saying the wrong thing. It was something they had all veered away from, being uncertain if Saul was going to be fit enough to return to that long, hard learning road.

Think I might change courses, he typed on. *Study furniture design.*

Cathy had been surprised, but Saul had persisted with the theme and had looked about as close to animated as he had since Terri's death, until he had grown too tired to go on typing and had lain back, the sadness back in his eyes again.

She supposed he was pretending about the doctor v furniture thing, perhaps for her sake because he knew how badly she felt. But Cathy knew a thing or two about faking recovery, about that particular brand of pretense, and sometimes, she knew too, you could almost kid yourself into feeling better.

Almost.

For her, the thing that still helped the most was running.

'You run,' Kez had told her, first time they'd met, 'like you're trying to escape.'

Which was fine, she had added, so long as Cathy was 'in charge'.

Not in charge now, that was for sure.

She still went running though, as she always had.

But these days wherever she ran, on a track, in Haulover Park or on the beach, in her mind she was always back in Naples, running shoulder to shoulder with Kez.